DEATH FROM A
TOP HAT

CLAYTON RAWSON (1906–1971) was a novelist, editor, and magician. He is best known for creating The Great Merlini, an illusionist and amateur sleuth introduced in *Death From a Top Hat* (1938), a rollicking crime novel which has been called one of the best locked-room mysteries of all time. Rawson followed the character through three more novels, concluding the series with *No Coffin for the Corpse* (1942). In 1941 and 1943 he published the short-story collections *Death Out of Thin Air* and *Death From Nowhere*, starring Don Diavolo, an escape artist introduced in the Merlini series.

In 1945 Rawson was among the founders of Mystery Writers of America. He served as the first editor for the group's newsletter, *The Third Degree*, and coined its famous slogan: "Crime Doesn't Pay—Enough." Rawson continued writing and editing for the rest of his life.

OTTO PENZLER, the creator of American Mystery Classics, is also the founder of the Mysterious Press (1975), a literary crime imprint now associated with Grove/Atlantic; Mysterious Press. com (2011), an electronic-book publishing company; and New York City's Mysterious Bookshop (1979). He has won a Raven, the Ellery Queen Award, two Edgars (for the *Encyclopedia of Mystery and Detection*, 1977, and *The Lineup*, 2010), and lifetime achievement awards from Noircon and *The Strand Magazine*. He has edited more than 70 anthologies and written extensively about mystery fiction.

DEATH FROM A
TOP HAT

CLAYTON RAWSON

Introduction by
OTTO PENZLER

**AMERICAN
MYSTERY
CLASSICS**

Penzler Publishers
New York

Published in 2018 by Penzler Publishers
58 Warren Street, New York, NY 10007
penzlerpublishers.com

Cover image: Andy Ross
Cover design: Mauricio Diaz

Paperback ISBN 978-1-61316-101-2
Hardcover ISBN 978-1-61316-109-8

Library of Congress Control Number: 2018947037

Distributed by W. W. Norton

Printed in the United States of America

9 8 7 6 5 4 3 2 1

DEATH FROM A
TOP HAT

INTRODUCTION

MORE THAN one scholar has suggested an analogy between magic and mystery novels with respect to each one's use of deception to fool an audience or readership. It appears to be a fair comparison.

A magician takes the stage and changes a tiger into a woman, makes an elephant disappear, pulls a rabbit from a hat, and saws a woman in half. The entire success of the performance relies on the ability to create the illusion that the feats performed are credible. Somewhere in the back of our brains we know that, no, the magician did not actually run a buzz saw through the midsection of his assistant. All the evidence indicates that that is precisely what he did do. We saw it with our own eyes.

Or did we? In most cases, such illusions depend on the magician's ability to misdirect the attention of the audience away from the action of the trick. Perhaps a cloud of smoke distracts viewers while a lever is pulled, or a hand calls attention to its waving as the other pockets a card for later. It happens so quickly that the eye doesn't even notice it has been misguided, thus producing the seamless experience that produces the audience's disbelief.

In many ways, the writer of mystery stories works in a similar realm. To say nothing of the illusory nature of fiction in general and its ability to conjure imaginary worlds from thin air, mystery stories, like magic tricks, depend upon misdirection to give structure to their plotlines. The story doesn't begin with a solution; instead, it begins with an act whose perpetrator, in league with the author, has worked to obscure his or her motives and methods. The narrative winds its way through false clues and red herrings, each precisely placed to take the eye away from the truth of the crime committed.

But there is a stark difference between the mystery writer and the magician: while the magician profits from the befuddlement of his audience, the author must also eventually reveal the truth behind the trick's misdirection. No reader of mysteries would be satisfied by a novel that did not ultimately reveal the criminal, and so the author must also include, alongside the illusion they construct, the tools of its own dismantlement. For every false clue, they must include a real one.

As a magician and an author of instructional books on the topic, Clayton Rawson was well-prepared to juggle these opposing elements and blend them into a series of outstanding mystery novels and short stories. His fiction featured a magician, The Great Merlini, whose help was often sought by the New York Police Department when a seemingly impossible crime had been committed.

Merlini's name, obviously, was an homage to Merlin, the master of ancient wizardry, just as Houdini had chosen his name in honor of the father of modern conjuring, Robert-Houdini. Rawson gave his character a backstory worthy of the illustrious lineage suggested by his name: Born in a Barnum and Bailey circus car, Merlini worked as a carnival and circus magician for four years before developing his own show and touring the world. Eventually, he settled down in New York City to open a magic shop called Miracles for Sale, which is where readers first encounter him in *Death From a Top Hat*.

Like Merlini, Rawson was one of the country's most famous illusionists and a member of the Society of American Magicians. Before turning to writing, he was an artist, specializing in magazine illustration and advertising. Rawson was also a distinguished editor for such publications as *True Detective Magazine*, Ziff-Davis Publications, Unicorn Books, Simon & Schuster's Inner Sanctum

Mysteries, and *Ellery Queen's Mystery Magazine*. In 1945, alongside Anthony Boucher, Brett Halliday, and Lawrence Treat, he founded Mystery Writers of America.

Few writers of his time were more beloved than Rawson, a quality that my own experiences with the author helped me understand. As a reasonably young fan of twenty-eight, I was able to attend my first Edgar Awards banquet in the spring of 1970. Before the ceremonies began, Rawson invited a friend and me up to his hotel room where he performed one astonishing magic trick after another. That year ended his tenure as editor of *EQMM* (he died a year later), so he was training Eleanor Sullivan to take over. She tells of coming to work one morning and finding a telegram on her desk: THERE IS A BOA CONSTRICTOR IN YOUR BOTTOM DRAWER. STOP. DON'T OPEN UNTIL CHRISTMAS.

A trickster at heart, Rawson's playful sense of humor is displayed throughout the four Great Merlini novels and twelve short stories; at the same time, the author was utterly serious about constructing plots, all of which are "impossible" locked-room crimes.

In his first novel, *Death From a Top Hat* (1939), magicians are the victims in a series of murders and some of their colleagues, expert at deception and illusion, are the key suspects. In the second Merlini novel, *The Footprints on the Ceiling* (1939), the police are baffled by the murder of a man found in a room that has, yes, footprints on the ceiling, seemingly possible only by magic. In *The Headless Lady* (1940), the ruthless killer performs his deadly tricks under the circus big top. In the fourth and final Merlini novel, *No Coffin for the Corpse* (1942), the retired prestidigitator is called to investigate the murder of a neurotic millionaire who was apparently killed by a man everybody "knew" to be dead and buried.

Rawson's short stories are no less inventive. In "From Another World," a man is found stabbed to death in a locked room in which all the doors and windows were sealed with tape. An unconscious iv

man who happens to be naked is discovered in a locked room in which a man has been shot to death in "Nothing Is Impossible," but there is no murder weapon. In "Off the Face of the Earth," a man disappears from a phone booth that has been under constant observation.

Given Rawson's mastery of the locked room story, it comes as no surprise that the most famous author of impossible crime fiction, John Dickson Carr, ranked Rawson as one of the six greatest writers of detective fiction of all time. *Death From a Top Hat* ranks among the most distinguished examples of the form; in it, the magician's expertise finds its perfect fictional application.

—OTTO PENZLER

Table of Contents

Chapter 1
The Voice in the Hall

But see, his face is black and full of blood,
His eyeballs further out than when he liv'd,
Staring full ghastly like a strangled man . . .
            Shakespeare: *King Henry VI, Part II*

THERE WERE times during the investigation of the case of the Dead Magicians when the New York Police Department's official attitude toward the infernal arts of witchcraft and sorcery was damnably inconvenient. It had the annoying disadvantage of leaving us with no explanation at all.

Some of the evidence in the case would have seemed vastly more appropriate had it been reported from the forbidden interior of Tibet or from that other famous home of magic, mystery, and tall stories—India. A murderer who apparently leaves the scene of his crimes by walking straight through solid walls of brick and plaster and by floating in midair out of second story windows would, however, be uncanny enough even in Lhassa or Hyderabad. In modern Manhattan he becomes doubly incredible and rather more frightening.

As recently as two hundred and fifty years ago the authorities would have ended the matter by simply applying those bloody and infamous instruments for crime detection, the pincers and the rack, and obtained a confession of sorcerous activity from the nearest innocent bystander. But this easy technique was denied us, and we were left, armed with logic alone, to do battle with irrational dragon shapes. . . .

Inspector Gavigan's ordinarily jovial and assured blue eyes held an angry worried look that stayed there until Merlini finally exorcised the demons and produced a solution that satisfied the Inspector except as to one thing: he couldn't understand why he hadn't seen it all along. I knew exactly how he felt. I was in the same boat. All we need have done, as Merlini pointed out, was to realize *exactly what it was that all the suspects had in common* and *just what the two things were that one of them was able to do that no one else could possibly have done.*

Except for a number of things the murderer had already accomplished, the action began on a Monday evening. I had worked all week-end and through Sunday night until five in the morning on a free-lance job of advertising copy at Blanton, Dunlop & Hartwick's, one of those madhouse advertising agencies in the Graybar Building. Their star client, after a full week of agonizing indecision, had made up his mind at 4:30 on Friday afternoon that the proposed national campaign for Sudzex Soap Flakes was lousy. He didn't know what was wrong with it—clients never do—but his wife said it wouldn't sell *her* any soap flakes, and his secretary didn't like the illustrations. So would B. D. & H. please show him a new set of comprehensives on Monday morning.

My phone rang as I was dressing for a dinner date, and Paul Dunlop had to jack his price twice before I said yes. Always after one of those incredibly hectic and sleepless jobs I promised myself it would be the last time, yet always, somehow, I managed to think of something I could do with that much money.

When I left the agency, a crew of bleary-eyed layout men and artists were still at it, putting a bit of everything into those damned ads, including, in this case, that usually excluded item, the kitchen sink. After toast and coffee at an all-night cafeteria I walked the few blocks to my apartment on East 40th Street, took a warm shower, drew the shade against the first gray streaks of dawn, and got into bed.

I awoke to see the alarm clock scowling at me reproachfully, the corners of its mouth turned down and indicating 5:40. Reaching out an arm, I flipped up the shade and then lay there for a moment enjoying the warmth of the bed, reluctant to face the cold air breezing in at the window. Warm squares of yellow light shone out from the dark face of the apartment house opposite. I heard the deep moan of a foghorn from the near-by river that moved, dark and silent, between Manhattan and the twinkling wilderness of Long Island. In the northwestern sky a faint blur of red glowed sullenly where low-lying clouds reflected the neon brilliance of Times Square.

Presently I got up, showered, shaved, dressed, and went to the corner restaurant where I ate leisurely with a book propped up against the sugar bowl. Returning to the apartment, I folded myself up in the big armchair and tried to enjoy having nothing to do but read. I soon found, however, that I couldn't relax comfortably so soon after the nervous, driving pace of the past few days. The book seemed pallid and dull. I dropped it, went to the kitchen and put together a Scotch and soda.

In the living room once more, I switched on the light at my desk, placed my glass on a coaster beside the typewriter, and tore open a new package of copy paper. I twisted a sheet into the machine and lit a cigarette. From the top drawer I took out a small loose-leaf notebook and removed the half dozen pages on which I had scribbled notes for a magazine article. Luncheon the week before with Dave Merton, editor of Greenbook, had resulted in a commission to do two thousand words on the state of the modern detective story. At the top of the sheet I typed off a tentative head, *Death Takes a Holiday,* x'd it out, and wrote two more, *Mur-*

der Is Hackneyed and *The Corpse on the Publisher's Hands.* I left them to age a bit and began to click off a rough outline of my main argument, a listing of my reasons for *not* writing detective fiction.

The detective story is a unique literature form, a complicated species of jigsaw puzzle that is not so much written as constructed; and that, according to almost mathematical formulae. It is a mental contest between reader and author that has evolved its own private *code duello;* a set of rules now so familiar to every detective story fan that the sales of the authors next book suffer if he so much as infringes a minor ordinance.

These rules require that the story of detection be cast in a regulation mold, fashioned according to a standard pattern that once may have seemed capable of kaleidoscopic variation, but which is now sadly worn.

The essential jigsaw pieces are these: the detective, the murder device, the clues, and the surprise solution. These elements are few, and their individual permutations rather less than infinite. The detective story has been a gold mine for many writers, but the steady demand of the last decade or so has almost entirely depleted the mother lode. Why write a detective story when all the good plots have been used, all the changes rung, all the devices made trite?

Take the detective, for instance. Take, in more or less chronological order, such characters as Dupin, Inspector Buckett, Sergeant Cuff, Lecocq, Ebenezer Gryce, Sherlock Holmes, Martin Hewitt, Dr. Thorndyke, Violet Strange, Craig Kennedy, Prof. F. X. Van Dusen, Father Brown, Dr. Priestley, Dr. Reginald Fortune, Eugene Valmont, Hercule Poirot, Hanaud, Colonel Gore, Max Carrados, The Old Man in the Corner, Frank Spargo, Dawson, Rouletabille, Uncle Abner, Arsène Lupin, Philo Vance, Lord Peter Wimsey, Anthony Gillingham, Philip Trent, Pagglioli, Mr. Tolefree, Perry Mason, Mr. J. G. Reeder, Inspector French, Superintendent Wilson, Ellery Queen, Charlie Chan, Anthony Gethryn, Roger Sheringham, Dr. Fell, Thatcher Colt, Sam Spade, Lieutenant Valcour, Hildegarde Withers, Henry Merrivale, Mr. Pinkerton, Nero Wolfe, etc., etc. Now try to invent a detective whose personal idiosyncrasies (the formula says they are necessary) are unique without being fantastic, a sleuth whose manner of deduction is original and fresh.

I stopped for a moment and, drink in hand, reviewed my listing of detective talent. With a pencil I made several additions in the margin: Nick Charles, the Baron Maxmilian Von Kaz, and Drury Lane. Lighting a new cigarette, I continued.

Consider the murder device. All the garden varieties of homicide have been exploited: shooting, stabbing, bludgeoning, drowning, suffocating, gassing, strangling, poisoning, decapitating, pushing from high places. The variations on these basic methods of dealing death have reached fantastic heights: icicle stilettos, rock salt bullets, air bubbles injected into the veins, daggers fired from air guns, tetanus lurking in the toothpaste, and all that huge assortment of concealed automatic mechanisms, the mere description of some of which is enough to scare a person to death—which, incidentally, has also been done!

And the clue. The author can ring more changes with this element, since clues depend upon time, place and circumstance. The clues of the gas tap and the missing bustle have been superseded by the clue of the electric cigarette lighter and the stolen brassiere. The list of clues, however, that have served a useful life and should be allowed a peaceful retirement is a staggering one. The clue of the barking dog, the cigar ash in the fireplace, the lipstick on the cigarette, the burned documents, the cipher letter, the missing pants button, the (collect more examples) . . .

Any writer's ingenuity may be excused from balking when it surveys the depleted forest of clues, but the surprise solution—there's the big headache. The problem consists in achieving it without leaving the reader feeling as though he had just lost his roll in a three-shell game. You're allowed seven or eight suspects, not more, and at one time or another each and every one of them has committed the foul deed. The helpless looking baby-faced blonde; the curly haired, forthright young hero; the victim's strait-laced maiden aunt; the doctor; lawyer; merchant; chief; even Grandma, who has been a paralyzed invalid for time out of mind; not to mention little Ethelinda, age 9, nor her pet kitten with the poisoned claws.

They've all done it, separately and together, and the reader knows it. In trying to escape this dilemma of exhaustion, many authors have slyly ventured outside the ordinary list of suspects, and foisted off the dirty work on the detective and the prosecuting attorney, the judge, the foreman of the jury, and, finally, in the last desperate attempt at novelty, the story teller himself. After that, there seems to be little left, except—if you can do it—the publisher of the book—or the reader!

As I see it, all that remains to be done is . . .

I broke off and glanced up from my typewriter with a frown. Someone out in the corridor was pounding on the door of the apartment across from mine; and now and then I could hear the low buzz of a doorbell. Two or three voices, fusing in a jumbled excited chatter, filtered through my door. I sat back helplessly to wait until they would decide to give it up and go away. Once, when I had worked on a newspaper, I had been able to write under all sorts of conditions, most of them noisy. There is something about the rhythmic clatter of a newsroom that is conducive to work, but this disturbance was merely aggravating.

Someone was evidently anxious to see the occupant of the

apartment which shared the third floor with my own, though I couldn't quite understand why. The tenant was a crusty, antisocial old so-and-so who never seemed pleased to see anyone, as far as I knew. After a tentative "good morning" once that elicited a black scowl as its sole response, I gave up trying to be neighborly. New York isn't the town for that, anyhow. And this bird was probably as unneighborly a specimen as could be found in the whole metropolitan area.

He was tall and had Cassius' lean and hungry look. His slicked dark hair came forward to a sharp V above his high forehead, and his eyes, wet and shiny black like an insect's, peered coldly from a face that might have been carved from soap. In spite of all that, his erect carriage and the incisively hewn symmetry of his face made him almost handsome in a strange foreign way. He had an annoying habit of looking suspiciously back over his shoulder when I passed him in the dark hall that made me think of Count Dracula. He was, somehow, just a shade too fantastic; and his name, which I had noticed on a card at the bell push, was equally odd. It was Dr. Cesare Sabbat.

Suddenly I swung around in my chair. The voices outside took on a quickened tempo, a new throb of excitement—one of them, a woman's, lifted above the rest. It was a curiously flat voice, charged with hysteria, a slow hypnotic tenseness, and a touch of what, oddly enough, sounded like studied horror. Six words came wading through the silence that instantly ensued and hung trembling in the air over my desk.

"There is death in that room!"

It was too much. I got up, scowling, and jerked open my door. "What is this?" I protested. "A game?"

Dr. Cesare Sabbat's apartment as the police found it.

Chapter 2
Death of a Necromancer

Facing to the northern clime,
Thrice he traced the Rhumic rhyme;
Thrice pronounced in accents dread,
The thrilling verse that wakes the dead . . .
— *The Samundic Edda*

IN THE dim light of the hall I saw three people. A man and a woman stood with their backs toward me, peering over the shoulder of another man who was down on one knee looking into the keyhole of Sabbat's door. When I spoke they pivoted together like precision dancers. A monocle tumbled out of the crouching man's right eye, bobbed twice at the end of its black cord, and was promptly replaced.

For a second no one spoke. The man with the monocle examined me closely, a cold scrutiny in his eyes that was vaguely disturbing. Finished with this leisurely, impudent survey, he turned a sudden disdainful back and again applied his eye to the keyhole.

"Scram!" he said. The acid in his voice made my annoyance boil over into anger.

"You took the word right out of my mouth," I replied with feeling. Before I could expand on that theme, there was a prefatory cough at my elbow, and the other man edged in front of me, hat in hand, an ambassadorial smile on his face.

11

"Excuse me," he said in a silky, oratorical voice. "I'm Col. Herbert Watrous. We have an appointment with Dr. Sabbat. Perhaps you know if he's in?"

Stepping back so that the light from my room caught his face, I took a good look at him. He was a small, gray-haired man whose short legs were oddly inconsistent with a wide-shouldered muscular torso. There was a cropped military mustache in the exact geographical center of his fat face. Pince-nez glasses perched astride the bridge of his nose and were fastened to a slight gold chain that looped back over one ear and swung in uneven time to his movements. His chin waggled above a white muffler which was tucked neatly into a sprucely fitted dark overcoat.

I stared with frank, ill-mannered curiosity at this unexpected personal appearance of a figure whom until now I had always half believed to be an invention of the Sunday Supplement feature writers. I began, with some interest, to wonder what "the foremost psychical scientist in America" could be doing here, pounding on Sabbat's door.

"How do you do," I returned, with minimum politeness. "I don't know if your friend Sabbat is in or out. Considering the racket you've been making, the latter seems indicated. And now, why don't you people be considerate and go away—quietly? I'm trying to work."

"I'm sorry if we've disturbed you," he said, his hands fiddling with the ivory top of his walking stick. "But we . . . ah . . . that is, Dr. Sabbat was expecting us, and it does seem a bit odd, I might even say . . ." He hesitated, casting a nervous glance at the woman who stood beside him in what seemed to me an unnaturally rigid position.

"Alarming!" he finished abruptly. "Our host was quite insistent upon our arriving no later than 6:30." He turned to the other man as if for confirmation, got none, and continued: "It's not at all like him to . . ."

The woman swayed stiffly, and Watrous, with a swift motion,

caught her arm. He looked at her anxiously and seemed to have forgotten about completing his sentence. The woman remained trance-like and soundless.

Stalling, and trying to fathom the queerness which hung around this group in the hall, I made conversation, inquiring, rather pointlessly, "What is Sabbat anyway, a chemist?"

The Colonel, eyes still on the woman, echoed absently, "A chemist?" Then after a pause he brought his attention back to myself.

"A chemist?" he repeated. "No, not … exactly. Why do you ask?"

"I just wondered. It smells that way now and then." I became aware, as I said it, that the hall smelled that way now.

Watrous smiled faintly. "The hermetic art," he said, half to himself, "*is* an odorous pursuit." And then more directly: "The Doctor's field is anthropology, with special emphasis on primitive magic and religions. He is not only a widely recognized authority on cabalistic theory, but also a practical student of many of the occult sciences. Furthermore . . ."

"Furthermore," said the kneeling man quietly, "you talk too damned much."

As he stood up and faced us I got a better look at him, though the light in the corridor was too shadowy for details and he seemed to avoid the additional illumination which came from my doorway. He was a man of medium height, in his late thirties. His body was admirably proportioned, and there was an unmistakable look of tense, willowy strength and trained coordination in his movements. I was puzzled by his clothes until I discovered who and what he was. His top hat was as shiny as they look in the advertisements, and an opera cape hung from his shoulders over evening dress that was obviously Bond Street. His face, twisted into a sardonic slant by the monocle he was wearing, had a taut, hair-trigger look. An inch-long strip of adhesive tape angled along his left lower jaw, strikingly out of key with his otherwise impeccable appearance.

Watrous pulled up momentarily, frowned, and then went on quite amiably as if nothing had happened.

"Allow me to introduce Mr. Eugene Tarot, of whom you have doubtless heard. Mr. Tarot—Mr.—" He glanced at the card tacked to my door "Harte, I think."

I nodded coldly. The Great Tarot, of whom I *had* heard, was busily scowling at Watrous and didn't even bother to nod coldly. Along with a considerable share of the public, I knew of him as the Card King, a sleight-of-hand performer of polished excellence, whose clever dexterity, chiefly in the manipulation of playing cards, had won him top theatrical bookings. He was, currently, garnering national publicity and pocketing a fat pay check for playing the title role in *Xanadu, the Magician,* a radio serial of his own devising that was presented nightly by a prosperous automotive sponsor.

Watrous blandly continued: "And this is Madame Rappourt, who is on her way to being recognized, if I may say so, as the greatest psychic personality of our day. The press has been so kind of late as to give her some of the attention which she so rightly merits. You have probably read . . ."

The Colonel's introduction, continuing for another paragraph or so, began to sound like a side-show barker's build up, and he lost my attention. The woman's name was one that I half expected. Madame Rappourt was the Colonel's discovery and *protégée,* a spirit medium who had created no little scientific and quite a lot of journalistic fuss in European circles. For the past two weeks, since her arrival in this country, the newspapers had showered the pair with publicity, largely favorable, which, paid for at line rates, would have amounted to plenty. I suspected that this was due partly to a prevailing lack of colorful news and partly to a smart press agent. When I discovered later that it was Watrous who had managed to induce the notices, I began to respect his flair for showmanship.

According to what he had given the papers, Madame Rappourt was a native of Hungary. A large, huskily built woman, with swarthy masculine features, she almost towered over the abridged Colonel at her side. Her eyes, imbedded in a blunt, yet somehow handsome, face were black holes, in each of which a tiny spark of light burned fiercely. She had an immense amount of jet-black hair which possessed an astonishing look of vitality and almost seemed to be growing before my eyes, in slow burnished movement. She wore a black evening wrap which she clutched around her awkwardly, as if she were cold.

I knew that she must be the owner of that oddly haunted voice, which, coming through my door, had talked of death.

Tarot shattered the Colonel's rush of incipient oratory with simple directness. Without my noticing it, he had resumed his kneeling position at the keyhole, and I now saw that he held in his hands a key ring on which were a number of queerly shaped, angular bits of metal. I knew, intuitively, that they were picklocks.

"Turn off the spiel, Watrous," he cut in, "and go see if that kitchenette door is locked."

The Colonel stuttered in mid-sentence and then quickly did as he was told, going toward another door some twenty feet down the hall. Tarot caught my look of surprise as I saw the implements in his hand.

"You think," he said, "that Sabbat is out. I don't."

"Nor do I!" As Madame Rappourt spoke I was looking full at her. Her lips did not move.

"That milk bottle,"—Tarot pointed at a pint of coffee cream standing near the door—"has presumably been there since early this morning. It is now six-thirty P.M. He hasn't been out today, and besides . . ." He sat back on his heels and announced, with measured intonation, "This keyhole has been stuffed up from the inside!"

I watched the vague ghost of a smile materialize around Madame Rappourt's mouth.

Watrous exclaimed loudly, "What!" and began pounding noisily on the kitchen door.

"Here, take this." Tarot drew one of the picklocks from the ring and flung it toward Watrous. It rattled along the floor. "See if that keyhole's stuffed too." Tarot started probing again at the lock, one of the mortise-knob type with the large keyhole such as is ordinarily found on connecting doors.

Involuntarily I sniffed, and was again conscious of a vague laboratory odor. "I'd better call the police," I said, turning.

Tarot whirled on me.

"You'll do nothing of the sort—yet!" he said threateningly. "Watrous!"

"This lock's stuffed up too!" Watrous shouted, his voice pitched high. His velvety bumbling gone, he almost squeaked, "I think I may be able to push it out, though." He fumbled at the lock.

"Try it." Tarot scowled and then added quickly, "Hell, no! Don't be a fool. If he's stuffed the keyhole, he's probably thrown the bolts he has on these doors. Picking the locks won't do us a damn bit of good. We'll have to break in."

Watrous came running back to where we stood. His face had taken on a purplish hue. He quavered breathlessly, "Perhaps Mr. Harte here has something we can smash a panel with." He looked at me.

I was still glaring angrily at the officious Tarot. I turned without answering, went into my apartment and got the heaviest stick of firewood I had. Returning, I ignored Tarot's outstretched hand and shoved it at Watrous. Then I walked back in to the phone and dialed Operator. "To hell with Tarot," I was thinking, "he can't push me around." I told the operator to get me Police Headquarters and to snap into it.

Outside I could hear the battering of wood upon wood as I explained to an official, somewhat bored voice at headquarters that someone at 742 East 40th Street had possibly committed suicide by gas. I went back to the corridor and found that Watrous had succeeded in splintering one panel of the door. Another powerful swinging blow cracked it open, and a heavy cloying odor came out.

"Can you reach the bolt?" Tarot demanded.

Watrous crooked an arm through the opening, and we heard the sound of sliding metal. His hand was busy an instant longer, and then he withdrew his arm.

"This was in the keyhole." He held up a wrinkled square of blue cloth and stood looking at it a bit uncertainly. I reached over and took it from him. It was the torn quarter of a man's blue linen handkerchief.

Tarot meanwhile had gone into action with his picklocks. He tried one, and almost immediately we heard the catch click over. I shoved the cloth into my trouser pocket and stepped forward. Tarot, hand on the knob, was pushing at the door. It gave an inch or so, then stopped as if impeded by some heavy object. Tarot applied his shoulder, and the door moved slowly. He threw his whole weight against it, and we heard something scrape across the floor inside as the door swung inward far enough to allow an entrance. Tarot squeezed in and was silhouetted against a flickering yellowish light.

"You'd better stay here, Eva," Watrous advised the woman and disappeared after Tarot. I started in. Madame Rappourt stood, tensely expectant, against the corridor wall, watching. Then she moved after us.

The others, having gone five or six feet into the room, had rounded the end of a davenport that had blocked the door but now slanted inward, angling away from the wall. They stood motionless, staring toward my left, within the room.

I jerked my head in that direction.

The air was misty with smoke. Four ovoid shapes of light that were tall candle flames wavered in the haze. They balanced delicately above the stubby ends of thick, black candles that stood in massive candlesticks of wrought iron. These, with a fifth in which the shortened candle had guttered out, were circularly arranged in the middle of the floor. The darkness, held off by their uncertain gleaming, lay thick around the walls and was heaped up in the corners of the room.

I saw only this at first. Then Tarot moved forward quickly, deeper into the room. Madame Rappourt behind me made a queer choking sound in her throat. On the bare, polished floor I saw the body of a man. He was clad in pajamas and dressing gown. His puffy, congested lips were drawn back from the jutting teeth in a fixed, distorted grimace; his eyes bulged hideously from their sockets and stared with an unblinking, fish-like intensity at the ceiling; his face, swollen and livid, was contorted into a grotesquely carved mask that bore not the slightest human expression. With difficulty I recognized Cesare Sabbat.

He lay on his back, symmetrically spread-eagled in the exact center of a large star shape that had been drawn on the floor with chalk, his head, arms, and legs extending out into the points. At the tip of each point stood one of the candles, and around this whole fantastic tableau ran a scribbled border of strange words, also in chalk.

Tetragrammaton . . . Tetragrammaton . . . Tetragrammaton—Ismael . . . Adonay . . . Ihua—Come Surgat . . . Come Surgat . . . Come Surgat!

The candle nearest Tarot, which had burned down to its socket, gave a final dancing flicker and went out. The darkness against the walls came closer.

Chapter 3
Suspects in the Dark

Faustus sold himself to the Devil,
Slashed his wrist and wrote in blood.
Pledged his soul to the Prince of Evil,
  Old Dr. Faustus.
  Bold Dr. Faustus—
Turned his face from the good.
    —George Steele Seymour: *Faustus*

TIME STRETCHED itself out intolerably while we stood there, staring. The draught from the open door snatched at the candle flames, and the body almost seemed to move as the dark shadows beneath it crawled on the floor. At last Watrous broke the straining silence.

"Sabbat!"

His voice now was harsh, cracked, and his hands trembled. No one else spoke.

I rubbed my palms against my trousers, wiping away the dampness, and glanced quickly around the room. On the left, beyond Sabbat's feet, a heavy marble fireplace towered, dominating that end of the room. Above it dull gleams of coppery light picked out the raised portions of a great circular plaque and traced a complex design of intersecting circles and unfamiliar symbols. To the right of the hearth a folding screen partially concealed what appeared to be a large worktable bearing the scattered glint of glassware.

On the floor near me, against the high, carved legs of the davenport, lay a black carpet, neatly rolled. On the side of the room opposite the door dark hangings, closely drawn before a large studio window, reached from ceiling to floor. The right half of the room was lined shoulder high with solidly filled bookshelves. The savage, eyeless faces of half a dozen ceremonial masks peered with feverish distortion from the walls and contrasted violently with the businesslike desk and steel filing cabinets in one corner, which, with several chairs, low tables, and a floor lamp or two comprised the remaining furniture. In the center of the right hand wall, slicing into the rampart of shelves, I saw the black rectangle of an arched doorway that led, I suspected, as did my own, into a short inner hall from which opened the entrances to kitchenette, bedroom, and bath.

Watrous was incredulous. "Is—is he—dead?"

Tarot took his eyes from the body and narrowed them on the Colonel. His voice, except for an incisive sarcasm, was emotionless.

"What do you think? 'S a damn funny place to *sleep!*"

"But I," Watrous jerked, "I don't . . . understand. There's no gas."

"Gas?" Tarot looked puzzled.

"Yes—the stuffed keyholes. This smell is incense—from that burner." He indicated a squat bronze object on the mantelpiece. "It's not—"

"Use your eyes, man!" Tarot snapped. "Look at that face. Asphyxiation, yes. But not gas. He's been strangled."

The thought had crossed my mind, yet I started when I heard the words. Rappourt moved and caught my attention. I saw that her rigidity and labored respiration had gone. She was bending forward, keenly alert, her eyes wide, with white showing beneath the black staring pupils.

I said, "There'd be marks of some sort on his throat, wouldn't there?"

Tarot stepped over the chalked circle closer to the body and looked down. "There should be—and there aren't. But that's no queerer than the rest of this . . ." He was starting to kneel.

"Maybe you'd better not touch him," I warned. "The police are on their way."

Tarot straightened. Somehow I felt that I had put a dent in that colossal self-confidence of his which was so annoying. His monocle flashed at me.

"While we were smashing in the door, eh?"

I nodded, watching him.

"But," Watrous argued doubtfully, "you're saying that Sabbat—"

"Was murdered!" Tarot finished. "And since these windows look directly on to the river, it's quite possible that the murderer . . ." His voice had lowered and was speculative. Leaving his thought half expressed, he turned to face the now forbidding darkness of the inner doorway. Together with his turning I saw a smooth motion of hand to pocket, and then blue metal highlights glittered in his hand. He held a square-nosed automatic.

"Get some lights, somebody! That switch by the door."

I jumped at it. I flicked it with my thumb . . . once . . . twice . . . Thin metallic clicks came, but that was all. Tarot yanked a candle from its socket and moved toward the black hall. I grabbed the next nearest and started after him. He looked over his shoulder, stopped short and spun around. His gun, held stiffly before him, seemed to point at me.

"You stay where you are!"

I kept on going, partly because I disliked Tarot's self-appointed leadership, partly because I felt that he was being a bit too melodramatic. The odds were against finding a murderer hidden on the scene of his crime.

"All right, sap!" he said. "Take the bedroom."

He slipped into the doorway ahead of me, turned right, and

vanished through a swinging door into the kitchen. I went on several paces and stopped before the single door on the left. Kicking it open, I held my candle high and fumbled inside for the switch. I found it and got another empty, ineffective click. I hesitated for an instant on the black brink, and then stepped in, suddenly, as if entering a cold shower.

My candle flame dipped precariously at the quick motion, and I slowed cautiously. The room contained a bed, dresser, and chair. The bed was made. I looked under it and then investigated a clothes closet. That exhausted the hiding places. There were two windows; one faced the blank rear wall of another apartment house and overlooked a bare stone court three stories below; the other, on the river side, dropped sheer to the water. Both were securely fastened.

"*Tarot!*"

I had one hand on the window catch, trying it, when I heard Watrous yell. I turned around so fast my candle flapped out. One bound took me through the door into the hall where I smacked solidly against Tarot as he shot out of the bathroom. We both swore.

Watrous ran at us, blurted excitedly, "She's fainted! Give me that." He snatched Tarot's candle, which was miraculously still alight, and popped into the kitchen. I heard running water splash in the sink as we hurried back into the living room.

Darkness had moved in threateningly on the two remaining candles. Madame Rappourt was a limp huddle on the floor. We lifted her into a large armchair. Her head rolled, mouth open. Watrous came with a glass of water, and Tarot leaned forward to support the medium's head as the Colonel tipped the glass against her pale lips. Water dribbled down the side of her face and neck, and she began to come out of it, choking.

She moaned slightly and mumbled indistinguishably in a

blurred, fuzzy voice. Her eyelids fluttered and then stayed open. She looked at the Colonel, who had put aside the glass and was bent over, awkwardly rubbing her wrists.

"I'll be all right in a moment," she said thinly. "Then you must take me home."

Watrous nodded and opened his mouth.

Tarot spoke first. "Mr. Harte's friends, the police, won't like that, you know, Watrous."

I let that crack pass and spoke to Watrous. "You might take her across to my room where it's light, and there isn't any . . ." I gestured at the body.

"Perhaps I'd better," he assented. But he made no move. He frowned thoughtfully and inclined his head toward the inner hall. "In there, you found nothing?"

I shook my head. Tarot put the gun back in his pocket and said, "No."

Watrous nodded, one hand holding Rappourt's arm, and looked across at the body. "That would have been disappointing. You know, this business is beginning to interest me highly. The authorities all state that unless very precise and proper precautions are taken during an evocation the demon may turn on the sorcerer and wring his neck. Many such instances have been recorded, though I haven't yet found any well-authenticated modern ones. I'm beginning to think that maybe the police are going to have a bit of a job on their hands."

"Slow down for the corners, Colonel," Tarot said cynically. "Your imagination's running wild again. Maybe the dead can return to jiggle tables and blow trumpets, though I should think they'd feel damned silly doing it. But when you insinuate that some demon twisted Sabbat's neck for him . . . eyewash! And you know it."

That was the wrong way to rub the Colonel's fur. He argued,

"But if there's no one else here, and the doors were all locked and bolted, and the windows . . ."

I walked over and pulled back the velvet hangings. A pale hint of moonlight filtered in. I glanced at the window fastening. "The windows in the other room and in here," I announced, "are all locked."

"You see," Watrous said. "What else . . ."

"At the moment I don't know what else," Tarot snorted. "But there's *some* way out of here. Duvallo should be able . . ." He stopped thoughtfully.

"Duvallo!" Watrous exclaimed. "I wonder what's delaying him. He should be here by now."

"That is queer." Tarot pushed back his cuff and glanced at a silver wrist watch. "It's six-forty-five."

"Is *Duvallo* expected?" I asked, moderately thunderstruck.

Watrous nodded. "He was to meet us here."

This was getting "curiouser and curiouser." The Society of American Magicians would shortly have enough members present to constitute a quorum.

With Watrous' help, Rappourt rose. He had started with her toward the door when a voice said:

"Hello, folks. What's up? Why all the dim religious light? Sabbat giving one of his séances?"

A man in evening clothes, topcoat on arm, hat tipped far back on his head, stood just inside the door at the end of the davenport. A woman stood beside him. She wore an evening gown that shimmered in the light and a white fur jacket with a high collar. The slightly foolish smiles on their faces indicated that they were both half seas over. The woman rocked a bit and hung more tightly to her companion's arm. "LaClaire!" Watrous piped. "What are you doing here?"

"Well, why not? We—er—thought there might be a cocktail in the shaker." His eyes strayed unsteadily around the room. "Where's Sabbat?" Then he saw the thing on the floor, and the bottom dropped out of his voice. A blank look of consternation washed the alcoholic grin from his face. The woman said, "Oh!" and I could hear her suck in her breath.

"Strangled!" Watrous said, with a consummate absence of tact. As they stood there, staring, he blurbled a quick, condensed story of our breaking in. Tarot walked to the window and stood with his back to us looking out. His fingers tapped impatiently on the pane. Rappourt dropped back into her chair. A vague psychic sense I didn't know I had responded to a faint hint of some new quality in the room's atmosphere and sent an uneasy shiver wavering within me, a cold feeling of danger near-by and waiting.

I looked at the newcomers and saw the bleached platinum blondness of the woman and the dark, long-lashed eyes that were now almost perfect circles. I saw the man's oddly disturbing combination of green eyes and blond hair, and noticed, when he nervously drew his right hand across his jaw, that the forefinger was missing and that the others were strangely twisted. He turned, his uncertainty suddenly gone.

"Come on, Zelma, let's get the hell out of here."

Zelma, however, had been oppositely affected by the sight. Hand at her mouth she ran quickly toward the bathroom. Her face had a pallid sickly color. LaClaire blinked at her comprehendingly and followed.

"Aren't there any lights in this joint?" he threw back.

"They're out of order," Watrous explained. We heard them fumble at the bathroom door, and then it slammed.

"You'd better stick around, Alfred," Watrous began, as LaClaire came back into the room. "Harte here has called the police."

"Harte?" LaClaire asked, giving me a suspicious scowl.

"Mr. Harte, Mr. LaClaire," the Colonel officiated. He was a

sucker for etiquette, and it occurred to me that he'd probably go around introducing people at a fire. "Harte lives across the hall." And to me, "The LaClaires have a most interesting mental routine presenting Mrs. LaClaire as *The Woman with the Radio Mind*. I doubt if anyone, even the Zancigs, have ever attained as high a degree of skill in the presentation of the second-sight trick."

The Colonel was a natural public relations counsel. I groaned inwardly when I heard this bit of ballyhoo. Another brace of magicians! If Duvallo, when he showed up, would only bring along a couple of acrobats and a man who could play *Humoresque* on the saw, we could go to town with a full evening's show. I could do my trick with the matches.

"Listen," LaClaire said to Watrous. "We're going to beat it. We're playing a date tonight and if the cops get here . . ."

We all heard it. The muted wail of a siren from the street outside.

"Well, that's that," LaClaire said and was silent. A moment later there were running footsteps on the stairs. We watched the door. Two red-faced cops came through it. The scent of cold air still clung to their uniforms. Halting just inside, they looked at us, their badges and buttons winking like stars in the candlelight.

I heard a second siren, its pitch rising as it came nearer.

Chapter 4
The Locked Room

From goolies and ghosties,
From long-legged beasties,
From things that go bump in the night,
Good Lord deliver us.

—Old Scottish Prayer

THERE WAS a small click, and we blinked stupidly at the light which an electric torch poured into our faces. The policeman that held it said nothing, but swung it in a slow circle, washing the walls with brilliance. The masks on the wall jutted out in sharp relief and revealed details of caricatured line, form, and color that were starkly exotic. Hanging with them, I now saw framed reproductions of Peter Breughel's *Mad Meg* and Hieronymus Bosch's *The Mouth of Hell*, two painted medieval imaginings that would make any psychiatrist stop and think twice—uneasily. In another place, near the faded colors of a Tibetan prayer flag, the light glowed yellow as it touched upon a gold crucifix whose inverted position was distinctly ominous.

The light reached the floor, jerked and stopped. The straining lifeless face centered in that bright theatric circle might have been a mask fallen from the wall.

The cop, moving swiftly, knelt by the body and touched the cheek. Again he turned the flashlight on us.

"What's wrong with the lights?" he demanded.

The Colonel, somewhat shakily and with an uncharacteristic lapse into understatement, explained that they didn't seem to be working. He started to plunge from there into an account of what had happened, but his introductory sentence was cut short by the arrival of a white-coated intern carrying a pulmotor. Outside another siren screamed hoarsely.

The man with the flashlight stood up. "We won't need you, Doc. You're way too late. The medical examiner can handle this one. Joe, you run down and tell one of the boys who just rolled in to keep an eye on the door. Phone the station and get the Homicide Squad started. Then see about these lights."

Joe said, "Okay, Steve," and left.

Steve went on, "You people stay where you are at that end of the room, and you," he poked a finger toward Tarot who stood in the dark shadow at one side of the window, "join 'em." Tarot obeyed, leisurely. Steve looked at us a moment in an uncertain way and then placed his torch on the edge of the desk. Its bright rounded eye looked at us with inappropriate gaiety.

"Who phoned headquarters?" Steve inquired finally, unbuttoning his coat and extracting a notebook and pencil.

I pleaded guilty to that and then quickly gave him the rest of the story. Steve interrupted several times with questions, and just as I finished Joe came back and got busy on the phone. He was followed by a third man in uniform. To him Steve said:

"Find the light box, Nick." And then, notebook ready and pointing his pencil at Rappourt, he added, "Now, I'll have all your names please."

But before Madame Rappourt could answer, Nick's voice came back from the inner hall into which he had disappeared. His words were hard and brittle. "I've got you covered! . . . Come outta there and keep your hands up." Steve's gun came from its holster before

Nick had finished speaking. He peered past us into the hallway, his eyebrows lifting.

Nick backed out, grinning. "Look what I found! A blonde!"

Zelma LaClaire followed him, hands half raised. "Say," she said, "can't a lady go to the bathroom . . ."

"How long you been in there?" Steve cut in.

Alfred LaClaire answered. "That's my wife, Officer. We came to pay a social call, just before you arrived. And—and we'd like to go and come back for the questions later. We're in the floor show at La Rumba and due to go on at—"

"Forget it, Mister," Steve cut in. "You'll stay put until the Homicide Squad gets here. Then you can tell it to the Inspector."

Alfred subsided, and Nick, gun in hand this time, resumed his investigation. Joe, leaving the phone, reported that the light company was sending a man and then joined Nick in the kitchen, where I shortly heard them at work on the light meter.

Steve licked the point of his pencil and again began collecting names and addresses. I watched my companions. Madame Rappourt shook her head and Watrous replied for them both. He also tried to interpolate extraneous information which Steve calmly ignored. Alfred LaClaire spoke for himself and his wife, impatiently. Zelma, somewhat steadier since her visit to the bathroom, stood with her back against the book shelves and stared at the corpse fascinated, as if expecting it to move. Tarot was smoking a cigarette, and I remember wishing I had noticed whether he had produced it from mid-air, already lighted, or whether he had merely fished it from a crumpled package like any other mortal. He briefly supplied his name and address in a voice that, though low, was filled with an irritating condescension, all of which was quite lost on Steve.

Suddenly, without benefit of siren, there were steps outside, and two men came through the door, three more crowding behind them. Even in that half light there was a vague indefinable something about them that said detectives—the un-civilian squareness of their shoulders, perhaps, or the quietly confident way in which they strode in.

I recognized one of the men. He wore a belted topcoat with the collar turned up, a smartly fresh hat, and a brown tweed suit. Quotation marks at the corners of his straight mouth indicated a capacity for humor that softened the hard, angular set of his jaw. Heavy eyebrows shaded frosty blue eyes. It was Inspector Homer Gavigan, one of the department's brighter lights.

Steve said, "I'm glad to see *you*, Inspector. This looks like one of those rip-snorters. There's the body."

Gavigan nodded, his sharp eyes busy and interested. "Lights?" he asked.

"Officers Hunter and Forelli are working on that now, sir. And the Edison Company is sending a man."

"Right. Check with them, will you? If it's going to take long, we'll rig a temporary light. Malloy, let's have the torch."

One of the other detectives deposited a large black suitcase on the davenport and, opening it, took out a large electric torch which he passed to the Inspector. The latter clicked it, and the body was again circled with light. The detectives stood looking down at it.

Steve returned, reporting, "Forelli says it's just a blown fuse and he'll have it right in a minute or so."

Gavigan nodded. "And who are all these people?"

Steve handed over his notebook. "Those are the names. Four of 'em broke in and found the body. The other two showed up just after. They were all here when we arrived." Steve then proceeded to rattle off a quick resume of what he had found and of what I had told him. When he mentioned the triply sealed door and exhibited the torn blue fabric that lay on the desk, Gavigan went over to look at it.

"What other doors are there?" he asked.

"I think there's one in the kitchen. I haven't had time to look at it yet."

"There's a job for you, Brady."

The dick who had brought in the suitcase went toward the kitchen. As he did so the floor lamps gave a bright, short flicker. Hunter's voice in the kitchen kibitzed, "I thought you said you were an electrician, Nick."

A cop stepped in from the hallway and reported, "The Edison man is here, sir."

"Let's have him," Malloy said. "The boys seem to be having their troubles."

The repairman came in and went through to the kitchen, stepping aside for Brady as he returned, a Five Star Final expression on his face.

"The kitchen door is bolted on the inside and there's some blue cloth, like that other, in the keyhole!"

Gavigan removed his topcoat and tossed it at the davenport. "It looks like work, Malloy," he said. Then, looking at me, "I suppose you've already phoned a flash to your paper, Harte?"

He rather startled me with that. I had never talked to him except at mass interviews and then only once or twice. His reputation for possessing one of those legendary headwaiter memories evidently had foundation.

I reassured him. "No, I'm an ex-newspaperman now. Mr. Hearst and I didn't get along. I write for the magazines now, the pages in the back. 'They Laughed When I Ate Off the Mantel. Drive a Straight Eight; It's Kind to Your Fanny.' That sort of thing."

"Oh, better hours, I suppose," he commented, little knowing what a howler that was. "Well, if you start itching to call a rewrite man—would you mind not doing it until I say yes?"

I assented and then added a hasty amendment, "If you'll sort of keep me up to date."

He grinned. "Blackmailer!" Then he nodded, "Okay, but be good. And now, if you don't mind, I'd like to put some of these people on ice in your apartment for a while."

"Sure," I said. "Go right ahead."

He turned to Malloy. "Captain, put them across the hall and have O'Connor go along."

Alfred LaClaire spoke up. "Inspector, my wife and I are due to go on in the floor show at La Rumba down on Sheridan Square. If we could leave and come back later . . ."

"Sorry. That's impossible. O'Connor will phone the club for you and tell them you'll be delayed. And, Malloy, on the way out see that no one touches that davenport or disturbs the present position of that door. That's all." He turned away, and Malloy and O'Connor began shooing them out.

The Inspector caught my eye. "You stick around," he said; and then, his voice rising, "What's the delay on these lights?"

Nick came out. "Looks like monkey business. New fuses blow as fast as we put 'em in. The electrician says there's a short somewhere and it may take a while."

"Well, we're not owls. Tell him to come in here first, run an extension from Harte's apartment, and connect up a couple of these floor lamps. Have Hunter go out and stay on the door, and you go find out who else lives in this building and what they know, if anything. The medical examiner . . ." Gavigan stopped. He was looking toward the desk in the corner. Then he said, "Okay, Forelli, get at it."

Nick did a right-about-face while the Inspector scowled in an annoyed way at Tarot, who, instead of leaving with the others, had seated himself on the edge of the desk. He sat there idly swinging one leg. Steve, who had evidently counted noses and found himself one shy, poked his head back in the door and said ominously, "The parade went up *this* street, Mister."

Tarot ignored that with a practiced air and spoke quickly. "A little light does seem to be indicated around here, Inspector. In more ways than one. I think I can help you, but if you want to hear it before I leave, it'll have to be now. I broadcast over a national network from WJZ five night a week. This is one of them. The Xanadu program goes on the air at ten, and the previous hour is devoted to rehearsal. I need ten minutes to get there. You can't dismiss that as lightly as Alfred's night club date." He glanced at his wrist watch. "I can give you fifteen minutes."

Gavigan put his hands in his pockets. Without turning, he said, "I'll handle this one, O'Connor. Go keep your eye on the rest."

O'Connor went. Gavigan eyed Tarot for a moment as if he were something in a store window. A sound at the other end of the room attracted our attention, and we saw in front of the hearth a rear elevation of Detective Brady. He was bent over, the upper half of his torso projecting into the fireplace, and poking with his torch up the chimney.

"What are you looking for, Brady?" Gavigan asked brusquely. "Chimney swallows?"

The detective produced his invisible upper section and straightened. There was a smear of soot across his nose.

"I was hoping I'd find one of those P. T. Barnum signs reading 'This way to the Egress.'" He dusted his hands. "But no such luck. Every cockeyed window in this joint looks out on a sheer wall. Two of them drop smack into the drink. And if you suggest a rope let down from the roof, or ladders being poked up from private yachts, it's a waste of breath. First, all the windows are bolted on the inside. Second, none of the panes have been removed and replaced—all the putty is old and cracked. Third, the bolt are so stiff it'd take a hammer to knock 'em loose. The late deceased must have been a nut on the subject of ventilation."

"He was," Tarot said. "He used to bundle up like a deep-sea diver before going out, which wasn't any oftener than he could help. He once fired a maid when he caught her trying to open a window in order to shake a rug. That was just one of his large collection of batty notions."

Brady went on. "A cat could get out of this flue, maybe, but nothing any larger. At the moment there's just one way out of this place. Through there." He gestured with his light at the hall door with its splintered panel. "If that was locked too, I give up. I took a peek at the inside of the lock. And it shows picklock scratches, which jibes with Mr. Harte's story about breaking in. I haven't found anything else as yet."[1]

At that moment one of the floor lamps blossomed light, and the electrician moved toward a second.

The Inspector said, "Take the fingerprint outfit, Brady, and go get the prints off that mob across the hall. No use dusting around here until we get a lot more light; and Quinn, you'd better get your pencil out."

Brady departed, and Quinn went to a chair under the lamp and opened a steno's notebook across his knee. Hunter's voice outside the door said, "Hello, Doc. Go right in."

A gnome-like man with abnormally rounded shoulders entered, following a huge cigar.

"Been wondering where you were, Hesse," the Inspector greeted him. "Go to it, if you can see anything. There's very little light on your subject."

The medical examiner smiled wearily, as if used to such con-

---

1   The examination of a lock's interior without removing it is accomplished with the aid of a cystosopic device, consisting of a viewing tube with a small electric bulb and a mirror at its end. The irregular searching movements of a picklock or skeleton key leave traces in the coating of oil and grease usually present in lock mechanisms.

ditions, the Inspector's puns included. He took off his coat and, picking up the flash light that Malloy had left on the davenport, stepped carefully over the chalked design on the floor and busied himself at the body.

"I want an estimate of the time of death as soon as possible," Gavigan said, and then turned to face Tarot once more.

The examiner mumbled, "Haven't I told you and told you that . . . oh, all right!"

Hunter at the door announced, "The identification squad is here, sir."

"Send the photographer in. Have the rest of them wait. And don't let anyone else in unless it's the D.A. himself." Gavigan addressed Tarot. "You can begin by telling me how you and those others happened to stop up here tonight."

"Suppose I start with my alibi, Inspector," Tarot replied. "You're going to be asking for it sooner or later, and we might as well get it over with."

Gavigan nodded, studying him.

"After leaving the radio station last night, I went directly to a party at 566 East 96th Street, Mr. and Mrs. Knowlton. There were a number of radio and theatrical people there, most of whom I knew. And since they had me doing card tricks most of the night, I'm pretty well supplied with witnesses."

I caught a glimpse of Captain Malloy making an unobtrusive phoneward exit from the room.

"That's very interesting, Mr. Tarot," Gavigan commented dryly. "When I get an alibi pushed at me, it usually means there's a motive in the woodpile. What's yours?"

Tarot smiled. "I see your point, Inspector, but this must be the exception that proves the rule. I had no motive for killing Sabbat. I was as good a friend as he had, I think."

"And why *did* you want to get that alibi off your chest?"

"Merely a desire to be of help and speed matters up. I've got to be on my way. Afraid it was the wrong thing to do. Your suspicions are easily aroused."

Gavigan followed through with a body blow. "Perhaps. And then again, maybe not. Just how do you know Sabbat was killed during the time covered by your alibi?"

Tarot acted as if he were playing the lead in a Noel Coward dinner jacket drama. "Elementary, my dear Watson. I talked to Sabbat on the phone just after my program last night, and before leaving for the party. So I know he was alive as late as eleven. The body is clothed in pajamas and dressing gown, and the morning milk still sits out in the corridor, and—oh, you saw the bedroom, Harte. Has the bed been slept in?"

I shook my head, "No."

"You see. He was killed after eleven and shortly before his bedtime, which I doubt would be as late as six this morning, the time when I left the party. And these lights—if they were intentionally put out of commission . . . well, why do that in the daytime?"

Gavigan made no reply to that argument. Instead he asked, "Is that what you had to tell me?"

"No." Tarot stood up. "I wanted to suggest one or two things. The LaClaires, for instance. I wouldn't waste too much time chasing them. You'll find soon enough that Zelma and Sabbat were having fun and games behind Alfred's back. Zelma's that way; she has considerable difficulty remaining for long in a vertical position. All of which give Al an A No. 1 motive. But I don't think this is the sort of murder he'd pull off. He's such a direct person, he'd probably walk up to Sabbat, slander his family tree, bash him one—and get caught doing it. I don't know why he hasn't done it before now."

Tarot dropped his cigarette on the carpet and stepped on it, grinding with his heel.

"The Colonel," he went on, "is a possibility except that military men usually run to guns, and Madame Rappourt . . . hmmm . . . she's the dark horse. Strangling isn't a woman's crime, I don't suppose—but you'd know about that. At any rate, I'd suggest you pay no attention to anything she may bring up in one of her psychic trances. Any way you slice that, it's still baloney."

"You're quite the amateur detective, Mr. Tarot. And so what?"

"Nothing, except that your clue to the murderer is as plain as day. It stares you—or me at least—right in the face. It's so obvious that—well, maybe that's why he thinks he can get away with it. Though I wouldn't care for that technique myself."

Another flash bulb flared brilliantly, putting a bright exclamation point on Tarot's sentence. The photographer said, "Okay, Doc. Take him away." Dr. Hess looked at Gavigan, who nodded, and then he and the photographer lifted the body and, stepping gingerly over the surrounding inscription, carried it to the davenport. Gavigan stepped forward, bent down and picked up a small white oblong from the spot on the floor where the body had lain. He gave it an astonished blink, and after staring at it for a long moment said:

"Go on, Mr. Tarot, what is it that's so obvious? The circles on the floor, the incense and candles, the occult setup?"

Tarot sniffed. "No. That says Sabbat invoked some demon out of hell and that the bogey got his dander up and wrung Sabbat's neck. Storybook stuff! Maybe Sabbat *was* playing at his occult games; he did that sort of thing. Or maybe the murderer set the stage this way—I don't know. That's not important. The locked room is your cue. All you have to do is find someone who could have gotten out of this apartment, leaving it with the doors locked on the inside as found. That narrows your choice of culprits no end. Every magician knows something about methods of picking locks and handcuffs, ways of escaping from rope ties, nailed boxes, and locked coffins. I used to do a milk can escape myself in the Keith circuit days. But this stunt has me guessing. I don't get it yet, and I don't like to admit it, either."

"The point being, I suppose, that you do know of someone who could do it?"

Tarot nodded. "That's the general idea."

"Well, out with it," Gavigan prodded.

Tarot shrugged. "Don't you ever read the papers? Haven't I said enough?"

The Inspector waited a moment, but Tarot remained silent. Gavigan nodded, then: "Yes, you've said enough."

He came over to the desk against which Tarot still leaned. On its top he placed the small printed business card he had been holding by the edges. Tarot and I leaned over it. It read:

DAVID DUVALLO

The Escape King

Booking Offices   Residence
1765 Broadway   36 Van Ness Lane

Chapter 5
Sleight of Hand

The hand is not quicker than the eye; but it's cleverer.
Merlini: *The Psychology of Deception*

"THAT," TAROT said slowly, "would seem to be that."

The Inspector, watching him intently, hinted, "You dislike the man?"

"On the contrary, we see a good bit of each other. But if he's going to go around strangling people . . ." Tarot made a helpless gesture. "Even though Sabbat may have had it coming to him."

"What do you mean by that?"

Tarot glanced toward the davenport where Dr. Hesse was working over the body. "Sabbat was a candidate for a sanitarium. Damnedest psychopath I ever met. His persecution complex was a honey. He was always accusing his friends of the most fantastic plots against himself. When his friends naturally got fewer, that only aggravated the condition."

"Who were his friends?"

"Zelma, of course, and myself. I was interested in him because, though he was bats, he did have lucid streaks, and he could be an excellent conversationalist. I introduced Dave to him recently, and he's been nosing around the old boy a bit, hoping to catch on to some of the inner workings of Sabbat's parlor Voodoo tricks. Watrous, I think, knows him, and Alfred, though those two didn't pal around much, naturally. I think Sabbat's psychopathic ailments included the one called satyriasis, so you may have to question some blondes. You know, Inspector, the papers are going to have a Roman holiday with this case. It has everything. An impossible mystery romantically trimmed with magic and witchcraft, and a cast of characters picked right from the headlines. Then, when Dr. Casanova Sabbat's sex-life gets an airing—what a dish to set before a city editor!"

"Know any of the women?"

"No. I prefer amateur talent myself." Tarot grinned and lit a cigarette. I noticed this time; he didn't produce it from airy nothing, but took it from a gold cigarette case.

"Then you think Duvallo killed Sabbat and the card cinches it? What about motive?"

Tarot shook his head. "I don't know. You've got a situation that cries aloud for an escape artist, and then you find Dave's card. But I don't quite understand why the Great Duvallo should fumble it so badly. He squirms out of packing cases that have been nailed shut and dropped in the harbor, and now here he is all tangled up in a revolving door. Rather out of character, isn't it?"

I couldn't decide whether Tarot just liked to run off at the mouth or whether he couldn't resist this unique chance to play the Great Detective. I felt an urge to do the latter myself, only I realized that the first act on the program would be to explain the locked doors, and somehow I didn't feel so confident about that.

Gavigan let Tarot run down, and then he brought him back to the starting point.

"Suppose you tell me why you, Watrous, and Rappourt showed up here when you did, Mr. Tarot."

"Oh, yes, of course. He said he could photograph thought, and he wanted to try it on Rappourt when she was in a trance state. That was the immediate reason for the gathering, I think."

Malloy came back just then, and I saw him, behind Tarot's back, spread his hand in the manner of a baseball umpire signalling "safe." I took that to mean that Tarot's alibi had been checked and not found wanting.

Tarot continued, "Dave and I were here Saturday night, and Sabbat mentioned Madame Rappourt. He'd been reading some report on her mediumship that Watrous had published in one of the psychic journals. Dave knew Rappourt and Watrous, and Sabbat wanted him to bring them up. Dave said . . ."

Gavigan interrupted. "I thought you said Watrous and Sabbat knew each other."

"Yes, but I gathered they haven't been speaking for the last ten years or so. I don't know why. Sabbat told Dave he was willing to bury the hatchet in order to meet Rappourt, and Dave promised to relay the invitation. This afternoon Dave phoned me, said they'd accepted but that he was unavoidably detained, and would I pick them up and escort them over to Sabbat's. He'd follow along as soon as he could. I discovered then that the party had gotten rather elaborate and that they were all having dinner together at Lindy's. I hadn't intended to stop in until after my broadcast; but, since Duvallo asked me, I went over, introduced myself to the Colonel and Rappourt, and brought them here, intending to eat with them, go to the broadcast, and return in time for the monkey business. It looks as if I don't eat at all now."

"What's detaining Duvallo?"

"I don't know. He acted as if he was in a hell of a hurry and said he'd explain when he saw us."

"Janssen," Gavigan said, turning to one of the other detectives, "get headquarters on to it. I want him at once. Have them try his home, his office, Lindy's, and—and put some men on the railroad stations."

"You might warn them," Tarot added with a grin, "that they'll be fooling with an escape artist and that handcuffs don't mean a thing."

Janssen got busy on the phone. Hunter poked his head in at the door and was joined by Gavigan for a whispered conference. Both Hunter's gestures and Gavigan's evident interest indicated developments. When the Inspector finally sent him off and turned back into the room, I took the opportunity to get something off my chest. I'd been impatiently waiting a proper opening and this seemed as good as any.

"May I suggest something, Inspector?" I asked.

He nodded and I took the plunge.

"I don't want you to think I'm telling you how to run your business, but—you don't do any parlor tricks yourself, do you? As a hobby?"

"No. Aren't there enough magicians around here now?"

"That's just it. There are far too many. And I'd suggest getting in one more. The cure this time might be a hair of the dog that's chewing us." I talked fast trying to stave off objections. "So far the suspects are all conjurers of one sort or another. Madame Rappourt's the worst of the lot. She claims to be the real honest-to-goodness McCoy, a magician in the original sense of one who has supernatural power—a twentieth-century witch.

"I don't know if Watrous practices sleight of hand, but he does know how—plenty. I wrote an article once on the spiritualistic community at Lilydale, and for background I skipped through four hundred pages of concentrated trickery entitled *Fraudulent Mediumistic Methods*. Watrous wrote the book. I'm not trying to belittle the ability of yourself or the Homicide Department, but I'll place a little bet with you that a technical expert who knows all the tricks of the trade will come in darned handy. You couldn't lose anything, and you might . . ."

"You have someone in mind?" Gavigan asked.

"Yes. Merlini."

Tarot said, "You think he'd do better than I, Mr. Harte?" His voice was refrigerated, each word a hard, frosty ice cube.

I rebutted that, addressing myself to Gavigan. "What we'd want, I should think, would be a disinterested expert, one who's not mixed up in the case." I was rather pleased with that thrust, especially when I saw Tarot's scowl.

"I know the man, Inspector," he argued, "and I'd advise against it. How do you know he's not mixed up in it? He knows all these people, and he might very well have a motive—"

The Inspector was, I think, pretty well fed up with Tarot as a self-appointed amateur detective and with his snooty superior air. His objection bounced off Gavigan's Irish temperament and boomeranged.

"I happen to know him myself," Gavigan said, "and I agree with Harte. If he knows all these people that's another good reason for having him here."

I stood slightly behind the Inspector, and I answered Tarot's dirty look by pantomiming the business of laughing up my sleeve. Gavigan was still talking.

"As it happens, I'd already thought of it. Merlini gave some lectures and demonstrations at Police College a couple of years ago explaining the tricks of card sharps and con men. He knows his business. Try and get him on the phone, Malloy."

Tarot dismissed the subject and said, "I've got to be going, much as I'd like to be here when Duvallo arrives—if he does. I'd like to hear his explanation for that card and to know why he made such a hash of things. It's really not so hard to fool people, you know—even policemen."

"Oh, so?" Gavigan asked coolly.

"Yes. Watch."

He turned his left side toward us and held out his right hand, which was still gloved. He turned it showing back and front. Then, with a swift, deft movement, he seemed to pick from the air a fan of about a dozen playing cards. He transferred them to his left hand and squared them up. His face now wore its professional smile, a disarming one, so apparently good-natured that it sugar-coated any chagrin his audience might feel at this double-crossing of their senses. It was the conventional grin conjurers use to nullify the conceit such an exhibition of superiority implies. But on Tarot's sardonic countenance it worked a startling transformation. He hardly seemed to be the same person who had been scowling at me so blackly a moment before.

As we watched he produced another handful of cards in a neat fan, and he repeated the gesture twice more with easy precision until he was holding a full deck. It was a slick performance, marred only by the fact that he did it with his gloves on. This variation, Merlini had once told me, was originated by Cardini, and the number of small fry who have pirated it are merely admitting their own lack of originality. I wondered why Tarot, a top-notch card man in his own right, descended to that sort of thing.

Gavigan, I saw, was consciously suppressing an openmouthed attitude. I suspected that he was one of those persons who dislike being fooled, whose alibi is always, "Oh, well, of course the stage is riddled with trap doors," and who get a bit of a jolt when a conjurer for the first time comes right up close, and with no trap doors about, hoodwinks them just the same.

Tarot came forward, fanned the cards in front of Gavigan, and voiced the conjurer's stock request, "Take a card, please."

The Inspector half hypnotically put forth his hand, and then withdrew it, scowling.

"For crissake!" he flared. "This is no time for parlor tricks!"

Tarot shrugged and dropped the cards into his pocket.

"Sorry!" he said, "I must be going anyhow. I'm late now." He headed toward the door.

"Not so fast!" Gavigan said quickly. "I won't take a card, but I'll have something else. Those picklocks, please."

He held out his hand.

Tarot stopped, grinned, and bringing out the key ring he tossed them at the Inspector. They jingled and flashed in the light as the latter caught them.

"Quite a professional assortment," Gavigan said. "Let's hear about them."

"Poor Dave even has circumstance working against him. They're his. I borrowed them Saturday night to work on a trunk whose key I had mislaid. I intended to return them to him tonight. Perhaps you'll see that he gets them."

"He'll see them all right. And now the gun, please."

"I've a permit for that, Inspector."

"Let's see it."

"It's at my hotel."

"Okay, then I want the gun." Gavigan's hand went out again. "You can have it back when I see the permit."

Tarot shrugged and held it out. "I hope you'll leave me some small change, Inspector. I need carfare. Anything else?"

Without replying, the Inspector crooked his little finger through the trigger guard and with the gun hanging crossed the room and placed it carefully on the blotter pad at the desk.

"Yes," he answered, "leave your fingerprints with Brady across the hall on your way out. I'll expect you back after the broadcast, and don't stop to look in any store windows on the way. Understand? Hunter," Gavigan raised his voice, "go downstairs and tell the boys to let Mr. Tarot out."

Hunter's voice came from outside, "Right," and we heard him go down the hall.

Tarot nodded. "Okay, Inspector. I wish you luck." He bowed slightly, stepped quickly through the door, and pulled it to after him.

Gavigan scowled at the place where he had been and said, "Damn him anyway! I wonder if he did that purposely."

I didn't get it for a moment; then I remembered Gavigan's orders, delivered in Tarot's presence, that the door was not to be touched.

"Janssen," Gavigan ordered, "you go tail him. I want a full and detailed report, and God help you if you lose him."

"Yes, sir." Janssen started off in high, then stalled as the Inspector warned, "Careful of that knob!"

The detective turned the knob carefully, grasping the shank between forefinger and thumb.

"Well, Doc," Gavigan began, "what's the . . ." He stopped short as if someone had clapped a hand over his mouth. I have since seen the Inspector conceal his surprise, and I have seen him when he couldn't conceal it, but this was the only time I've even seen his jaw literally hanging. It sagged as if the maxillary muscles had suddenly been severed. I looked where he was looking and understood. Sabbat's body lay on the davenport, and Dr. Hesse, standing near it, held a playing card, the ace of spades, between his right forefinger and thumb. Watching it intently, he made a quick throwing gesture and the card vanished, his open, empty palm stretched flat. He reached down and pulled the card from behind his right knee. With grave concentration he repeated the maneuver, twice more.

Gavigan bellowed, "Dr. Hesse! What the blazing hell are you doing?"

The card, which the doctor was again producing from behind his right knee, slipped from his startled fingers and fell to the floor. Dr. Hesse looked up foggily and said, "What?"

The Inspector couldn't think of any more words, and Hesse, noting the amazement in his face, realized its cause.

"Sorry, Inspector," he said, a bit shamefacedly. "I couldn't refrain from practicing that one while it was fresh in my mind. Standing behind Tarot as he produced those cards, I could see some things that you couldn't. I noticed that he has an original variation on the basic sleight used in that manipulative series, an improvement on the standard Thurston method. It's so simple I can't think why it had never occurred to me . . ."

"But that card . . . what . . . where?"

"Oh, I always have a deck in my pocket. Sleight of hand is my hobby. Nothing unusual in that, you know. The medical profession is represented in the ranks of amateur conjurers to a greater degree than any other, more doctors being enrolled in the Society of American Magicians than any other single profession. The practice of surgery, I suppose, predisposes us toward a hobby that is so largely pure manual dexterity."

Gavigan began to recover. "Oh, dissection leads to deception, does it?" He groaned. "Since you know, how did Tarot pull those cards out of nothing and how do you—"

Dr. Hesse grinned and shook his head. "Magicians, even amateurs, aren't in the habit of divulging their secrets to idle curiosity seekers. Of course, if you're seriously interested in acquiring the art . . . ?"

"God forbid! And besides, Mrs. Gavigan wouldn't allow rabbits in the house," Gavigan said, and added, "Maybe you knew Sabbat, or know some of the witnesses we've collected. Tarot, the LaClaires, Colonel Watrous, Madame Rappourt, Duvallo?"

"Hmmm, that's a pretty good bill. I don't know Watrous and Rappourt. The others I am acquainted with slightly, having met them at S.A.M. meetings. I don't, however, attend very regularly any more. The murder rate in this town keeps me too busy."

"Well, I'll hear what you know about 'em later. Let's have your report."

Dr. Hesse picked up his ace of spades and placed it in his coat pocket. "The present corpse," he said, "met death by strangulation. The usual soft marks are present. If you look closely you'll notice a pale groove in the neck with a slight surrounding suggilation. It indicates that the strangulation was accomplished with the aid of some soft material such as a woman's hose or a towel. Find anything of that sort?"

"No. The body was just as you found it."

"Murder then, of course. But that's odd."

"What is?"

"There aren't any bruises on the body. When a person is strangled it almost always entails a struggle that leaves some sort of trace. Usually bruises on the back. Their absence suggests that he was drugged or stunned first, though I see no outward signs of that. Something to look for in the post mortem."

"The time of death, Doctor?" Gavigan asked.

Dr. Hesse sighed. "I wish it were compulsory for the victim's watch to be broken and stopped during the death struggle. That makes it so much simpler."

"Come on, quit stalling, Doc. You make pretty good guesses."

"Well, rigor mortis is quite complete, no signs of decomposition yet, and the interior body temperature—well, say around three this morning, with the usual margin for error. That do?"

Gavigan nodded. "Thanks," he said, and began investigating the pockets of Sabbat's dressing gown. He took out a bunch of keys, a piece of white chalk, an indelible pencil, and then, just as Malloy came into the room, the torn half of a blue-bordered handkerchief.

"Spence was the only one in the house with any information, Inspector," Malloy reported. "The old maid downstairs wears one of those amplifying gadgets hung on her ear, and she could live right under a bowling alley and not know it. I've got ten men push-ing doorbells on this street trying to scare up witnesses that might have noticed something. Merlini is on his way and . . . oh, yes. Tar-ot's alibi checks and double checks. The Knowltons gave me half a dozen names, and they all swear he was the life of the party every minute. There doesn't seem to be any question about—"

Brady came in, carrying his fingerprint paraphernalia. "I've got their prints—all except . . ." He looked around in a surprised way. "Where's the swell with the monocle?"

Gavigan choked. "Haven't you . . . didn't he come in there and let you ink him?"

Brady replied with an open-mouthed no.

Inspector Gavigan emitted a crackling, neon-colored stream of high-voltage profanity. Malloy jumped for the hall, and I heard him going down the stairs, two steps at a time.

Chapter 6
The Great Merlini

. . . only to the privileged few has that precious link been given, that transcendent rapport with the Unseen World been made manifest. These chosen ones are outside the Law; their confluence with the Astral Force makes possible all those Dark Things which earthlings pretend are mere flights of imaginative fancy, all those thaumaturgie realities of Abaddon which would swathe their pigmy minds, their shriveled souls with Insensate Fear.

Dr. Cesare Sabbat: *The Secret Heresies*

INSPECTOR GAVIGAN was phoning headquarters and still throwing out intermittent bursts of lava when Malloy came back and reported that Tarot had last been seen in a taxi headed north, Detective Janssen in his wake.

Gavigan barked into the phone, "Send a couple of men to NBC at once and pick up a guy named Eugene Tarot. He's on the ten o'clock program, and I don't care how many million people are waiting to hear him. I want him at once! Bring him directly here and hurry it!"

He banged the receiver. "Malloy, Headquarters is sending more men. You can put them to work collecting data on those people in the next room. Quinn, you nose through the desk and filing cabinets. I want to know lots more about the cadaver."

Malloy went out followed by Dr. Hesse, and Gavigan, motioning Brady to follow, moved toward the kitchen. "I want to see that other door for myself," he said as they disappeared.

I lit a cigarette and stood for a moment or two by the window, listening to the foghorns and watching the lighted outline of a ferry boat that moved slowly across the dark nothingness of the river. I heard a step behind me and turned to see a tall figure come through the door and move toward me around the end of the davenport. Then, as at some stage manager's cue, the ceiling lights and the green shaded desk lamp flicked on, chasing the darkness at last from the corners of the room and with bright accommodation giving Merlini a good entrance. As he stood there, blinking a bit in the light, I half expected him to take a bow and proceed with his opener, in which one of his white gloves, tossed into the air, became a dove that circled and disappeared into the wings.

Merlini's off-stage appearance is, for a magician, oddly lacking in peculiarity. Those rubber stamp stigmata of the conjurer, the curling mustachios and the unharvested crop of bushy hair, have little existence today, save in the cartoonist's imagination. Merlini's face was clean shaven and his haircut altogether normal.

At first you do not suspect him of any connection with show business. This despite the fact that the Riding Merlinis have been one of circusdom's top equestrian acts here and abroad for five generations. You would not guess that Phineas T. Barnum had been his godfather, that his initial entrance on to this earthly stage was made in a circus car en route somewhere between Centralia and Peoria, Illinois; or that he made his first public appearance at the age of three in the role of a small, burnt-corked Nubian, who held grimly to the side of a swaying howdah as it was borne around the arena on the back of the immortal Jumbo.

It is not until he speaks that you suspect his profession. His voice belongs to the theater; richly resonant, it exhibits an unusual range of depth and tone. Merlini can be, and at times is, completely self-effacing, then suddenly he speaks and in that instant has captured everyone's complete attention. If he is "working" he proceeds at once to double-cross his listeners with smooth misdirection. His speech, habitually dry, ironic, and humorous, has a habit of shifting with subtle celerity to a compelling delivery that is not far short of hypnotic. It is utterly impossible to tell when he is being serious and when he is pattering in preparation for a minor miracle. He could sell you anything; and he does sell you impossibilities.

The planes of his face are forceful though asymmetric, one wayward ear projecting with rakish nonconformity considerably further than the other. His hair and eyes are black; and the latter shine with an intense curiosity. The good-humored crinkles at the corners of his mouth often bracket a faintly lopsided smile. He carries his tall, spare body with an almost conceited air of confidence. At rest his hands look large and masculinely awkward; in motion they take on that special grace and delicately co-ordinated economy that spells long discipline.

There is no predicting his dress. At times it is as impeccable off stage as it always is on; and at other times it achieves an inimitable disorganization, as comfortable as it is slack. His pockets are always loaded with the smaller appurtenances of his profession— cards, thimbles, silk handkerchiefs, and, I suspect, other gadgets of a more secret sort.

Merlini likes surf bathing, table tennis, puzzles, Times Square, and Mrs. Merlini. He can smell any circus that approaches within a radius of one hundred miles, and he promptly disappears in that direction. He dislikes subways, beer, inactivity, grand opera, and golf. I suppose that he sleeps, but I have never caught him at it. He has authored three books: *Legerdemainiacs, The Psychology of Deception,* and *Sawdust Trails.* He is the proprietor of a shop which supplies the conjuring fraternity with its illusive paraphernalia.

As the light came up Merlini looked at me and started to speak, when his eye caught the rigmarole of words and circles traced on the floor. His eyebrows lifted the tiniest bit, and then flattened in a frown. He glanced swiftly around the room. His eyes came back to the chalked diagram, and he asked,

"What the devil have you—or rather, what have you and the devil been up to, Ross?"

"Breaking and entering, for one thing. Discovering a corpse for another."

That announcement got me some attention.

"That doesn't sound like a gag."

"It isn't. Look behind you."

He turned and saw the covered form on the davenport.

"The gentleman's name," I went on, "is—or rather was—Cesare Sabbat. He—"

"Who?" Merlini's steady calm evidenced a slight wobble.

"Dr. Cesare Sabbat. Know him?"

Merlini took two steps and lifted a corner of the dressing gown. He looked at the face a moment.

"Yes, but—" He regarded me thoughtfully. "The face doesn't exactly suggest an easy death, and, judging from the numbers of the forces of law and order outside, I'd guess it was far from normal."

"He was strangled," I explained. "And since there was no noose of any sort found, he could hardly have accomplished it unaided."

"And yet you had to force an entrance." He eyed the splintered door panel. "This is an interesting contradiction. Quite, particularly since the dressing gown is incomplete."

"The dressing gown—what's the matter with it?"

"There are loops on each side which indicate that it's built to tie around the middle. I don't see the cord. By the way, what am I wanted for?"

I stared at the dressing gown and answered, "Not for murder—at least, not yet. I think Inspector Gavigan of the Homicide Bureau would like you to explain how the Walking-Through-A-Brick-Wall Trick is done. It looks as if Sabbat's murderer knew the answer. So far, the Homicide Squad hasn't been able to discover any other way out of this apartment. The doors, both of them, were locked, bolted, and the keyholes stuffed, from the inside. The windows haven't been opened in months."

"You're off to a swell start, Ross. Don't stop."

With studied calm I produced another thunderbolt. "What's more, all the witnesses hereabouts seem to be customers of yours. There are so many magicians floating around that they positively get in your hair."

"Some of them do that, singly," Merlini said dryly, and then with entreaty, "Harte, will you please stop running on in this Scheherazade manner and tell me what's happened? And don't put all your climaxes in the first scene. It's bad theater. Besides, I'm punch drunk already."

"So you can't take it?" Gavigan's voice preceded him into the room. They shook hands and the Inspector asked, "Have you met the corpse?"

"Yes," Merlini answered, "Ross did the honors. But I knew him before, some ten years ago. He used to be rated tops as an anthropologist in the magic and primitive religion line. Then he dropped out of sight so suddenly and completely that I rather thought he must have gone to continue his other-world researches closer to their source."

"What caused the sudden eclipse?" Gavigan asked interestedly.

"His subject ran away with him. He began taking such things as vampires, werewolves—and maybe pixies, for all I know—seriously. He even hung the traditional sword and sprigs of garlic on his door as a vampire preventive. Odd, because he looked a bit vampirish himself. There was a Lon Chaney–Boris Karloff feel to him. You almost expected him to bare a set of yellow fangs at any moment and say boo! Last time I talked with him, he was full of some new experiments in what he called modern alchemy."

Merlini gestured toward the worktable and the bottle-laden shelves in the further corner of the room. "Still at it, evidently. Then he began writing books and articles that his scholarly colleagues couldn't swallow. *Lycanthropy Today* and *The Secret Heresies* were two of the titles I remember. The latter book treated Telekinesis, Cryptesthesia, and Astral Projection as established facts. The editors of scientific journals began sending him rejection slips, and his scholarly reputation nosed over into a power dive."[1]

"But what about his disappearance? What did he do, start pouting and go hide?" Gavigan asked impatiently.

"He had a frightful temper, and he nearly killed an eminent German archeologist at a scientific congress by clubbing the poor man over the head with his own umbrella. He'd been trying to convince the old boy that Pyramidology was an exact science. The Herr Doktor swore out a warrant for his arrest and Sabbat skipped. No one ever seemed to know where."

"Pyramidwhatsis wasn't taught at Public School 67, as I remember. What is it?"

Merlini shucked his overcoat and dropped it with his hat on a near-by chair.

"It's one of the fancier divination systems and is based upon certain measurements of the Great Pyramid of Cheops, notably those made in 1864 by Piazzi-Smyth, the Astronomer Royal of Scotland. The occultists say that this is the world's oldest existing structure and was built 100,000 years ago by the Atlantaeans just

---

1   His more scientifically acceptable books were: *Daughters of Hecate, The Road to Endor—A History of Prophecy,* and *Studies in Superstition,* this last an encyclopedic six volume work that is still the standard authority on the subject.

prior to the sinking of their continent, as a repository of learning and a temple for the initiation of adepts. Similar temples are said to have been set up somewhere in the unexplored—oh, always the unexplored—portions of either Brazil or Yucatan—the authorities disagree—and in Tibet, where the Great White Lodge of the Himalayas is supposed to be today the one remaining active chapter of this ancient priesthood.[2] Their thesis is that if a pyramid inch—they invent their own inches—is taken as a year of our time, then the course of the Pyramid's inner passageways predicts the course of world history and civilization. According to that science the world came to an end at 4 A.M. on September 16, 1936. Did you know?"

"Sabbat," the Inspector broke in, finally, "was trying to convert the German professor to that theory?"

Merlini nodded.

"Well," Gavigan said emphatically, "we know one thing then. He was as batty as they come. Which explains a lot of things in this room." He scowled up at a Balinese devil mask on the wall, whose varnished fury, glistening in the light, showed that its owner had been a discriminating connoisseur of the hideous.

"There are people who would dispute that conclusion, Inspector. Even in this streamlined Twentieth Century there are plenty of people outside of nut houses who believe firmly in that sort of thing. Southern California is full of them. I could name you a dozen books issued quite lately by reputable publishing houses whose authors state their belief in all sorts of black magic, from teleportation to levitation, werewolves to banshees. Sir Oliver Lodge, William Crookes, and Professor Zoellner were convinced of the

---

2   A colony of 1000 Lemurians (from the Pacific's even more ancient lost continent of Mu) was reported as late as 1932 to exist on the slopes of Mt. Shasta surrounded by an invisible wall of force that prevents approach by either man or forest fires!

truth of spiritism. Conan Doyle took photographs of fairies—the winged variety—and Dr. Alexander Cannon, a member of the British Medical Association's Executive Council, says he has made thought take objective form and seriously warns his readers to beware of the evil forces set up in the ether by black magicians. And he cites instances. Madame Blavatsky still has her followers, and Evangeline Adams' writings on that hardy perennial of the divinatory systems, astrology, are still best sellers. A recent convention of the National Association of Fortune Tellers in Trenton, New Jersey, voted to picket all tearooms employing non-association tea-leaf readers. They also introduced to a waiting world a new method of divination or skrying, beer suds reading. Pennsylvania still has its witches, the rite of exorcism for diabolic possession has by no means fallen into complete disuse and Satanic Masses are still—"[3]

Gavigan held up his hands to stem the flood of information and said, "Sure, sure, I know. I've got a niece who believes in Santa Claus and has a theory about storks. So what? I still think the Doctor was off his nut." The Inspector hastily dismissed the whole subject and addressed me, "Harte, you bring Merlini up to date while I clean up a few odds and ends before we get those vaudeville acts next door in here for questioning."

I assented, and he turned to issue a brisk flow of orders. Brady was busily messing up the place with an insufflator that belched clouds of aluminum powder. Gavigan began a painstaking examination of the room, part of the time on his hands and knees. I

---

3   See Montague Summers : *The Vampire in Europe,* Dutton, 1929, and *A Popular History of Witchcraft,* 1937; Alexander Cannon: *Powers That Be,* Dutton, 1936; Hamlin Garland: *Forty Years of Psychic Research,* Macmillan, 1934; Charles Fort: *Wild Talents,* Kendall, 1932; Maurice Magre: *Magicians, Seers and Mystics,* Dutton, 1932; etc.

And if you really want to go to town, see Harry Price: *Short-title Catalogue of the Research Library from 1472 A.D. to the present day,* University of London, Council for Psychical Investigation, 1935.

noticed that he kept an ear tuned in on the rapid resume which I rattled off for Merlini.

When I mentioned the difficulty with the lights, Gavigan added a marginal note. "The electrician found all the fuses blown. And new ones popped out as fast as they were put in. He deduced a short. Then he found a penny in a light socket. After removing that he blew some more fuses. Then finally he discovered that pennies had been put in five different outlets. He blew about four sets of fuses finding that out. Does that information mean anything to anybody?

"Doesn't sound very illuminating, to say the least," Merlini commented. "Let's hear more, Ross, lots more."

As my recital progressed, his eyes beamed like those of a small boy with his first bicycle. His quick, alert movements indicated a growing inner excitement, though his face, except for the eyes, was bland and inscrutable. I took my story up to the arrival of the Homicide Squad, and Gavigan, rejoining us at that point, added a brief summary of the subsequent events. Merlini inspected Duvallo's card and the pieces of torn handkerchief, Gavigan having brought the one from the kitchen back with him.

"No sliding panels or secret exits," Gavigan concluded. "Three walls of this apartment are outside ones. The fourth, along the hall there, is plastered on both sides, and you can't conceal a door in a wall like that. And anyway, just to be sure, I've looked. Ditto for the ceiling, of course. As for the floor—well, with the carpet rolled aside you can see for yourself, and, besides, Malloy says that a trap door would drop one straight into the bedroom of a maiden lady who'd yell bloody murder at the very thought. Just why the blazes a murderer has to go and commit a murder like this, I don't know. It's the damnedest—"

"It's a swell alibi, isn't it?" Merlini said. "If you can't explain how it was done you can't convict. You might know who the murderer is, place him right on the scene, and have a dozen witnesses, but just as long as he isn't actually seen within or leaving this room, he's quite safe—as long as the impossible situation isn't punctured, of course. It's also possible that he may be a murderer with some regard for others and doesn't want any innocent person convicted. As long as it looks impossible, we can't even do that. Or perhaps he couldn't manage to manufacture any proof that he was somewhere else at the proper time—he may even have been seen near here at the time of the murder. The impossibleness of the murder gets over all that."

"Sure, and that's your job. Puncture the impossibility. Tell me how someone got out of this room, and it's a ten-to-one shot we'll know who it was."

"Give me a chance to warm up, will you? I'm pretty well grounded in locked room theory, and I supply the profession with escapes from leg-irons, lead coffins, strait jackets, and the like, but—well, this situation is something of a honey. All the usual locked room trimmings, plus a new one. And that's obviously going to be the headache. Those keyholes. . . ." He broke off, frowning thoughtfully at the door. Then he said, "Inspector, let's see you put on your Torquemada act. Before I hand in a report, I'd like to hear what those witnesses have to say for themselves."

"That's fair enough," Gavigan answered. "Brady, we'll start with Rappourt. Shoo her in."

Brady withdrew, and the Inspector held a quick whispered conference with Malloy, who then went out, stepping aside at the door for Madame Rappourt. She glanced briefly at the covered figure and then quickly at the Inspector. Though more composed than before, she held herself stiffly alert, and her gaze was restless. Merlini, as she came in, retired suddenly to the bookcases where he began browsing.

"Sit down," Gavigan said, pushing forward a chair. Madame Rappourt moved her head negatively and stood, waiting.

"How long have you known Dr. Sabbat?" the Inspector began. Behind me, at the desk, Quinn scribbled shorthand.

Rappourt's voice was deep, almost masculine, and mysteriously pleasing.

"I'd never met him," she said, speaking with the abnormal precision of one whose native language was not English. "We were to meet tonight for the first time."

"You knew of him?"

She nodded. "Yes. I've read some of the things he has written."

"Colonel Watrous knew him?"

"Yes."

"Do you know why Mr. Sabbat invited you here?"

"He wanted to study my trance state, I believe."

"I see." Gavigan said that as if he *did* see. "Perhaps you know of someone who might have desired to kill Mr. Sabbat."

"No. I do not."

"Please detail your movements from say ten o'clock last night up to now."

Impassively and without hesitation she replied: "At ten o'clock last evening I was in my apartment at the Commodore Hotel. There were several persons present, including Colonel Watrous. They stayed until after three o'clock. I slept late this morning and did not leave my room until I came here. At four this afternoon Colonel Watrous arrived, and shortly after Mr. Tarot called for us."

"Who was present last night besides Watrous?"

"Is that information quite necessary?"

"It is." Gavigan was polite but firmly emphatic.

She hesitated slightly, then flatly, as if repeating a grocery order, named two Columbia University professors, a distinguished physicist, a well-known, syndicated editorial writer, and a radio news commentator.

"You were holding a séance?" the Inspector asked.

"We were conducting an experiment."

"In what?"

"Astral duplication."

Gavigan sighed a bit helplessly. "What's that?"

"I'm not sure I could explain it so *you* would understand it." The impression she gave was that, further than that, she didn't intend to try.

"Okay. I'm not very interested anyhow. Besides, I can ask the professors or the Colonel."

She made no reply to this, and Gavigan's inquiry made a right-angle turn.

"How did you know there was death in this room tonight before you entered it?"

She closed her eyes. "I could feel it."

"Clairvoyance, I suppose?"

She frowned slightly, then nodded as if she didn't like the way he said it.

"Could you turn some of it on now and tell us who killed Sabbat?"

For the first time her voice was something other than flatly expressionless. There was a hint of anger in it as she said:

"Do I look like a fool, Inspector?"

"Meaning that you could but won't?"

"Meaning that you wouldn't believe that any information I gave had been clairvoyantly obtained. Madame Blavatsky used her occult powers once in pointing out a murderer for the Russian police. Their gratitude took the form of trying to arrest her as an accessory."

"I suppose there's something in that," the Inspector admitted. "And if I promised immunity?"

Rappourt shook her head. "I wouldn't trust you."

Gavigan stepped closer to her. "You know, of course," he said threateningly, "that I can arrest you for the séance you have admitted holding. Perhaps if you told me who the murderer was . . ."

"I know nothing of the sort." Rappourt's shiny black eyes glistened angrily. "You are bluffing. I collected no fee."

"Maybe not, but you're out to get yours one way or another. And you'll do well to remember I've got an eye on you from now on. Can your guests of last evening swear that you were at the séance the whole time?"

She smiled now, for the first time, in an unpracticed sort of way, hesitated a moment, and then with cool amusement said:

"For two hours during the latter part of the evening I was in a deep trance."

"And how do I know you didn't walk in your sleep?"

"Because, as my guests will tell you, I was sitting in a large, thoroughly examined canvas bag, the mouth of which was drawn tightly around my neck and the drawstring tied with many knots to the back of my chair. The knots were sewn through with needle and thread and covered with sealing wax. Ropes around my legs and body outside the bag held me to the chair, and the chair was screwed to the floor of a cabinet whose door was triple locked with all the keys held by the sitters."

There was a slightly adenoidal expression around the Inspector's mouth. Visibly he collected himself and started to speak, but Rappourt had not finished.

"Tapes had been sewn and sealed about each of my wrists, and their further ends, which passed out through two small buttonhole openings in the bag and through an air vent in the door of the cabinet, were held constantly by the experimenters."

Gavigan glanced helplessly toward Merlini's back, but the latter gave no indication of having heard. The Inspector nosed about for a more fruitful line of investigation. "What," he asked Rappourt fiercely, "do those hentracks on the floor mean?"

"They are obviously some form of invocation. Sabbat seems to have been a black magician."

"What other kinds are there?"

"Black magic is occult power applied for evil; white magic is occult power applied for good. According to Manley P. Hall there also exists a gray and a yellow magic. Gray magic is the unconscious perversion of—"

The Inspector had had enough of that. He cut in, "Who is Surgat?"

"I don't know that. There are many demons."

Gavigan turned toward Merlini, scowling. "Do you know?"

The latter pushed a large dusty folio back into place.

"No," he said, and then faced us, his eyes on Rappourt. "But if we don't find it here, this reference library isn't as complete as I think it is. May I ask Madame Rappourt a question?"

This, I think, was what the Inspector wanted. He nodded.

Merlini smiled at her innocently and asked, "Was your séance—pardon me—your experiment conducted in the darkness usual to the production of that type of phenomena?"

He had only half done when Rappourt began acting strangely. Her eyelids dropped; her arm swung up jerkily; the back of her hand pressed against her forehead. She swayed backward, and then forward, stiffly, and too far.

Gavigan caught her as she dropped.

Chapter 7
The Ghost Hunter

Witchcraft is not dead, nor are Satan's winged hosts entirely banished to the Limbo of Myth. Psychic phenomena have, through the ages, been so intertwined with superstition, mental aberration, and religion, and the issue so clouded by fraudulent imposters, venal quacks, and the clumsy exposés of prejudiced conjurers that Science, engrossed in the mysticism of modern Physics and prostituting itself on the couch of commercial Chemistry, disdains to investigate, afraid that it might—as it would—uncover some shining Truth its materialistic philosophies could not explain.

Col. Herbert Watrous: *A Plea for Psychical Research*

THE INSPECTOR placed Rappourt in the armchair, and Quinn, like a well-trained jack-in-the-box, sprang up from his chair and was swiftly at the department's black suitcase. He brought an ammonia ampoule which he held and broke under her nose. Merlini knelt at her side and began rubbing her wrists. After a moment her eyelids fluttered, and she moaned faintly.

The Inspector went to the door and stood there talking to Malloy, who was just outside. They spoke in undertones. Pretending to watch Rappourt, I backed in their direction until I was close enough to eavesdrop.

Gavigan asked, not very hopefully, "Well?"

Malloy said, "A blank. He doesn't think so, but he's not any too sure. Lousy witness. The over-cautious type."

The Inspector seemed to have a card up his sleeve, but apparently didn't know whether or not it was an ace.

Rappourt showed signs of reviving, when suddenly her body tensed. Her head jerked and her eyelids flicked back, exposing white eyeballs, no pupil. Her breath was expelled in a long whistling exhalation through clenched teeth.

Quinn warned, "Hey, Chief. She's going to throw a fit!"

Merlini, watching her closely, said, "I think she's going into a cataleptic trance, Inspector. Fresh air should help. You'd better get her outside."

Gavigan eyed her odd behavior with curiosity, and then alarm. "All right," he said, "see to it, Malloy. Put her in a taxi and have a couple of the boys deliver her back at her hotel. If she's not out of it by then they'd better get a doctor."

Malloy and Brady carried her out.

When they had gone Gavigan looked at Merlini speculatively, then growled, "What is this trance business, anyway?"

"I don't think she wanted to answer any more questions. She does the catalepsy well, don't you think?"

"Oh—just an act, huh?"

"I think so. Chafing her wrists gave me a chance to feel her pulse. Instead of being subnormal, it was excited."

"And what was the idea of aiding and abetting her by suggesting that I get her out of here?"

Merlini spread his hands wide. "What else can you do with a woman like that? Besides, you seemed to have finished with her— and she didn't seem to want to answer my question."

"Why not? Did it have any occult significance I didn't get?"

"I'll know that when we get an answer either from Watrous or the others who attended the séance. My main purpose in asking was to see if she'd recognize me."

"If that song and dance was because she recognized you, then your effect on the ladies is damned devastating. Explain yourself."

Merlini snapped open a cigarette case and held it toward the Inspector. "You may have noticed that I moved upstage when she came on and stuck my nose in a book. I've met the lady before. She's changed a good bit, and I wasn't quite certain until she spoke. But I couldn't mistake that voice. In 1915 she was in London, and her name was Svoboda."

"During the war, eh? I suppose she did a rushing ouija board business then?"

"Not ouija boards, Inspector. She's more original than that. But she did evoke quite a few spirits of the war dead for their relatives. She's obviously not English, and the Military Intelligence Department began eyeing her suspiciously. I was playing the Palladium, and a member of the department asked me to check up on her for them. They thought her séances might be a clearing house for spy information, foreign agents attending and going home to decode her spirit messages. 'Heaven is just too lovely. Having wonderful time. Wish you were here. Love. Cecil' meaning 'Convoy embarks Liverpool Friday. Midnight.' That sort of thing."

"Svoboda the Secret Agent," I said, "sounds like a dime novel."

"That's what I thought," Merlini answered. "If she was a spy, you would hardly expect her to go asking for investigation with a name like that. But the M.I.D. was taking no chances."

"Well," Gavigan asked, "what about it? Is that what she was doing?"

"I don't know. My presence on several of the London Psychical Society's investigating committees had given me rather more notoriety among mediums than I'd suspected. I wore a pair of dark glasses and was introduced as a blind man, but I should have taken more pains with the disguise. She recognized me, and the séance was a complete frost. All very ordinary and nothing startling enough to require either supernatural or fraudulent aid. So she may have been a spy, or she may merely have been hostile to conjurers. I never did find out. On the way back to the hotel that night I managed to be one of the few persons in London on whom the Zeppelins successfully dropped a bomb. I got a splinter in my arm that terminated my engagement, and I sailed for home the first boat out."

"I'll check London on that," Gavigan said. "What about these séances she's giving now?"

"I don't know. I'd have to see one. Watrous brought her over here just recently, and she's not given any public performances as yet. But if she is fraudulent and has Watrous fooled, she's got something good. He's nobody's fool, even though he does talk like it at times. Trouble is, he wants to find genuine phenomena, and that unconscious bias is his weak point. He's never bit on anything obvious though, and the few mediums to whom he has given his okay are still bones of contention."

"Well, just now it's a case of does he get *my* okay. O'Connor! Send Colonel Watrous in here."

The Colonel's entrance was excited and angry. He waved his hands. Meeting the Inspector's unsympathetic stare, he drew himself up, adjusted his pince-nez more firmly on his bulgy nose, and cleared his throat with a prefatory rumble.

"Where is Madame Rappourt?" he blurted. "What have you done to her? Why are you . . . I'll have you know . . ."

"Pull up, Colonel," Gavigan ordered. "I'll have you know something. This is a murder case, and since I happen to be in charge I'll ask the questions. You answer 'em. Madame Rappourt gave us some answers and now it's your turn. You were at the séance last night?"

The Colonel's carbonated sputtering went suddenly flat. His still open mouth plopped shut. Then, after a moment, it opened again. "I was at Madame Rappourt's apartment from ten until nearly three-thirty A.M. But what . . ."

"Who tied her up in that bag?"

"Why . . . ah, we all did . . . but what did she . . . what has that to do . . ."

"Stop asking questions! What happened after you tied her up? Come on. Talk!"

Watrous puffed up, pigeon-like. "I fail to see that any connection exists between our experiments last evening and the lamentable tragedy that has happened here."

"I don't see any myself, but that doesn't mean there isn't one. My job is to find out. All I know, at the moment, is that her specialty is the supernatural. And this case has more than its share of spook atmosphere . . ."

Watrous seemed to get the idea. He took off his glasses and tapped them nervously on his hand. "I'm not at liberty at this time to release any statements concerning the results of our experiment of last night."

"Was it a dark séance?"

Watrous looked puzzled, but nodded. "Yes, why?"

Gavigan threw a glance where Merlini had been, only to discover that he was back poking into the bookshelves again. He returned his attention to the Colonel.

"Then no one can testify that you were in the apartment continuously?"

The glasses weren't tapping now. "On the contrary," Watrous' tone was indignant, "two persons at least could swear I was there every minute. During the time that the lights were out we were arranged in the usual psychic circle, each person holding the hand of the one next to him. To establish a proper contact, you know."

Inspector Gavigan's patience looked a bit thin. He had examined three suspects so far and had drawn three gold-plated alibis. He left it at that for the time being.

"Who is Surgat?" He flung the question at Watrous.

"I don't know," the latter answered. "I've come across the name somewhere in my researches, I'm sure, but . . ." He frowned thoughtfully at the chalked incantation, shaking his head.

"Does the name Svoboda mean anything to you?"

Watrous answered with another apparently puzzled negative.

"You say you left the séance at three-thirty this morning. What did you do then?"

"I took a taxi home and went to bed. I rose at eleven, and I spent the afternoon writing up an account of the experiment in my day book. My meals were sent up. Shortly before four I left for Madame Rappourt's."

"Your relations with Sabbat were what?"

"I have had none for at least ten years. Before that time we were rather good friends. In 1925, however, I found it necessary through the columns of *The Occult World* to call attention to some rather grievous misstatements which Dr. Sabbat had made concerning . . . ah . . . concerning psychic doubles. Having been stationed for some years in India, having traveled with the Granby expedition through Tibet, I feel that I can lay some claim to first hand knowledge of that type of psychical manifestation. Sabbat, however, had traveled extensively in the East, but his none too adequate knowledge of Oriental dialects handicapped him. He took my purely impersonal criticism as a direct personal attack, even going so far as to threaten me with bodily harm. He was quite capable of carrying out such a threat, and I avoided him. I never saw him again until tonight."

"How'd that happen?"

"Mr. David Duvallo informed me that he had recently met

Mr. Sabbat, and Saturday, I think it was, he said that Cesare was extremely anxious to meet Madame Rappourt and that our old quarrel had been forgotten. Under other circumstances I might have been loath to revive such a distressing acquaintanceship, but the reports of certain occult experiments he was making quite intrigued me."

"And they were?"

For a hard-headed skeptic who thought occult matters were on a par with the freaks at Coney Island, Gavigan was a bear for punishment.

"I am told," Watrous said, "that he claimed to have produced levitation phenomena in himself that equalled those amazing, still unexplained, experiments of D. D. Home. I felt that this, at least, deserved investigation, though, when I knew him last, he was trying to rediscover such chimerae as the lost hermetic formulas for invisibility and the Universal Alkahest.[1] I was somewhat skeptical. But since *a priori* skepticism among scientific investigators is what has for so long kept the psychical sciences in a rudimentary state, I couldn't very well—"

The Inspector had heard all he thought necessary of that. He came over on a new tack.

"Where do the LaClaires come into this?"

"I don't know. They were not invited to the gathering here this evening, so far as I know."

"You know them well?"

"Alfred's father did Indian duty in my regiment."

What do you know about Sabbat and Mrs. LaClaire?"

"Pardon?" Watrous asked. "I don't believe I quite understand."

"Were they having an affair?"

---

1 The Universal Alkahest was the alchemist's ideal solvent, a super-hydrofluoric acid that would act on any and every thing. It never was decided just what sort of container to keep it in once it was found.

Watrous mounted his high horse and went into a dignified canter.

"I know no particulars as to Mr. Sabbat's ah—er—love life, except that he did have an unsavory reputation where the ladies were concerned."

"When are you and Madame Rappourt going to release the results of last night's hand-holding in the dark?"

"When we are in a position to refute quite positively such skeptics as yourself, sir."

"You may have to do that sooner than you think—if I need the information. You are fully satisfied then, I take it, that Madame Rappourt is bona fide?"

Watrous flushed slightly and then said stiffly, "My integrity as an investigator has never been questioned by any competent critic. I have discovered, as anyone who has read my books would know, several genuine instances of psychic phenomena, inexplicable on any materialistic basis. As for Madame Rappourt, I think I may safely say that if her mediumistic powers are the result of trickery, then she is by far the cleverest impostor I have ever met. And I might add that if she is genuine, modern science will be faced with something it cannot ignore. Her telekinetic phenomena, in particular, are so remarkably . . ."

"Who," Gavigan cut in impatiently, "do you think might have killed Sabbat?"

Watrous said slowly, "You are sure that *someone* killed him?"

"Suicide is out of the question."

"Yes, I know. I also know that a similar case occurred in Devonshire in 1903 and that many investigators have considered it explainable only on the assumption that some enemy who held a malign control over etheric vibrations must have . . ."

"Strangled by vibrations?"

"There have been stranger things, Inspector."

Gavigan sniffed, then said abruptly, "Okay, you can go. But just stay handy. I'll want you again."

The Colonel placed his pince-nez firmly on his nose, glared at the Inspector a moment, then wheeled and stalked out. I thought I detected a flicker beneath his mustache of what may have been a faint smile of amusement.

When he had gone Gavigan said, "That old dodo shouldn't be allowed out alone. He needs a nurse—and a psychoanalyst."

Merlini walked over from the bookshelves, bringing with him, one finger between its leaves, a large and dusty volume. "Don't judge the Colonel too hastily. I had a feeling there at the last that he might have been spoofing you a bit. He shouldn't be a bad actor, you know. His father was the famous Shakespearian actor, Sir Herbert Watrous. And besides, some of what he says sounds silly only until you've looked into it a bit. He's right when he says that science should take the field of psychical research a bit more seriously. A few men are beginning to do it. Professor Rhine's experiments in parapsychology at Duke University have pretty well demonstrated that something suspiciously like telepathy may exist. And J. W. Dunne's book, *An Experiment with Time,* gives me the willies every time I look into it. I find it difficult, though, to believe that the dead can come back, largely because they seem to act such idiots when they do return. It shouldn't really be so difficult for a disembodied spirit to show a conjurer aces and spades. As for the occultists, if they'd just forego the dark and bring but one of their dog-headed Elementals out into the light of day—"

"I wish to heaven," Gavigan said, "that you and Rappourt and Watrous wouldn't be so damned technical. I'm going to have to have an occult glossary compiled for me before I get out of these woods. What in hell is an Elemental?"

Merlini laughed. "An Elemental in hell, Inspector, is at home.

There's quite a tribe of them, Ginn, Ginee, Salamanders, Undines, Efreets, Poltergeists, etc. Hindu authorities place them in the scheme of reincarnation as unattached human spirits who are waiting their next incarnation. Madame Blavatsky, whom the Colonel mentioned, used to have them about. On one occasion, when a small one pestered her by pulling at her skirt, she said that it wanted something to do. Olcutt, the Theosophical Society's president and her mentor, suggested that she have the sprite hem some towels he had purchased. She locked the material in a bookcase with needle and thread. Twenty minutes later they heard a mouse-like squeaking, which she translated as meaning that the work was done. Olcutt opened the bookcase and found the towels hemmed, though, as he said, 'after a fashion that would disgrace the youngest child in an infant sewing class.'"

"In other words," Gavigan said slowly, almost absently, and without the ghost of a smile, "the hemstitching was elementary."

Merlini threw a startled glance in my direction, and as Gavigan moved away toward the window, followed it with a delighted wink and whispered, "A policeman who puns! He's defying all the ancient tradition, every canon of criminal investigation!"

"I suppose I can expect anything now," I whispered back. "Yours are always a fearful earful when you have competition."

The Inspector stood looking out the window thoughtfully. Half to himself, he said, "That Rappourt woman gets me down. I've heard alibis in my time that were miracles of watertight ingenuity, but she can pick up the marbles and take 'em away. And Watrous matched it! Three suspects questioned, and we get three alibis that are too damned slick for any good use! I never saw such a good batting average in all—"

His soliloquy petered out Merlini, seated now, was again absorbed in his book.

Gavigan shook his head wearily and turning said, "Merlini, you've been nosing about in those books long enough to have discovered something about our mysterious Surgat, the demon nobody knows. Let's have it."

Merlini nodded. "Yes, it's about time we cleared up his identity. Listen to this."

He glanced down at the book, open across his knees, and began to read.

Chapter 8
The Grimorium of Pope Honorius

> Like one that on a lonesome road
> Doth walk in fear and dread
> And, having once turned round, walks on
> And turns no more his head
> Because he knows a frightful fiend
> Doth close behind him tread.
>
> Coleridge: *The Ancient Mariner*

MERLINI'S FACE was solemn and his voice low and serious as he read: "Pliny states that the dried muzzle of a wolf is efficacious against enchantments and that perfume made of peewits' feathers drives away phantoms." He looked up at us, grinning.

The Inspector said, "Sure, and a stew made of nitwits' brains is what causes 'em. Is that the sort of stuff those books are full of?"

"There's a good bit of that sort of thing here, yes. And there are some that are more serious. That book, for instance," he drew out a large musty looking one, "is Sprenger and Kramer's *Malleus Mallificarum,* one of the most important of the source books on witchcraft. It's a guide for the use of judges in witchcraft trials, the inquisitor's handy manual. And it'll give any imaginative person who reads it the holy horrors, because it smells to high heaven of blood and torture and sadism. This is the early 1489 edition, bound in human hide. The rarity of the item is due almost entirely to its date of issue; a great many of the source books on this subject have that type of binding."

He replaced it on the shelf and indicated another volume nearby, a small one bound in faded red leather. "King James the First's *Daemonologia,* the *vade mecum* of the professional witchfinders, who, in the seventeenth century, set themselves up in the business of legalized murder and travelled from town to town consigning harmless old women to the flames at so much per head—reductions on gross lots." He ran his finger along the shelf. "Gaule's *The Mag-astro-mancer, or the Magi-call-astrologicall-diviner posed and puzzled,* Hedelin's *Des Satyres, Brutes, Monstres et Demons,* Jacquerius' *Flagellum Daemonum Fascinariorium,* Saint-Hebin's *Culte du Satan,* Jules Delassus' *Les Incubes et les Succubes,* Glanville's *Saducismus Triumphatus,* Cotton Mather's *The Invisible World Displayed*—he's got them all, from Apollonius of Tyana right on up to Eliphas Levi, Arthur Edward Waite, Manly P. Hall, Montague Summers."

The Inspector frowned, not at all sure what, if anything, Merlini was leading up to. He waited silently, somewhat interested, I think, in spite of himself.

"This section," Merlini said, moving over, "is devoted to the alchemists, Nicholas Flamel, Saint-Germain, Althotas, Roger Bacon, Albertus Magnus, and Alain de l'Isle, who is reputed to have actually discovered the *elixir vitae*—he lived to be 110. Here's a biography of Raymond Lully, who had an alchemical laboratory in the precincts of Westminster Abbey about 1312, where, years later, a quantity of gold dust was found. The fly-leaf bears the signature of Dr. John Dee, Queen Elizabeth's astrologer, and alongside is the Doctor's own quaintly titled work, *A true and faithful relation of what passed for many years between Dr. John Dee and some spirits.* Also present are the more sober anthropological authorities—Frazer, Breasted, Budge, Murray, Thorndyke, *et al.*

"Oh, oh!" He grabbed at another book. "This is a bit out of place. *Les Secrets des Sorciers*. It's about witchcraft, all right, but it's an original manuscript, and the shelf numbers plainly indicate that it is the property of the British Museum. Perhaps you'd better take charge of it, Inspector."

"I wish you'd get on with it," Gavigan said, his impatience beginning to overflow. "I'm after a murderer, not a book thief. I don't see that this literary chat is getting us anywhere."

Merlini didn't seem to hear. He had crossed to the shelves in the corner behind the desk and, pointing to a row of yellowed paper-bound pamphlets, explained, "Here's a particularly choice collection of the English pamphlet literature. I don't know how they ever sold any of the things. Their authors had an odd journalistic habit of telling almost the whole story on the title page. Listen to this:

> The Wonder of Suffolke, being a true relation of one that reports he made a league with the Devil for three years, to do mischief, and now breaks open houses, robs people daily . . . and can neither be shot nor taken, but leaps over walls fifteen feet high, runs five or six miles in a quarter of an hour, and sometimes vanishes in the midst of multitudes that go to take him. Faithfully written in a letter from a solemn person, dated not long since, to a friend in Ship-Yard near Temple-Bar, and ready to be attested by hundreds . . . London, 1677.

Merlini showed signs of continuing indefinitely, but Gavigan put his foot down. "Harte," he said, "does Merlini have these spells of talking like a book collector's catalogue very often? He's *worse* than Philo Vance!"

I shook my head. "I think he's better," I said. "At least he hasn't annoyed us with any quotations from the *Bhagavad-Gita* in the original Sanskrit."

Merlini smiled a bit sheepishly. "I'll be good, Inspector," he promised. "But when you turn a bookworm of my inclinations loose in a pasture like this—" He gestured at the shelves and shrugged helplessly. "However, we are getting a more revealing picture of Sabbat than any description his friends might be able to provide."

"And a very pretty picture it is," Gavigan commented acidly.

"Here's a shelf full of assorted occultism, presentation copies of those remarkable works on Theosophy by Helena Blavatsky, and most of Churchward's and Spence's books on Mu and Atlantis. On the shelves by the window you'll find all the important works on the modern witchcraft, spiritism. Richet, Podmore, Lodge, Doyle, Flammarion, Zoellner, Crookes, Price, Carrington—the whole lot—and a nice set, in good condition, of bound volumes of the *Proceedings of the Society for Psychical Research*. Watrous would have a picnic over in that corner."

He made an inclusive gesture at the shelves. "It's all quite complete. If you want to know anything about the sorcery of the Esquimaux, Maori Tohungaism, Negro Voodooism, the Berserkir of Iceland, or Indian Shamanism, it's here. He must have spent a young fortune collecting this library. He didn't swipe *all* the books, and some of them are pretty rare items."

Inspector Gavigan was fidgeting again. Merlini, noticing it, spoke faster.

"For our purpose, the more important books of the lot are these." He indicated that section just to the left of and handiest to the desk. "They are the Black Books, the Rituals of Magic, fourteenth century treatises that describe and illustrate the instruments necessary for conjury and divination, with all the necessary pentacles, prayers, invocations, and suffumigations."

He ran his finger over the titles. "*The Claviculae Salmonis, The Legmegton or Lesser Key, The Books of Cornelius Agrippa*, the *Mag-*

*ical Elements ascribed to Peter of Albana,*and the *Sacred Magic of Abramelin the Mage.* Those five are the Rituals of white and black magic. And these, the famous *Grimorium Verum, The Grand Grimoire,* and the—*The Grimorium of Pope Honorius the Great* are the Rituals devoted solely to black magic. Here you can find, if you are interested, recipes for the flying ointment with which the witches greased themselves before their wild ride through the sky to the Sabbath.[1] And the formula for pact-ink, should you want to draw up any agreements with Lucifer.[2] What's more important, just now, you'll find here a comprehensive demon directory which lists the names and offices, and pictures the personal seals of the members of the infernal hierarchy, the Almanac de Gotha, the DeBrett of Hell. Surgat should be on the list, and I don't think we'll have to spend much time hunting him. The Pope's *Grimorium* is not in its place." He indicated an empty space in the otherwise closely packed shelf. "It lies on that table." We followed his glance toward the low coffee table that was partly hidden by the armchair near the door. We moved over and stood looking down at it. It was a large folio in only fair condition. The binding was scuffed and the pages wrinkled with damp, but the richly intricate gold leaf tool-

---

1 Two of the formulae as given by Weyer are as follows: 1. Water Hemlock, sweet flag, cinquefoil, bat's blood, deadly nightshade and oil. 2. Baby's fat, juice of cowbane, aconite, cinquefoil, deadly nightshade and soot. It is interesting to note that, in the opinion of Prof. D. J. Clarke, the use of aconite and belladonna as an unguent is likely to produce the sensation of flying.

2 In signing on the dotted line of any compact with His Satanic Majesty you will, of course, write your signature with your own blood, but the body of the deed itself requires a special ink. Arthur Edward Waite in *The Book of Ceremonial Magic* gives this formula: Gall-Nuts, 10 oz. Roman Vitriol or Green Copperas, 3 oz., Rock Alum or Gum Arabic, 3 oz. Dissolve this powder in river water using a new varnished earthenware pot, and bring to a boil over a fire laid with sprigs of fern gathered on the Eve of St. John and vine twigs cut in the full moon of March, and kindled with virgin paper.

ing and the warm patina of age that covered the binding gave it a mysterious dignity.

"I wonder," Merlini continued, "if someone kindly left that out—so we'd be sure not to miss it?"

He bent to pick it up, and Gavigan cautioned, "Careful. There may be prints."

Merlini nodded, "I suppose so. Though if we have a demon to contend with, I doubt if his prints will do us much good—unless, of course, he's been previously arrested for some misdemeanor. And if the murderer is mortal, I'll bet that any fingerprints he may have left belong to someone else."

He lifted the book gently and turned it over so that the open leaves faced us.

We all bent over, staring at the open pages, and then Merlini said, "Someone has been very considerate. Look."

He pointed at the left hand page and ran his finger down a list of names that appeared there.

> Lucifer—Emperor
> Beelzebuth—Prince
> Astaroth—Grand Duke
> Luciferge Rocale—Prime Minister
> Satanachia—Commander-in-Chief
> Afaliarept—Another Commander
> Fleuretz—Lieutenant General
> Sargatanas—Brigadier Major
> Nebiros—Field Marshal and Inspector General

> *The Seventeen Sub-Spirits*

> Frucissiere who brings the dead to life
> Trimasel who teaches chemistry and sleight of hand
> Sedragossam who makes girls dance stark naked
> Humots who transports all manner of books for thy pleasure

At the next name his finger stopped. The line read:

Surgat who opens all locks.

Following each of the sub-spirit's names was an invocation guaranteed to summon that demon from the infernal depths. Surgat's began near the bottom of the page, and Merlini read it aloud.

For Sunday, to Surgat (otherwise Aquiel). . . . This experience is to be performed at night from eleven to one o'clock. He will demand a hair of your head, but give him one of a fox and see that he takes it.

Gavigan's attitude was irreverent. "Foxes," he said, "are red. What does a gray-haired sorcerer do?"

Merlini ignored this arrant skepticism and read on, tasting each syllable with obvious enjoyment, but delivering them with all the solemn dignity of an earnest Archbishop.

I conjure thee, O Surgat, by all the names which are written in this book, to present thyself here before me, promptly and without delay, being ready to—Merlini stopped.

"Well," prompted the Inspector, "let's have it. We're all of age."

Merlini pointed to the center of the folio where a ragged fringe of paper was all that remained of a leaf that had been roughly torn away. The pages were aged with yellow, but the serrated edges of the tear were white and fresh.

Inspector Gavigan made a noise like a string of firecrackers. The whole damned business, in his opinion, was blithering, four-starred, purple-hued nonsense.

His expert flow of pungent Anglo-Saxon was interrupted by Malloy, who put his head in at the door and announced:

"Mr. Duvallo just walked in downstairs, Inspector. Do you want him brought up?"

Chapter 9
Ask Me No Questions

Faustus lived a life of pleasure,
Kissed the lips of the Maid of Troy
Wealth and power beyond all measure,
    Bad Dr. Faustus,
    Mad Dr. Faustus—
All were his to enjoy.

           George Steele Seymour: *Faustus*

THE INSPECTOR's fulminations were forgotten. He said, "Yes, but not just yet. I want LaClaire first. Get him."

Merlini said, "There's a candid camera shot of His Nibs here, Inspector, but perhaps in your present state of mind you'd rather not—"

The pendulum motion of Gavigan's irritated pacing slowed, then stopped. "Okay, I can take it. Now what?"

Merlini swung the book around. Gavigan took one look and walked off, snorting.

I saw a full-page reproduction of a woodcut in the tortured fifteenth-century style. The word "Surgat" appeared there, together with the incomprehensible assortment of cabalistic symbols that comprised his personal seal. Surgat himself was a leering, furious monster belonging to the genus Pink Elephant. A jigsaw scramble of animal life, his head was that of a brute with a flaring snout, dark-rimmed pop-eyes, and trailing, curled fangs. His body was constructed on the general architectural plan of man's except for great, limp bat wings that protruded from the shoulders and a torso covered with lizard scales. A bristling cluster of spikes and a thorny, curved tail growing out of his behind must have considerably complicated the art of sitting down. The monstrosity stood on two emaciated hairy legs that terminated in long-clawed talons, four-pronged like a bird's. One oddly gnarled hand clutched a large, unlikely looking key. The artist must have been, at the very least, a Surrealist hophead suffering from acute delirium tremens. Beneath Surgat's name I saw the startling inscription, "Drawne from the Life."

Gavigan's sarcasm was heavy. "That, I suppose, breaks the case! We hand that tintype to the papers, captioned 'Wanted, Dead or Alive' and wait for someone to phone in saying they saw him boarding a subway train at Times Square, or shouting 'boo!' at the children in Central Park. Maybe we'd better phone the Zoo in case he's been turned in to Doc Ditmars. Hmmpf!"

Merlini, managing a straight face, replied, "We'll hope not, Inspector. I doubt if Dr. Ditmars would give up an exhibit like that without a struggle. Even though you offered him a whole cageful of assorted bushmasters, vampire bats, and duck-billed basilisks." Then turning his attention to the book again, he reflected aloud: "It would be nice to know about that missing page—and the rest of that invocation. If we can locate another copy of this book . . . Rosenbach maybe, or—"

"And I," Gavigan said, underscoring each word, "don't want to hear any more about it. Just one more mention of hobgoblins, and I'll have someone's scalp."

Alfred LaClaire came in then. He stopped just inside the door and stood there woodenly, his hands in his pockets, his green eyes scowling. He saw Merlini, started slightly, and nodded.

Gavigan turned to him and went to work, sharp staccato questions streaming like ticker tape from his mouth. Quinn scratched busily in his notebook. LaClaire stated that on the previous evening he and his wife had done their usual three turns nightly at La Rumba, one of the village hot spots. Their routine was a twenty-minute one, and they appeared at 9:30, 11:30, and 1:30. He had left after the last show, at about two o'clock, going direct to Tony's Place, a bar on Sullivan Street.

"Proprietor know you?" Gavigan asked.

"Yes."

"How long were you there?"

"Until four o'clock. Some damn fool put me in a taxi at that point and the fare home was three bucks."

"A little bit hazy about then?" Gavigan suggested.

LaClaire nodded. "Some, yes. Too many stingers."

"You didn't notice the number of the cab or see the driver's name, then, I suppose?"

"Hardly."

"You haven't mentioned your wife. Wasn't she with you?"

"No, I left her at the club. Look, Inspector, was—was he killed last night?"

Gavigan said, "Maybe. Did Mrs. LaClaire go right home from the club?"

His pause was just a shade too long. He nodded slowly. "That's where she said she was going."

Gavigan closed in on that. "And where did she go?"

"She was in bed when I got home."

"All right. You don't know where she went. What do you think?"

Alfred walked over to a chair. I noticed the lithe spring to his step and the careful poise of his body. He turned at the chair, looked at the Inspector a moment and sat down.

In a low, very slow voice he said, "She may have come up here."

Gavigan's calm was professional. "Let's hear about it." LaClaire seemed to be having trouble finding the words and Gavigan helped out. "She do that often?"

The expressions on LaClaire's face were a mixed lot and not easily sorted. He said, "I've reason to think so, yes."

"And last night? Just what makes you think she came here?"

Alfred looked up at him. And suddenly began talking fast, as if trying to get it over.

"She phoned Sabbat from the club last night. I heard her. When she thought I'd gone, I was outside the door, and I heard her say, 'Cesare, I'm coming up.'"

"What else?"

"That's all. It was enough. I went out and got plastered. I've known about it for some time. I guess it's no secret by now. What I can't understand is why she wants to play around with that old goat. If she has to sleep out like an alley cat, she might at least . . ." He leaned forward suddenly and put conviction in his voice. "But she wouldn't have killed him, Inspector. I know that."

Somehow I had a definite impression that, on the contrary, he thought her quite capable of it.

"And yet," Gavigan said, "you go on living with her. Why is that, Mr. LaClaire?"

He felt in his pockets for a cigarette but found none. Merlini offered his pack. LaClaire took one. "Thanks, Merlini. You explain it to him, will you? I think you understand."

Merlini nodded and then spoke to the Inspector in a flat, non-committal voice. "Mr. and Mrs. LaClaire's act, Inspector, consists in apparent extra-sensory communication. Mental telepathy or clairvoyance or both, depending on how you look at it. That sort of act is the result of long practice and close cooperation. The two members of such a team must have worked together so consistent-ly as to have acquired the ability of almost predicting each other's actions and thoughts. Breaking in a new partner is a tedious, highly speculative job. And since one can't earn while one learns, there would be no income during the process. I think you get the idea."

Gavigan said, "Bring her in, Malloy."

LaClaire looked up quickly. "Listen, I've got to know. Was Sabbat killed *last night?*"

Gavigan nodded, "Yes."

"When?"

"That's one of the questions I'm supposed to ask."

"You're going to tell her I said she might have come up here?"

"If necessary, yes. I've got to know if she did."

"I'd better warn you, then." LaClaire spoke quickly. "I'll deny it. You've had your hint. Use the information any way you like, but don't ask me to back you up. Understand?"

The Inspector glanced toward Quinn bending over his notebook at the desk.

"Yes," LaClaire said, "I know, you've got it on paper, but I haven't signed it. And I won't."

Merlini, behind LaClaire, was frantically trying to signal the Inspector, jerking with his thumb toward the bedroom.

Gavigan scowled. "Brady, take Mr. LaClaire into the next room."

LaClaire didn't move from his chair until Gavigan added, "Come on, snap into it." Then he stood up and walked out. Brady closed the door behind them.

"What's all this thumb jerking about?" Gavigan asked suspiciously.

"The general underlying theory is that telepathists, even pseudo ones, should be questioned separately. Even then, you never know. Those two could toss hints, whole paragraphs even, back and forth right under your nose and you wouldn't catch them at it. Not sure I could follow through myself. They all have their own variations . . ."

We heard Malloy's voice. "This way, please." Merlini stopped, watching the door.

Zelma LaClaire came in, walking toward us with considerable self-assurance and rather more sway amidships than necessary. She was the luscious type, the smoldering sort that the out-of-town buyers who frequented La Rumba would get hot about. Her evening dress encompassed an interesting assortment of curves that were, for my tastes at least, a shade too adequate. Her hair, bleached almost white, and her peaches-and-cream store complexion gave her a youthful appearance that appeared somewhat forced. She wore too much eyeshadow, and her finger nails flashed blood red as her hands moved in the light, flicking cigarette ash to the floor.

Gavigan had an astonished look on his face. "Hello, Babe," he said, "I didn't know you were married."

The dark, too thin line of her eyebrows flattened. "Do you have to bring up that Babe stuff?"

"Haven't seen you lately. Not since we had to close the Elite Burlesque house. Gentlemen, meet Babe Colette, Queen of Strippers, the gal with the Tiffany G-String. Or was that a publicity gag?"

"Skip it, Inspector! I'm not in that racket now. So lay off."

Gavigan indicated a chair, and she sat, crossing her legs and looking up at him as if he were a news photog with a flash bulb ready.

"Okay, forget I mentioned it. Let's hear your story."

"My story?" she asked, her blue eyes turned on full.

"Yes. What are you doing here? Where were you when Sabbat was killed? That sort of thing. You can start with last night about this time."

She seemed more used to policemen than had Alfred. Gavigan didn't pull his punches, and she took it as a matter of course. Her story began like Alfred's.

"I left ten or fifteen minutes after Al did, took the subway home, and . . ."

"Seventh Avenue to Times Square and change there for Queens, crosstown on 42nd?"

"Yes. I got home just before three. Al came in plastered and woke me up at 5 A.M. trying to undress himself. I got up at the usual time, around eleven, and spent the afternoon getting a permanent. At five Al and I came in to a cocktail party in Tudor City. When we left there we came over here."

"Why did you stop in here?"

Her fingers tightened ever so slightly on the purse in her lap. "We thought maybe Sabbat might furnish another drink."

"Known him long?"

She shook her head. "Six months, maybe. Eugene Tarot introduced us. Sabbat was interest in mental telepathy. We've seen him off and on since."

"Who do you think might have killed him?"

"I haven't the faintest notion."

"Anything else you'd like to tell me?"

She shrugged. "What else do you want to know?"

Gavigan's eyes were hard. "Who did you phone before you left the club last night?"

If she reacted, I didn't catch it. "Who did I phone . . . ? I don't know what . . ."

"Listen, Babe. You're a good actress. You always were more than just a strip artist. But don't try it on me. I'm not guessing. Come on, spill it."

She sat up straighter in her chair.

"Nuts! I didn't just blow in from the sticks. I don't have to answer questions like that. And you know it."

"So that's your line. Okay. Suppose I know who you phoned?

What if I've got a witness who heard you talking to Sabbat? Anything to say to that?"

Zelma's mouth was a thin hard line. She stood suddenly on her feet, and her voice was harsh, biting. "This washes me up with that dirty, lying—! Al handed you that line, didn't he? I haven't phoned Sabbat all week. Put me on the spot, will he! The . . ." Her phrasing was masculine.

As she slowed, Gavigan stepped in quickly. "Then you have phoned Sabbat before?"

"Yes, but it's none of your business."

"If you weren't talking to him last night, who did you call?"

"No one, and that's straight! Alfred thought I did, because . . ."

There would have to be an interruption at a spot like that! I should have expected as much. Merlini had wandered over to the radio and had tuned out the police calls. Mrs. LaClaire was cut short when he suddenly turned up the amplifier bringing a brassy blare of trumpets from the speaker. I glanced at my watch. It was 10:30, time for the Tarot program.

The suave voice of the announcer came into the room, meticulous, impersonal. *"This is the Xanadu program, presented to you each night at this hour by the Emmalene Motor Company, featuring the Mysterious Tarot in another thrilling adventure of mystery and magic."*

We all faced the radio now, intent.

"Have you seen the new Emmalene Eight with its Magic Motor? Visit any Emmalene Dealer and let him explain the mystery of Floating Control, that masterpiece of scientific sorcery that makes possible the thrilling adventure of a smoother ride!"

A temple gong sounded three times, and against the muted background of a few bars from Rimsky-Korsakov's *Scheherazade* the announcer continued:

"Yesterday, Xanadu and our friends, Tom and Marian, were trapped in the subterranean cellars of the haunted castle by the Green Ghoul and his henchmen. The room is fast being filled with a deadly gas and poisonous spiders. Can Xanadu's magic save them?"

The sound effect department supplied thunder, lightning, and hissing gas. Then Xanadu spoke.

"We've got just one chance! The Lascar at the door is watching us through the glass. I may be able to hypnotise him! Keep your faces covered and don't breathe any more than you have to! I'll try and make him open the . . ."

There was more to his speech, but I didn't hear it. Merlini was frowning at the radio. Gavigan was goggling at it.

"Well, I'm damned!" he shouted. "If that's Eugene Tarot, who in hell passed himself off on us as Tarot? The voice of the guy that was doing card tricks up here was just a poor imitation of that. Of all the impudent . . ."

"No," Merlini said, "you've got the cart before the horse. *That's* not Tarot's voice."

I agreed. It certainly wasn't the voice of my friend with the monocle. It had a similar high hat confident air, but the timbre was different, the tempo changed.

Gavigan jumped at the phone. "Well, then, who the devil . . ." He reached it and dialed rapidly. Finally he managed to get someone on the wire at NBC who had some comprehension of what he was talking about.

"Is Eugene Tarot playing Xanadu on that Emmalene program, or isn't he? . . . *I* want to know, dammit! . . . Inspector Gavigan, New York Police, Homicide Bureau . . . What! . . . Yes . . . That's what I'd like to know too!" He hung up violently. "An understudy! Tarot didn't show up. They've been hunting him frantically for the last hour."

The phone, as if in protest at the Inspector's rough treatment, rang sharply. Before the initial ring had been completed Gavigan had the receiver at his ear.

"Hello!" he said, and then: "Yes, Gavigan talking . . . Speak louder . . . This connection's lousy . . . *Who's vanished?*"

The voice in the phone took the Inspector at his word. We could all hear the reply, faint but unmistakable. It was Detective Janssen's voice and it said,

"*Tarot!*"

Chapter 10
Into Thin Air

I saw a man upon the stair,
A little man who wasn't there.
He wasn't there again today.
I wish he'd go away and stay.
After Hugh Mearns

IT WAS at this point that I began to see myself writing a detective story after all. If things kept on happening at this rate, I'd only need to do a simple, straight-forward job of reporting. Even if the case fizzled at the finish, which didn't seem indicated, I'd still have one hell of a good running start.

The remainder of Detective Janssen's report cinched it. With a "sock" like that at the start of his story, one might have expected the rest to be anticlimatic. It wasn't.

Gavigan glanced sharply at Captain Malloy and jerked a thumb toward Zelma LaClaire. Malloy took her out into the hall.

The Inspector scolded into the phone. "All right, Janssen. You lost him. Let's have your alibi, and make it good."

We could hear the blurred metallic sound of the detective's voice, talking fast. Merlini and myself got his report in a disconnected fashion. We heard, first, the Inspector's share of the conversation, which didn't make sense; and then his quick resume of what Janssen had said, which didn't make sense either. Janssen later repeated his half of the conversation for my benefit, and I report it here with the Inspector's conversation as it occurred.

"It's good and cockeyed, Chief. Maybe you can tell me where I went wrong. Listen. When I left you I went downstairs and told the boys at the front door to let Tarot out when he showed. Then I hiked to the corner and grabbed a cab. Just as I climbed aboard, I saw Tarot hurry out and do a line buck through the mob of reporters that had collected on the front stoop. I thought for a minute that they had him stopped, but he held one arm over his face, lowered his head, and did a line buck right through. I don't think the pictures they got were worth much. That little fat photog from the Mirror got a poke in the slats that sent him backwards over the hedge. He landed flat on his Graflex.

"Tarot headed my way, got himself a cab, and came north. In a hurry too. I tagged along. And behind me a whole cabful of nosey Parkers.

"We turned west on 42nd Street to Grand Central. Tarot got out and paid off the driver. The rest of us dittoed. I made the newspaper boys scram, and then kept right on Tarot's tail, because this didn't look like Radio City to me. He went in and picked up a suitcase he had salted away in one of those dime-in-the-slot lockers near the subway entrance. It began to look like a sneak. But instead of heading for the Concourse, he goes upstairs and ducks out the Vanderbilt Avenue exit, and gets another taxi from the stand there. I followed suit.

"We cut over to Madison, uptown to 49th, and turned toward Fifth. I started to breathe easier. It looked like Radio City might be on the itinerary after all; but we sailed right past. At Eighth Avenue he started acting like a dope. He got out at the corner, paid off the cabbie, and started walking north on Eighth. That's not such a flossy neighborhood, and everybody eyed the topper and opera cape. I stuck to my cab, just in case he took it into his head to ride again. He did. What does he do but walk once around the block and come right back to where he started. Don't ask me why. He didn't do a damn thing but walk; I had my eye on him every second. He didn't even speak to anyone. When he got back near Eighth again he speeded up a bit and ducked around the corner with me right on his heels. And there was that same cab still there. He popped into it, and the driver stepped on the gas pronto, as if he'd been waiting for him. Maybe taxis make him seasick or something and he has to take the air every so often. I don't know. The whole layout was funny as hell. I wish now I'd grabbed him then, but you said follow him, so I did. Besides, he hadn't done anything he shouldn't, except not go where he said he was going.

"We headed up and across town, and then over the Triborough Bridge into the Bronx. I was right behind him the whole time. After a while he started stepping it up, zigzagging crosstown, and, in general, acting as if he was trying to shake me. He didn't have any luck at that, though. We nosed right after him. And listen, Chief, I want to say right here that from the minute old high hat got into that bus until we caught up with it, the car wasn't out of my sight once! And my driver will ditto that.

"It began to get interesting now, and, after he'd sailed through two stop lights without noticing them I decided to pull him in. I told James to step on it, but they kept ahead of us. By this time we were going along at a pretty good clip. We sailed through another red light, and a big beer truck with the right of way came along, and smacked our car up against an El pillar! I didn't have to be no Einstein to know damn well, by this time, that Tarot was up to something funny. After all the trouble I'd had chasing him—not to mention the cab fare—I wasn't going to lose him like that. So I piled out and took a couple of pot shots at his cab. I planted one bull's-eye through the little back window, and it showered glass all over the inside of the car. The driver lost control—he got cut up a good bit—and the cab did a one and a half spin, bounced off another El pillar, and rolled over on its side.

"I ran up and opened the door on top. And this is straight! There was just one guy in that hack, the driver, and he was out— cold! He had a nice big bump on his head, and he was sort of bloody. But that magician must have crawled into his silk hat and pulled it in after him! *I saw him get in; I know damn well he didn't get out; and yet, he wasn't there!* That's the story, and it looks like I'm stuck with it."

Inspector Gavigan objected, "Why couldn't he have jumped out on the way? It's not so damned light at this time of night. Are you sure—?"

"Sure, I'm sure," Janssen protested. "That's just the trouble. "I was right close to his tail every minute. I swear there wasn't a chance, and my driver'll tell you the same."

"All right, then you only thought you saw him get into the cab."

"Just as you say, Inspector. Only, in that case, how come I found his suitcase in the cab, after it had updumped?"

"The suitcase!" Gavigan's eyes lit up briefly. "What was in it?"

"Nothin'," Janssen said. "It was empty."

"Has the driver come to yet?"

"No. We've got an ambulance here, and the doc's going over him now."

"Hang on," Gavigan ordered. Turning to us, he quickly summarized Janssen's story. "This is your department, Merlini," he finished. "Could Tarot pull a stunt like that, or has he got Janssen hypnotized, or what? I've seen magicians vanish ducks, but this—" He shrugged doubtfully.

Merlini sat on the edge of the desk, listening. His fingers, unwatched, played absently with a half dollar that twinkled in the light as it alternately vanished and reappeared. Now, in answer to the Inspector's question, he looked meditatively down at the coin and then flipped it, spinning, into the air. He caught it deftly in his right hand and held the closed fist out toward the Inspector. A half smile touched his lips as he opened the hand slowly, fingers spread wide. The half dollar was not there.

"Hypnotism not needed, you see," he said. "Ask Janssen just why he's so sure he saw Tarot get back into that cab."

After a minute of phoning, Gavigan reported, "He says he didn't actually see Tarot get in, but he'd bet two months' pay that he did. Tarot ran around the cab and got in on the off side. He heard the door slam, and there was no place else for him to go. The car drove off immediately, the pavement was empty, and Tarot couldn't possibly have reached a doorway unseen. There was no one else within thirty feet of the cab, and no manhole covers nor anything to hide behind. That corner is well lighted with street lights and illuminated signs."

"Good," Merlini said, grinning. "That settles it. Tell Janssen to make thorough search of the cab, and then call us back. And if the driver comes to—well, he'd call us in that case anyway."

"What should he look for? Don't tell me Tarot is hiding under the seat?"

"Something like that. Tell him to look there first."

Merlini's tone was far from facetious, and so Gavigan, after a moment's hesitation, passed his instructions on, ending with, "Get going, and phone back at once!"

He clicked the phone rest and dialed headquarters. "And where should I *really* have 'em look for Tarot?" he asked Merlini.

"I don't know. If the men you sent to his hotel haven't picked him up, as seems to be the case, I haven't the slightest idea where he has got to."

Gavigan started uneasily. "I thought you sounded as if you were going to explain this hocus-pocus?"

"I am."

The Inspector told headquarters to send out a general alarm for Tarot. Then he tipped back in his chair and said, "Okay, let's have it. But don't tell me it was done with mirrors or trap doors. Not in a taxi. If you can clear up a mess like this, maybe we can go to town on this locked room headache. Tarot leaves a taxi without using any of the usual means of exit, such as doors; and a murderer left this room in the same way. Though, offhand, I'd say the taxi stunt seems to be the most difficult."

"They're both good," Merlini said. "But then, so is Tarot . . . and so is our murderer."

"I'm not so sure they're two different people. That alibi of Tarot's is going to get a raking over. If I can break that—"

"I'm afraid that an explanation of the Great Taxi Trick isn't going to help much with our locked room tangle. The two effects are, as you say, similar; but the means of accomplishing them were quite different."

Gavigan sat up straight. "Then you know," he almost shouted, "how this locked room escape was managed?"

Merlini eyed a bronze sacrificial knife that hung on the wall just behind and over the Inspector's head. "I didn't say that, Inspector. But I know that the methods *must* be different, because the cab, after Tarot had vanished, contained a living, though unconscious, driver; whereas this apartment, after the murderer's escape, held only a dead man."

"Come on, speak English," Gavigan muttered.

Merlini wasn't going to have his climax rushed. He continued in the same even, unhurried, tantalizing tempo.

"Deception is eighty per cent psychology and is mostly accomplished by hindering the audience's observation in some manner, so that it is either incomplete or incorrect. That's the primary principle. Even a trained observer cannot possibly see more than a portion of the things within his view at one time, nor can he look in more than one direction at a time. It only remains to place the device or stratagem that works the trick among those things that are not seen, or if seen, not properly observed. The end result is actually a normal one, but, thus distorted, has the *appearance* of impossibility, of magic, sorcery, legerdemain, hocus-pocus, conjuring . . ."

Gavigan's fist pounded on the desk. "I didn't ask you for a lecture on the psychology of swindling, dammit! There's a murderer running around loose, and it's my job to catch up with him. Get on with it!"

"Objection sustained, Inspector." Merlini bowed apologetically. "The theory class is dismissed. The situation as it stands, then, is this: You are annoyed because Janssen's story states an impossibility. This means merely that some one of his statements is false, that somewhere along the line he was cleverly misled into thinking he saw something that didn't happen, or into missing something that did happen. Or a little of both.

"He and other bystanders swear that Tarot was not in the wrecked cab. He and his driver both swear that Tarot could not have left the cab en route without being seen. And, finally, they both insist that he entered the cab because he couldn't have gone any place else. Suppose we assume the opposite of each statement in turn and see what happens. Suppose, first, that Tarot *was* in the cab when it overturned. That merely leaves us with another miracle. Tarot must not only have been invisible, but also impervious to flying glass."

Gavigan, irritated by Merlini's round-about approach, interrupted, "And, if he left the taxi without 'Eagle-Eye' Janssen seeing him, that makes him invisible, too. So what? This isn't a story by H. G. Wells."

"Suppose he didn't get into the taxi the second time, then. Suppose he didn't even go near it. He wouldn't have to be invisible to do that."

"Merlini," the Inspector begged, "will you *please* stop giving an imitation of an assistant instructor in beginning logic and talk so it makes sense? He wouldn't have to be invisible; he'd have to be the opposite of invisible. He'd have to appear to be some place he wasn't. Now you've got me talking that way!" Gavigan's growl was distilled frustration.

"But that's exactly what he did do, Inspector! He only appeared to get in the taxi. Janssen saw him? How does Janssen *know* it was Tarot? He was following him; he didn't see his face, merely the back of his head, the hat, the opera cape, and the suitcase. Someone else could have"

"So! It wasn't mirrors or trap doors. Just a confederate! Now, all you have to explain is how this Mr. X you've invented got out of the taxi. If you so much as hint that he was a vampire who dissolved into thin air on the stroke of twelve and went back to his grave, I'll . . . I'll . . ."

"You'd have an apoplectic fit, so I won't suggest it. Anyway, it happened before midnight." Merlini took out a package of cigarettes and selected one. "No, it's much simpler than that. Mr. X, once in the cab, simply stayed there. He was in it when it crashed— and he wasn't invisible at all!" Merlini's match scratched along emery paper and flared brightly.

Gavigan stood up. "It won't wash! You're saying that the cab driver, dressed in some of Tarot's clothes and carrying his suitcase, walked around the block, got back into the cab, and took Janssen on a wild goose chase, Tarot in the meantime having vamoosed. The hat, which folded, and the cape, you want us to believe, were hidden under—"

He stretched out his arm and snatched at the phone receiver

before the initial ring had been completed. He listened, and then said:

"Under the seat! Damn! How about the driver? . . . What! . . ." He listened intently, amazement and understanding spreading over his face. At last he said, "Get a stenographer up there and get that on paper, with witnesses!" Then he hung up and scowled sheepishly at Merlini.

"You win," he said. "Janssen found the hat and cape under the front seat-cushions. And the driver just woke up and talked himself blue in the face. But I'm going to be mean and make you come through with the rest of it—if you can."

"On the spot, eh?" Merlini smiled. "I'll take a chance. When the cab stopped at 49th and Eighth the driver got out, wearing the hat and cape, and carrying the suitcase, all of which Tarot had shoved over from the back seat. Janssen wasn't in a position to see that his quarry came out through the forward, rather than the rear, door of the cab; the driver, probably feeling pretty silly in such unfamiliar get-up, took his mysterious and seemingly senseless promenade around the block. Tarot, meanwhile, vanished by simply going away from there. Returning, the driver again prevented Janssen's getting a complete picture of what was happening by entering on the off side of the cab. It wouldn't have looked quite right for Janssen to have seen Tarot popping into the driver's seat. The give-away, of course, was the fact that although the man was in a hurry he circled clear around the car before getting in. Inconsistent. Only reason, obviously, was concealment.

"Tarot made Janssen think he saw the exact opposite of what really happened. Tarot *left* the cab on the very spot where Janssen and his driver swore he must have *entered* it!"

The Inspector's bark was softer now and more respectful. "So far, so good," he approved. "But you don't explain how Tarot managed to pick a taxi at random from the Grand Central stand

and get an accomplice for a driver. Asking a lot of coincidence, isn't it?"

"I suppose so," Merlini admitted, "but that's not too important. I only know that's how it must have been done. I hope coincidence doesn't enter; it's less artistic. What did the driver say?"

Gavigan seemed pleased at having a chance to explain something. "Tarot is going to be a slippery customer to deal with. He must have done some damned fast thinking, because the whole thing seems to have been impromptu. The driver had never set eyes on Tarot before. But he had heard of him; he has a couple of kids that soak up Tarot's radio program every night. Tarot handed him a line about being trailed by some dame's husband. He gave the driver fifty bucks, and his gold watch and chain as security that he wouldn't make off with the cab. Ten bucks would have done it. The driver says that because he was such a hot-shot celebrity it never occurred to him that they were being followed by the police. Not until he couldn't shake the other cab, even through the red lights. Then he got his wind up."

"Why did he trek clear over into the Bronx?"

"Tarot told him that after ditching the husband he should leave the hat, cape, and suitcase at 5416 Mercer Avenue. Janssen checked that and it's a skating rink! The Great Tarot is going to have to do some high, wide, and fancy explaining when I get my hands on him. After dishing out a nice neat alibi, he queers the whole act with this flum-gummery. What's he up to that's more important than that nation-wide broadcast, why did he avoid being finger-printed, and where the hell is he?"

"You've left out a question, Inspector," Merlini said, "and it might be more important than all the others put together."

"Yes?"

"Why," Merlini went on, "did the Great Tarot vanish at all? Why, if he merely wanted to avoid the police, didn't he simply lose

Janssen? There are lots of methods that are a lot simpler, surer, and much less expensive. Why take all the chances anything so spectacular necessitated? It's a knockout of a publicity getter, but, judging from the way he treated the news photographers outside, it looks as if, for once, that's just what he didn't want. Which is queer too, because ordinarily he can't get enough of it. That's why he affects that opera cloak. It's his trademark."

"If it wasn't for the corpse we've got," Gavigan said acidly, "I'd say the whole dithering mess was some press agent's brainstorm."

"Why," Merlini suggested, "don't you send someone over to Tarot's hotel to take a peek at his rooms? He was in evening clothes and hatless, and I'd expect him to do something about it. His hotel is only a few blocks from where he disappeared."

"What do you mean, a few blocks?" Gavigan almost shouted. "He gave an address on 121st Street."

"I wouldn't know about that," Merlini said, "but he lives and always has lived at the Barclay Arms, 250 West 50th Street."

The Inspector pounced on the phone and stabbed angrily at the dial with his forefinger.

Merlini turned to me. "Ross, do you think that suitcase was empty when Tarot picked it up at Grand Central?"

"I'll give you odds that it wasn't," I said.

"No sale. Inspector, how about getting that suitcase over here where we can take a look at it?"

"Janssen said he was sending it," Gavigan growled.

"Good."

"He might," I suggested brightly, "have had a spare opera cape in it."

Gavigan spoke across the phone. "That smells. If he had an extra hat and cape planted, it means he expected to be tailed and intended all along to perform that fancy vanish. In that case, why didn't he make previous arrangements with a taxi driver and avoid taking chances with that obviously impromptu irate-husband story?"

I couldn't think of a good answer to that, so I shut up.

Over the phone Gavigan gave Tarot's address as supplied by Merlini and commanded that someone be sent there at once. When he had hung up, he looked toward the door, put two fingers in his mouth, and whistled a long, shrill note.

Chapter 11
Alibis Wanted

CAPTAIN MALLOY came in, answering the Inspector's summons.

"What did Spence say about Mrs. LaClaire?" Gavigan asked.

"Not much," Malloy answered. "He says that if you'll make her kick and scream a bit and cuss some, maybe he could tell. He was two floors below, and all he'll swear to is that it was a woman's voice and she was mad. He's stuck at that."

"All right. Send her in again."

Merlini settled himself on the davenport and crossed his long legs. "This suspense about Spence is terrific," he said. "Who might he be?"

"Reporter." Gavigan glanced in my direction. "House seems to be crawling with 'em. I ought to report it to the Department of Health. Spence lives on the first floor. When he let himself in at three this morning, he heard some female, up on this floor, pounding on a door and cussing like a longshoreman. Seemed to be mad at somebody. I'd hoped he would recognize Rappourt's or Mrs. LaClaire's voice, but his answers aren't promising. It could have been Zelma. She could have left the subway at Grand Central and stopped up here on her way home. Or it may have been some girl friend of Harte's banging on *his* door?" He inspected me questioningly.

"No," I protested, "I don't know any longshorewomen. Sorry."

"And when Spence came down the street," Gavigan added, "he

saw a man leave this building. Everyone else in the place says they were sound asleep at that hour and, except for the spinster on the floor below, they all sleep in pairs and back each other up. She could have been entertaining him, I suppose, only Malloy says that Spence describes the guy as walking, and in his opinion any male that left her apartment at three A.M. would be running like hell."

"Description?" Merlini asked.

"Short, maybe forty-five, round face, decked out in derby, carnation, spats, and cane."

Merlini lifted an eyebrow at that description, but Gavigan didn't notice. He had turned toward the doorway through which Zelma LaClaire came, swaying. The light glinted coldly on the platinum brightness of her hair and hotly on the full red mouth. Her poise was smooth and unruffled.

Gavigan wasted no time. "Let's have the rest of that fairy tale. You've had time to polish it up and round off the edges. So it should be good. You were saying that you didn't phone Sabbat, but your husband thinks you did because—?"

She scowled. "If you don't believe it before you hear it, what the hell chance have I got?"

"Get on with it," he said shortly.

"Anybody got a cigarette?" Her voice was calm, confident.

I supplied a cigarette and held a match for her. She puffed absently, without inhaling.

"Al," she said, talking through the smoke, "thought I was calling Cesare, because I wanted him to. I *had* intended to phone him, but I caught a glimpse in my mirror of Al listening at the door, so I kept my finger on the hook and carried on a one-way conversation. I only intended to give him something to worry about. Maybe I gave him too much."

Gavigan's nose wrinkled as if at a bad smell.

"You see!" she said, "I knew you wouldn't like it. But it's true."

Merlini was playing with that half dollar again, watching it speculatively as it flickered in his fingers, vanishing and reappearing like an uncertain ghost.

"Malloy!" the Inspector snapped. "Get LaClaire in here."

Merlini's coin fell floorward, spinning. He grabbed quickly, snatching it from the air. "Wait, Inspector!" he said quickly. "May I ask a question first?"

Gavigan didn't take his eyes away from Zelma. "Shoot," he said.

She half turned toward Merlini, waiting, alert.

"Mrs. LaClaire, is the phone in that dressing room a wall phone or a desk set?"

"It's—it's a hand phone."

"And a dial phone, of course." Merlini still eyed his coin. With a quick motion he made it invisible, and then, a second later, extracted it deftly from nowhere.

Zelma and Gavigan both watched him now, frowning. I wasn't so clear about things myself.

"How would you like to go back with the circus, Mrs. La-Claire?" he went on solemnly. "Billed as 'The Woman With Three Hands'? That's what your story amounts to. It's the only way you could hold a receiver to your ear, dial a number, and keep a finger on the hook all at the same time. With a wall phone, the hand holding the receiver can double in brass. With a desk phone—perhaps you'll show us how it's done?" He indicated the phone on Sabbat's desk.

"You go to hell!" she said briskly.

"All right, Babe!" Gavigan threatened. "That tears it. Start talking, and make it mean something!"

She tilted her face up at the Inspector and switched on the sex appeal. "Okay, what if I did twist things a bit? I don't want to get mixed up in a murder case."

"You missed a train, Babe. You *are* mixed up in one, and you're going in the wrong direction for an exit. Come on. You told Sabbat you were coming up. What happened when you got here?"

Suddenly her eyes were wide, startled. "Say, is that when he was killed, at—at about three this morning?"

"Maybe you should tell me?"

She took an uncertain step or two backward, away from us, and then, feeling the chair against her legs, she sat down slowly. Her body was tense, her eyes wide.

"Well?" Gavigan persisted.

She focused on him, and then abruptly relaxed, leaning back in the chair and drawing deeply at her cigarette.

"Okay," she said easily, "but you might have said so before. I did call Sabbat, but I didn't come up here—and—and I can prove it. Sabbat put me off. He'd been doing that lately. Cesare and I argued a bit, then made a date for tonight, after the show. After that I went straight home."

"And how do you go about proving it?"

"Alfred phoned me just after I had got there. It was just three o'clock. Ask him. He was checking up on me. Maybe he does want a divorce. But his luck wasn't so hot. I was home, and that means I didn't have any time left over to stop off on the way. I don't understand why—why he didn't tell you . . . unless—" She drew the back of one hand slowly across the bright red of her mouth. "—unless he doesn't intend to—*Inspector!*" She was on her feet clutching at his arm and gripping it desperately. Her purse and cigarette dropped to the floor. "Inspector! He's framing me . . . you . . . you've got to make him tell . . . you must—"

"Get him, Malloy!" Gavigan snapped.

Zelma still clung to his arm. The last female witness had fainted. This one was about to have hysterics. The Inspector pushed her toward the chair and got her into it.

"You sit there and keep quiet," he ordered.

Malloy brought Brady and LaClaire from the bedroom. The latter threw a swift inquisitive glance toward Zelma, faced Gavigan, and stood waiting. His underlip had a tight, drawn look.

Zelma, leaning far forward in her chair, pleaded in a voice that, though low, had all the piercing quality of a scream, "Alfred, for God's sake . . . you must tell him . . . you can't hate me like that! You know I couldn't—"

Gavigan stepped in front of her, swiftly, took her by the shoulders and shoved her back into the chair.

"Another word out of you, and I'll smack you one. I'm running this show. Now calm down."

He swung on Alfred. "You said you had no idea what time your wife got home last night?"

Alfred looked at the Inspector for a second, steadily. Then he said, "Pardon me, Inspector; I don't think so. You didn't ask me that."

"All right, I'm asking now."

"She was home at three o'clock, I know that. I phoned the house and she said she had just come in."

"You expect me to believe that?"

"Yes."

The Inspector looked at them both grimly, his jaw hard. He threw a hopeful glance at Merlini, but that gentleman was back at his coin tricks. Wearily, he said, "Brady, get these two out of here. Have somebody take 'em downtown in one of the cars."

Mrs. LaClaire went out hurriedly. Alfred hesitated just slightly, then followed her.

Gavigan said, "Any idea what all that means, Merlini?"

The latter tucked his coin away in his vest pocket. "Well, for one thing," he replied, "it would seem that Sabbat was still alive and kicking at 2:00."

"I got that. What else?"

"I rather got the impression that Zelma LaClaire is considerably more quick-witted and imaginative than the general run of platinum-blonde burlesque queens. She's also a good liar and an accomplished actress."

"Can you pick out the lies?"

"Most of them, I think. She didn't know Alfred was outside her door when she dialed Sabbat. When we told her he'd heard, she pretended she had known and presented us with the 'pretending to call' version. She hadn't warmed up yet, and that was a foul ball. If she had pretended to call her lover in order to get her husband's goat, she wouldn't say, 'I'm coming up,' and then let herself be argued out of it. She'd give him something worth listening to. Check?"

"I never try to predict what a woman will do. But that sounds all right."

"Just to be sure, I took that long shot with the question about dialing a French phone while holding down the receiver rest. If she *had* only been pretending to call Sabbat, she'd have known the right answer. But since she wasn't, and since she was under a bit of a strain, she didn't think of it."

"And how do *you* do it?"

"Receiver in the left hand, dial with the right, any number, and then break the connection with the right hand. You don't have to do all three at once. Or you can dial your own number and not have to break the connection at all."

"The voice of experience speaking?"

"Maybe." Merlini grinned. "It's not a criminal offense, is it?"

"Depends on whom you're pretending to call. But go on. What about that alibi? Alfred checked with her on it. If she invented it as she went along . . . how come he had the same story? They had no chance to . . . Damnation!"

"Exactly, Inspector. I warned you to keep that pair in separate cages. You must catch their act sometime. He goes down into the audience and takes a peek at someone's watch. Standing on the stage, blindfolded, she immediately begins spouting a description that includes the make, the number of jewels, the inscription on the cover, and so forth. She clutched at your arm and got hysterical so you wouldn't think to shoo her out of the room before getting him in. Then she cued him and transmitted the whole alibi. She was playing a long shot too, unless he's scared of her and she knows it. Anyway, he played up and she won."

"Why'd you ask Zelma if she wanted to go *back* in the circus? They don't have strip-tease artists, or at least not when I was a boy."

"No," Merlini grinned, "no strip artists yet. The pink tights are scantier, but they're still relatively modest. Zelma and Alfred both used to work with the Al G. Robinson Combined Shows. Believe it or not, she did one of those hanging by her teeth butterfly acts. He was a trapeze artist, one of the best until he fell and smashed that hand of his. They left the circus then, and she got a job with Minsky. He was unemployed for a couple of years. Then he worked up this second sight routine."

"That's what's meant by checkered careers, isn't it?" Gavigan said. "If Spence could only identify the dame he heard. Zelma's a two-to-one shot unless—oh, the hell with it! I'll take them over the bumps again later. Malloy, chase Duvallo in here. I've been saving him for dessert."

I sat up and opened my eyes all the way.

The man that followed Malloy through the door carried a faded blue overcoat on his arm and held a battered black felt hat. He stopped just inside and glanced quickly around the room, his gaze resting interestedly on the pentacle and candlesticks. His movements were all impatient, alert ones that indicated abundant vitality, and his poise held the assured self-confidence of the athlete. His face, even when he smiled, was taut with the obstinate determination that one might expect to see in a man who made his living escaping from impossible situations. He was of average height, in his late thirties; and I was sure, somehow, that I had seen him before, probably on the stage, though I had no remembrance of it.

In looking us over he saw Merlini.

"Hello!" he said. "What are you doing here?"

Merlini nodded. "Hello, Dave." Then he introduced the Inspector, Malloy, and myself. Duvallo bowed and waited. Gavigan began:

"You know what's happened up here?"

"I've got a hazy idea, yes. The reporters outside seem to be under the impression that Sabbat has been murdered. Judging from the number of squad cars and cops cluttering up the neighborhood, I'd guess there was something in it."

"There is," Gavigan informed him.

Duvallo indicated the splintered door panel and asked, "I see you had to break in. Door locked?"

"And bolted. But before we go into that . . . I understand you knew Sabbat quite well. Maybe you can tell us what all this is about?" Gavigan motioned toward the chalk marks.

Duvallo walked over and took a closer look. "Strikes you as screwy, I suppose. Well, Sabbat was screwy, pretty much. I knew him well enough to know that. Though I wasn't a close friend by any means. He didn't have 'em. Not the sociable type, unless it was with the ladies."

"Who, for instance?"

Duvall shrugged. "Different ones. He liked variety."

"Mrs. LaClaire, maybe?"

He lifted an eyebrow delicately. "You've been reading Winchell."

"Well, is it so?"

"Yes. But I'd rather not be quoted."

"How long have you known him?"

"A couple of months. I met him through Tarot."

"Was he in the habit of rolling back his rug and marking up his floor like this?"

"I wouldn't be surprised. He was apt to do most anything. The circles are obviously for the conjuration of some demon named Surgat. I've heard Sabbat talk about such things as if he believed in them. But he wasn't altogether batty. He put across one or two fast ones that had me guessing. That's why I persuaded him to ask Watrous . . . by the way, Watrous was here, wasn't he?"

"Yes, he and your other friends found the body."

"I seem to have missed all the excitement," Duvallo said regretfully, "but where's Sabbat and just what did happen? My curiosity is about to boil over."

"I'd rather get your statement first, if you don't mind."

"You make it sound ominous, Inspector. But you're the boss. Only I'd feel more at ease if I knew what I was stepping into."

"Dave," Merlini said, coming to life, "what was it Sabbat did that had you guessing? First time I ever heard you admit that."

Duvallo smiled. "That's why I never told you about it. I thought maybe I could get on to him first. He had a couple of parlor tricks that were Grade A. The Inspector here is going to think I'm batty if I describe them."

"I'll take a chance," Gavigan said brusquely.

"Okay. You asked for it. I sat up and took notice first when he materialized a first class spook one night that I'm damned sure wasn't made of the usual cheesecloth and luminous paint. Then once we got into an argument about Home's levitation phenomena. He got pretty steamed up about my skepticism—his temper was lousy, anyway. Finally, to shut me up, he said he could duplicate anything Home ever did. That was a good-sized mouthful, and he had to back it up. He went through some ritualistic gibberish, and I was beginning to feel sorry for the old boy and his delusions, when I'm damned if he didn't float right up off the floor a good foot and a half and just hang there. He let me pass my hands under his feet, and in full light too. He stayed there almost a minute and then, his eyes almost popping out with strain, he said in a low whisper, 'I can't hold it any longer!' and he came down with a thump. I didn't get any sleep for a week trying to dope out that one."

"And did you?" Gavigan inquired.

Duvallo shook his head slowly, smiling. "Maybe. And if I did, now that Sabbat's dead, I don't think I'd broadcast the answer. I'd have an exclusive on it."

"Then it was a trick and not black magic?" Gavigan asked.

"What do you think?"

The Inspector growled, "Do I have to join the Conjurer's Club, or whatever it is, and take the 33rd degree before I make any headway on this case?" He scowled at Duvallo. "You didn't like the man particularly, did you?"

Duvallo's glance was amused. "That's what they call a leading question, isn't it? No. I didn't. His persecution complex was particularly annoying, and he was as suspicious as—as a detective. Thought people were after his secrets. That's why those big bolts on the doors."

"It looks now as if he had some reason to be suspicious, doesn't it? Who do you know that might have wanted to kill him?"

"Nobody. I didn't think anyone took him that seriously."

Gavigan sat down on the edge of the desk and pushed his hat back on his head. "Suppose you give me an account of your movements since last evening, say about this time."

"Why since last night? When was he killed, anyway?"

"Let's take my question first, shall we?"

Duvallo shrugged, sat down on the davenport, and then, in a straight, level monotone reported on himself. "I've been working night and day since I got back from the road two weeks ago. Getting a new show ready for an opening next month. I was dead tired, and I hit the hay early for a change. I'd worked all night the night before on a new triple-locked coffin escape. I want to see you about it, Merlini. I'm having a little trouble with the—"

Gavigan broke in. "You live alone?" he asked.

"Yes, 36 Van Ness Lane, near Sheridan Square. I was up at nine, worked all morning and until four this afternoon, going out only to eat. A phone call—"

"Just a minute, Dave," Merlini interrupted. "See anyone you knew when you went out to eat?"

Duvallo's head jerked round at Merlin. "What—why, yes. The waiters at the lunch stand on the corner know me. But—"

"Go on, Duvallo. A phone call . . ." Gavigan reminded.

"A phone call caused me to rearrange my plans. I asked Tarot to pick up Watrous and Rappourt and bring them here since I'd have to be late. I had an appointment to see a man about a dog. After that I came on here."

"Let's hear about the dog, please," Gavigan insisted. His tone was polite and pleasant, but stubborn. "It took longer than you expected, didn't it?"

Duvallo stood up, and now, for the first time, he seemed nervous. He walked back and forth. "Yes, Inspector, it did. And I don't think I like it much. It seemed funny at the time, and when I come up here and run smack into a murder investigation—it begins to look queer as hell."

"Mind telling us what you're talking about?"

"I had a phone call," Duvallo said slowly, "from someone I don't know, a Mr. Williams. He'd heard I collected old and rare locks. He said he had a Spanish pin-lock that dated from 1400. He was in town only for the day, and if I'd meet him uptown some place he'd have it along. It sounded like a good buy, so I told him I'd meet him at my office. He said okay and then wanted to know if I'd be alone. I cooled a bit on the proposition when he said that. It sounded like maybe the lock didn't belong to Mr. Williams at all. But he gave me some more sales talk that made me decide it was worth a look, anyway. I went up there and waited. He didn't show up, and I was just about to pull out and come over here when he phoned to say he'd been held up and couldn't get there for another half hour. I waited another—say—!" Duvallo stopped and looked curiously at the Inspector. "Did you send somebody to hunt me up?"

The Inspector said, "I did."

"Now I know I don't like Mr. Williams. Just after he called someone knocked on the door. I knew it wasn't Williams because he hadn't had time to get there, and there were two of them. Anyway, knowing Mr. Williams wanted peace and solitude, I kept mum like a damned fool and didn't answer. You may as well get out your handcuffs, Inspector. If Sabbat was killed while I was sitting there on my fanny busily avoiding the best witnesses I could have had, then I am in a spot."

"How about Williams?" Gavigan asked. "Won't he testify that he talked to you over the phone?"

"I waited almost an hour and a half after that phone call and he never showed up. I thought it must be somebody's perverted idea of a practical joke, but it doesn't look like a joke now. Or am I imagining things?"

"I couldn't say," Gavigan answered. "Sabbat was killed early this morning around three. Are you sure you didn't recognize the voice?"

"No, I never heard it before. But that doesn't mean much. I know a lot of actors, and if one of them wanted to disguise his voice . . ." He shrugged.

Gavigan scowled, turned and looked down at the desk where the business card lay face down.

Duvallo regarded the door. "Since this door was smashed in," he said, "I suppose the kitchen door was locked too. Was it bolted as well?"

Merlini answered. "Yes. And I'd like to know what you think of the setup. The keys to both doors were in the pocket of the bathrobe Sabbat was wearing."

Duvallo closed the door, tried the bolt a couple of times, and then, leaving it in the locked position, stood back and looked at it. He turned after a moment, and said, "How about the windows?"

"Same thing there. All locked on the inside."

"Then you've got some very good reason for calling it murder and not suicide? Bullet in his head and the gun missing?"

"No, worse than that," Gavigan said. "He was strangled."

"He couldn't have strangled himself?"

"Suicides can do that only by hanging; otherwise they lose consciousness before the job is completed. Sabbat was lying flat on his back on the floor in the middle of that—that pentacle."

"Hmmm. Let's take a look at the other door." Duvallo started for the kitchen and we followed. He looked at the door and, getting down on his knees, ran his fingers along its bottom edge. He shook his head. "You couldn't throw the bolts from the outside with a string running under the door. Both doors fit too tightly in their jambs. But if the string was looped around a thumbtack or something of the sort in the wall, to attain a sideward pull, it could go out through the keyhole. And the matter of the lock is simple enough. It's an easy—"

Merlini broke in, "Perhaps, before you go too far with that theory, you'd better know that both keyholes were plugged up from the inside, with quarter pieces of Sabbat's handkerchief, the remainder of which was, with the keys, in his pocket."

Duvallo stopped, hand on the bolt. He regarded Merlini closely. "Listen," he said, "if you really want my help why so secretive?

I'd do a lot better if I didn't get information by installments. What's the idea?"

Gavigan, I noticed, had brought along the business card and was turning it over in his hand. There was an awkward silence, and then Duvallo threw the bolt over, impatiently.

"Tarot and party," he asked, "are quite sure no one was hidden in the apartment, someone who might have sneaked out after they broke in?"

"You tell him, Harte," Merlini said. "You were here."

"That was the first thing we thought of," I said, "and we searched the place. Result: zero."

"How does one get to the roof?"

"There's a trap in Harte's apartment," Gavigan replied.

Duvallo spoke, avoiding my gaze. "How about a rope from the roof and replacing a windowpane after locking the window from outside?"

"Harte's alibi has been checked. The putty in the panes is all old."

So he'd checked up on me, had he? I was beginning to think that working all night did have its advantages.

Duvallo looked a bit worried now. He turned to Merlini. "What do you think?" he asked.

But Gavigan cut in, "You're not licked already, Mr. Duvallo? I understand that your business is squirming out of packing cases that have been nailed shut and dropped in the bay. This should be pie, after that sort of thing."

"Yeah, I was afraid that was going to be your attitude. Don't you see what a lovely pickle that puts me in? If I admit I'm stuck, there goes a nice big hole in my reputation. Big headlines in tomorrow's papers: *Escape King Meets Defeat.* And if I say 'Sure, I could get out of here like rolling off a log,' then you'll immediately figure that's just what I did. No thanks. Particularly since I slept alone last night and haven't any witnesses to swear I was in bed when the dirty work was done. If you don't mind, I think I'll skip it."

"If the answer is no, I'll promise that the reporters won't hear about it," Gavigan said. "And if you can show me some way anyone could have gotten out of this room . . . well, I'd have to have more than just that, before I took your case to a jury. That fair enough?"

Duvallo hesitated, then said quickly, "Okay, I'll chance it. The answer is no. I couldn't have gotten out of this room and left it as you found it. Satisfied?"

Gavigan's face wore a cat-at-the-mousehole expression. He replied softly, "No. I'm not."

Duvallo's black eyes gleamed angrily. "And how do I go about proving I *can't* do something?"

"It might help," Gavigan said, "if you'd explain this." The Inspector turned the card so that Duvallo saw its face.

The latter looked at it a long moment before he lifted his eyes to Gavigan's. "So you did have that something else necessary to take my case to a jury." His jaw muscles were tight and his voice held a dark undercurrent of anger. "Where did you find it?" The Inspector touched off his cannon cracker.

"It was lying on the floor of the living room. Under Sabbat's body!"

Duvallo digested that and then said slowly, "It's that bad, is it?"
"Yes."

"May I see?" Duvallo held out his hand.

Gavigan drew the card back with an instinctive movement. Duvallo scowled, thrust his hands into his pockets and said, "I won't touch it."

The Inspector held it up and Duvallo examined it closely.
"Well?"

"It's mine, all right," Duvallo admitted. "But I haven't the slightest idea how it got where you say you found it. What happens now? Handcuffs and the Black Maria?"

"No, nothing quite so dramatic as that, but I'm afraid you may have to be a house guest at headquarters for a day or so until we get this ironed out."

Duvallo looked at him a moment; then he took a cigarette from his pocket, tapped it on the back of his hand and put it in his mouth.

"All right," he said slowly, "I'll tell you how the murderer got out of this apartment."

Chapter 12
Solid Through Solid

Man has contrived no lock that some other man
with the aid of ingenuity cannot pick.

David Duvallo—from an interview in
the *New York American,* August 17, 1937

GAVIGAN BRIGHTENED perceptibly, but he said nothing, waiting. Duvallo began speaking rapidly, self-assured once more, his voice colored with condescension as if lecturing a class of not too bright pupils.

"If you remember I said that *I* couldn't have gotten out of here, leaving the layout as you found it. I didn't say no one could. Watch!"

Omitting the conjurer's usual polite request for the loan of a gentleman's handkerchief, he reached out and deftly flipped the brown-bordered one from the Inspector's breast pocket He shook it out, and, gripping it in both hands, gave it a quick twist that ripped it in half. Discarding one piece, which he deliberately dropped to the floor, he calmly proceeded to tear the remaining portion again into halves.

"Suppose that I'm the murderer." He spoke coldly and with obvious sarcasm. "After killing Sabbat, I lock and bolt the living room door, and poke this piece of cloth," he indicated the torn square in his left hand, "into the keyhole. The keys and the larger piece of handkerchief I put back in Sabbat's pocket. Then I come out to the kitchen."

He glanced quickly around the kitchen, and reaching down, pulled a tin wastebasket from under the sink. He rummaged in it, threw out an assortment of waste paper, and finally, straightened up, having fished out a two-foot length of string.

"Anyone got a pencil?" he asked.

I took one from my vest pocket and handed it over.

He folded one of the small squares of cloth in half, and using the point of the pencil punched a hole through both thicknesses of cloth midway along and a quarter of an inch from the folded edge. Threading the string into the punctures, he drew it through until the cloth dangled halfway between the two ends. Gathering both ends in his right hand, he held the device up; his other hand made a waving conjurer's gesture. He turned, pulled the door open a foot or so, and, kneeling, threaded the two ends of the string together into and through the keyhole. He stood up, holding the ends of the string that were now on the corridor side of the door, and surveyed the Inspector coldly.

"I will now go out and close the door. If you gentlemen will watch the little piece of cloth closely—" His voice mimicked the parlor magician. As he began to shut the door after him, Gavigan spoke sharply:

"Not so fast!"

The Inspector looked at Malloy, and jerked his head toward the hall. Malloy sidled out, and the door closed after them.

Duvallo's voice penetrated the door, calm, didactic. "Using a duplicate key, picklock, or what have you—I could do it with a paper clip myself—I lock the door. And then—"

The string drew itself and the quarter handkerchief up and into the keyhole. The cloth jerked spasmodically once or twice as it was pulled tightly in.

"Now, by pulling one end only," Duvallo's voice went on, "I can remove the string completely . . . and that's that!"

We heard their footsteps go up the hall, and, re-entering the apartment through the living room, they returned to where we waited in the kitchen.

Gavigan didn't appear overly impressed. "And the bolt?" he asked.

"Can't some member of the class finish the demonstration?" Duvallo grinned maliciously. His eyes questioned Merlini.

"I wouldn't want to steal your thunder, Dave," said Merlini. "You tell him."

"The murderer left the door just as you see it, Inspector. Since the discovery of the body and before the arrival of the police, someone got out here and finished the job by throwing the bolt!" Duvallo reached over and pushed it home.

"Tarot, Watrous, Rappourt, the LaClaires, and yourself, Harte," Merlini said quietly. "How many of them qualify?"

"Tarot came out here," I answered, "when he and I searched the place. Watrous did when he got the glass of water for Rappourt. Mrs. LaClaire was in the bathroom for some time, and might possibly have made a side trip in here, unnoticed. Alfred took her to the bathroom, but came back immediately. I'd rule him out. Neither Rappourt nor myself came in here at all."

Gavigan squinted critically at Merlini. "You're not satisfied with this hocus-pocus, are you?"

"It's not bad . . . so far," he replied.

"Yeah, so far," Gavigan grunted. "But that's not far enough. The pieces of cloth we found in the keyholes, if you remember, had no holes poked in them."

"How about a needle and some strong thread? A woman might have done it that way," Duvallo suggested. "The holes wouldn't be so obvious."

"I said there were *no* holes." The Inspector's voice was metallic, precise. "But there were very obvious indelible pencil marks, showing that the cloth must have been pushed, not pulled, into the keyholes. You said yourself that the piece in the living-room door was pushed in. Both pieces present an identical appearance."

Duvallo grinned impishly. He reached out and pulled at the protruding ends of the cloth he had pulled into the keyhole, jerking it out.

"Like this?" he said, handing it to the Inspector.

Gavigan spread it out. Malloy and myself leaned nearer. Somehow the piece of cloth had undergone a startling transformation. The holes we had seen Duvallo punch in the cloth and through which he had threaded the string were not there. But there were pencil marks, like the ones on the torn pieces of Sabbat's handkerchief, except that they were not indelible.

We examined it with varying expressions of astonishment, all except Merlini who, not having bothered to look, was still leaning comfortably against the door jamb. "Dave's got a nice neat little theory there, Inspector," he said.

"I can see that." Gavigan reached down and picked up the half of his handkerchief that Duvallo had dropped on the floor. Then he held out his hand. "That other quarter piece, please."

Duvallo smiled, and held up his right hand. On its palm was a second crumpled square of brown-bordered handkerchief. He tipped it into the Inspector's hand. Here, in this piece were the missing holes!

"This is the piece you pulled into the keyhole with the string," Gavigan stated. "Just now, when you jerked it out and handed it to me, you switched it by sleight of hand for this other that has the pencil marks."

"Sure. And I added the pencil marks when Malloy and I were out in the hall. The murderer switched pieces too. He left half of

Sabbat's hanky in Sabbat's pocket, one quarter in the living-room door keyhole, and the other quarter he took away with him. This keyhole was filled with a piece from some other handkerchief, and was drawn in as I showed you. When he came into the kitchen tonight to throw the bolt he replaced his own handkerchief with Sabbat's, poking it in with a pencil. And there you are."

The Inspector seemed a bit appalled at such minutely planned deception, and somewhat incredulous. Noting it, Merlini said, "That's peanuts for a magician, Inspector. Sometime I'll explain for you the inner workings of a good trick, and show you with what infinitesimal details a conjurer will concern himself. That, in itself, is the whole secret of a number of tricks; the audience overlooks a possible explanation, because they don't think the performer would go to all that trouble for a mere trick. But he does—and if the trick is murder—"

"When it's murder we can expect anything," Gavigan exclaimed, "and that seems to be what we're getting."

Malloy suddenly came out of his retirement and fired a brusque question at Duvallo. "Well, which one of them did it? You act as if you had a pretty good idea—"

In the living room the telephone whirred brightly. Before it had had time to repeat its summons, Gavigan was lifting the receiver. The rest of us moved after him.

"Hello," he said. ". . . Yes, this is Mr. Sabbat's residence. I'll call him." He cupped a hand over the mouthpiece and blurted at Malloy, "Trace this call. Hurry!"

Malloy raced for the phone in my apartment.

Gavigan stalled a bit, then turned again to the phone. "Mr. Sabbat can't come to the phone at the moment. Who is calling, please? . . . Ching what? . . . How do you spell it? . . . *Ching Wong Fu!*"

Merlini edged in quickly. "Let me take it, Inspector. Before he hangs up."

Inspector Gavigan, a really incredulous look on his face now, handed over the receiver and slid out of the way. I heard him mutter disconsolately, "That's all this case needed. A Chinese menace!"

Merlini said, "Hello, Ching. Merlini speaking. Where are you? . . . Good. Listen. Get a cab and shoot over here right away. It's important. I'll tell you later. Hurry!" He hung up.

"That was Donald MacNeil. Ching Wong Fu is his stage name. I don't think he can resist the lack of information I gave him. He'll be along."

"Wonder why he was calling Sabbat?" Duvallo mused. "I didn't know they knew each other."

Merlini said, "I met Sabbat through him, ten years or more ago. They knew each other quite well then."

Malloy came back. "No luck. He hung up too soon."

Merlini sauntered over to the davenport and picked up a flashlight which one of the detectives had left there. "Ching said he was calling from his home. Apartment hotel on 23rd Street. Number 233, I think." Merlini snapped the flashlight on and off a couple of times, experimentally.

From the radio against the far wall a bored voice was repeating mechanically, "Calling car 42. Calling car 42. Go to 110th Street and Lennox Avenue. Code 13. Go to 110th Street and Lennox Avenue. Code . . ." I turned a dial in my head, tuning him out.

Duvallo sat on the desk's edge and lit a cigarette. The Inspector, facing him, said matter-of-factly, "Captain Malloy asked you a question. What's the answer?"

Duvallo looked around for an ash tray, found one near him on the desk top, and carefully placed his match in it. "Do you understand, now," he asked, "why I couldn't have gotten out of this apartment, though someone else could?"

The Inspector was cautious. "Yes. It doesn't look as if you could have gotten out using the method you demonstrated. But you don't get a clean bill of health until I'm quite sure that's the only method." He was holding Duvallo's card in his right hand, and he tapped one edge slowly against the knuckles of his left.

"Then I won't worry. That happens to be up my alley, and I can tell you that there is no other . . . unless Merlini—" He peered inquisitively across toward the davenport where Merlini sat playing thoughtfully with the flashlight.

Merlini said, "You should know, Dave."

"I think I do. It's the Inspector who seems uncertain. And because I'm sure there's only that way, I know that either Tarot, Watrous, or Zelma must have committed the murder. They are the only ones who could have left this room as found. Which of them did it, I wouldn't know. But you should be able to carry on from there, Inspector."

"You're damn sure of yourself all the time, aren't you?" Gavigan asked.

"We're discussing my specialty, aren't we? Why shouldn't . . . oh! So that's it." He frowned at Gavigan and I had the feeling that a good seismograph might have detected a tremor in his self-assurance. "Say, do I have to look guilty to make you realize I'm not, like the innocent but jittery suspects in a detective story? I could, I suppose, only it rather looks as if someone has been aiming to save me the trouble."

"Or else you've been trying to make it look as if someone had."

"Oh, it's heads you win and tails I lose, is it? I get it in the neck either because I did do it or because I've arranged to make it look as if I was being framed. I suppose I left that business card of mine lying where you found it for that reason. Come, Inspector. I can think of safer ways for a murderer to avoid suspicion."

"Yeah, so could I," Gavigan said. "But if I was an escape artist and had committed a crime that called for an escape artist, I might think it was a good idea."

Duvallo smiled grimly. "When I do commit murder I won't make it look as if an escape artist must have done it! Or do I look that dumb? And what's more, I wouldn't leave my card lying around in hopes that the cops would deduce it was planted by someone else. I didn't suspect, until now, that they were that smart." There was a thick icing of sarcasm on that last crack.

Gavigan came right back at him. "Maybe you didn't realize that they were clever enough to see that a clue as obvious as that one must have been planted. And a clue that's obviously planted, that's meant to look planted, could only be left by the person whom it implicates."

Gavigan was in rare form. That was the Fourth of July sparkler sort of logic I should have expected from Merlini. I was dazzled a bit, but it seemed to sound all right.

Duvallo made a helpless gesture with his shoulders. "Merlini," he asked, "what is the matter with this man? Why is he so keen on having my head? He suggests the card was planted and then says that's the reason I planted it. I don't—Hell! It's about time I got my lawyer." He reached for the phone. "I'm allowed one call before you jug me, I think."

"Hold it, Dave," Merlini's voice came. "That may not be necessary just yet." Merlini had pulled the rolled up rug to one side and was lying flat on his stomach, head and shoulders out of sight beneath the davenport. He backed out, sat up, and snapped off the flash light. Rising, he said, "I think the Inspector may have something there, at that. If he only knew just what. May I have that card for a moment?"

He reached for it and Gavigan let it go uncertainly. "What," he said, "were you looking for under that davenport, Merlini?"

"Something I didn't find. You haven't looked this card over for fingerprints yet, have you?"

"Haven't had time. The laboratory will have a go at it later. But they won't find any." The Inspector eyed the davenport with a puzzled frown.

"Suppose we take a look now." Merlini went toward Sabbat's worktable behind the screen in the corner.

"Hey, not so fast!" Gavigan hurried after him. "What do you think you're up to?"

Merlini surveyed the bottles that lined several shelves against the wall. He took one down and removed the stopper. The label read "Iodine Crystals."

"I read a magazine article the other day called *G-Man Methods*. It explained all the latest techniques for bringing out fingerprints. Here, light this bunsen burner." He shook some of the flaky black lumps from the bottle into a beaker. Gavigan scratched a match. "You go slow," he said. "Hot iodine fumes work fast, and it's damned easy to get too much."

"I'll let you boss the operation, but I want to do it. I'm a confirmed putterer, and playing at chemistry is one of my pet brands of puttering." He placed the card in the beaker, blank side up and so that it leaned across the bottom at a forty-five degree angle directly over the crystals. He covered the beaker with a flat dish and held it above the flame.

"Why are you so concerned over my doing it wrong, Inspector? I thought you didn't expect to find any prints."

"I don't, but just the same I wouldn't be surprised at anything in this case."

"I would," Merlini replied. "I'd be surprised to find fingerprints. But there may be something else. The card has a glossy surface, and when I first examined it the light struck it at such an angle that a dull rubbed-looking spot was plainly visible on its back. As if something had been written there and erased. You wouldn't know, would you, Dave?"

Duvallo, who with myself had edged close to watch Merlini's alchemical fiddling, shook his head slowly. "No," he said.

The card had begun to take on a faint sepia tinge, and now I could see a faint purplish glow hovering above the crystals. The coloration on the card increased, and then two darker smudgy areas began to show. One that was a long streak across the center of the card and the other a round blob near one corner.

"Look at that!" Merlini exclaimed, "There is a fingerprint, after all. We were both wrong!"

The corner spot came up stronger and showed definite whorls and loops. Then, in the midst of the other brownish smudge, I could begin to make out the faint, brownish ghosts of lines, smeared and blurry. Gavigan's nose was close to the glass. He began to spell. "Q-U-E-E . . . *Quee of words* . . . whatever that . . . There's an N and what looks like it might be an S. *Queen of Swords!* What in hell does that mean? Duvallo? Recognize the handwriting?"

Merlini quickly took the beaker from over the flame, removed the cover, and retrieved the card.

Duvallo said, "There's no particular reason, Inspector, why I should know who may have written on one of my business cards, dammit. I give a lot of them out. That's what they're for."

"Then you don't know?"

"Yes, as it happens, I do. The Queen of Swords is the name of a playing card. The original suits of our present-day cards were Cups, Wands, Coins, and Swords. I wouldn't recognize the script or the fingerprint, but I'll tell you who wrote those words."

Merlini turned out the bunsen flame. Duvallo went on, sounding a bit as if he couldn't believe it himself. "I did a trick for him once, weeks ago. A common enough billet-reading gag. Mental telepathy, clairvoyance, sympathetic psychic vibrations, or what have you. He knew the trick, of course; I had merely worked out a new wrinkle of my own and was demonstrating it. He evidently kept the card afterward for future use."

"One of the people who could have fixed that kitchen door. I can see it coming," Gavigan said suspiciously.

Duvallo said slowly, "I'm afraid so. It was Eugene Tarot."

Gavigan's expression was classifiable as the "I might have known it" type. He turned to Malloy. "Send someone out to look over those Knowltons and check with some of the other people at the party last night. I've got to know for sure if Tarot's alibi is . . ." He stopped, listening.

Then we all whirled together to face the radio, staring as if it were some infernal machine threatening to explode. The voice that came from it was speaking in its usual precise manner, though at a slightly faster tempo.

"Calling cars 12 and 36. Code 18. Code 18. Proceed at once to 36 Van Ness Lane. Calling cars 12 and 36. Proceed at once—"

We stared hypnotically as the message was repeated.

Gavigan pulled out of it first.

"Get headquarters!" he barked at Malloy.

Malloy ran.

"Code 18," the Inspector said slowly, watching Duvallo, "indicates a crime of violence. And 36 Van Ness Lane is a damn funny place for it to happen just now. Who's down there?"

"N-no one, when I left, Inspector. I don't see how—"

I looked at my watch. It was just 10:40 P.M.

Gavigan roared, "Quinn! Get that kit together. We're going places!"

Chapter 13
Designs for Escape

Stone walls do not a prison make,
Nor iron bars a cage . . .
Richard Lovelace: *To Althea, from Prison*

WE THREW MALLOY to the wolves, those ravenous journalistic ones that were howling lugubriously on the outer doorstep. He had been supplied by Gavigan with a shrewdly contrived statement that included enough blood and thunder to still the baying for the moment, but not so much that the news hawks would think they were being ribbed. Some of the facts in this case would have strained the credulity of even a gypsy tea reader's clientele.

Gavigan, Merlini, Quinn, and myself made a dash for the Inspector's car, Duvallo having been left behind to follow with Malloy.

The car whirled crosstown, pedestrians staring after us as our siren screamed like a hoarse banshee. The new snow glistened softly in the brilliant splash of the headlights, and the tall buildings rose around us ghostly and dark into a black sky.

Gavigan took out his pipe and fumbled with it. "It's high time we had our sleight-of-hand technician's report," he declared. "You have the floor, Merlini."

Merlini took it and unexpectedly broke out in rhyme.

There was an old demon at Sabbat's
Who, from hats, could produce many rabbits.

> He escaped to the hall,
> Oozing right through the wall,
> Murmuring "That's just one of my habits."

And before anyone could stop him,

> He was noted for one other vice,
> And no one considered it nice,
>   For he liked to twist necks,
>   Regardless of sex;
> And then blame it all on the mice.

One school of thought holds that the most effective procedure, in such cases, is the maintenance of a cold, dignified silence. The Inspector and I tried it. Merlini was, however, a hardened offender. He chuckled.

"Your criticism is probably sound. I find it difficult"—we turned a corner with a sickening skid—"to compose while traveling at this rate of speed."

Then, with sudden seriousness, he asked, "Ever heard of Dr. Fell, Inspector?"

Gavigan's grunt was negative.

"Harte?"

"I'm way ahead of you. You're thinking of his 'Locked Room Lecture' in *The Three Coffins*.[1] Right?"

Merlini nodded, his eyes twinkling. "Yes. Dr. Fell, Inspector, is an English detective of considerable ability, whose cases have been recorded by John Dickson Carr. Locked rooms are a specialty of his. And, in the book Harte mentions, he outlined a fairly comprehensive classification of the possible methods of committing murder and contriving to have the body found in a sealed room— minus murderer.

---

1 Harper & Bros. 1936.

"He mentions two major classes: A. The crime that is committed in a hermetically sealed room which really is hermetically sealed, and from which no murderer has escaped, because no murderer was actually in the room, and B. the crime that is committed in a room which only appears to be hermetically sealed, and from which there is some more or less subtle means of escape."

Gavigan puffed at his pipe and I listened carefully.

"The first class includes such devices as," he ticked them off on his fingers,

"1. Accident that looks like murder.

"2. Suicide that does the same.

"3. Murder by remote control, in which the victim meets death violently, and apparently by someone's hands, but in reality through poison, gas, or at his own hands, being forced to it by outside suggestion.

"4. Murder by a long list of mechanical lethal devices, some of which, as they occur in detective fiction, are pretty silly.

"5. Murder by means of an animal, usually a snake, insect, or monkey.

"6. Murder by someone outside the room, but which looks as if the murderer must have been inside; dagger fired through windows from air guns—that sort of thing.

"7. Murder by illusion, or the Cockeyed Time Sequence. The room is sealed, not with locks and bolts, but because it is watched. The murderer kills his victim and walks out; then, when the observer has taken up his place before the only door, he makes it appear that the victim is still alive. Later, when he is discovered foully done in, it appears impossible.

"8. The reverse of 7. The victim is made to appear dead while he is still alive, and the murderer enters the room just in advance of the others, and accomplishes his dirty work then.

"And, finally, No. 9 is perhaps the neatest trick of them all, because essentially it is the simplest. The victim receives his mortal wound elsewhere, in the conservatory or the music room; and then, still traveling under his own power, enters the room in question, preferably a library, and manages to lock himself securely in before popping off."

"They don't do that when they've been strangled," Gavigan protested.

"No," Merlini agreed. "Sabbat's murder doesn't seem to fall in Class A, unless you can conceive of some mechanical contraption that will strangle a man and then evaporate. Icicle daggers or bullets that vanish by melting may be practical, but offhand I'd say a man couldn't be strangled very efficiently with a piece of ice."

"You forgot method No. 10," Gavigan added quietly. "Murder by the supernatural, which includes such damn foolishness as homicidal pixies who can dematerialize and Watrous' theory of strangulation by etheric vibrations. Proceed, professor. Get the rest of it out of your system."

"You've got the patter down very well, Inspector." Merlini grinned. "It begins to get interesting now. Class B, the hermetically sealed room that only looks that way because the murderer has tampered with the doors, transoms, windows, or chimneys; or because he has been thoughtfully provided with a sliding panel or secret passageway. The last contingency is so whiskered a device that we'll pass it without comment. Doors and windows, however, can be hocused by

"1. Turning the key which is on the inside from the outside with pliers or string. The same goes for bolts and catches on windows.

"2. Leaving at the hinge side of the door, without disturbing either lock or bolt, and replacing the screws.

"3. Removing a pane of glass and reaching through from outside to lock the window, and replacing the glass from the outside.

"4. Accomplishing some acrobatic maneuver that overcomes

the seeming inaccessibility of a window—hanging by one's teeth from the eaves or walking a tightrope.

"5. Locking the door on the outside, and then replacing the key or throwing the bolt on the inside, *after* breaking in with the others to discover the body.

"Duvallo's explanation is a neat combination of methods 1 and 5. The kitchen door was locked *from the outside* with some sort of picklock, and the stuffing was pulled into the locks with a string *from the outside,* while the bolt was thrown and the cloth switched *from the inside* after the discovery of the murder."

"We don't seem to have any choice," Gavigan said. "We've eliminated all the other methods. Duvallo's must be right. But, Merlini, wouldn't you say that it was just a little too complicated for him to have figured out as quickly as he did?"

"You forget that he's an escape artist and he's trained himself to think quickly along exactly those lines. Suppose something goes wrong when he's inside a locked milk can filled with water? He has to be able to think fast. Besides, I'd figured that method out myself before he came through with it. And I'm not claiming any superior deductive ability. It's merely that since I'm a magician, I have to know something about the mechanics and technique of deception. I stalled you off because I wanted to hear what Duvallo had to offer."

"You agree then that Duvallo's answer is correct? You seem to have mentioned all the possible methods and a lot of highly improbable ones."

"Improbable!" Merlini sat up. "Improbable, Inspector? Perhaps you can tell me something that, on close examination, isn't improbable. This afternoon I would have considered it eminently improbable that I should now be veering across town in a police car expounding locked-room theory to an Inspector of Police! Some people think detective fiction is improbable. Sure! So is all fiction.

So is life. Hmmpf! Have you ever studied the life history of the liver fluke? Did you ever see a wilde-beeste, a spiral nebula, a fly under magnification or . . . or a bustle? They're all as improbable as hell. And what have the physicists been doing these last few years but reducing matter itself to a vague improbability . . . an improbability so utterly—"

"Hey!" the Inspector yelled. "Stop it! Just consider I didn't mention the subject."

Merlini spluttered a bit, then calmed down. "There is," he announced unexpectedly, "one more class of locked-room flim-flam. Class C."

The Inspector gaped. I chuckled to myself. When the Great Merlini rolled up his sleeves and started coaxing surprised rabbits out of a hat, he really worked at it.

"Class C," he continued calmly, "completes the outline. C'est finis! Kaput! There is no Class D, and matters are thus simplified. We've just two and only two possible methods—"

"The hell with Class D!" the Inspector thundered. "What is Class C?"

"It's something Dr. Fell didn't mention, as I remember. Superintendent Hadley was always interrupting him in the most interesting places."

"If this Fell person always had to work up a lather of suspense on his listeners before he came out with it, I don't blame the Superintendent. Get on with it!"

"Class C includes those murders which are committed in a hermetically sealed room which really is hermetically sealed and from which no murderer escapes, not because he wasn't there, but because he stays there, hidden—"

"But—" Gavigan and I both started to protest. "Stays there hidden until *after* the room has been broken into, and leaves *before* it is searched!"

"Harte!" Gavigan turned on me. "What about it?"

"Not a chance," I said, and then, almost before my words had traveled a foot, I saw it. I grimaced; it was so ridiculously simple. Our attention had been so occupied with the triplicate sealing of the doors, the locking, bolting, and keyhole stuffing, that we had overlooked the obvious. Gavigan saw me start. "Now what?" he asked. "It's easy as pie," I said excitedly. "The movies' mildewed old gag of hiding behind the door and walking out after someone comes in, behind them. Only this time the murderer crawled under the davenport when he heard us in the corridor, and when we pushed into the room he wriggled out the opposite side, straight into the hall. Even if we'd been actually watching the door we couldn't have seen him, and the rolled-up rug would have screened him in the unlikely event that anyone had his face down at floor level."

The Inspector scowled at Merlini. "So that's why you were poking around under that davenport!" He was silent a moment Then he said, "No. I don't think so. Would any murderer be such a confounded ass as to stay in a locked room for sixteen solid hours, with only the body of his victim for company, waiting for someone to come and please let him out? If he did, we've got a loony to hunt for."

"Of course," Merlini said, "we must remember that this isn't the usual garden variety of murder case, and that we do not have the ordinary run-of-the-mine grade of suspects. It's not entirely out of bounds to suppose that the murderer knew just when someone would show up . . . and perhaps even who. Maybe he arranged for it. Then again he may not originally have planned to have the murder occur so early. Or perhaps the person or persons he expected didn't show up on schedule. I don't know. I'm just letting the possibilities crowd in. I understand it's bad form not to examine *all* the possibilities. Sometimes the least likely one turns—"

"You're being trite now," Gavigan criticised, "and besides, those aren't possibilities you're letting crowd in, they're improba—" He caught himself too late.

Merlini sighed exaggeratedly. "Yes, of course. Have it your own way. So what? You've got an improbable kettle of suspects, and you've got a devilishly improbable murder. An improbable method would, at least, be consistent. It's a damn sight better than a downright impossibility, which is what has had us on our ears all evening."

"But look, Merlini," I said, as an idea occurred to me, "suppose we had entered by the kitchen door instead. There's Mr. Murderer, all nicely curled up under the davenport, and no place to go. And how would he plan on accounting for that sixteen hours? It's hard enough to fake a good alibi covering sixteen minutes. All we'd have to do is locate someone who can't give a corroborated account of his whereabouts from 3 A.M. to 6 P.M."

"Can you?" Merlini asked.

"The Inspector's already checked that. I was working until 5 A.M. and I've got a dozen witnesses."

"Inspector?"

There was a mildly thunderstruck expression on Gavigan's face. He blinked rapidly. "Damn you, Merlini," he growled. "No, I can't. When I hit the hay at midnight I was shy two nights' sleep after finishing off that Bryant Park case. I slept all day and arrived at the station just a few minutes before the call came through that brought us to Sabbat's. I didn't see a soul I knew the whole time!"

Merlini roared.

"Funny, is it?" Gavigan said testily.

"Yes, it's so damned *improbable*. I'm in the same fix. Mrs. Merlini is visiting relatives in Philadelphia. I spent the day at home working on a new Guillotine illusion. I made two phone calls, but I could have done that from Sabbat's. I don't understand, though. I didn't see you under the davenport, Inspector."

Chapter 14
The Man Who Laughed

"He flew through the air with the greatest of ease . . ."

VAN NESS Lane is a shrunken, lost little backwash of a street, its only connection with the outside world a dark arched opening, iron-grilled, squeezed uncomfortably in between two elderly apartment buildings. Several squad cars, an ambulance, and a small but growing crowd clustered about the entrance when we arrived.

Inspector Gavigan spoke briefly to an officer standing by one of the cars, and we went in, down several steps, to meet an India-ink blackness that was only accentuated by the thin artificial glow from Quinn's torch. The yellow splash of the light moved before us and disclosed a pattern of dark splotches on the thin carpet of white, a hurried trail of footprints leading inward.

Fifty or sixty feet back the walls on either side fell away, and we emerged into the Lane proper. On our right a large lonely house slept behind the blank eyelessness of shade-drawn windows. Two smaller buildings were on the left, one a low brick carriage house and the other, No. 36, a three-story, red brick building in the obsolete Village style. The Lane ended in a high blank wall.

From the partly opened door of No. 36 a narrow oblong panel of light came hesitatingly forth and fell crookedly down across a flight of stone steps. At the left of the door, and on the same level, were a pair of large French windows opening out on to a narrow wrought-iron balcony. Two of the several sets of footprints continued on up the steps and in at the door, only to come out again and join with the others that made a confused track toward the windows. Below the balcony they stopped.

Burke leveled his light at the window. The right half was just slightly ajar, and near its center edge where the catch would be one pane had been smashed. A thin sliver of light streaked the opening, and the sound of voices came from behind heavy drawn curtains.

"I guess we go in by the window," Gavigan said, "but keep clear of those prints."

Inside the voices stopped, the window swung inward, and the black shape of a man stepped on to the balcony. "Don't worry about those tracks," he said, "they're ours."

"Oh, it's you, Grimm," Gavigan replied.

Leaning over, Grimm offered his arm to each of us in turn as we hoisted ourselves up and swung over the railing.

Merlini and I followed the Inspector into the room, stepping carefully past a small end table that lay overturned just inside. On the floor around it lay the shattered pieces of what had been a lamp with a pottery base. Light sparkled in the deep-piled rug from the bits of glass that had formed the bulb, and the parchment shade was crushed and torn.

Beyond a davenport that stood a few feet in from the window, back toward us, were four men, facing us. Three of them were uniformed officers from the squad cars, the fourth, a young ambulance intern. Gavigan started around the end of the sofa, stopped short, and stood looking down at something it concealed. I followed Merlini as he stepped forward.

At first I saw only the face; I couldn't take my eyes away. It was dark with a deep tan, and horn rimmed glasses were wildly askew on a sharp nose. There was a small mustache, shiny black hair worn somewhat long, and that same horrible constriction of facial muscles that we had already seen on another face. The eyes bulged, and the mouth, with its swollen tongue protruding, gaped as if still gasping for that last agonizing breath of air. The lips, drawn far back, exposed the teeth in an ugly, inverted grin.

But what really brought us up short was the position of the body. Flat on its back on the floor, arms and legs spread wide, feet toward a fireplace, it lay in exactly the same position as had the body of Sabbat.

The man's clothing was shabby, ill kept, and disordered, as if death had been accompanied by a struggle. There was a ragged tear in the trousers at the knee, and a battered black hat lay crushed on the floor, stepped on.

I pulled my eyes away, finally, trying hard to retain control over the uneasy roller-coaster feeling in my stomach.

Gavigan said, "Who found him?"

Grimm, from behind me, answered, "I did."

"Who is it?"

"We don't know. Haven't looked at his pockets yet. Headquarters said you were on the way, and to hold everything."

Gavigan looked at Merlini. "You know?" he asked.

Merlini still watched the body. For a moment he made no answer, then, at last, he shook his head in a slow negative and turned abruptly to frown at the debris on the floor.

I looked around at the rest of the room, and saw, suddenly, a sixth man sitting uncomfortably on the edge of a low divan beyond the fireplace. He was a small, furtive-looking individual with a pallid, washed-out face and a shock of wiry, sand-colored hair. He sat stiffly and gazed with a curious, frowning intensity at Merlini's back.

Gavigan saw him too. "Who's that?" he demanded, pointing as if the little man were something for sale.

"Says his name's Jones," Grimm replied.

Merlini swung around and returned the man's stare with a surprised lift of his eyebrows. He seemed about to speak, but Grimm continued, "He was with me when we broke in."

The Inspector dropped to one knee and began a closer examination of the body. I looked about the room. It was large, perhaps twenty by forty feet. Two tall glass cabinets stood at the far end of the room and had shelves that were filled with a strange array of metal and wooden shapes, locks, keys, handcuffs, leg irons. Against the black wall, between two windows, sat an exceptionally odd affair, the dummy, life-sized figure of a bearded man wearing the turban and native dress of a Turk. He sat, cross-legged, behind a desk-like cabinet in the front side of which were numerous doors. From under lowered lids he gazed solemnly down at the cabinet's top which was laid out as a chessboard and on which chessmen stood. The fingers of his left hand were closed about a Bishop while the right hand held a clay pipe of extraordinary length.

Old playbills and faded, but still exciting, posters announcing the magical performances and listing the repertoires of famous conjurers lined the walls: Breslaw, Pinetti, Houdin, Anderson, Alexander, DeKolta, Herrman, Kellar, Houdini, Thurston. The largest poster, a three sheet in full color, hung above a radio on the mantelpiece. It depicted Duvallo and his Chinese Water Torture Cell Escape.

The Inspector got to his feet. "All right, Grimm, let's have the story."

Grimm began, talking rapidly, with a matter-of-fact assurance that was flatly contradicted by the puzzled look in his eyes. He spoke as if sure of what he had seen, but as if he couldn't quite believe it.

"You had headquarters send a car here looking for Duvallo. They reported no one home. I was sent along from the Charles Street Station, with orders to stick around in case he showed up. It began to snow just as I got here, at ten o'clock. Regular blizzard. Everything was quiet until just a couple of minutes before ten-thirty when this guy," he indicated Jones, "came into the Lane. I waited until he had gone up the steps and was putting his key in the lock. I said, 'Just a minute, Mr. Duvallo,' and followed him up the steps. He said, 'Sorry, it doesn't look as if Mr. Duvallo is in. You'd better stop back later.' He stepped inside, snapped on the hall light, and tried to close the door in my face; but I eased in after him and flashed my shield. He started to get on his high horse, said it wasn't his house, he couldn't let me in and would I go away. I told him, 'Sorry, I'm already in, and, if you're not Duvallo, how come you're letting yourself in with a key, this time of night?' Before he could think up a good answer to that—"

"Inspector," Jones blurted angrily, "I don't have to stand for that. I can explain. You see—"

"Take it easy, Jones," Gavigan said. "We'll get to that."

Jones shut up, but the look he threw at Grimm had poison in it.

"Before he could think up a good comeback to that," Grimm repeated doggedly, "we heard voices in this room. Looked as if someone had been in there, quiet like a mouse, all the time I had been waiting out front. I motioned Jones to keep his lip buttoned and plastered my ear against the door. The door is plenty thick, and I couldn't make out much, except that there seemed to be two persons arguing about something, both plenty mad.

"Jones didn't like my snooping, so he sings out 'Duvallo!' a couple of times. It didn't get any reply. The argument inside was going strong, and they kept right at it as though they hadn't heard or didn't give a damn. Then one of them laughed—Inspector, you remember Hatcher, the screwball who killed because it made him feel good?—well, it was a laugh like his."

The look on Grimm's face seemed to add that he would just as soon not hear it again.

Gavigan nodded silently, his eyes on the body, and Grimm went on. "Just then I caught a few words clear. The man who laughed stopped suddenly and said, '*And the police will never know!*' I didn't wait for any more. I pounded on the door and told 'em to open up. I didn't have any better luck than Jones did. The argument just got hotter. Someone screamed. I shouted that I was coming in, and one voice yelled something I couldn't get, but it didn't sound reassuring by a hell of a ways. There was a crash—then dead silence. I threw myself at the door and found out how solid it is. I took a chance of hitting somebody and put a couple of shots into the lock. But that only jammed it, and so, figuring the window would be a lot quicker—"

Merlini broke in, "Wait. You mean that lock's jammed so the door can't be opened at all?"

Grimm nodded. "Exactly. It won't budge. I've tried it from both sides."

Merlini looked at Gavigan, smiled grimly and said, "That locked door's here again! Go on, Grimm."

Grimm did, looking even more bewildered. "I took those front steps three at a time. Jones trailed along, and when I climbed on to the balcony I pulled him up after me so's he couldn't lam. I smashed a pane, pushed the catch over, and came in. That light was on—I hadn't seen it before because the curtains had been drawn tight. At first I thought the joint was empty. Then I saw the body. It couldn't have been a full minute since I'd been listening to two people, and now all I find is one guy—and he's dead! I made for that rear door—it was open—and went in with my gun handy, expecting a scrap. . . ."

Grimm came to a full stop. Gavigan said, "Well?"

There was an odd expression on Grimm's face, and he spoke slowly and with emphasis. "That door leads to a study—and something screwy. It's the queerest damn setup I ever—it doesn't make any sense at all." He started toward the door. "Come, take a look for yourself."

We followed. It was then that I became more fully aware of something I had before noted only subconsciously. The temperature of these rooms was no higher than that outdoors. And the reason was that a steady stream of cold air came in through the open door of the study.

It was a comfortable little study. There was one window, a large flat-topped desk, two chairs, steel filing cabinets, and, hanging on the walls, more lock collection. Great wooden Chinese pin-locks; ornate, intricately worked Spanish ones; crude cumbersome affairs from the Middle Ages; and small, delicately wrought animal locks from Egypt. In one corner, standing on end, was a large box that was like a brightly painted coffin.

The Inspector glanced at it suspiciously, and Merlini said, "That's a Spanish Iron Maiden. Lined on the inside with sharp spikes. Duvallo used to escape from it."

The inner machinery of what appeared to be the time lock of a large safe lay scattered on the green blotter covering the desk top. The further edge of the blotter was dark with damp, where snow had blown in through the open window. Gavigan leaned over the desk and put his head out.

"Let's have the torch," he said. "There's a ladder out here."

Grimm handed over the light. "Yeah," he grumbled. "A ladder. And it goes all the way down to the ground. But if the murderer left by it, then . . ."

The Inspector pulled in his head. There was an angry, determined twist to his mouth.

"Look at that Merlini," he said.

As Merlini peered out, I edged over and got a glimpse. Fifteen feet below (the ground level was lower here than in front of the house) was a garden surrounded by a high stone wall, and at its far end, fifty feet from the window, stood a lone ailanthus tree. What annoyed Grimm and Gavigan was the fact that the garden was covered and the foot of the ladder completely surrounded by snow. Snow that was entirely innocent of footprints, as white and unmarked as a new sheet of paper.

"Shades of D. D. Home and Apollonius of Tyana!" Merlini said softly, his eyes bright. Then he finished Grimm's sentence.

". . . if the murderer went this way, then he must have been able to float in midair!"

Duvallo's apartment just as it appeared after Grimm and Jones broke in.

Chapter 15
Death in Disguise

IN THE living room once more, the Inspector dismissed the intern, put one of the patrolmen on duty outside, told Burke to phone Dr. Hesse. Standing in front of the fireplace, he flicked the switch of the radio, frowned irritably at the absence of any answering glow from the pilot light, and snapped it off.

"Grimm," he said suddenly, "go take a look at those prints in the snow out front and find out if anyone back-tracked in them."

Grimm shook his head. "The answer is no. I've already seen to that. The only footprints in that snow before the squad cars came were mine and Jones', and they were all kosher. What I want to know is: is there a trap to the roof? Though even then I don't see—"

"There is," a heavy voice from behind us said. Two patrolmen came in at the window, and the first continued, "But it's padlocked on the inside. And we went over the other rooms and looked under all the beds. Nobody home."

Gavigan acknowledged their report and then asked, "Grimm, were both the voices you heard those of men?"

Grimm pondered. "I don't know," he said slowly. "That door's so damn thick . . . those words I heard, that was a man's voice, but the other—I don't know."

"What would you say?" The Inspector addressed Jones, who

still sat on the divan, not so stiffly now. I noticed that he never looked at the body.

He nodded quickly. "Yes—that is—I mean no. I wouldn't know. I heard the voices, but not well enough to distinguish. *I* wasn't eavesdropping at the keyhole!"

The angry glance Jones threw at Grimm bounced off that gentleman like a rubber ball, and the skeptical stare with which he was regarding Jones only deepened.

"What's your full name?" Gavigan asked.

"Marvin Ainsley Jones."

"Address?"

"248 Bank Street."

"You know who that is?" Gavigan jerked his thumb at the body.

"I never saw him before. That's what I've been trying to tell Grimm, but he doesn't seem to believe anything I say. I don't get it. Wasn't I outside with him in the hall when it all happened? What could I have to do—"

"Forget it, Mr. Jones," Gavigan said. "Grimm is used to gangsters who wouldn't appreciate tact. Also he's a bit upset. Suppose you tell me your story. How did you happen to stop in here, and what about the key?"

"I stopped in to leave the key. I stayed here temporarily while Duvallo was on the road. I only moved out a few days ago, and I had forgotten to return the key."

"Where were you at 3 A.M. this morning?" Gavigan asked innocently, but his tone failed to conceal the oddity of the question, or at least, Jones didn't think so. His eyes popped, birdlike. "Three A.M.?" he said. "I don't understand. What does that have to do with—"

"Maybe nothing. But I would like to know."

"I was in bed, sleeping. I usually am at that time of morning."

"Can anyone verify that?"

"No. I'm afraid not."

Gavigan, catching that, said, "You know this man, Merlini?"

"Yes. I knew his father. He was ringmaster for many years with Barnum and Bailey."

"And how did you spend the day today, Jones?" Gavigan continued.

"I spent the morning seeing about a job. I stopped in to see Merlini at the shop this afternoon, but he wasn't there. I met a friend of mine there, and we had dinner together uptown, afterwards going to his apartment where I stayed until just before coming here."

"Friend's name, please."

"Ching—Donald MacNeil."

I glanced toward Merlini at this and saw that he was only half listening. He stood by the davenport, blinking thoughtfully at the body, a faint trace of wear and tear beginning to mar that enigmatic calm of his which so annoyed the more irritable Inspector.

Suddenly and quietly he spoke. "Grimm, is that what I think it is, there on the floor partly under the edge of the davenport?"

"Oh, yes—I was coming to that. It was around his neck when I got to him. I cut it away, thinking I might be in time to bring him out of it—but no such luck."

Grimm held it up. It was a long strip of silk two inches in width, dark maroon in color, with tasseled ends, one of which tied back on itself and formed a loop that was now cut through.

"The missing piece of Sabbat's dressing gown," Merlini said. "I've been wondering when and if that was going to turn up."

The Inspector raised an eyebrow at this. "Oh, so you missed that too, did you? Well, it's the straw that breaks the camel's back. When I get two locked-room murders in one day, there *would* seem to be some connection, unless Congress has repealed *all* the laws of chance. But when the body is lying in the same position and both men have been strangled with the same . . ." He broke off and went toward the body. "We'll take a look through his pockets. It's about time we got an identification."

Kneeling by the couch, he went quickly through the dead man's clothes. Then, holding a small object in his hand, he sat back on his heels and looked up.

"We don't seem to be able to find anything about this case that's ordinary," he grumbled. "A man's suit has thirteen pockets, and even a bindle stiff carries more in them than this." The corrugations on his brow were impressive as he regarded the thing on his palm. It was a small egg-shaped black stone, like a piece of highly polished cannel coal, perhaps two inches long. Gavigan contemplated it curiously for a moment, then shrugged his shoulders and laid it along with the cord on the mantel.

Merlini lit a cigarette and looked meditatively at the match flame before flicking it out. Then he said, "I've a great curiosity to see if there are any more business cards under this body, Inspector. I thought I caught a glimpse of something white, like paper, when you were going through his pockets—just there under the hip."

The Inspector lifted the coat a bit, took hold of something with his thumb and forefinger, and pulled forth a folded square of paper. He stood up and gingerly opened it out.

When I saw the ragged edge that ran down one side I knew what it was—the missing page from the *Grimorium of Honorius*.

Merlini recited, "*I conjure thee, O Surgat, by all the names which are written in this book, to present thyself here before me, promptly and without delay, being ready to . . .* to what, Inspector?"

Gavigan read aloud, "*To obey me in all things, or failing this to dispatch me a Spirit with a*—" He stopped, mouth partly open.

Then he closed it firmly and looking up said, "Merlini, someone is amusing himself at our expense, someone with a damned perverted sense of humor."

He glanced again at the page and read on: ". . . *with a stone which shall make me invisible to everyone whensoever I carry it! And I conjure thee to be submitted in thine own person, or in the person of him or those whom thou shall send me, to do and accomplish my will and all that I shall command, without harm to me or to anyone, so soon as I make known my intent.*"

Inspector Gavigan's glance was sour. "Merlini, you don't need to hint that the murderer, made invisible by that stone, is still here in this room, laughing at us! I can make that deduction myself. I suppose now you'll suggest that we spread flour around on the floor and shoot when we see his footprints. Damn such a case, anyway."

"I doubt if that would help. This murderer doesn't seem to leave footprints. May I see the paper?" Gavigan passed it over, and Merlini, following the Inspector's lead, held it lightly between thumb and forefinger at one corner. Examining it, he said, "More invocations; Morail, Sergulath, Mersilde—Hummpf! The paper tells us one thing. Inspector. We can eliminate Surgat, in spite of that mysterious black pebble you found. Since its removal from the book, this page has been folded . . . twice . . . so that it will go into a pocket . . . or a handbag. Demons don't have either and would find folding quite unnecessary, or is that too far-fetched?"

"Yes, and you know it." Gavigan was curt.

"Is this any better? Among some of the curios lying about at Sabbat's apartment I noticed a small leather case lined with velvet. A card in the lid of the case bore the inscription, 'Dr. Dee's Crystal.' Other than that the case held nothing. There was a hollowed depression in the velvet, however, that I'm pretty sure would fit very snugly," he pointed at the mantel, "around that stone."

"The black stone," Gavigan said, "the torn page, the dressing gown cord, the position of the body, and the sealed rooms. Two murders and one murderer. That seems clear enough. The first locked-room headache was bad enough, but the trimmings on this one are even fancier . . . and we've one suspect who's demonstrated that he's an expert vanisher. Burke, find out how many men are on the Tarot assignment and . . . have it doubled."

"Of course, Inspector," Merlini said, "the really difficult crimes to solve, as you know, are the ones in which anyone might have popped in and done it. But when, as in this case, it seems that no one could possibly have murdered either man, it means that, once we find out *how* they were done, we will know *who* did them. The impossible situation, by its very uniqueness, ultimately limits the possibilities."

"If you're trying to say that impossibilities don't have many possibilities, I agree. Now, if you'll just tell me how—"

A phone rang insistently from behind the closed door of the study. Burke, who had already started phoneward, went into high, and Gavigan, dropping everything, chased after him. Merlini laid aside the *Grimorium* page, and wandered over to stand beside the body. Something about it seemed to fascinate him. I saw him bend over, touch the side of the cheek, and then look curiously at his finger.

Gavigan was reading a riot act to someone over the phone. When he came back he spoke to the patrolmen. "Take some tools from that case and get the pins out of those doorhinges so we can get in and out of here." He superintended the removal of the door, and after it had been put to one side against the wall addressed Grimm. "Take Jones upstairs and make him comfortable. I'll see him again later."

Jones stood up and went obediently toward the door. Then he stopped, asking, "Am I under arrest, Inspector?"

"No. You're being held as a material witness, though. Do you want to make anything of it?" Gavigan's tone was pugnacious, nettled. Evidently he had heard something over the phone that hadn't agreed with him.

"I just thought I'd ask," Jones said. "One likes to know. Merlini, I wish you'd tell him that I'm not the type that goes around throttling people."

"Oh, people, is it?" Grimm said, stepping toward him. "What do you know about anyone else being strangled?"

"I don't know what—Oh, so that's why you wanted to know so much about my movements?" He looked at Merlini. "Who was it?"

Gavigan said, "Cesare Sabbat. Know him?"

Jones' face was blank. "No. Who's he?"

Gavigan looked sharply at him for a moment, then said, "You can read about it in the papers tomorrow. Take him out, Grimm." He turned to us. "I'm going to have a look-see around upstairs. Quinn, you keep your eye on our friends here. I don't want any amateur detecting going on that I don't know about." He turned to go.

Merlini asked, "Who was that on the phone, Inspector? Mind? I thought I heard you mention Col. Watrous?"

Gavigan stopped in the doorway. "That was Byrd, the tail who was supposed to keep tabs on Watrous. He and Janssen make a lovely pair. He thought he had Watrous bedded for the night, so he parked across the street from the old boy's apartment and sat on his hands. Watrous went in and the light in his room came on at 9:55. Byrd decided he'd better report just now when he saw Watrous go in again! It seems that there's an exit through a drugstore, and Byrd was watching the wrong mousehole. Unless he's twins, Watrous went out, immediately after he got there, for all we know, leaving a light burning in his room. Wherever it was he went, he'll sleep better tonight if he can produce witnesses. He could have *walked* here from his place in fifteen minutes, and arrived soon enough after the snow began that his footprints would have been covered."

Gavigan stepped through the doorway and was gone.

"The Inspector is something of an actor, himself," Merlini commented. "That was a very good exit. And now, under Quinn's watchful eye, I'll do a little amateur sleuthing."

Hands in his pockets, Merlini wandered about the room. There seemed to be little purpose in his explorations and little result. He viewed the lock collection critically and spent several minutes studying the arrangement of chessmen on the board before the Turk. Presently I grew bored watching him, and, thinking again of an idea which had occurred to me in the last few minutes, I hunted in my pockets for paper and pencil.

I was busy for the next five or ten minutes, until suddenly I heard Merlini saying, "Inspector, take a look at this."

I glanced up from my paper. Gavigan had returned. Merlini stood behind me, impolitely reading over my shoulder.

I had listed our suspects in the order of their appearance, and had noted, in separate columns, the whereabouts of each at the times of Sabbat's and X's murders. I boxed those alibis which, to me, seemed sufficiently corroborated.

Burke, who had been busy with the phone in the study, came in and followed Gavigan across the room. He looked at what I had written and suggested, "You might fill in those blanks after the La-Claires. Jennings says they were on the floor doing their turn at La Rumba at ten-thirty."

That amendment made, the result looked like this:

SUSPECTS   *ALIBIS*

	Sabbat's murder 2-3 A.M.	X's murder 10:30 P.M.
Watrous	Séance	?
Rappourt	Séance	?
Tarot	Party	?
Alfred	Tony's	Night club
Zelma	Subway	Night club
Duvallo	Bed	At Sabbat's
Jones	Bed	With Grimm

"Two murders," Gavigan said unhappily, "and all the suspects covered for one or the other. Watrous and Rappourt are going to supply answers for those question marks, but I'd give a month's pay right now to know where Mr. Eugene Tarot was at 10:35 and where he is now."

Merlini struck a match and held it to a cigarette. He might just as well have applied it to a stick of dynamite.

"I'll take you up on that offer, Inspector," he said. He paused, smiling, then went on, speaking with a slowness of tempo that was technically sound, artistically perfect, and damned exasperating.

"At 10:35 Eugene Tarot was in this room. And now . . . well, he's still here, or rather, his body is."

We all turned and stared at the dead man.

Chapter 16
The Red-Haired Wench

"Here's the blood of a bat
Put in that, oh, put in that.
Here's lizzard's bane
Put in again.
The Juice of toad, the oil of adder
Those will make the yonker madder.
Put in; there's all, and rid the stench;
Nay, there's three ounces of the red-hair'd wench
Round, around, around . . ."

Middleton: *The Witch*

As WE stood there waiting for the Inspector to verify this amazing assertion, the sound of voices and footsteps came from outside the window.

"Damn!" said the Inspector. He stepped into the hall, and as the front door opened, we heard him order, "Malloy, you'll find Detective Grimm upstairs. Take Duvallo up there. Bennett, you come in here and get busy with that camera. Who's this gentleman?"

"Ching Wong Fu, Inspector. He showed up just after you left."

"All right, he goes up with Grimm, too. Then you come in here."

"Dammit, Inspector," Duvallo's voice said, peevishly, "what's the idea? Malloy has to spend a half hour dictating a report before he leaves, then he stops on the way and putters around at the station house and takes half the night to get here. What's happened here, anyway?"

Gavigan's reply should easily reach the finals in any contest for the best understatement of the year. "I'm not quite sure yet," he said. "But you'll hear about it soon enough. In the meantime, please do as I suggest."

His tone made it obvious that there was no alternative.

Duvallo gave in reluctantly. "I'm getting fed up with this nonsense." Then he went slowly up the stairs, Ching and Malloy following.

Bennett came in and busied himself over the body with camera, tripod, and lights. In a few moments Malloy returned and, while we waited, Gavigan gave him a hasty summary of the situation. When Bennett finally said, "Okay, Chief," we gathered around the body.

Gavigan lifted the glasses from the still face, looked through them and said, "Dime store." Then he pulled tentatively at the mustache and found that it peeled off.

"I didn't get a decent look at Tarot in good light at Sabbat's," he said, "but this still doesn't look much like him to me."

"That facial expression, of course," Merlini said, "is hardly characteristic of the suave Tarot, and the absence of the monocle makes him look positively naked. I've never before seen him without it. But what makes the greatest difference is the sun tan." He ran his finger across the dead man's cheek and held it up. There was a yellowish-brown smear on the finger and a pale streak across the face.

"Make-up," he said.

Gavigan leaned forward and twisted the head to one side, looking closely at the right side of the jaw.

"You win," he said gravely.

I saw it too. The strip of adhesive that had seemed so out of place on the immaculately groomed Tarot was there, covered and partially concealed by the cosmetic."

Merlini, seeing it for the first time, scowled. "Tarot had that on his face before?"

Gavigan nodded, and then reasoned, "He could just about have made it. After ducking out of that taxi at 49th Street, he could have made a quick change at his hotel, and then . . . well, the subway would get him here in under fifteen minutes. Allowing another fifteen minutes for the change into this disguise, he'd have arrived here maybe five minutes to ten, but not any earlier. A taxi's no faster than the subway for that distance. That gets him here just before the snow and no trouble about footprints. But why the disguise?"

"Maybe," I suggested, "he was doing a little private detecting. He seemed to think Duvallo was the guilty person, so he might have come here to hunt for evidence. The disguise was to prevent his recognition should Duvallo happen to be at home."

"He seems to have done a bit of 'breaking and entering,' at any rate. He's got no key and, this time, no picklocks, so he must have come in by the ladder. But Grimm was out front from ten on, saw and heard nothing. What was Tarot up to during that half hour?"

"I wouldn't know that," I said. "Something sinister, probably, and the murderer coming along caught him at it, recognized him, and let him have it."

Gavigan made a wry face. "Harte," he protested, "if you're going to submit theories make the words mean something. The murderer just 'comes along,' does he? Isn't it bad enough that he got away without leaving footprints? You've got him coming in that way."

"If he did it once," Merlini said, "he might have done it twice."

"Sure, but it would be a damn sight simpler to suppose he came in like Tarot, before the snow. That leaves us a little less to explain."

"Does it?" Merlini asked. "It leaves me wondering what two

people, murderer and victim, did to amuse themselves so quietly during the half hour Grimm was outside."

"Any way you look at it, there's plenty to wonder about. For instance, where did that ladder come from in the first place?"

"The murderer," Merlini said slowly, "may, as you say, have entered by the ladder; but if we could prove he left by it, then we'd know one very interesting fact about him."

"Such as?"

"We'd know that he was a *Lung-Gom-Pa.*"

"That would be *such* a help," Gavigan said, suspecting where this was leading. "I don't want to hear about it." He turned and busied himself examining the catch on the window and then, stepping part way out, surveyed the balcony.

Grimm, however, was interested. "What is it in English?" he asked.

"Madame Alexandra David-Neel," Merlini said, watching Gavigan out of a corner of his eye, "a Frenchwoman who lived in Tibet for eighteen years and who claims to be the only white woman ever to have made the dangerous trip, in disguise, to the holy city of Lhassa, writes that one day when travelling she came upon a naked lama whose sole wearing apparel consisted of heavy chains wrapped about him. Inquiry disclosed that this conception of what the well-dressed lama should wear was not as lacking in logic as might be supposed. Through the practice of *Lung-Gom* the fakir's body had become so light that, without sufficient ballast, he was always in danger of floating in midair."[1]

Gavigan studiously avoided any appearance of interest. Grimm snorted, "Does Barnum and Bailey's know?"

"In order to get off that ladder," Merlini went on, "without having disturbed the snow that surrounds its foot, Mr. X would have had to float in midair, no less. Just what the practice of *Lung-*

---

1 *Mystery and Magic in Tibet*, Claude Kendall, 1932.

Gom is, Madame David-Neel neglects to say. One of the breath-control systems, probably. Nevertheless it's the only practicable method of getting off that ladder. I have many times caused a young lady assistant to float some six feet above a stage floor and then passed an examined hoop completely over and around her body. I didn't resort to *Lung-Gom*, and the method I did use is, in this instance, quite useless."

Quickly, before Merlini could go on, Gavigan put in, "That's your way of saying that the window and the ladder are out. Okay. Perhaps you know how the murderer did get out? Let's have it, and no moonshine about Tibetan lamas, Transylvanian werewolves, Javanese hobgoblins, or witches on broomsticks. It may be entertaining table talk, but we're supposed to be busy catching a murderer."

"Hmm," Merlini said speculatively, "sailing out the window on a broomstick. I missed out on that one." He pushed his cigarette, lighted end first, into his closed fist, and by squeezing gently made it vanish. Gavigan's face flew storm signals, and he took a step toward Merlini.

Quickly the latter said, "Perhaps it *is* time we looked into the possibilities. There's one method in particular—"

"Oh, so there are a couple of methods, are there? All right, Mr. Magician, bring out your rabbits."

Merlini turned to me. "How about you, Harte? Doesn't our recent review of Dr. Fell's outline suggest anything?"

"Yes," I said not too cheerfully, "it does. But I don't like it. It would be an awfully flat finish to what is so far a really writable mystery yarn."

"Class B, method 2, the secret exit?" Merlini asked.

I nodded.

"That would be lamentable," he agreed, "though, unless he's still in it, you'd also have to postulate a tunnel that would bring him out a block or so away in order to duck that snow. Still, I suppose we'd better look into it."

"I intend to," Gavigan said. "Duvallo's a magician, and this house is probably riddled with secret passages. If he denies it, we'll take the place apart."

"Don't count your chickens too soon, Inspector. The Merlini mansion doesn't have those conveniences. Mrs. Merlini says secret passageways gather dust and attract mice. Grimm, have you any ideas?"

Grimm was disgruntled. "Oh, sure," he said sarcastically. "The murderer might have had an Autogiro parked in the air outside the window, only I'd have heard it. Or he could be one of those human cannon balls they have in the circus, and he shot himself through the window, landing over on Barrow Street somewhere, only I haven't seen anything that looks like a cannon. If Tarot only *could* have strangled himself."

"Has anybody," Merlini asked, "thought what an odd feature of this case that is—both here and at Sabbat's? Usually when a corpse is found in a locked room the murderer uses a means of death consistent with suicide. Much more logical. There's always the chance that the police may fall for it." He gestured toward the study. "As to your preoccupation with the open window, Grimm, there's a simpler and somewhat more practical possibility. Duvallo mentioned it at Sabbat's. Rope."

The Inspector spoke to Patrolman O'Connor. "Get Duvallo's keys and open that trap door to the roof. Look for footprints, and—and you might include the top of that carriage house next door while you're at it."

"Not counting Grimm's pulp magazine suggestions," Merlini said, "two methods have been submitted. And I think Gavigan is toying with number three. A variation on the davenport theory. Am I right?"

"Any reason why not? It's still the simplest. The murderer hid behind that chair near the French window. After Grimm and Jones came in and dashed madly into the study, he slipped out on to the balcony and hoisted himself from the top of the railing to the roof of the carriage house next door. It's low enough so that it wouldn't require any abnormal acrobatics."

"I knew Jones had something to do with it," Grimm broke out, apparently taking to the Inspector's idea. "If that's what happened, he knows it. He didn't follow me into the study. He was still standing just inside the window when I came out of the study."

"If O'Connor finds tracks on the roof, you can take Jones apart." Gavigan turned to Merlini. "There are three possible solutions to an impossible situation. I don't suppose it's too much to ask *you* for a fourth, and a better one?"

"No, not at all," Merlini grinned. "Do you know what that is?" He pointed at the silent Turk who sat rigidly, contemplating his chessboard.

"No, do you?"

"It's an exact replica of Maelzel's Automaton Chess Player, the original of which was destroyed when the Chinese Museum in Philadelphia burned in 1854. Mechanical marvels weren't common as dirt in those days, as they are now; and a machine that could apparently think through the complicated moves of chess, and, what's more, almost invariably win, created what Variety would term 'a hit playing to stand-up biz.'"

Merlini walked over and opened one of the doors in the face of the cabinet, disclosing an intricate mass of cogwheels, springs, and pulleys. "These doors are for the purpose of showing that the innards are purely mechanical. Maelzel opened a door in the rear and held a lighted candle there to show that this compartment contained nothing but cogs and gears. Edgar Allan Poe, for one, however, demonstrated very ably that a chess genius, by name

Schlumberger, who was connected with Maelzel's party, but who was never in evidence when the automaton was playing, could have concealed himself in the compartment behind those other doors and then, when Maelzel had closed the rear door, could move over behind the machinery so that the two remaining doors could be opened."[2]

Gavigan's hand came from his pocket gripping an automatic.

"Open those other doors," he commanded.

Merlini pulled with both hands and swung them open simultaneously. Gavigan's gun pointed squarely at the black opening, and from behind him Malloy flashed a torch. The interior was empty. Merlini stepped behind the cabinet and opened the rear door he had mentioned.

"Nobody home," he said. Coming around to the front again, he knelt and stuck his head inside, peering about interestedly. "Well, there goes solution number four. If the murderer had never left this room the mystery of the absent footprints would dissolve. It would have been the simplest solution of the lot." Grimm suddenly turned and went into the study. He came back almost at once announcing, "And that Spanish Maiden contraption is just as empty."

There were steps on the stair and O'Connor came back. "The roof's clean as a whistle," he reported, "except for snow. And there's not a footprint in a carload."

"And the roof next door?" Gavigan asked.

"It's the same."

Merlini had been swallowed by the automaton until only his long legs projected awkwardly from one of the open doors. The Turk's hand lifted, with a jerky mechanical motion, and completed

---

2   "Maelzel's Chess Player," an article in the *Southern Literary Messenger,* April 1836. Or see *Poe's Complete Works,* Stedman and Woodberry, Vol. 9, Page 141 et seq.

the move with the Bishop which he had been studying so long. Merlini's muffled voice issued from the Turk's chest.

"Checkmate, Inspector! Three from four leaves one. You can get odds on your secret exit now, Ross." The Turk caressed his beard in deep thought.

Gavigan said, "Merlini, if you could pull those long legs of yours inside, I'd lock you in for the duration of this case. Crawl out of there and—"

He stopped, listening. In the hall a woman's voice was saying, "I want to see Mr. Duvallo at once." The voice was young and determined.

A patrolman appeared in the doorway, and Gavigan said, "Show her in."

The girl stopped abruptly just inside the door. "Dave . . ." she started, and then saw that he wasn't there. "Where's Mr. Duvallo and who—" Her blue eyes, frank and direct until they took in the body, grew suddenly wide, startled. She stepped back, one hand reaching for the door jamb.

Her tall, slim figure stood there, arrested in a pose that was at once graceful and rigid. Her face was cool, capable, and her complexion had a smooth, wind-blown look. She wore a short fur jacket over a smartly tailored blue dress and an oddly twisted snippet of cloth perched insecurely on her head pretending to be a hat. Her mouth was soft and crimson.

"Your name, please?" Gavigan asked.

As she turned her head, the light in her hair flashed warningly, a hot, bright red. The waves of her coiffeur swirled down from under the hat and broke in a foam of small curls at the back of her neck.

"You're the police?" she said.

The voice from the Turk spoke again, louder this time. "Miss Barclay, this is Inspector Gavigan of the Homicide Squad. Also Captain Malloy and Mr. Harte."

Merlini slid out of the automaton. "David is upstairs and will be down any moment."

The girl turned again toward the body and stared. Her shoulders shivered a little, then drew themselves straight.

"You know the man?" Gavigan asked gently.

"Yes!" Her voice was low and taut. "I didn't at first, but I do now. It's Eugene! But why is he here? What . . . what has happened?"

"He's been murdered," the Inspector said, stepping across the room so that he stood between her and the body.

From somewhere over our heads we heard a solid thump, a cry, and then feet came pounding down the stairs.

"Judy!"

Duvallo burst in at the door and took her in his arms.

"Dave," she said breathlessly, "I was afraid . . . I saw the police cars outside and I had to know—who did it?"

Duvallo glowered at the Inspector. "I'm fed up with being pushed around. When I heard Judy I tripped up my jailer and came on. What's going on in here anyway? Why—?"

Gavigan moved to one side, and Duvallo saw the body. His arm tightened around the girl, and he turned her so that she couldn't see. But he kept on looking over her shoulder. Grimm appeared in the doorway behind him, rubbing his jaw, revenge written all over his face.

Duvallo said, "Listen, kid, you wait outside for a minute. Then I'll take you home."

She moved away from him and took a seat on the divan. "Don't be silly. I'm of age. I want to know what happened."

He scowled at Gavigan. "I'd like to know myself."

The Inspector said, "Forget it, Grimm. And go watch Jones and that Chinaman before *they* take a run-out powder." And to Duvallo, "Now you're here you can stay, but you've put yourself right where I want you. One crack out of you at the wrong time and I'll run you in for assault and battery. That clear? Sit down."

"But what . . . ?"

"I said 'sit down!'" Gavigan's Irish temper was moving over a wet pavement, skidding.

Duvallo started for a place next to Miss Barclay.

Gavigan objected, "No, over here."

Duvallo looked at the Inspector obstinately for a moment, then obeyed. Taking out a pack of cigarettes, he tossed one across to Judy and took one himself.

The Inspector stood over Judy. "How did you happen to stop in here just now?"

She held up her cigarette and smiled at him. He took a paper of matches from his pocket and lit one for her.

"It sounds criminal, Inspector, the way you put it. I was on my way home when I noticed the police cars out in Grove Street. Naturally I was curious."

"You live near here?"

"On Bedford Street, just around the corner off Grove."

"And you were coming from—?"

"A movie at the Music Hall. Mystery thriller, full of policemen that barked. I didn't like it."

Gavigan elected to ignore that one. "You went by yourself?"

"Yes, I work at NBC in Radio City. Mother was having her evening of bridge tonight, so I stayed uptown for dinner and then went to the show."

"Alone?"

"Yes."

"Time, please."

"Oh, am I a suspect, Inspector?"

"I don't know. That's what I'm trying to find out." Gavigan saw

Duvallo edge forward in his seat as if about to speak. "Well? You were going to say something?" It didn't take a mind reader to gather that what the Inspector really meant was, "You aren't going to say anything."

Duvallo settled back. "I'm as quiet as a mouse, Inspector. Go ahead, browbeat the lady." But that wasn't what he meant either.

Judy broke in, "I finished work at five-thirty, dined at the Hotel Bristol from six to seven, and entered the Music Hall at a quarter to eight. I believe I still have my ticket stub." She looked in her purse and finding it, handed it to Gavigan.

"What do you do at NBC?"

"I write continuities for sustaining programs."

"Where were you at 2 to 3 A.M. this morning?"

Judy had placed her cigarette to her lips, but she took it away without drawing on it. "Do you always ask people that, Inspector, or do those times mean something?"

Duvallo straightened again, then relaxed as she went on, "I was home and in bed. I have to be at work at 9 A.M., you know."

There was a commotion at the door, and Dr. Hesse walked in. He started to take off his coat when he saw the pictures on the walls. He stood there, one arm in and one out, looking around the room with a mildly thunderstruck expression on his face. There was a covetous gleam in his eye as he surveyed the posters and playbills.

"Where are we anyway?" he asked. Then he saw Duvallo. "Oh, I see." He finished removing his coat and threw a distasteful glance at the corpse. "Hmm! Some more of the same. Is this going to go on all night, Inspector? Maybe I'd better just stick around. No sense in all this commuting."

"Stop griping, Doc. And get on with it. I'm busy." Gavigan faced Duvallo. "Do you own a twenty-foot ladder?"

Duvallo's eyebrows went up. "Yes. There's one in the garden. Lying by the wall. Why? Someone been using it?"

"Something like that. This is an interesting place you have here, Duvallo. Would you mind showing us the trap doors and secret passageways?"

"Oh, oh! Another locked-room gag." He turned and eyed the door, noticing for the first time that it had been removed from its hinges. Getting up, he went over and looked at the lock. "Sorry about the secret passageways, but those only come with castles. Walls aren't thick enough here. I'm thinking of buying a moat, though. They're useful things."

"It would be a lot less messy if you didn't take that line, Duvallo," Gavigan appealed. "I'd like to hear if you can give us as neat an answer this time. It's on your home grounds."

Duvallo looked at Merlini. "You at a loss again? Or is he just asking to hear *my* answer?"

"You're too suspicious, Dave," Merlini said, from where he sat near Judy. "He wants information. He's just had several answers shot out from under him, and he's looking for a replacement."

"Okay. If he'll stop snapping at Judy, I'll take a stab at it. Try anything once. What's the setup?"

Rapidly Merlini explained, and Duvallo listened eagerly, his bright, black eyes shifting impatiently, searching the room. Presently, as Merlini told about the window and the ladder, they went into the study. Judy followed, listening.

Just then Grimm's voice came from upstairs. "For Crissake! Will you stumblebums get the hell outta there! I mean it. Scram now!"

Coming up from the garden outside, a new voice replied, "All right, Juliet. Don't get sore about it. When's the Inspector going to feed the animals?"

The two windows near the Turk that were black empty squares flared briefly with bright, soundless flashes of light.

"Malloy," the Inspector exclaimed quickly, "get some men out there and keep those reporters from messing up that yard. Hurry!"

Malloy was gone before he had finished.

Dr. Hesse snapped his black bag shut and announced, "Same report as last time, Inspector. Death from same cause with same markings. Weapon still missing?"

"No. Grimm found that around his neck." Gavigan pointed at the cord on the mantelpiece.

Dr. Hesse examined it and nodded. "Yes, that's about what I'd expect."

The others came back from the study just then, and Gavigan faced Duvallo. "Well, was it another string trick? Or is it mirrors this time?"

Dr. Hesse stood in the doorway, putting on his overcoat. "Pardon me, Inspector, but haven't you forgotten something?"

"What?"

"It's not like you. You didn't ask me when he died."

"Thanks, but we know that. Ten thirty-five."

"Oh? Well, that's a help. Good night. There'll be a report on your desk in the morning."

He went out, and Gavigan reminded Duvallo, "Well?"

There was a deep scowl on Duvallo's face and a worried, restless look in his eyes. "Offhand, Inspector, I don't know. And this time that's on the level. I doubt if you realize how much I hate to have to admit that."

"Miss Barclay?" Gavigan asked.

"Me? Heavens, no! If Dave is up a tree, who am I to have a guess?"

"And neither of you have any suggestions as to who might have had a motive for killing Tarot?"

They both shook their heads.

"And you, Miss Barclay. Did you know Cesare Sabbat?"

"*Did* I know . . . ?" she turned to Duvallo. "Has he been—murdered, too?"

"Yes."

I saw her breast rise as she caught her breath quickly. Duvallo put his arm around her again, but her slender body was stiff, unyielding, except for the hand that held her purse and trembled.

"No," she said, keeping the tremor from her voice, "I didn't know Dr. Sabbat. I've heard Dave speak of him, but that is all."

Gavigan hesitated, eyed Merlini once, and then said, "All right, you two can go for now. Duvallo, you'd better camp out tonight. This is going to be a busy place, and you wouldn't get much sleep."

"I don't think I will anyway. This vanishing stunt has me worried. Come on, Judy."

The sounds in the hall indicated the arrival of more detectives. When Duvallo and Miss Barclay had gone, Gavigan had several of them in. His brusque commands crackled efficiently as he threw the switches that set in motion the routine machinery of detection. It was obvious that the Homicide Squad was going to meet the dawn sleepless. Watrous, Rappourt, the LaClaires were to be collected at headquarters and gone over by expert inquisitors. Their backgrounds, along with those of Duvallo, Judy, Jones, Sabbat, and Tarot were to be checked and double checked, as were their lives, loves, friends, fingerprints, and habits. Telegrams to the Federal Identification Bureau were mentioned, and cablegrams to Europe for information on Rappourt, Sabbat, and Watrous. The dressing-gown cord, the stone, the *Grimorium* and its torn page were to be taken to the laboratory for more thorough examination. Two men with insufflators began dusting the room for prints, and Bennett was told to finish his pictures, getting the usual shots of the room and some of the garden and the roof.

Malloy answered the phone once, and came back with a report from the detectives who had been going through Tarot's apartment. They had found his evening clothes—opera cape, hat, coat, trousers, vest, shirt, and tie—strewn about on the floor, as if he had changed in great haste. His monocle was there, and a towel with cold cream and make-up on it.

The Inspector told Malloy to send Jones over to the Charles Street Station, have him sign a statement, and then release him. And to bring in Ching Wong Fu. As Malloy left, Gavigan saw me fish in my pocket and bring out my alibi list.

"What are you going to do with that?" he asked.

"Add Miss Barclay's name," I said.

"And how are you checking her off?"

"One up and one to go. The movie isn't any great shakes as an alibi, of course."

Gavigan scowled. "I'm almost inclined to give her a clean slate, just because she's not a magician."

"Not so fast, Inspector," Merlini put in. "She's not a magician. There aren't many among her sex, but there are a lot of female magicians' assistants. You see, she used to work for Tarot. The lady he sawed in two."

Gavigan threw up his hands. "I might have known it!"

"He also used her in a transposition effect. He put her in a trunk that a committee from the audience locked, roped, and sealed. Then, when he clapped his hands she appeared at the back of the theater and ran down the aisle with a revolver, firing blanks and shouting, 'Here I am!' They were playing Detroit one day when Judy got a little mixed and came dashing down the aisle of a theater next door where an audience of Guild subscribers were viewing O'Neill's *Mourning Becomes Electra!* The *Detroit Free Press* next day captioned its story, 'Mourning Becomes Electrified.'"

"Oh," Gavigan said, "so she can disappear too. I wish we had just one suspect who couldn't vanish at the drop of a hat. Oh, yes—I forgot Jones. What does he do for a living?"

Merlini made no answer. He was thoughtfully regarding a handkerchief which he had spread out on the divan beside him. It was small and obviously feminine; white polka dots scattered on a deep maroon. I had last seen it tucked under one corner of the flap on Judy's purse. Apparently Gavigan also recognized it.

"How did you get that?" he demanded.

"Don't hound me, Inspector," Merlini replied. "I'll talk. I used a little sleight of hand of the pickpocket variety."

Merlini's hand delved in his coat pocket and with a slow conjurers movement drew out a second and nearly identical handkerchief. It had the same dotted design and differed only in that its color was blue.

"But I didn't *steal* this one. I found it. Pushed down behind the seat cushion of the armchair in Sabbat's apartment. Do you suppose, by any chance, they could belong to the same set?"

The Inspector was suddenly all business. "The boys at the lab can tell us if the cloth is identical, and they might even manage fingerprints." He knelt by the side of the divan and held a glass over first one, then the other, of the pieces of cloth. "And if both have touched her face there may be enough powder grains adhering that a microanalysis will establish identity. If we're lucky—" He stopped abruptly and bent closer. After a long careful scrutiny, he sat back on his heels and said:

"Here, Harte. Tell me what that is."

He gave me the glass and I looked through it where his finger pointed at a spot on the blue handkerchief, the one from Sabbat's apartment.

"It's a hair," I said. "And it seems to be red."

Chapter 17
The Heathen Chinee

"I FEEL AS if I were riding on a ferris wheel," Inspector Gavigan said. "First we're up, then we're down, but all the time we're moving in a circle."

Captain Malloy came in then, followed by Ching Wong Fu. I had been wondering what a Scotch Chinese Menace looked like. This one was, by a good majority, just plain American. He did have the short stature and bland, round face that made a Chinese make-up plausible, but he was no more Oriental, off stage, than a kippered herring. Or Scotch, for that matter; it was obvious that this branch of the clan MacNeil was several generations removed from its native heath. He used his stage name in private life as Tarot did his opera cape, for reasons of publicity. His personality was effervescent, supercharged with enthusiasm. He talked like a bottle of seltzer water, and his pudgy hands were full of nervous, hackneyed gestures. He wore a derby and spats, and carried gray gloves and a cane.

He bounced in, eyes round with excitement and, completely failing to catch either the mood or tempo of the scene, greeted brightly, "Hello, Merlini! What's all this international intrigue I'm surrounded with? Mysterious message asking for rendez-vous at hide-out of sinister alchemist. I depart in haste and fall smack into the arms of the law! Never saw so many cops and detectives! Thick as anything, and twice as uninformative. Somebody snatch the Crown jewels, or get away with the air defense plans, or—"

His roving eyes glimpsed the body, and his rapid-fire patter stumbled and fell headlong.

"Who . . . what . . . damn! I seem to have put my foot in it again."

The Inspector swung while Ching was off balance. "Did you know that man?"

Ching moved closer, hesitantly. "Yes," he said soberly. "It's Tarot. But what's—what—" He foundered completely.

"Why did you phone Sabbat tonight?"

Ching swung around. His eyes probed the Inspector's. "Why shouldn't I? And just what did happen up there anyway?"

"He was murdered too. Why did you phone him?"

Ching Wong Fu looked from Gavigan to Merlini, and back at Gavigan. I felt that somewhere behind his astonished face some fast thinking was going on.

Merlini helped out. "The inquisitive gentleman is Inspector Gavigan of the Homicide Squad. I think Emily Post would advise, in such circumstances, that you overcome your natural shyness and provide answers."

"Excuse me, Inspector," Ching said, "but you do have a nasty way of knocking a man all of a heap. I called Cesare to ask if he was home to visitors. I thought I'd fill in the evening with a social call. Anything wrong with that?"

"Where were you and what were you doing from midnight last night until 10 P.M. tonight?" I divined an eagerness about the Inspector that his gruff tone didn't quite cover.

Ching blinked and said, "What is this, a game of Twenty Questions?"

"Something like that, yes. Only when I play I do all the asking. Let's have it."

Ching took two slow steps toward the nearer sofa and then seated himself on it, his back to the body.

"From midnight until two-thirty," he said in a level monotone, "I was working at the *13 Club,* on East 48th Street. Dinner-table magic between floor shows. I left shortly before three and went home to bed. This morning—"

"You got home at what time?" Gavigan asked.

"It was just three-thirty. I remember because my watch had stopped and I asked the elevator boy."

"Take a taxi?"

Ching shook his head, "No. Subway. I walked to Grand Central and shuttled across to the Seventh Avenue line."

"And you didn't stop anywhere between the *13 Club* and the subway entrance in Grand Central?"

Ching regarded the Inspector searchingly; then, though his eyes didn't move, he half smiled and said, "From a magician's point of view you're a bad audience, Inspector, I see that. No deception allowed. You know too much. Mind telling me what brand of clair-voyance you use?"

"Not at all. I've a witness who saw you coming out of Sabbat's building at three this morning. Simple as that."

"Oh. Yes, I did pass someone. But he exaggerates. I wasn't com-ing out of the building, though I'm afraid it may have looked that way. I had intended calling on Sabbat, and I went there with that intention, but I . . . er . . . I changed my mind at the door."

"Sabbat expecting you at that hour?"

"I was under that impression. He's not an actor, but he keeps that sort of hours. I'd phoned him earlier in the day, and he had suggested that I stop in after my last turn at the Club."

"Sabbat was expecting you; you went there intending to call on him; and you were seen coming away from the building. What do you mean, you changed your mind?"

Ching put a cigarette in his mouth, scowled at a paper of matches, then scratched one and applied it. "I meant just what I said. It seemed rather obvious that Sabbat had forgotten all about my coming. He was a bit eccentric." He expelled a cloud of blue smoke. "There are two doors at the entrance of that place, the inner of which is locked, and the mailboxes with names and bell pushes are between them. When I opened the first door I saw a woman letting herself in at the second. Thought it was some tenant, at first, as she had her own key. Don't think she saw me, but she should be able to tell you that I didn't follow her up to Sabbat's."

"How do you know that's where she went?"

"That wasn't hard. The inner door is glass and, as it closed behind her and she went on toward the stairs, I recognized her. I didn't see her face, but I saw the platinum-blond hair and I recognized her—well—her walk. Knowing who it was I had a good idea where she was going and deduced further that, in this case, three might very possibly be a crowd . . . I came away. Do I have to explain any further?"

He didn't, but Gavigan wouldn't admit it. Instead he said, "You do, if you want me to believe any of it."

"Yes, I see that, though you don't put it very tactfully. Still, I hate to be telling tales out of school, you know."

"Listen, Mr. Fu," Gavigan said, apparently unaware that a Chinese surname is found at the front end of the signature, "you've just admitted you were right smack on the scene of a murder at the time it was committed. I would advise that you talk, that is, unless you're guilty."

"Oh, it's that bad, is it?" Ching's eyes were round. "Well, of course, in that case, there's not much—" He stopped and said it. "It was Zelma LaClaire."

After hearing his description, Gavigan, Merlini, and I had expected that. But, nevertheless, we all relaxed, and I put away the paper of matches whose flap my fingers has absently torn into an untidy fringe. Ching only remained tense, sitting very straight on the davenport, his hand that had been so full of gestures now very quiet on his knees.

"Then," Gavigan asked, "you went home to bed?"

Ching nodded.

"And today you did what?"

Ching looked at the floor and poked at a polished toe with his cane. "I spent the afternoon at the library looking over some books on Chinese magic in the Ellison collection. At seven o'clock I ran into a friend, Marvin Jones. We had dinner together at The Deep Sea Inn and afterwards went to my apartment for a few highballs. He left at ten, and a little while after he'd gone I phoned Sabbat."

"How long have you known Sabbat?"

"Fifteen, twenty years, I guess."

"Good friends?"

"Pretty much. I haven't seen him since 1927 up until a year or so ago. He was in Europe somewhere—Hungary, I think. I ran into him on the street one day, and I've been up to visit him half a dozen times since."

"How long has he been back in this country?"

"Two years."

"Did he ever show you," Gavigan asked warily, "any occult funny business that you, as a magician, couldn't explain?"

"No. He said magicians were prejudiced bigots and wouldn't admit there was such a thing as magic without trickery, even if they saw it. He said he wouldn't waste his time proving something he knew was a fact."

"He have any enemies?"

"He thought he did, but I've always suspected it was his imagination. He was quite sensitive and not easy to get along with. The lone wolf type."

"Was he well off?"

"I don't know, except that he has always seemed to be in funds, and without any visible means of support."

"Did you know Tarot?"

"Yes, very well." Ching seemed uneasy again. "He was one of my best friends. I don't know why anyone should want to kill him."

Gavigan pondered. Then, "That'll be all for the moment, unless—. Merlini, any questions you'd like to ask?"

Merlini sat on the divan with a deck of cards, playing an odd sort of solitaire. He laid out the queen of hearts between two deuces, face down.

"No, I don't think so, Inspector," he answered, without looking up.

He flipped the queen face up, only I saw that in some inexplicable fashion she had become a deuce. His favorite brand of solitaire was evidently Three Card Monte.

After Ching had gone, Gavigan instructed Malloy to find out how the roundup was progressing and to make sure that Zelma LaClaire, in particular, was being looked after.

"That wench is going to get a thorough going over, and no holds barred. She's been asking for it."

"Sounds as if she'd need a chaperone, Inspector," Merlini said, springing the cards in a long flutter from hand to hand.

"I don't blame you though. She parts with information on the strip-tease principle. A little at a time. But, now we've got her down to her pants, it should get interesting."

"What's the lowdown on this Heathen Chinee with the Scotch name and the innocent face?"

Merlini put the deck on the back of his right hand and with a sweep of his left spread them out along his arm. "He's quite good.

A very finished performer with a clever and entertainingly humorous presentation." Merlini's right arm dropped, and the cards hung for a fraction of a second spread out in space, then dropped. His right hand drew back quickly, and then shot forward, gathering them from midair. "He claims to have produced more rabbits from hats than any other magician. He specializes in children's parties, but has lately gone in for night-club work. He was born in China of missionary parents, and his magical training was preceded by the usual Oriental initiatory course in juggling. He's the only present-day conjurer to include plate spinning in his act."

"Plate spinning! What in blue blazes is . . . never mind. Don't tell me. I don't want to know. You'd get started on a history of the art, if it has one. Ross, get that list of yours out."

I produced it and added Ching Wong Fu's name.

Gavigan said, "Give him a nice goose egg for Sabbat's murder. Even though his times seem to check, he was on the scene, and it doesn't take long to strangle a man; instead of the walk and the subway, he might have used a taxi and, at that time of night, gained fifteen or twenty minutes. As for Tarot's murder . . . he says he phoned from 23rd Street, but there's a phone here. I wonder—"

Merlini put his cards away and stood up. "Grimm," he said, "let's see your watch."

Grimm drew it out, and Merlini compared it with his own. "Afraid not, Inspector. We both agree. Grimm heard two angry voices in here between 10:30 and 10:35. Ching was talking to you on the phone at 10:33, by my watch. He may not have called from 23rd Street, but if he used this phone, then there must have been three people in here, and that leaves us faced with *two* persons who leave no footprints. I object. Let's call it an alibi."

Gavigan didn't argue, so I wrote: *On phone*, and ringed it. The list now presented this none too promising appearance:

SUSPECTS	ALIBIS	
	Sabbat's murder 2-3 A.M.	X's murder 10:30 P.M.
Watrous	Séance	?
Rappourt	Séance	?
Alfred	Tony's	Night club
Zelma	On Scene!	Night club
Duvallo	Bed	At Sabbat's
Jones	Bed	With Grimm
Judy Barclay	Bed	Movie
Ching Wong Fu	On Scene!	On Phone

Gavigan said, "And the question is: which one of those alibis isn't what it seems. Where do you think *you're* going?" This last was directed at Merlini, who had wound his muffler around his neck and picked up his overcoat.

"I want food; then I'm going home where I can think. I can't do it around you. Too much going on. Suspects hopping in and out like mad, questions and answers popping six dozen to the minute, detectives swarming, Harte writing a book on the back of an envelope, photographers climbing all over me, fingerprint experts spraying powder down my neck, and every ten minutes the whole blamed case does a triple somersault over six elephants and lands on its neck. Once tonight I thought I had it all nicely figured out, and then, suddenly, my solution melted, all at once, like a Vanishing Bird Cage."

"So you're running out on me." Gavigan was scornful. "The murderer's little vanishing trick has the Great Merlini licked."

"No, Inspector, you can't draw me like that. I'll tell you this much though. We've discussed four methods of escape from this room and investigated three of them. There is a fifth one, but as yet I don't see how it fits and theory that will also explain why the lights were gummed up at Sabbat's, Duvallo's business card, why Tarot disguised himself, why he chose such a spectacular method to elude Janssen, or what the ladder means—especially the ladder—oh, definitely. But you get the idea. I want to sleep on it."

"When I have all those answers," Gavigan said, "I'll know how to do the vanishing trick myself."

"If you try it, Inspector, be sure you know how to reappear. And, oh yes, if you should happen to discover where Watrous went on his little walk, what Rappourt was doing at 10:30, what Zelma has to say for herself this time, how Judy explains the handkerchief, and who Mr. Williams is, I'd love to hear. Coming, Harte?"

I got my hat.

It was 4 A.M. when I crawled into bed in the Merlinis' guest room. I had just turned out the light when the door opened and Merlini's head appeared, silhouetted by the light in the hall.

"I was afraid for a moment there," he said, "that Gavigan wasn't going to let us get away without repeating that question of his as to what Jones does for a living."

"Don't tell me," I said, "I can guess. He's either a tightrope walker or a trapeze artist. He also does tricks with matches."

"You're warm but no bull's-eyes. His stage name is Signor Ecco."

The door closed gently after him.

And I had the devil's own time getting to sleep. I kept trying to imagine the look Grimm's face would have when he learned that the man with whom he had listened to voices through a locked door was a *ventriloquist*.

Chapter 18
The Invisible Man

To render oneself invisible, it is only necessary to possess
the stone called ophthalme. Constantine held one in his
hand, and in this wise became invisible.

Albertus Magnus: *De Secretis Mulierum*

The power of becoming invisible at will . . . is . . . ascribed
by Tibetan occultists to the cessation of mental activity . . .
material contrivances for causing invisibility . . . the *dip
shing* . . . the fabulous wood which a strange crow hides
in its nest . . . The smallest fragment of it insures complete
invisibility to the man, beast or object which holds it or
near which it is placed.

Madame David-Neel: *Magic and Mystery in Tibet*

FROM SOMEWHERE far away the irritable clamor of a bell came and
beat at me with a steady insistent demand. I reached out, grop-
ing for the alarm clock, and found, where the night table always
stood—emptiness. Turtle-like I pushed my head out from under
the covers and tentatively opened one eye. Gray morning light
came in through a window that was in the wrong wall. And then,
at last, the bell still ringing, I remembered where I was.

I threw back the covers and let the cold air wake me. Forc-
ing myself from the bed, I went to the window, threw it wide and

leaned out. The Inspector's shiny Lincoln waited at the curb, and below me the Inspector himself leaned on the bell push, whistling a flat but cheerful tune.

"Morning, Inspector!" I growled. "You're disturbing the peace, did you know?"

He took his thumb from the bell and looked up. "It's about time," he said, grinning. "I thought the battery was going to give up before you did. Do something drastic to that long-legged friend of yours, and then come down here and let me in."

I pulled the window down and got going. In the hall I thumped on Merlini's door, hailing, "Shake a leg, sailor. Company calling. The Inspect—"

Under my knocking the door swung inward, and I saw the bed. At the sight of the thing that sat there on the counterpane, I stood for a long instant stock still. Propped awkwardly against the pillows was the body of a midget with a grotesquely large head. From under the bulgy mass of crimson hair, fixed glassy eyes stared at me, motionless, and on the mouth a flat, dead smile had hardened.

Then I saw that it was a ventriloquist's dummy, a snub-nosed little imp with painted freckles. There was a white envelope in the small wooden hand, and across its face, scrawled large, I saw my name. I ripped it open and read the note, pencilled in a jagged, nearly impossible script.

The early bird gets the clues. See you at Duvallo's.

Hawkshaw

As we left the house I noticed that Gavigan slipped into his pocket the thin red-covered book from Merlini's shelves which he had been reading as he waited. I knew then whence sprang the Inspector's cheery whistling mood. I had only gotten a glimpse of the title, but that was enough. Its author was Arthur W. Prince and its title, *The Whole Art of Ventriloquism.*

Malloy, Grimm, and Brady were waiting on the steps of No. 36. They looked sleepy.

Gavigan asked, "Have you seen Merlini?"

Malloy shook his head. "No. Duvallo was here a few minutes ago. Said he wanted a clean shirt. We shooed him off. Shannon was still on his tail."

He held the door open for us as we went in. We were halfway down the hall when it happened.

There were two voices, rising faintly in angry excited tones, and they came from inside the living room. Suddenly these words, shouted, stood out above the rest:

"*And the police will never know*!"

Grimm's "What the hell!" was explosive.

We covered the remaining ten feet at nearly the speed of light. The door, which had been replaced on its hinges, was closed. Gavigan kicked it open, and the four of us crowded violently in, stopped and stood looking—at each other. There was no one else to look at. The voices had ceased; the room was empty.

Gavigan repeated Grimm's actions of the night before. He sailed comet-like toward the study with Malloy at his heels, gun in hand. Grimm, his jaw sagging, seemed incapable of movement.

Gavigan disappeared; Malloy stopped in the doorway. Then, almost at once, they returned. There was an angry bewilderment on the Inspector's face, and the line of his jaw was rigid.

"Not a soul," he said. "And this time the window's closed, just as I left it—"

He stopped, watching the thin thread of blue smoke that rose tenuously from an ash receiver standing on the floor by an empty armchair. It came from a lighted cigarette, long and new, that lay balanced there.

Grimm whispered, half sincere, "The place *is* haunted!"

As if in verification of that statement, an irregular ghostly tapping began, coming from the dark corner near the study door. We strained our eyes looking and saw something white that moved in the shadow. Malloy's gun pointed. We stepped forward. On a small single-legged table such as magicians use was a portable typewriter that seemed to be endowed with a life of its own. As we watched the keys jerked spasmodically, the type bars swung up, and the space bar danced. We closed in, uncertainly.

There was a sheet of paper in the roll, across which, above the ribbon, words were forming.

"*Dear Inspector: You not only can't believe all you see . . .*" We heard the bell and saw the carriage slide suddenly from left to right, double spacing as it did so. Other words clicked into being, letter by letter. "*. . . but you mustn't believe everything you can't see. Very truly yours, THE INVISIBLE MAN.*"

"Merlini!" Gavigan exclaimed. "But where—"

Suddenly all the keys on the keyboard jumped convulsively; there was a vague, swishy movement within the typewriter and a low, hissing, snake-like sound. Gavigan bent over, eyeing the machine warily. Then he lifted it quickly and peered under it, at nothing. Turning, he carried it to the light of the window where we examined it gingerly, to no effect.

Grimm, looking nervously behind him, suddenly pointed and pushed out one startled word, "Look!"

We wheeled. Gavigan almost dropped the typewriter on my foot. Merlini was sitting in the big armchair, smiling impishly and blowing smoke rings.

"Dammit!" Gavigan thundered. "I've had all the parlor magic I can stomach!" He dropped the typewriter back on to its table with a crash. "Here's where you do some fast, furious, and fancy explaining. How did you get in here? How did you disappear, and how did you get back? And don't give me any song and dance about invisibility! I won't—"

Merlini stood up. He dropped his cigarette into the ash receiver, not bothering to vanish it, and spoke rapidly. "In the literature of Psychical Research you will find some mention of a phenomenon known as Bilocation. Watrous mentions it, for one. It is defined as the presence of an individual in two different places at one and the same time. It is one of the rarer psychic manifestations. What few recorded cases there are lack any proper sort of authenticity—with one exception—and that, though occurring under rigid test conditions, was patently a trick. Duvallo called it *The Mystery of the Yogi*. He performed it before an audience of newspapermen in this room two years ago, just after his return from India, and it netted him a whole scrapbook of clippings.

"He had a couple of the reporters go out and buy several padlocks and a hasp. They fixed those on the inside of the door leading to the hall. You can still see the screw holes in the woodwork. The padlocks were locked and the keys held by the reports. Duvallo sat in this chair and dished out some high-powered pseudo-Yogi patter. He began by demonstrating the system of breath control and apparently slid off into a deep trance. With his customary flair for showmanship, he had a doctor standing by who poked a stethoscope at his chest every few minutes, kept a constant hand on his pulse, and exhibited a properly grave countenance. The reporters were naturally skeptical, but Duvallo got fairly respectful attention because they knew that he usually came through with something that rated page one. He held that trance for a good ten minutes, heating up suspense.

"Then finally the phone rang, and one of the reporters answered it. He heard Duvallo's voice, saying that he was at La Rumba, three blocks away. At the suggestion of the voice in the phone, several other reporters listened and were each given an earful. Their credulity balked a bit, and there were a few impolite snickers. One of them suggested to the voice that he hang up, and wait to be called back. They tried that, but the same voice answered. When they started to stall, the voice hung up. Then Duvallo rolled his eyes and, breathing heavily, began to come out of his coma.

"They immediately accused him of having employed a double, and began to razz him. 'Wait a minute, gentlemen,' he said. 'It's not quite over. Look out the front window.' Several of them did, and in a minute or so they all had their noses glued to the pane. A man was running down the street through the snow. As he came under the light from the window, he was, to all appearances, Duvallo. Everyone whirled, started for the door, and stopped. Duvallo had vanished. *He was no longer in the room.*

"They began on the padlocks. While they were unlocking them, someone knocked on the door. When they got it open, in walked Duvallo, big as you please, grinning and shaking the snow from his overcoat. He handed over a menu card, bearing the orchestra leader's and the headwaiter's signatures, with the hour and date. When they checked later they got a further shock. It had been celebrity night and Duvallo had been called on to stand and take a bow. So there were plenty of witnesses at both ends."

"Do you call that explaining things?" Gavigan protested.

"Yes. The reporters, of course, were right the first time. Duvallo did use a double, an actor who could imitate his voice. I would suspect Tarot. He was almost exactly the same build and height, and had features similar enough in general appearance so that properly applied make-up would do the trick, except before close friends. The bang-up finale, however, left Duvall's audience so goggle-eyed that they forgot their 'double' theory, and when they tried to find some other explanation . . . there wasn't any. Common principle in conjuring."

"And Duvallo got out of this room the way you did just now, after giving your little imitation of two people scrapping?"

"Yes. Harte's theory, trite as it was, is correct. This room does have a secret exit; and it's a honey. I figured that out when I read the account of Duvallo's stunt and saw the pictures in the papers. I've always suspected where it was, but, even so, it took me nearly fifteen minutes to find it."

"Stop bragging and get on with it." Gavigan was impatient.

Merlini walked back to the chair and squatted in the seat, Oriental fashion, legs tucked under. He braced his elbows on the chair arms. The fingers of his right hand pressed lightly on the under side of the arm where it curved over and the seat of the chair fell away, noiselessly. Merlini's legs dropped down into a dark hole, swinging. He found a foothold, took a step downward, and, as he ducked his head, the chair seat swung smoothly and silently back into place. The whole operation had taken less than five seconds.

"Regular Jack-in-the-Box, isn't he?" Grimm said, blinking.

The chair seat dropped again, and Merlini's voice said, "Come on down." There was a click, and light came up from the opening.

Merlini was standing on a stepladder arrangement, the steps of which were covered with sound-absorbing black felt. Gavigan said, "Brady, you stay up here and keep your eyes open."

Merlini went on, "When the reporters dashed for the window, Duvallo simply dropped through here and . . ."

"When I looked the cellar over last night," Gavigan said, "this end of it seemed to be full of boxes and packing cases."

"Camouflage. They go clear to the ceiling, and this is behind them."

Following Malloy, I climbed down the ladder and found myself in a small room less than ten feet in depth. The light came from a bare electric bulb in the ceiling. There was a work-table along one end wall, heaped with a queer miscellany of odds and ends. I saw a tambourine, several slates, a headless, undressed ventriloquist's dummy, a scattered pile of paper flowers, a rumpled quantity of cheesecloth. Hanging from hooks on the wall were several the-atrical costumes, among them a pair of completely black all-over tights with a peculiar all-enveloping hood. Two black gloves lay on the floor near a dusty jawless papier-mâché skull that had rolled into one corner.

"Behind the scenes with a spirit medium," Merlini observed. "Dave puts on a mean séance, as you might guess from these props." He pointed at the left-hand wall. "There's the door. Du-vallo, in working his Yogi Mystery, dashed through there and up the stairs, met his assistant in the hall, and took the snow-covered overcoat and the menu card. The latter came down here and lay doggo until the party was over."

"But there's no door on the other side," Malloy said.

"It opens into one of the packing cases and you leave through the hinged side of that."

"He was cutting it pretty fine, wasn't he?" Gavigan asked, frowning. "Suppose the reporters opened the door upstairs too soon?"

"That's why the padlocks on the door. They were not to keep Duvallo in the room, as everyone was led to suppose, *but to keep the reporters in*. In many tricks the very precautions that are taken to guarantee absence of trickery are what make it possible."

"Are all your magic tricks figured as closely at that?" Gavigan asked, somewhat incredulously.

"And then some," Merlini replied. "A magician can't take many chances, because when a trick doesn't come off—well, it's like that dream where you suddenly find yourself addressing the Woman's Club—minus clothes."

"I wonder," Gavigan said, "who else besides Duvallo and Tarot knew of this place. It doesn't seem . . ."

Malloy was nosing around the worktable. "Hey," he broke in, excitedly, "here's the insides of another trick." He had pulled the pile of cheesecloth to one side and disclosed a typewriter, identical with that upstairs.

"Yes," Merlini said, "the spirit typewriter. Duvallo has always claimed that it's the original one on which Madame Blavatsky's posthumously written memoirs were typed, but that was probably ballyhoo.[1] While I was typing, all the keys of this machine were connected with the keys of the one above by strands of this, strong, black fishline. It's a rather complicated setup, but it works. The strings ran up through that hole in the ceiling and through the single hollow leg of the table. Each string went over the arm of the proper key and came back, down to this hook." He pointed to a hook in the wall, near which hung a large pair of shears.

"When I had finished, I gathered the strings just above the typewriter in one hand, cut them at the other end close to the hook, pulled in rapidly, drew them over the arms of the keys upstairs and back down. There's some sound up at the other end which you many have heard, since I couldn't be there to cover it with patter. The hole in the table top has a spring-hinged cover that folds into place when the typewriter is lifted for examination."

"It's all done with trap doors and threads so far. I suppose the mirrors come next," Grimm observed.

Gavigan, who had been in a brown study with the door closed, came out of it and said, "Maybe I'm dumb, Merlini, but I don't see it. It might help a lot to know that Grimm's vanishing murderer escaped down this rabbit hole, but there's still the snow that surrounded the house, and even if he bid until after we left, early this morning—"

"Take a deep breath, Inspector," Merlini said, "and don't throw anything when you hear what comes next. This all had to be looked into anyway. You, Harte, can take that woebegone expression off your face, because I'm going to put your detective yarn back on its

---

1   *Posthumous Memoirs of Helena Petrovna Blavatsky,* Boston, J. M. Wade, 1896.

feet. The murderer *didn't* leave by this route. That door is locked on the inside!"

Gavigan grunted and, stepping forward, yanked savagely at the door knob. "I don't see any key," he said. "How do you know it wasn't locked from the other side?"

"Because it doesn't lock from the other side. There's neither doorknob nor keyhole. All the lock is in here. And, furthermore, the murderer couldn't have been hiding here until the coast was clear up above. I took a look before I came down the first time, and there was a nice, smooth, undisturbed layer of dust on the floor and on those felt-covered steps where, as you can see, our footprints show all too plainly."

Gavigan said nothing for a moment, staring at Merlini. Then he turned and started up the ladder. Two steps up he stopped and looked back.

"I wish," he said vehemently, "that instead of trying to make this investigation jump through hoops, you'd make yourself useful. Come on up here. We've wasted enough time."

As the Inspector's legs disappeared through the trap, Merlini said softly:

"I wonder?"

Chapter 19
Curved Sound

AFTER WE had all clambered back through the chair seat to the upper room, Gavigan turned to me impatiently.

"Harte," he said gruffly, "we're going to give one final twist to that alibi list of yours; and then, after this wand-waving practical joker has had a last chance to speak his little piece, I'm going to make an arrest."

There was a knock at the front door. Gavigan strode over to the window and looked out. "Brady," he said, "a couple of reporters got past our first line of defense. Go chase 'em away and then stay on the door."

"An arrest?" Merlini said. "It's come to that, has it? You must have unearthed a lot of answers during the wee small hours."

Gavigan ignored him. He strode nervously up and down the room, speaking in a thoughtful growl.

"Colonel Watrous," he stated, "was tailed into his hotel last night at 9:55. He spluttered like Old Faithful when he found that out. Thinks the police department are a lot of nosy Peeping Toms. He says that he was in his rooms until almost eleven; then he went out, going through the drugstore, where he bought two cigars, and took his usual before-bedtime walk. Five times around Union Square! The man's a whirling dervish!"

"Drugstore clerk remember him?" Merlini asked.

"Yes, but there were other customers, and he couldn't say if

Watrous was coming or going. The elevator operator says that's when he went out, but—well, there are stairs in the place."

"Yes," Merlini agreed, "it could be better. He might have ducked out immediately after arriving, and a taxi would have gotten him over here in ten minutes, just when the snow began, and just after Tarot's arrival. They chat for a half hour, until 10:30, when Watrous finishes him off, quietly dematerializes in Grimm's face, floats across the snow, in through the drugstore, walks up the stairs, and then comes back down in the elevator to go for his evening stroll. Simple as that."

"Sure, I know, you can say it so it sounds silly, but, just the same, Watrous can't prove he was in his room at 10:35, and he gets a goose egg. Put it down, Harte."

Merlini said nothing. He brought his half dollar out and absently started it through its now-you-see-it—now-you-don't routine.

"Madame Rappourt was taken to her suite at the Commodore. Brady stationed himself on her floor and watched her door until 2 A.M., when he was ordered to rout her out. He brought her to the station house, mad as a wet hen. When I asked her what her real name was she closed up tighter than a sub-Treasury Vault and all her answers from then on sounded alike: 'I want a lawyer.' We may hear from London this afternoon on that angle, but she doesn't look very promising. We'll have to give her an out, Harte."

I wrote "At Hotel" and ringed it.

Merlini said, "There goes the beautiful symmetry of your list, Harte. It's a shame. Everyone alibied for one or the other except the mysterious Madame, who's sitting pretty for both. As one detective fiction fan to another, I'd say that looks highly suspicious."

"Yeah, *you* would." Gavigan went on with his report. "Zelma and Alfred LaClaire were dropped at La Rumba by the squad car at 10:25, and, though that's suspiciously near here, in the next block, they seem to be adequately accounted for since they had only a few minutes in which to change and make ready for their next show."

"What result did your little set-to with Zelma have, Inspector? Did she finish her strip-tease information act?"

"She admitted, finally, that she was the woman in the hall whom Spence heard, yes. I had to confront her with Ching before she took down her black hair and had a good cry. Sabbat, it seems, had been trying to shake her. When he told her on the phone for the third time in a week that he was busy, she got obstinate and stopped off of her way home to have it out with him. She was sure Sabbat was still there, because she heard someone move inside. That's when Spence started hearing the rough language. Her theory now is that it was the murderer that she heard. That's *her* theory. But Sabbat might eventually have let her in, and she could have left via the string through the keyhole method, throwing the bolt and switching the handkerchief last night when she was supposed to be in the bathroom."

"And so far, she has the most obvious motive," Merlini said. "Hell hath no fury . . . and all that. But what about Alfred? Did Tony agree that he was in the bar for the whole period between leaving the night club and going home?"

"He did not. Two or three people remember him for part of the time, but there are large gaps. He gets a goose egg, too."

"And Dr. Hesse's report. What about that? Could a woman have managed the strangling?"

"Yes. Strangling isn't ordinarily a woman's method, but it's been done, and more unlikely things too. In this case it's quite possible. Both men were knocked out first. Hesse found several microscopic particles of a light gray paper fibre adhering to the back of both their heads. That's a cinch; we've met it before. You can knock out a man with a Manhattan telephone book and leave almost no external marks at all."

"No fingerprints on the phone books?" "None that shouldn't be there."

"Whose fingerprint was it that we developed on Duvallo's card?"

"Tarot's."

"Were his prints in your files?"

"No, nor in Washington."

"What about the *Grimorium* and the torn out page?"

"Some of Sabbat's prints in the book. That's all. And—oh, yes. We found his bank and checkbooks. Most of his checks were made out to rare book dealers, Ouaritch, Rosenbach, and so forth. But just lately he's been flat, or so nearly so it's the same thing. No rent payments for two months. His checkbook is full of a long list of withdrawals, and there hasn't been a deposit to amount to anything for two years. But that was a honey. On May 27, 1935, he deposited the nice round sum of $50,000, just like that. I want to know where it came from. I've got a couple of men going through his files, and they may run across some explanation. But 50,000 bucks! I'm betting the explanation will be a queer one."

"It probably will," Merlini agreed. "Everything about the man seems to be queer. Since you're so full of information this morning—did you tree any of those blonde playmates of Sabbat's, and did you examine that suitcase of Tarot's?"

"Yeah, we scared hell outta half a dozen dames. But we didn't turn up anything but iron-clad alibis. The suitcase was a cheap cardboard affair, and the lab's report wasn't enlightening. But we did find where it came from. A second-hand shopkeeper on Third Avenue saw Tarot's picture in the papers and reported that he sold it to him last week. He remembers the monocle. Not many of his customers wear 'em."

"What about the mysterious Spanish lock salesman, Mr. Williams, and what about the incident of the incriminating hanky?"

"Nothing on the first. You can't trace a call from a dial phone unless it's still in progress. As for Miss Barclay, she admitted the handkerchief was hers, but claims she lost it two or three weeks ago and hasn't the vaguest idea where, except that it wasn't at Sabbat's. Though for some reason she was nervous as hell all the time I was questioning her, I rather think I believe her. Her story is naïve enough to be true. It's possible she lost it while dating Duvallo, and he picked it up, intending to return it, but lost it himself, at Sabbat's."

"Did you ask her how long she's owned the handkerchiefs?"

"She lost the one in question the first time she carried it, the next day after she bought it."

"That rather leaves Duvallo out, doesn't it? He's been out on the road for two months and didn't return until a week ago.

"All right, then if Miss Barclay didn't leave it there, who—" Gavigan stopped as the phone in the other room began to ring. Malloy took it.

The Inspector started to speak again, then stopped, listening, as an excited undertone crept into Malloy's voice. Finally he hung up and came back.

"Here's a hot one," he said. "The permit issued for that gun has Sabbat's name on it!"

The Inspector looked at him blankly for a moment. "What gun is that, Inspector?" Merlini asked. "The one I took off Tarot. He said he had a permit, but we couldn't find it. So we checked back on the gun through the number. I suppose it all means something, but I'm eternally damned if—"

"It means," Merlini said slowly, "that Tarot dished out a preposterous number of tall stories. And that fact is distinctly a sour note; it's a whole chord in the wrong key. It almost looks as if he . . ." Merlini stared at the lady on his half dollar.

"As if he what?" Gavigan prodded.

Merlini shook his head. "No, that doesn't make sense at all." He looked up at Gavigan and changed the subject. "What was that you said about making an arrest, Inspector? Let's hear. You aren't going to put cuffs on Rappourt just because her alibi looks too good to be true, are you? And I don't see anything much in what you're reported that would warrant actually arresting anyone except Tarot."

"Oh, you don't, don't you?" There was the beginning of a baleful gleam in the Inspector's eye. "You might tell me why I shouldn't arrest *you* as an accessory. Just why have you been keeping to yourself the fact that—"

Abruptly Merlini jerked from his sleepy lounging pose in the chair to a stiff upright attitude. He threw up a warning hand and leaned forward, his body tense, his gaze fixed intently on the door.

"Listen!" he exclaimed softly.

We heard nothing, and Gavigan started, "What—"

Merlini said, "In the hall—"

Then we heard it. A low confused murmur, rising louder, and then, sharply, in a queer strained voice that was flat and in deadly earnest, "*. . . I've got you covered! You've seen my face and you'll have to take the—*"

The habitual nonchalance was washed off Merlini's face, exposing an expression of blank astonishment. Gavigan sprang to his feet, and Grimm, who was nearest, flung himself headlong at the door.

A gun flashed in his right hand as his left yanked at the doorknob. The door swung inward violently, and the opening framed Detective Brady, a quiet picture of repose, sitting balanced, somewhat precariously, on a chair tipped back against the further wall. His head bobbled up from the *Daily Mirror* he held, and he stared, jaw slack.

Grimm skidded to a stop, stared back at Brady, and then looked quickly to right and left along the hall. His gun held ready, pointed at Brady's midriff. The latter, eyeing the weapon nervously and Grimm with bewilderment, started to get out of his chair. The legs scraped on the floor and slid away from the wall. Brady grabbed the air convulsively; the chair's motion accelerated. Chair, Brady and all hit the floor together with a reverberating smack.

"What the hell's going on out here?" Grimm roared.

Brady emitted several words, none especially printable, and tossed Grimm one not very accurate word in reply.

"Nothing!" he said, and then, rolling over, began disentangling himself from the chair. He stood up, felt the back of his head experimentally, and grunted, "What the hell's going on in there? Did you see a ghost or somethin'?"

Grimm goggled at him. "Were you sitting there, reading that paper, and . . . didn't you hear anything?"

Brady's eyebrows rose. "Place quiet as a graveyard until you made such a racket."

Gavigan had settled back in his chair and was scowling at Merlini. Grimm said, "Maybe I'm crazy, but—" Turning quickly he caught Merlini's wide grin of amusement. He frowned uncertainly. "I smell a rat. What is this, another parlor trick?"

"Is that what you had in mind, Inspector?" Merlini asked.

Gavigan nodded. "Exactly. Thanks for the demonstration.

I was afraid it might be a little fantastic, but you've cinched it.

Grimm, you had better take this sitting down. Your pal, Jones— he's a ventriloquist."

I could see the idea penetrate Grimm's skull and begin to circulate. "So that was it," he muttered finally. "Last night when we stood outside that door—" He spoke slowly, picturing it to himself. "Jones threw his voice in here, same as you just threw yours out."

"I think the Inspector has some such idea, Grimm. Only you can't treat your voice as if it were a boomerang. That's a popular fallacy. Ventriloquists don't throw their voices. It only sounds that way."

"Well, it sounded all right to me. But I thought ventriloquists used a dummy. Charlie McCarthy . . ."

"That's only one way. And the easier. Almost anyone can do it passably with a little practice. It's merely a matter of talking without moving the lips. Only a few of the consonants offer any difficulty and those can be satisfactorily approximated by substituting similar sounds, such as *eng* for M, *fee* for P, or *duggle-you* for W. Of course, you use a voice that contrasts with your own and is the sort your dummy would have if he could talk. The ear depends on the eye for the localization of sound, and when the dummy's mouth is synchronized with his patter it *looks* and, thus, sounds as if he were speaking. Talking pictures utilize the same principle, and . . ."

"Yeah, but what about this behind-the-door business?" Grimm asked.

"That's the same thing, a bit more advanced. I drew your attention to the door and led you to expect something from that direction. Then I imitated a voice as it would sound coming from behind a door at about that distance. That's the hard part. It's done by tensing the diaphragm and speaking from deep down in the throat; it's known technically as the 'far-away voice.' The word ventriloquism literally means belly-speaking, from the Latin *venter*, belly, and *loquor*, to speak. Naturally Brady heard nothing. The sound was all on this side of the door."

Grimm's face indicated that deductive processes were simmering behind it. "Then Tarot," he said slowly, "was already dead when Jones and I came up the front stoop. Jones had already strangled Tarot, and he came back to stage his voice-throwing exhibition for an alibi!"

Merlini cocked an eyebrow at the Inspector. "That what you had in mind?"

There was a vague hint of skepticism in Merlini's tone that made the Inspector pause. "Well," the latter said truculently, "why not?"

"But I thought we'd decided that Tarot would have had to step on it to get here as much as five minutes before the snow and Grimm's arrival. And Jones, when the snow began, was still at 23rd Street with Ching. If he strangled Tarot, then he must have gotten in and out of this place in spite of Grimm and the snow. You explain the voices, but not the lack of footprints. You aren't going to try my *Lung-Gom-Pa* theory on a jury, are you?"

"Ching might be lying about the time Jones left. I've heard of stranger things."

"All right, suppose we suppose that. What then?"

"Well, say Jones left 23rd Street only twenty minutes earlier. He could have walked in here before the snow, and before Tarot arrived. Tarot shows and catches Jones red-handed at whatever he's at. Jones kills him and then, finding Grimm out front, leaves via the ladder before there's enough snow to matter."

"So. If Ching can be proved a liar, then the absent footprints are explained. Now if you'll tell us why Jones waited a half hour before confronting Grimm with his ventriloquism? Seems as if the logical thing to do would be to get it over with at once."

Gavigan sniffed at Merlini's objection. "Does a murderer have to be logical? I've met a few, and most of them didn't know the meaning of the word. You've got a point there, but we'll get the answer from the guy that knows it."

The Inspector walked to the phone and lifted the receiver.

As he began to dial, Merlini said, "Suppose he won't admit knowing it?"

"I can get it out of him."

"Inspector, I wish you'd leave that phone alone; you make me nervous. You see, I know that Jones couldn't possibly have left this room by that ladder."

"You what?" Gavigan held the phone limply.

"No one has used that ladder since it's been put against the side of this house except myself."

The Inspector threw the receiver back on the phone rest; and then, before he could get too hot under the collar, Merlini went on: "I got in here via that ladder this morning. But before I put foot on it I took a good look at the ground beneath. It hasn't frozen really hard yet, and the foot of the ladder rests in what was a flower bed. I marked the spot, moved the ladder a foot nearer the building, and came up a few rungs. My weight caused the ladder to make quite an obvious depression in the earth, a good quarter of an inch. There wasn't anything of the sort where the ladder had rested before."

"Grimm, you get out there and check on that. And, if it's as he says, see about getting pictures."

Gavigan walked away from us toward the far end of the room. He went ten feet or so and then turned quickly. "The more we know the less sense it makes. If no one used that ladder last night, then why was it there?"

"Well," Merlini said hesitantly, shifting his gaze to the floor, "perhaps someone intended using it and then didn't."

Gavigan apparently didn't think that answer worth much. He stood for a moment indecisively rubbing his chin. Then he strode toward the phone again. "I'm going to have Jones over the rocks anyway, dammit. He's still the only suspect with no alibi for either murder."

"Inaccessibility can't count as an alibi for everyone. As you say, Inspector, since Tarot actually was murdered, the impossibility of access and exit must be only apparent, and you've got to find out how it was done if you're going to make the District Attorney happy."

"We can't prove it, but we know damn well. . . . It's like sawing the lady in two. I can't prove it, but I know damn well that it's not done by witchcraft. If I had an ordinary list of suspects, I'd almost admit that there was such a bugaboo as Surgat roaming around loose, twisting necks and slithering out through keyholes. But what have I got? A whole stage full of magicians, people who make a business of escaping from lead coffins, vanishing bird cages, reading minds, pulling rabbits out of thin air, and pushing weejee boards." Gavigan was excited. "Inaccessibility, bah! And why shouldn't Jones, for instance, know a trick or two that you don't?"

He picked up the phone.

"And what," Merlini asked of no one in particular, "if there is someone else who, like Jones, has no alibi for either murder?"

Some minutes before I had taken out my alibi list and had been staring idly at it. When Merlini said that I saw it.

"There is!" I said, suddenly sitting up very straight. "Look! As soon as you assume that Tarot was killed at some other time than 10:30, then *all* the alibis on that side of the list go blooie. And with only three alibis for the time of Sabbat's death checked as good, that gives us five live suspects."

Gavigan stopped midway in his dialing. "Hey, not so fast," he protested. "We know that . . ."

"Wait, Inspector," Merlini said, "this is going to be good. I'll top that, Harte. Suppose you cross out Judy's alibi for the first murder, too."

"Reason, please," I insisted.

"On my way over here this morning I stopped and had a chat with her mother. She swears Judy was safely in bed long before 3 A.M., and she told the detectives you sent around the same thing,

Inspector. But she's not the most logical old lady in the world. She saw Judy go to bed at midnight and she woke her the next morning. But they do sleep in separate rooms, and the old lady is a bit hard of hearing. Judy could have gone out and come back. Her alibi won't do."

Merlini paused, and then, "That leaves us Rappourt, hog-tied in her cabinet, and Watrous holding hands in the dark. Suppose we cross out his alibi too."

Gavigan stuttered a bit. "Listen," he argued, "we've got two witnesses, and they both swear that they had a tight grip on him every minute."

"Yes, I know, but Watrous, you remember, said he was the one who turned out the lights. Suppose in the dark the two members on either side of him get each other's hands rather than Watrous'. That's one of the commonest ways for a medium to escape the circle. It's easier if one of the persons is an accomplice, but it's been known to happen without. It's such an old and such a good stunt that Harry Price, Secretary of the London Psychic Society, has gone to the trouble of devising an arrangement in which the sitters wear gloves, joined with wire and having contacts, so that when everyone joins hands an electrical circuit is completed, and no one can leave the circle without an immediate warning being sounded. The lights are controlled by an outside observer having no connection with and completely isolated from the circle.[1]

"Okay, but you can't break Rappourt's alibi. I never saw such a—"

"Who says I can't?" Merlini grinned.

Gavigan sighed and sat down. "I'm having the best time!" he said, scowling fiercely. "All right, Professor, bring on your rabbits. As I remember, that woman was inside a triple-locked cabinet, sitting in a canvas bag that was drawn tightly around her neck and

---

1   *Confessions of a Ghost-Hunter,* Putnam, 1936.

tied to the chair behind her. She was roped to the chair, and her audience held the other ends of the tapes that were sewn around her wrists. Maybe she could get out of that, but it would take her an hour to get out and another hour to get back in. Or am I wrong?"

"You are, by about fifty-nine and a half minutes. She would have gotten out of everything except the cabinet, while they were locking that up. And, since a medium's cabinet has trickery as its only excuse for being, she could be out a cleverly concealed rear door in half a minute, before the audience had gotten itself properly seated."

"What about the sack? She could cut her way out, sure. But she's got to get back in again without any traces."

"Suppose the seam around the mouth of the bag through which the drawstring ran had a small slit on its inner surface. She could reach in with a finger, catch the drawstring, and pull it a foot or two down into the bag before they got it drawn tight around her neck. Later, when she released the slack, the sack that had been drawn so tightly about her neck would simply drop around her. When she pushed the ends of the tapes that were sewn around her wrists out through the buttonhole slits in the bag, she could have pushed out duplicate ones. The tapes that the sitters held, instead of having Rappourt securely fastened to their nether ends, were merely tied to a couple of short pieces of dowel stick that were there to prevent the tapes from being pulled free of the sack."

"But how could she get any slack in the ropes that tied her to the chair outside the bag?" Gavigan asked weakly.

"She wouldn't need any. Her hands were free. She could merely cut the ropes free from herself and the chair. At the finish of the séance she steps back into the sack, ties herself anew with duplicate ropes that have been secreted, either in the cabinet or on her person, pulls in the slack of the drawstring, and then, when the tapes that the audience has been holding are released, she quickly draws them back inside the bag. While the cabinet is being unlocked she rolls them up and hides them. The more locks on the cabinet, the more time she has—seems to me I explained that principle once before this morning."

"If Rappourt left the hotel," Gavigan asked, not quite convinced, but weakening, "and took a three-block side excursion for the purpose of killing Sabbat, who is responsible for the manifestations that occurred during her absence? Her Indian control. Chief Rain-Water, or whoever she uses?"

"Watrous could have covered for her there, and he could also have thrown the bolt the next evening when he went to Sabbat's kitchen for a glass of water—for her, too, you notice."

"But why—oh, hell! I never saw such a mess." Gavigan's blue eyes twinkled, but the sparks that flew were fiery and hot. "Every time I draw a breath this case does a lightning change act and turns up wearing a set of false whiskers and a putty nose. Last night we were stymied because, at one time, though we had four possible outs from this room, all the suspects were alibied for one murder or the other. And now, after we've eliminated all four methods, you throw cold water on a fifth one and then blow holes in every single alibi! Who told you that was any way to solve a murder case?" Gavigan gave a good imitation of a dark thundercloud about to unleash crashing jolts of atomic force. He growled stubbornly, "I still think Jones did it."

Grimm echoed somewhat less emphatically, like a second carbon, "And so do I."

"And *you* can't prove he didn't," Gavigan scowled and then, in his best cross-examining voice, argued, "Another thing, Harte was a bit hasty when he threw out some of those alibis—and you know it." He poked a thick forefinger at Merlini. "Why are you trying to cover up for Jones?"

"I'm not trying to cover up for anyone. I only know that you don't have a case against Jones—and—" Merlini spoke seriously and straight at Gavigan, "the person who murdered those two men isn't the sort who is going to cry 'Kamerad' as soon as a police inspector speaks harshly to him. Someone has planned this thing so carefully and so cold-bloodedly that it's a bit frightening. Particularly since we don't know the motive nor who else it includes. You aren't going to make this murderer cry 'Nuff!' until you have a nice near airtight case, and don't forget it."

Gavigan stuck out his chin. "Are you trying to tell me how to investigate this case?"

"No," Merlini said, "but if you were to ask me nicely, I might."

Hoping that it would break the tension, I introduced a question. "What," I asked, "is all this loose talk about my being hasty?"

Gavigan answered, still scowling at Merlini, "If the murder took place just after Tarot's arrival, before the snowfall, then both the LaClaires do have an alibi. They were in the squad car en route from Sabbat's to La Rumba. And Duvallo was explaining his string hocus-pocus to us at Sabbat's. Judy's alibi is uncorroborated, and Watrous and Rappourt didn't have any. Ching Wong Fu and Jones say they were together at his apartment, *but* . . . if Ching is lying, or perhaps is mistaken about the time Jones left by twenty minutes or more, then we have one possible way of explaining how one of our suspects could have accomplished both murders."

"Ching didn't happen to inform you last night, did he, Inspector, that the latter half of his act consists of a very able ventriloquial routine? And did you notice the vent dummy downstairs on the table? Duvallo began as a ventriloquist at Coney Island. And Tarot was tops at it. It's merely a special type of magic—auditory conjuring, and many magicians fool around with it."

"So what? Jones was the guy outside the door, wasn't he? Don't tell me Ching can throw his voice twenty blocks, or that Duvallo can throw his a mile. And if you so much as hint that it was Tarot's ghost throwing his voice from the astral sphere . . ." Gavigan snorted, made up his mind, and went determinedly toward the phone again. "I'm going to put Jones through the mill."

"And," Merlini said, talking fast, "just how does that theory explain the baffling presence of the unused ladder? Can you tell us, then, why Jones remained, as he must have, in Sabbat's apartment with his victim for sixteen hours? Why did he leave Duvallo's card with Tarot's writing on it under the body? Why did Rappourt think there was death in that room? Why did Tarot avoid being fingerprinted? Why did he come to Duvallo's; why was he disguised, and why—oh why, as I've insisted before, did he have to vanish from that taxi so spectacularly? And do you think that Jones is so dumb he'd try to create an alibi using ventriloquism, when it's common knowledge that that is his profession?"

The first few questions slowed Gavigan's phoneward progress, and the rest brought him to a halt. His eyes, on Merlini, suddenly had in them a new spark of interest.

"You sound as if you had an idea. Suppose you get it off your chest. If Jones didn't do it, then we have to explain how Watrous, Rappourt, or Duvallo could have worked the voices. Even at that, we're right back where we started, and there must be a sixth way out of this room."

Merlini sat very still, and his face had a ventriloquial calm as he said:

"*There is!*"

Chapter 20
The Garrulous Ghosts

THE INSPECTOR EXPELLED a fervent "Oh, my God!" and subsided weakly into an armchair. He sat there quietly, looking as if he had at least decided that it might be a good idea to allow Merlini's conversational flow an unobstructed channel. Merlini, sensing this attitude, took immediate and full advantage of it. He deliberately recited another limerick. The smoothness of his delivery, however, made me suspect that it was one he had previously composed and carefully hoarded against the proper moment.

> There was a sealed room hereabout,
> Locked ever so tight, without doubt;
>   But a young man named Beazle
>   Contracted a measle,
> And escaped, by just breaking out.

Gavigan, like a momentarily quiescent volcano, waited. Merlini lay, rather than sat, in his chair, his long legs trailing.

"And that," he went on, "might be a seventh method, except that none of our suspects exhibit the proper symptoms. But escape method No. 6 is, in several respects, positively alluring. It explains not only the Mystery of the Impossible Voices *and* the Perplexing Puzzle of the Absent Footprints, but also that Irritating Enigma of the Open Window and the Unused Ladder!"

The rest of us sat up and took notice.

"I don't understand why it hasn't occurred to Watson—er—I mean Harte, here, before now. The device has been used so often in detective fiction that, fully ten years ago, S. S. Van Dine, in one of his critiques, voted to outlaw it as a cliché. But perhaps Oscar Wilde's dictum that Life imitates Art has a corollary stating that Crime imitates the Detective Story.

"Suppose that the murder did take place earlier than first appeared. Suppose that it took place, as you suggested a moment ago, sometime between Tarot's arrival here and the beginning of the snow. And the killer vanished not by the ladder but by simply walking out through that door and away from the house just before Grimm showed up."

"All right. That's substantially what I said Jones did. And I might as well admit that Doc Hesse's report hinted that he wasn't quite satisfied with 10:35 as the time of death. He said that although the low temperature of the room, the muscularly well-developed physique of Tarot, and the fact that death was due to asphyxia all made an early onset of rigor mortis likely, on the other hand rigor was rather more complete and the body temperature had fallen further than he would have expected. Go on."

Merlini smiled, his dark eyes sparkling. "We next consider the Useless Ladder. It had a purpose in the murder scheme, a very definite one, but it was accidentally distorted, and that's where we got into trouble. The ladder was there, not to aid the murderer in his escape, but to aid the police in escaping from the otherwise impossible situation which this room would present. We were supposed to think that the murderer left by the window. However, this carefully laid—"

"But," Grimm objected, "it *didn't* look as if the murderer had just gone down that ladder. The snow proved that no one could possibly have—"

"As I started to say," Merlini cut in, "this carefully laid red herring didn't hatch out. The Weather Bureau double-crossed the murderer when its Delphic pronouncement for Monday failed to mention snow. The snow cancelled out the ladder; and when we try to fit it, as a factor, into our equation we put ourselves out on a limb. We run smack into the very impossible situation our master mind wanted us to avoid. I rather think that snow has worried him a bit."

"He's got a lot more worry ahead of him, if I've got anything to say about it," Gavigan hinted darkly. "But why all the trouble to *avoid* presenting us with an impossibility? It's hardly consistent with the rest of his actions."

"And if it hadn't snowed?" Merlini answered. "Grimm would have heard the voices, broken in, and found what he did find. Everyone would assume that the murderer left by the window, and no one would suspect that the crime might have been committed earlier."

"And the voices?"

Merlini looked at Grimm. "It has already been suggested," he said, "that this room is haunted."

Gavigan's sigh was resigned, but there was hope in his eyes.

"That theory might bear investigation, because it's just possible that Grimm, Jones & Company did, in a way, hear ghosts." Merlini watched the smoke curling up from his cigarette to fuse with the blue haze around his head. He looked quickly at us and went on, the barest hint of a smile showing on his mouth. "Not the voices of ghosts,—but the ghosts of voices, spectral sound waves, conversation from behind the Beyond. There's a chapter tide in that for you, Harte: *The Garrulous Ghosts,* or perhaps, *The Leprechaun Speaks. Poltergeist Patter* is good, too, though perhaps a bit esoteric, and—"

Gavigan, lying back with his eyes closed, stirred uneasily and spoke to Malloy. "Send someone over to the station house for a rubber hose. We've got to make him talk so it means something."

"But, Inspector," Merlini protested. "Use your imagination. If the murderer wasn't in the room, and if Tarot was already dead when Grimm heard the voices . . . and if ventriloquism is left out of it for the moment—Well, what other means of faking voices are there?"

Then at last I tackled an idea as it went past and threw it. "I get it," I said. "The long-whiskered device of the phonograph recording, set and timed to spout at the proper moment. No detective story is complete without it! But, I'm damned if I can see—"

The Inspector pulled himself to his feet. "Yeah," he blurted. "There are several things I don't see, but . . . but . . . Malloy! Grimm! That's your cue. Take this place apart and locate a gadget that could have produced those voices."

Grimm looked around uncertainly and frowned. Malloy took his hands slowly from his pockets and started to shed his coat.

Gavigan regarded Merlini and added, a bit wistfully:

"It seems to explain a helluva lot, but I do wish it didn't sound so blamed much like a pulp-writer's pipe dream. Are you *sure* you haven't read too damned many detective thrillers?"

"What choice have you, Inspector? A murderer that floats in midair? That's a damned sight more far fetched. Even a detective story fan wouldn't swallow that one. He'd send the author poisoned chocolates in the next mail. Besides, what if I have read too many detective stories? Perhaps the murderer has too."

"You've got this phonograph business a little too pat. You know where it is. Come on, fess up."

"I wish to high heaven I did knew. I haven't the faintest notion. But Grimm and Malloy should be able—is that the right time?"

He pointed at the clock which Grimm was investigating, holding it gingerly as if it might explode at any moment. Grimm mumbled in what would have been his beard if he had had one, "There's got to be a time arrangement of some sort, but this seems to be on the up and up."

The hands of the clock pointed to 11:50.

"Come on, Inspector," Merlini said, getting up and reaching for his coat. "Let's knock off for lunch. I knew something was wrong. I need food. There's a place up on 49th Street that has really scrumptious Smorgasbord."

"Oh, no you don't, my fine feathered friend," Gavigan insisted. "We've going to find that phonograph."

"I wish you luck," Merlini said. He picked up my hat and scaled it at me. "Come on, Harte, and while we're eating, I'll explain a few ideas I've got about that alibi list of yours." He started for the door.

"Hey, wait a minute," Gavigan protested. "If you must act like one of those amateur detectives who are always stopping in the middle of an investigation to take in a symphony or go water their orchids—Malloy!" They held a hasty conference and then Gavigan came after us.

"That last crack, Inspector," Merlini objected, "was the unkindest cut of all. I'm no amateur criminologist, merely a professional conjurer."

"I suppose you think that's preferable," Gavigan snorted, pulling on his coat.

As he went out into the hall Merlini called back at Malloy, "You might search out here for that phonograph, too, you know."

The Inspector looked at him as if he were a two-headed calf. He almost spluttered. "Do you—are you—you're not suggesting a phonograph record with a ventriloquial recording on it!"

"What's the matter with that? I've read about crazier notions."

"Shows the sort of tripe you read!" The Inspector stomped out the door, and as he went down the steps he muttered, "My idea of a congenial non-official investigator is a deaf-and-dumb mute."

The Inspector's car pulled up before Merlini's restaurant in 49th Street, and we climbed out.

Merlini pointed. "Look, Inspector. Tarot's hotel is just down there. You know, I could still my hunger pangs for fifteen minutes if you'd take us up for a look at his rooms."

"Smorgasbord, my eye!" Gavigan said. "I thought that's why you picked this restaurant. All right. Come on. I've been wanting to do that myself."

The apartment consisted of a living room, bedroom, and bath. It was like many another hotel apartment, Tarot's individuality having been impressed on it but little, though his profession was more or less in evidence. There were at least a dozen decks of playing cards lying about, and on one table several decks lay scattered in a jumbled heap. A queen of hearts looked down at us with her wide eyed stare from a curious position, resting quietly on the ceiling.

Gavigan eyed the card, frowning, and Merlini explained: "That's the trick in which a chosen card is shuffled back into the deck and the deck thrown against the ceiling. The cards fall in a shower, but the selected card remains sticking there. I'll show you sometime."

Several red and green silk handkerchiefs and two or three steel hoops from a set of Linking Rings lay in one chair. On the floor near the bedroom door I saw a dress tie. And inside we found the dress clothes strewn about on the floor and on the bed. The monocle lay on the dresser.

"Everything's been left just as it was found," Gavigan explained.

Under my watchful eye, Gavigan and Merlini nosed about as if engaged in a game of Hunt the Thimble. The Inspector began investigating the contents of a desk in the living room. Merlini's survey seemed aimless, but his quick eyes darted about, probing, scrutinizing. Finally he strolled into the bathroom and I followed.

The towel with the make-up on it lay on the floor. Merlini examined it intently, then walked to the medicine cabinet and opened it. He regarded the contents briefly, started to close the door, and stopped.

"That's odd," he said. He looked for a moment longer and then examined the ledge of the wash basin, which held a bar of soap and a tube of toothpaste without a cap. He got down on his knees and made a hasty but thorough search of the floor. He got up, a pucker between his brows, then silently turned and walked out.

I opened the cabinet and took a look for myself. The contents consisted of shaving brush, shaving cream, a safety razor, a box of blades, several used blades lying loose, a box of aspirin, a bottle of shampoo, a mouth wash, Witch Hazel, a packet of flesh-colored sticking plaster, Mercurochrome, a jar of cold cream, and the stubby end of a styptic pencil. A toothbrush hung in a holder affixed to the inside of the cabinet door.

I didn't see anything particularly odd in that collection. Except for the cold cream, I had all those things in my own cabinet at home.

I went after Merlini and found him in the bedroom, busily going through the drawers of Tarot's dresser. Whatever it was he was looking for, I gathered from his expression that he was unsuccessful. He had just finished and was scowling thoughtfully at himself in the mirror when Gavigan let out a surprised snort that carried clear from the other room.

"Listen to this," he said as we came in. He held a bankbook and read from it, "May 27, 1935, $50,000."

"Hmmm," Merlini said, "Sabbat deposits $50,000 and on the same day Tarot withdrew fifty—"

"No," Gavigan said excitedly, "He didn't withdraw it. It's a deposit."

"What!"

"You heard me. I suppose there could be two people in New York City who would each deposit an even $50,000 on any one day, but if this deposit was made in cash too, then—"

"The chances of its being a coincidence aren't much," Merlini finished.

"And," Gavigan added, "the chances that it's blackmail are good."

"Obviously," Merlini said. "But how do we connect that with the murders? None of our suspects are in any position to pay a blackmailer, or a couple of blackmailers, $100,000. Watrous is probably the wealthiest, and I'm sure that amount would have cleaned him out. What about the other entries? Tarot wasn't stony like Sabbat, was he? According to Variety he's been collecting almost a grand a week lately, with his radio acting and writing and his Rainbow Room engagement."

"No, he's pretty well fixed, though not as well as he should be. He's evidently dropped a good bit on the market. There are a flock of checks made out to Kneerim & Belding, Brokers. But he's still a few thousand ahead of the game."

The Inspector picked up the phone and dialed. Sabbat's number. He flicker through the pages of the bankbook interestedly as he waited.

"Parker, this is Gavigan. Have you found any explanation of that fifty grand yet? . . . Well, keep at it. It gets queerer by the minute . . . You what? Who's the beneficiary? . . . Mrs. Josef Vanek! Who the hell's she?" Gavigan listened, and I gathered from his attitude that Parker had not been idle. Finally he told Parker to report to headquarters and have them get on it. Then he hung up and said, "Did you ever hear of Joseph Vanek and wife?"

Merlini shook his head. "I haven't had the pleasure. What did Parker find, a will?"

"No, a life insurance policy for $75,000. And Josef Vanek's

handwriting, according to Parker, is identical with Sabbat's. What do you think of that?"

"Looks as if it might be a reason why no one seems to have heard of the man during his ten-year absence."

"Exactly. And when we locate Mrs. Vanek, maybe we'll turn up something in the way of a motive."

Gavigan gathered up the check-and bankbooks, and we left the apartment. In the elevator he asked, "And did you find what you were looking for, Merlini?"

"No," Merlini answered, scowling at the back of the elevator operator's neck. "But what's worse, I didn't find something I wasn't looking for."

"All right, Hawkshaw," Gavigan said, "but you won't convince me you're not an amateur detective until you stop trying to be cryptic."

"*Trying* to be cryptic?" Merlini said. "It is cryptic. So much so that I can see only one explanation, and that's utterly fantastic."

"I can believe that. If *you* think it's fantastic, it certainly must be. You can have it."

Chapter 21
Dead End

It is almost axiomatic that great detectives are fastidious gourmets. Merlini, when he selected his Smorgasbord, flew straight in the fact of tradition. He merely started at the nearest end of the table and worked around it to the left, gathering the hors d'oeuvres as he came to them with all the dainty discrimination of an automaton. Inspector Gavigan did no better, differing from Merlini only in preferring a counterclockwise route.

They brought their heaping plates back to our table and began pecking at the food abstractedly. Before long Gavigan gave up even this pretence, and with his fork began drawing on the tablecloth a complex, interlocking design of squares and circles. After a bit he spoke, as much to himself as anyone else.

"If we do find a talking machine," he mused, "it would seem to let Jones out. He'd naturally be somewhere other than in front of that door when the thing began spouting. And yet, except for Duvallo, he had the best chance to set any such an arrangement. He lived there for some weeks, and he had a key to the house. Of course, one of the others might have had a duplicate made—" He grabbed at a passing waiter. "Where's the phone in this place?" he demanded.

As Gavigan bustled off, Merlini abstractedly began building a tower of sugar cubes, using a card house structure. It was five high when the Inspector came back and sat down grumpily. The sugar edifice toppled and collapsed.

"I just had Malloy examine the lock on Duvallo's front door," Gavigan announced. "He found paraffin traces." He scowled at his water glass. "Someone coated a blank with paraffin, put it in the keyhole, and turned it so that it touched the lock mechanism. The marks left by the points of contact served as a guide for filing the key to the proper shape."

Merlini shook his head slightly as if to straighten out his thoughts. "Now," he said, "that's positively illuminating."

"In other words, you don't know what the hell it means. Neither do I. It certainly doesn't help eliminate anyone, except maybe Duvallo and Jones, who, having keys, wouldn't need to make one."

"And our friend Surgat, who, though not having one, wouldn't need one anyway."

"Merlini, you know these people. Which of them could have a motive for both murders?" asked the Inspector thoughtfully.

"Well, Jones and Rappourt disclaim knowing Sabbat, while Watrous and Rappourt say they hadn't previously met Tarot. Of the others, only the LaClaires have an obvious motive for killing Sabbat. I'm not *au courant* enough with Zelma's sex life to know if Tarot figured in it too, but I wouldn't say it was impossible."

"Tarot," Gavigan said, "acted as if he had it in for Duvallo, and if that's true the reverse is likely. Ching knew Sabbat better than the others and thus could have had more opportunity for acquiring a motive. Judy—"

"Yes?" Merlini prompted.

"Well, sex could rear its lovely head there. Sabbat might have made lecherous motions, and since she worked for Tarot—umm, he might have—"

"You have a lewd mind, Inspector. He might have been blackmailing her because she's the comely leader of a gang of dope runners, while Ching, a member of the Baluchistan Secret Service, is trying to steal from Greenland's high command the blueprints of a collapsible submarine which Tarot had snitched from Sabbat, and was carrying sewn into the lining of his underpants. Now go on with the story."

"Say," I wanted to know, "who's writing this yarn, Oppenheim?"

Gavigan said, "He doesn't think a discussion of motive is going to help. It won't, the way it's being discussed."

"Do we have to have murder with our meals?" Merlini asked as he took out a pencil and began drawing on the tablecloth an odd geometrical diagram only slightly more sensible than Gavigan's aimless cross hatching. He started guiltily when the waiter, arriving with the soup, gave his draftsmanship a cold Swedish stare. He covered his embarrassment by reaching for a roll, breaking it open, and shaking from its center a shiny half dollar. I was one up on the waiter, who retired uncertainly as Merlini reached for more rolls; I recognized the coin.

Gavigan, whose realistic soul disliked the unsettling effect of Merlini's small miracles, ignored the incident and pointed with his spoon.

"What's that diagram? I suppose it's too much to except that X marks the spot where we find the phonograph?"

The design had this appearance:

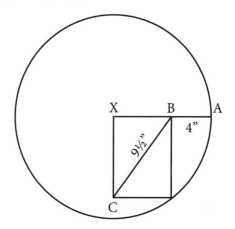

"X," Merlini announced, "is the center of the circle; BC is 9½ inches long, and BA is 4 inches. What's the diameter of the circle? No calculus required. Nothing but common ordinary sense. Par for the course is one minute flat." Merlini added a psychological handicap by glancing at his watch, and then began on his soup.

I eyed the diagram suspiciously and hazarded, "The square of the hypotenuse of a right angled triangle is equal to the sum of the squares of the other two—"

"That's it," Gavigan said. "Nine and one half squared minus the square of—of—" He bogged down. "No. We can't solve a triangle with only one side and one angle given. We've got to know the length of XC in order to find XB."

"Not this time you don't," Merlini grinned.

The Inspector glared at the diagram and I helped him without result, until finally Merlini said, "Time's up. Go to the foot of the class, both of you. Misdirection wins again. That's my favorite brain teaser because it's a perfect diagrammatic example of misdirection. The answer is right in front of you all the time. I asked for the diameter and I gave you the radius. You can multiply by two, can't you?"

"You gave us—" I started and then we both saw it.

Merlini continued, "The two diagonals of a rectangle are equal, anybody knows that, and I told you that one of them measured 9½ inches; the other, the undrawn one, is the radius. Twice 9½ is nineteen. Q.E.D. The answer stares you in the face, and you don't see it because that superfluous four-inch red herring neatly misdirects your attention and leads your reasoning up a blind alley to a dead end. You vanish handkerchiefs and watches the same way; focus the audience's attention on the right hand and they completely fail to see the nefarious operations in which your left is—"

"That's how our murderer vanished, I suppose," Gavigan said with some sarcasm.

"Sure, why not? When you meet an impossibility, it only means that there's been some faulty observation or some bad logic somewhere—either that, or the science of physics is haywire and Surgat and his infernal friends do exist. And note that faulty observation. It's the more important. A whole audience of impeccable logicians can be fooled if their observation is properly misdirected. I might cite the case of Gavigan and Harte and the Puzzle of the Circle's Diameter. Misdirection, then, is the first fundamental principle of deception. The other two—and they are all used by magicians, criminals, and detective story authors alike—are Imitation and Concealment. Understand how those principles operate, and you should be able to solve any trick, crime, or detective story. It's only necessary—"

"Careful, Merlini," Gavigan warned, "or you'll have to back that up by delivering some high, wide, and fancy deducing. And if you don't pull it off—"

"It won't be the fault of the method; it'll be because I haven't applied it properly. That's just the trouble. There are a lot of nice deductions in this case, but they don't all come out together."

"I've noticed that," Gavigan said acidly. "I thought you didn't want to discuss murder while you ate."

Merlini looked at his now cold soup ruefully. "I don't seem to be eating, and I wasn't talking about murder. I was explaining the principles of deception to a very inappreciative Inspector of Police."

"Be good, you two," I broke in. "If I'm going to write up this case I'd like a little harmony between the forces of law and order."

"I don't follow that, Ross," Merlini said. "I thought the amateur detective and the Chief Constable were always at loggerheads."

"The novelty would be nice, and besides, a little co-operation might catch your murderer."

"Oh, I see," Merlini smiled. "He's worried for fear we won't provide him with a good last chapter. By the way, suppose you had written this case up to date and were completing it without further help from life. What would happen next?"

"That's easy," I said. "This is the chapter where the investigators repair to the old inn to guzzle beer and compare notes in a manner carefully aimed at befuddling the reader more than ever. Then just as the great detective smacks his brow and shouts, 'Eureka!' the chapter ends—*with another murder!*"

Gavigan nearly choked.

Merlini chuckled and said, "Well, if we're going to play the game according to Doyle, let's get on with it. Get out that alibi list of yours again."

"I wish someone would do something to it. It's pretty well chewed up." I produced the paper and laid it on the table before us.

Merlini tapped it with his finger. "Since the phonograph device explains so much, let's start from there. We've agreed that it obviously sets a new time for the murder. It would seem that Tarot must have been killed between his earliest possible arrival at 9:55 and the beginning of the snowfall at 10 o'clock, or within a few minutes after that." Merlini stopped, scanning the list intently.

"Go on," Gavigan said.

"Item Number One, Watrous. At present listed as having no alibis at all. That obviously lets him out."

"Oh, sure," Gavigan agreed sarcastically. "No alibis, so that lets him out. Merlini, will you please stop dithering?"

"Dithering? If the murderer used a phonographic device, he

did it to establish an alibi at 10:35, didn't he? And if Watrous has none for that time . . ."

"He doesn't have one, therefore he does. Watch the professor, children. Nothing up his sleeves except his arms, a couple of ducks, and—"

"And G. K. Chesterton," I finished.

"But what," Merlini inquired seriously, "is wrong with that?"

"Nothing much," the Inspector said, "only merry-go-rounds always did make me dizzy. I suppose you want to make out the same sort of case for Rappourt and Miss Barclay?"

"I was working up to that, yes."

"Which would leave us the LaClaires, Duvallo, Jones, and Ching as the suspicious parties who *did* have alibis for 10:35. And at 10 o'clock the LaClaires were in a squad car en route to La Rumba, Duvallo was at Sabbat's being questioned by ourselves, Jones and Ching say they were together at Ching's place. Alibis all down the line!"

"It's worse than that," Merlini said mildly. "Rappourt is also alibied for Sabbat's murder, because, though she might have slithered out of her fastenings at the séance, she couldn't have been under the davenport, and she had no chance to throw the bolt."

"And," I jabbered excitedly, checking off suspects by twos and threes, "Duvallo, Jones, Ching, and Judy couldn't have thrown the bolt because they weren't there to throw it; and Alfred, though there, didn't go to the kitchen. That leaves Watrous and Zelma as the only possible suspects in Sabbat's murder, since either of them might have thrown the bolt, but *all* the entries for the Tarot sweepstakes are scratched."

The list, with each valid alibi boxed, now had a positively formidable appearance. I scaled it to the center of the table.

SUSPECTS	ALIBIS	
	Sabbat's murder 2:30-3:00 A.M.	Tarot's murder 9:55-10:00 P.M.
Watrous	Séance?	Lack of alibi
Rappourt	Couldn't throw bolt or be under davenport	Lack of alibi
Alfred	Ditto	In squad car
Zelma	On Scene!	In squad car
Duvallo	No bolt or dav.	At Sabbat's
Jones	Ditto	With Ching
Barclay	Ditto	Lack of alibi
Ching	Ditto	With Jones

The Inspector regarded it sourly, then looked up at Merlini.

"Haven't you eliminated just a bit too much?"

Merlini picked up the list and frowned mightily at it, though he didn't quite manage to conceal the twinkle in his eye.

"Maybe I did, at that," he said.

"It was your shilling-shocker phonograph theory that put us where we are. It may seem to explain the lack of footprints and the presence of the ladder, but if it's going to place the murder at a time when *no one* could have done it, then it's no sale. I don't want it. And—St. Patrick and all the saints!—why didn't I think of it before? How the hell would the murderer know that Grimm and Jones, or anyone for that matter, would show up just when the phonograph spoke its piece?"

"But it was such a lovely theory," Merlini said regretfully. "It did explain so many things."

"Wait a minute, Inspector!" I protested suddenly. "If you two are going to jettison the talking machine—it's another case of eliminating too much. We've considered six methods of escape from that room, and now you want to cancel out the last one! Don't tell me there's a seventh way out!" Gavigan looked at Merlini. "Well?"

The latter spread his hands wide. "Sorry, but the quota of rabbits from that hat is exhausted."

"Is that final?"

"Yes," Merlini said slowly, "the only methods that remain are the supernatural ones, the flying ointment and the witch's broom, Surgat and dematerialization, *Lung-Gom-Pa* and astral doubles."

"And what," Gavigan said, suddenly eager, "about Sabbat's apartment? Do you realize that we've discussed six methods for getting out of Duvallo's place and only two for leaving Sabbat's? Come, come, Merlini, you can do better than that. You're holding back something for the grand blow off. I want it now!"

"Sorry, Inspector, I'd love to dazzle you with a fresh new exit, but I told you when we reviewed Dr. Fell's outline that Class C closed the books. We have the davenport theory, and the hocus-pocus with the string through the keyhole. We've got to get along with those. There is no other way, I promise you."

The Inspector pushed back his chair, threw his napkin on the table, and stood up, just as the waiter came with the meat course. Gavigan scowled at him. "The check, please, and hurry!" Then he shook a finger at Merlini. "This is the last time I listen to an amateur gum-shoe. Why did you have to dish out this lunatic, impossible talking-machine theory anyway? We've wasted more time—"

"I dished that out, Inspector, because I was seriously considering it. That's really why I sneaked into Duvallo's ahead of you this morning. I didn't think the secret exit would help much because of the snow. I spent most of my time looking for the phonograph."

Gavigan started apprehensively. "You—you didn't . . . find it, did you?"

"No. And if Grimm and Malloy have had no better luck—"

"They haven't, or they'd have phoned me. We'd better go call them off before they wreck the place. There can't be any such dingus. And I don't want to hear any more about it.

Come on!"

We piled into the Inspector's car, and the driver was instructed to step on it. He did. The shrill howl of the siren rose and fell as we raced down Seventh Avenue. Merlini was slumped in his seat, eyes closed, his lean face grimly preoccupied. Gavigan peered gloomily out at the flying, swerving panorama, and his finger drummed an impatient tattoo on his knee. We passed 14th Street before anyone spoke. The Inspector had just reached out and flicked a switch. Faintly, under an explosive scattering of static, we heard a blurred, chopped-up voice. "Car fifty-seven . . . your station house . . . car fif . . . report . . . station house . . . car fifty-sev . . ." Gavigan frowned and turned it off. "Sellers," he said curtly, "that damned thing's out of order again. See that it gets fixed so it stays that way."

"Yes, sir," Sellers said, shooting across Sheridan Square and nicking a piece from the fender of a delivery truck as it scuttled belatedly from our path.

Merlini opened his eyes and stared at the back of the driver's neck.

"So that's it," he said softly. "We find the diameter when we see the radius."

Whoopee! I thought excitedly, Two-Gun Merlini rides again!

The Inspector made a face. "He's being cryptic again!"

Merlini said, "We've been had, Inspector. We'll do a bit of un-eliminating now."

We found the searchers ill-humored. The room was in an advanced state of disarray, and Grimm had a dirty smear across one cheek and a pair of very grimy hands.

"There's a funny assortment of junk in this place," Mallory reported discouragedly, "but no talking machine. Except for Grimm here, who's just decided that the voices were made by a parrot that disappeared out the window."

"Well, anyway," Grimm said, shrugging, "a parrot has wings, and wings would explain a lot."

"You aren't so far wrong, at that, Grimm," Merlini smiled. "The talking machine we're about to unveil is a parrot-like contrivance. But it doesn't have wings; it's still here, in this room."

"Sure," Grimm replied. "You said that before. The point is—where?"

"Inspector, may I present the undrawn radius that's been smack in front of us the whole time—there on the mantel—the unseen radio."

Grimm sank wearily onto the divan. "But that damn thing's out of kilter. It won't talk. It was that way when we got in here yesterday. The Inspector tried it himself and didn't get a peep."

"Just the same, it is the one contrivance in this room that could have made those voices." Approaching it, he took hold and swung it around so that its open back was outward. "Perhaps you've noticed what an efficient dust catcher the interior of a radio is. Even the most talented maid seldom gets that far, and yet the innards of this set exhibit an astonishing lack of grime, about as I'd expect it might look if someone had been cleaning up to make sure they'd left no fingerprints." Merlini started for the phone. "There's a radio shop at the corner. I'll have them send a man over. I want to know why it seems to be out of order."

Gavigan sighed. "Merlini, didn't we just decide that a talking machine would leave us worse off than ever?"

"I told you you weren't going to like it, Inspector. But don't take it out on me. I didn't commit the murder."

"Maybe not, but it's just the kind I'd expect if you did."

Grimm, who was peering eagerly into the radio, said, "Never mind the repairman, Merlini. I'm an old hand at radios. And I think I can tell you what you want to know!" Hastily we crowded about the machine, listening to Grimm's excited voice, "See those two pieces of copper wire coming up the side of that amplifying tube? Notice that their ends almost, but not quite, meet? And see that blob of wax on top of the tube? It's as simple as pie. The wax held the wires together, in contact, and the set would work. But as soon as the tube got hot enough, the wax melted, the wires spread apart, the circuit was broken, and the radio just up and died. Give me a knife and a piece of wire, and I can do that to any radio in five minutes."

Gavigan had lost his lofty detachment, and his head had joined ours surrounding the radio. "And a few experiments would indicate just how thick the piece of wax should be to hold the connection for any desired lapse of time. I give in. That's how the machine was turned off, and that's why it's now out of order—but how was it turned on? Who turned it on? And why—"

"You've got me there, Inspector," Grimm said. "I don't see how *anyone* could have turned it on. The main switch on the outside of the cabinet has been disconnected."

Merlini moved, walking quickly around the room, following the lead-in cord which ran along the lower edge of the baseboard. As he disappeared into the hall he called back, "Grimm, don't worry about the main switch. Put those wires back in position as you say they were, with the wax holding them together."

I heard a click in the hall and saw the hall light go out. Merlini came back and stood in the doorway. "Say when, Grimm."

Grimm scraped up the blob of wax with a penknife and wedged

it between the top of the tube and the lower end of wire, so that it raised one wire and held it contacting the second one. "When!" he said.

"Ladies and gentlemen," Merlini began, "we shall now have a demonstration of the Little Wizard Radio Unit. Like our friend the Turk over there, it's a machine that thinks. It starts by itself. It stops by itself. The Lazy Man's Friend." He turned, vanishing into the dark hall. There was a click, and the hall light shone again. As Merlini returned to the doorway, the radio, its pilot light now glowing steadily, warmed and in a moment a wave of dance music came from it, soft at first, then rising quickly to full volume.

"The wiring in these old houses," Merlini explained, "was an afterthought, and, quite contrary to all fire ordinances, much of it has been installed by the various tenants. The base plug into which that radio hooks is a dime store product, the kind that screws on to the baseboard, and the wire leading from it gets its juice in the hall"—he pointed to where it crept along the baseboard, hugging the floor and disappeared into the hall under the saddle of the door—"and is controlled by the light switch out there."

Gavigan started to speak, when the glow from the pilot light blinked out and the music stopped. The wax had melted again.

"And if you hadn't fiddled with the tuning dial last night, Inspector," Merlini pointed out, "we'd know now what station the set was tuned on and whose were the voices Grimm and Jones heard."

The Inspector directed a scowl at Merlini. His mouth was a thin, tight line.

"You realize, of course," he said in a level monotone, "that the man who turned that radio on was *Jones!*"

Chapter 22
The Absent-Minded Suspect

> Sherlock Holmes sprang from his chair with an ex-
> clamation of delight.
> "The last link," he cried exultantly. "My case is
> complete."
>
> Conan Doyle: *A Study in Scarlet*

MERLINI WASN'T listening to the Inspector. He said, half to himself, "And so we know that Tarot wasn't killed because he knew too
much. The radio indicates preparation so far in advance that the
murderer must have planned Tarot's death even before Sabbat was
killed. Hmmm. What did you say, Inspector?"

"I asked if you realized that Jones was the man who started that
infernal machine talking? He pushed that light switch."

"Yes, of course," Merlini said, eyeing Gavigan warily. "Jones
was the man. And so what?"

The Inspector snorted. "Don't 'and so what' me! Goddallmighty,
man! Jones is a liar, that's all. He couldn't have 'just happened' to
stop in here. He set those voices going; therefore, he came for just
that purpose. No murderer's going to put together a setup like this
and then trust to luck, to a million-to-one chance that someone
will pull the trigger for him. Jones is either the murderer or an
accomplice. There's no other answer."

"No?" Merlini asked significantly. "Suppose the murderer did make arrangements for himself or an accomplice to poke that light button? Jones may have entered accidentally and too soon, the unpredictable human element no criminal can foresee."

"And the next person who entered after Jones, other than ourselves, was Miss Barclay. No, this isn't a woman's crime. All this expert vanishing and slipping out through keyholes sounds like someone with narrower hips. Women aren't magicians; they don't saw people in two; they're always the sawees."

"Yes," Merlini admitted, "conjuring is largely a male pursuit; woman's love of mystery is concerned with something else. But you mustn't forget that the great majority of mediums are female and that the magic profession has the fraudulent ones among them to thank for some of the best and subtlest conjuring devices in the whole field of deception. Besides, this present vanishing and escaping isn't necessarily a question of rope ladders and flying leaps. I've told you about misdirection. It may not be safe to rule out everyone who's not an acrobat."

The Inspector shook his head slowly. "No, Miss Barclay's out. You're clutching at straws. If it had been anyone *but* Jones at that door . . . The fact that he's a ventriloquist makes the irony too perfect, the coincidence appalling. And that radio dialogue Grimm caught; it was far too appropriate. The odds are a hundred to one that if the radio had been turned on by accident and too soon, he would have heard Cab Calloway, or cooking recipes, or—or Charlie McCarthy." Gavigan faced Malloy, "Find out what that program was. Get me the scripts of all programs that went on the air from stations in this area at 10:30 last night." He started to turn away when a thought struck him. "Oh . . . er, you might try NBC first."

"I'm prostrate under the Juggernaut of your logic, Inspector," Merlini admitted, inclining his head slightly. "But aren't you forgetting that Grimm was there? Can you account for that?"

"Say!" Grimm burst out, "is he insinuating that *I* turned that radio on?"

"No, not that," Merlini said. "I merely want to know how Jones, or, if he's only an accomplice, the murderer could have predicted that Grimm would be there as a witness. If Jones is an accomplice, he wouldn't start the radio and simply expect us to take his word that he heard voices. He could simply lie about them, and there would be no need for the radio. If he's the murderer the same holds true, though I don't know why a ventriloquist would bother with the much clumsier device of the radio. The point is, in either case he'd supply himself with at least one witness. He might have brought Ching along. But he didn't. He came alone."

"But Grimm had been out front for a good half hour before. The murderer could have known that far in advance." Gavigan objected half heartedly.

"Now you're clutching at straws, Inspector. The gimmicked radio proves that the murderer's plans were laid well in advance of Grimm's arrival. No, the fact that Jones was the man who pushed that light switch merely takes us up another blind alley—a damned dark one, too. I know who the murderer is, Inspector. I've known for some time. But the mystery is still there, and almost every time we discover something it gets deeper. Perhaps the murderer is too smart for us, perhaps . . ."

He paused discouragedly; then suddenly his head jerked up, his shoulders straightened. "Inspector," he said, "I've got to get out of here and think. Somewhere along the line there has been some A No. 1 misdirection, some smooth criminal slight of hand. I haven't caught all of it, and I don't like it. I'm supposed to know about such things." He picked up his hat and jammed it on his head. "Come on, Harte. I'll need you."

Gavigan stood between Merlini and the door. "So you know who the murderer is, do you? I'll call that little bluff. Let's have it."

Merlini shook his head obstinately. "As long as I can't prove it, it's slander. I'll keep it under my hat until I can. Besides, you wouldn't believe me; and I know better than to try to sell you a bill of goods that doesn't make sense."

Gavigan hesitated, measuring Merlini with his eyes. Then he stepped aside. "I wondered how long it was going to take you to find that out. All right. Go on. Take your run-out powder, but think fast, Captain Flagg. Eliminating suspects by letting the murderer kill them off may be all right for rental library fiction, but it isn't department procedure."

Merlini stopped in the doorway. "You won't do anything drastic without calling me, will you? We'll be at my place."

"I'll think about it," Gavigan said.

Merlini said nothing until we had let ourselves in at 13½ Washington Square North. Then he said, "What logic there is in this case is about as neat and tidy as a tornado. And the trouble is dat ole debbil, faulty observation. We're going to work on that. There's a chance you may have seen something, Ross, which, in your hasty recitals to Gavigan and myself, you overlooked because it seemed small or unimportant. I want you to sit down at that typewriter and put on paper in minute detail everything that happened from the time you heard Rappourt's voice outside your door until I arrived. And I mean everything."

I jerked off my tie, rolled up my sleeves, and, lighting the first of a chain of cigarettes, went at it. While the typewriter was warming up, Merlini hunted up Scotch and soda. The pages fell from the typewriter in swift succession while Merlini waited hungrily, reading them as they came.

I had been typing for perhaps an hour and was halfway down on a new page when I noticed that Merlini had not leaped to pick the last one from the floor. He held the penultimate sheet unnoticed in his lap, and was lying in his chair, long legs thrust out, eyes closed. I thought he was asleep. But as the rattle of the typewriter stopped he raised his head and looked at me, a bright sparkle dancing in his eyes.

"Ross," he said, "you've done it. The solution I've been shying from because I couldn't quite believe it isn't all airy logic any more. You've given it a solid base of observed fact. But don't stop. I want more."

He snatched at the page on the floor and read avidly. I retrieved the sheet he had held and ran through it. So, I'd done it, had I? I read it a second time. I didn't see it, and if he suspected the person I'd just been writing about, then something was screwy as hell. I knew better than to ask for explanations, so I began pounding again at the keyboard, slower now, my thoughts circling like Sonja Henie.

I typed for another half hour until the phone interrupted, ringing with a nervous uneasy jangle. While Merlini answered it, I took time out and filled my glass again.

He came back. "Gavigan's just discovered that the radio program was broadcast from WJZ. The dialogue Grimm caught was the beginning of a sustaining program, one of those blood and thunder serials for the kiddies called *Crime Doesn't Pay*. And it was written by Tarot himself!"

"Oh, for Crissake!" I said. "It would be. Every interesting lead we get takes us straight to a dead man, and they don't talk. If Rappourt's the real McCoy, it looks as if she'd be the one to solve this case."

"You forget, I've solved it. Though you're right about Rappourt in one way. If she could bring back Sabbat or Tarot, I could get some evidence I badly need. But the radio program isn't what has the Inspector all atwitter and agog. He's just found out who Mrs. Joseph Vanek is. Ching supplied the information, said he thought it might be pertinent. It is."

"Just a minute," I said. I reached for my glass and killed the rest of the drink. "All right. Let's have it. Another surprise package, I suppose."

Merlini poured three fingers of Scotch into my glass and the same in his own. "Better have another, Ross. Mrs. Josef Vanek is Madame Eva Rappourt!" Merlini drained his glass and added, "Gather up those papers and let's go. Gavigan is rounding up all the suspects. He has a bee buzzing in his bonnet, and unless we're there I'm afraid he may get stung."

A police car stopped before Van Ness Lane as we came abreast of it. The LaClaires got out, accompanied by several detectives. We went in with them. Entering the hall, we heard the Inspectors voice:

"I'd like to see that trick with the business card, Duvallo. It sounds—Oh, hello. Come in."

Duvallo, Judy, Ching, and Jones, along with Malloy, Grimm, and Quinn were already there.

When we had taken seats, Duvallo said, "Yes, of course, Inspector. Do you have a card?"

"Suppose we use yours."

"Sure. I usually borrow one; it looks better. That wasn't necessary when I did it for Tarot because he knew the trick and it was more of a technical demonstration than a performance." He drew a card from his billfold and passed it to Gavigan. "Write a word or draw any simple design on the back of the card."

The Inspector took a pencil and sketched something quickly.

"Now, I can discover what you've written by using either clairvoyance or telepathy. The latter is a little more certain, but you have to help by broadcasting a few thought waves. You can do that by freeing your mind as far as possible of all else and concentrating on the word or diagram. I shall try to reproduce it."

"Never mind the ballyhoo," Gavigan objected. "What is it?"

Duvallo smiled. "Careful, you might have to eat those words. Hold the card, back toward me, up before your eyes, and give me a break by concentrating on it, anyway. Just to make quite sure I couldn't possibly see what you've written—here." He drew out his handkerchief and dropped it over Gavigan's hands, covering the card. Then he stepped back some distance from the Inspector, took another of the business cards from his pocket, and held a pencil over it, frowning. The Inspector didn't play fair. He watched Duvallo like a hawk.

Then, slowly, Duvallo began drawing on his card. Suddenly he made two or three last quick strokes and looked up.

"Are you trying to scare someone, Inspector?" he said, turning the card so that we all could see.

On it there was a drawing of a gallows.

The Inspector dropped his hands and nodded resignedly. "Okay. I don't get it. How's it done?"

"Keep your illusions and stay young, Inspector," Merlini said. "The truth would disappoint you. Here, drop that card and pencil into this envelope." He produced a plain, white, letter-size envelope and held it open. Gavigan complied, and Merlini immediately closed the flap and sealed it. Then, holding the envelope at his finger tips and always in full view before him, he said, "Give me a number, five or six digits."

Glumly Gavigan said, "Six eight nine two four."

"Added, they total what, Inspector?"

"Twenty nine."

Merlini winked broadly at Duvallo. "There are unseen forces in the air about us, Inspector, imps from some fourth dimension who have strange powers." He ripped the end from the envelope. "Hold out your hand."

Gavigan did so and Merlini shook the pencil and card out on to his palm. Gavigan took one look and said, "Goddammit!"

I'd seen Merlini do that little stunt before so I knew, without looking, that Gavigan had found, pencilled on the card, the figure 29. I was standing quite near and directly behind him, however, and I saw that, this time, something more was written there in Merlini's uneven script: "*Ask hall light but don't mention radio.*"

The Inspector put the card in his pocket just as the front door banged. Colonel Watrous came in, protesting every step of the way. He was followed quietly by Madame Rappourt and two detectives. The latter stopped on the threshold, and Gavigan dismissed them with a wave of his hand. Watrous stomped toward the Inspector like a turkey cock with its tail feathers ruffled. His voice was angry and rose too high in a strident, almost feminine pitch.

"You'll regret this, Inspector. I intend to sue. I want to call my lawyer."

Gavigan looked down at the little red-faced man. "Sue for what?"

"False arrest, and what's more—"

"Skip it, Colonel. I haven't arrested you . . . yet."

"Then just what do you mean by this high handed—this—" Watrous' choler seemed to have retarded his mental responses. As the meaning of that "yet" finally penetrated he left the rails and plowed to an uncertain stop.

"Grimm," the Inspector said, "put the Colonel over there on the divan and treat him gently, but if he starts to yap, take him across your knee." Gavigan seemed a bit fed up with the Colonel.

Watrous flounced across and sat down with his outraged dignity next to Madame Rappourt, who was already seated there. She sat quietly, only the black eyes moving restlessly in the white stillness of her face. I glanced at her hand, looking for a wedding ring, and saw none.

"This is a familiar looking scene, in detective fiction, at least,"

Duvallo said. "All the suspects present and accounted for. Are we about to unmask the murderer?"

Gavigan looked at him thoughtfully and then glanced at the others, his gaze travelling slowly. Duvallo's question hung suspended over us. Judy sat in the armchair, apparently at ease, but as the Inspector's eyes met hers she looked down and fumbled in her purse for a cigarette. Ching Wong Fu MacNeil, the customary grin missing from his found face, was furtively eyeing Zelma, who in turn watched the Inspector cat-like. There was a clouded expression in her eyes, and she shifted uneasily in her chair.

"The murderer," Gavigan said slowly and in a way that made me wonder why he should criticise Merlini for building up suspense, "is, I have reason to believe, in this room."

If you have ever stood in a room filled with purring dynamos and inhaled the crackling pungency of ozone, you know what the atmosphere in that room was like. Alfred LaClaire took his cigarette slowly from his lips. Duvallo was sitting on the arm of Judy's chair, and his right leg, which had been swinging, stopped. Jones stood in the shadowed background, leaning with Merlini against the bookcases. He was like the rest of us, tense, but I caught no other reaction. Merlini alone seemed at ease, his eyes half closed, apparently gazing in abstraction at the floor. But some sixth sense told me that he was watching someone, waiting for some histrionic flaw, some tell-tale false action.

Having allowed his preamble to sink in, Gavigan said suddenly, "Duvallo, do you use that hall light out there in the daytime?"

Duvallo raised an eyebrow. "No, there's enough light from the glass transom above the door. Why?"

"When was the last time you used it?"

"Night before last when I came in, I suppose." He looked curiously at the door to the hall and then back at Gavigan.

"You gave Jones a key to this apartment?"

"Yes."

"Anyone else?"

"No."

"Can you think of anyone who might have gone to the trouble of making a duplicate key to your front door? There are traces of paraffin on the wards of the lock."

"Oh? Perhaps that's how Tarot got in. I've been wondering about that."

"I doubt it. He would have planned on using those picklocks of yours that he had. And since Grimm was out front within a few minutes after Tarot's arrival, it looks as if the murderer was already here. He could have let Tarot in."

"Inspector," Jones said hesitantly, "I can tell you about the paraffin." Heads turned, looking at him. "I made the duplicate key. While I was staying here during Duvallo's absence, I mislaid the one he gave me and locked myself out. I took a paraffin impression on a blank key and had a locksmith cut it out."

"Where'd you lose it?" This, Gavigan's tone said, began to look interesting.

"That's what worried me. I've said nothing about it before, because, well, it was the day after the party that I missed it. But I found it this morning in a pocket of this suit. I thought I had looked there, but I guess—"

"Party?" Gavigan growled. "What party?"

"Tarot, Ching, the LaClaires, and Judy were here one Friday night. It was just an end of the week party."

The Inspector's face was stormy. "If you people would tell me things as they happen we'd get ahead a lot faster." Everyone looked at him so damned innocently that he got mad. "You, for instance, Madame Rappourt."

"I?" Her voice had that full deep-throated quality again.

"You heard me. I'm not talking to myself."

She looked straight ahead at nothing and said, "I know nothing at all about your murders, nor do I care to."

Watrous started up. "I warn you, Inspector, that—"

Grimm's hand shot out and hooked into the Colonel's collar. He pulled and Watrous flopped back on his fanny. "Sit down, you!" Grimm said.

"But you do know quite a lot about Cesare Sabbat, don't you?"

"Yes," she said, without moving her lips.

Gavigan followed through, quickly. "Tell me about it."

The trance-like monotone she used gave her voice the flat, dead feel of a legal document. "I married him in Paris five years ago. He called himself Josef Vanek. I didn't know until yesterday that that wasn't his right name. I lived with him two years. Then we separated. I had not seen him since, until I walked into that room and saw him lying there on the floor."

"Why did you separate?"

"I left him. The man wasn't—wasn't sane."

"You knew that he had taken out an insurance policy with you as the beneficiary? For $75,000?"

"Yes . . . but . . ." She wasn't so still now; she looked at the Inspector, as if startled. "But he would have changed that."

"No, he didn't. And it would be nice if you could prove you didn't know that. Perhaps now you've something more to say about that prediction of yours last night. Have you?"

She nodded slowly. "Yes, I'll admit that was not psychic. I had been told that Sabbat was very precise about appointments. There was the milk bottle that hadn't been taken in, and the room inside was so very still, I felt that something was wrong; and—I shouldn't have but I did—I took a chance and said that there was death in that room. When we found that the keyholes were stuffed up, I was sure of it, but I didn't—I never knew I'd find Josef there."

The Inspector, I gathered, wasn't quite sure whether he believed that one or not. "So, just a play for publicity. Nothing lost if you missed; everything gained if you were right, and the Colonel would see to it that the reporters were informed."

"Yes. But when we went into that room and I saw Josef . . ."

"Yes, I know, you fainted. But what about that second faint? Wasn't it to prevent Merlini questioning you? Wasn't it?" Gavigan stood over her and thundered down. She twisted her hands and started to nod, when Watrous, who could contain himself no longer, blurted:

"Don't pay any attention to his filthy accusations, Eva. You *couldn't* have killed Tarot. You were at the séance."

The Inspector, his eye warning Grimm to stay clear, pounced on Watrous. "So she was at the séance, was she? Maybe you can prove that? She was out of your sight for two hours. You've admitted that."

"But I told you how we tied and fastened her. There can't be any doubt as to where she was."

"No? And suppose I explain to you with diagrams how she could have wriggled out of all those fancy Boy Scout knots and later returned, leaving no traces?"

Watrous blew up completely. He bounced to his feet and yelled, "It's impossible, I tell you! Merlini, you're responsible for this. You've primed him with one of your fake conjuring explanations. I'll show you, all of you. She'll repeat it and I defy any of you . . . you magicians to explain . . ."

Merlini said, "Or better yet, Colonel, suppose you tie me—or Duvallo, for that matter—the same way you tied her. And let us try getting out."

This challenge seemed to set him back a bit. "Yes, of course, I'll do that; but you can't . . . you couldn't . . ." There seemed to be a hint of uncertainty in his voice, of suspicion, as Gavigan broke in.

"Suppose," he said, and his tone was a red flag, waving. "Suppose I should admit all you say. Suppose you tie Merlini and he *can't* get out. Do you know what that leaves me, Watrous?"

The Colonel said nothing, but there was apprehension in his bloodshot eyes, and his pink tongue licked once across his lips.

"It leaves yourself! *You* could have left that séance even more easily than Rappourt, and don't waste our time denying it. The room was in total darkness, and the sitters had their attention focused on the cabinet. You could have come over here when you were supposed to be walking circles around Union Square last night. You could have left the light on in your rooms to make the detective think you were still there. After killing Tarot, you could have gone back and let the elevator operator see you for an alibi. *You* could have killed them both!"

Gavigan laid it on rather thick, and he didn't say anything about snow. The accusation, hammering at Watrous, seemed to act like cold water. His apoplectic symptoms vanished, and he gained control of himself. He was suddenly calm, icy.

With what, for him, was abnormal steadiness, he said, "You're a bloody ass, Inspector. I never saw Tarot before in my life. And you'll have to show more than opportunity—some sort of motive before you present that case to the State's Attorney."

"All right. How's this? You knew that Rappourt would get $75,000 when Sabbat died, and, being a smart man, you could steer a course from there. As for Tarot . . . you had to kill him. He'd found you out."

Watrous fixed his pince-nez more firmly on his nose and his hand shook, but his voice was hard. "You can't prove any of that. I want to phone the British Consul, at once."

"Is that all you have to say in your defense?"

"At the moment, yes. Where's the phone, please?"

Gavigan glared at him with an angry frustrated scowl. "In there," he said, indicating the study. Watrous went out, Grimm hooked on behind like a trailer.

Gavigan hesitated briefly, then addressed Judy. "Have you remembered where you lost that handkerchief of yours yet, Miss Barclay?"

Her voice was nonchalant, but the blue eyes wavered. "I've told you I lost it weeks ago. I haven't the slightest idea where."

Duvallo looked from Judy to Gavigan, suspicious and alert.

A new voice broke in—Zelma's. "Is the handkerchief maroon with large polka dots?"

We all looked at her. Gavigan said, "Yes, what do you know about it?"

"I can guess where you found it. I left it there. Judy and I had lunch together uptown a couple of weeks ago. She dropped it, and I picked it up after she had gone, intending to return it; but I lost it myself, at Cesare's, the last time I saw him."

Something like relief sprang alive in Judy's eyes. "Thanks, Zelma," she said. "She's right, Inspector. I do remember, that must have been the day."

The Inspector's batting average was low this afternoon. Every line of inquiry was beset with snags. He pulled at his mustache, eyeing Judy with indecision. And then Merlini stepped forward from the shadows and spoke quickly.

"Inspector, your case against Watrous sounds pretty complete."

Oh, oh, I thought, the Great Merlini is up to something. That didn't sound right at all, not after the arguments he'd given us before.

"But," he continued, "I'm not thoroughly satisfied. I'd like to try something else, a little experiment that may show whether you're right or not."

The Inspector hesitated a moment, then stepped back and sat down. "Go ahead," he said. "The floor's yours."

"Thanks, but there's one thing more before you commit yourself. I must have your word that you will not, under any circumstances, interrupt me. I want ten minutes of absolute freedom minus any assistance from the police department. Without that I can do nothing."

The latter said, uneasily, "I don't like that. I small rats." But then he gave in, nodding, "But go ahead; let's hear it."

Gavigan put his trust in Merlini's smiling face, and forgot that the man was a conjurer, his livelihood consisting in a polite kind of con game whose main principle is the double-cross. In a few minutes he was busily regretting his assent.

Merlini gave a final reflective flip to his half dollar and returned it to his pocket.

"Though it may never have occurred to you," he said, "I think all of you here can easily appreciate the similarity that exists between crime and conjuring, between the murderer and the magician. It should also be obvious that the underlying technique in both fields of endeavor is—must be—the same, that the basic principles of deception used are identical. And if the murderer of Sabbat and Tarot is, as the Inspector says, among those present, these murders especially can be expected to show very definite symptoms of conjuring."

Madame Rappourt was glaring at him spitefully, apparently annoyed at being included with the tricksters. If Merlini noticed it, he gave no sign.

"You all know that in every trick, in every effort to present an illusion or false appearance, there is always some tell-tale clue that points straight at the secret. The purpose of misdirection, of course, is to gloss over that danger point, to hide or camouflage it from the observer's notice. If murder is like conjuring, then it too has its weak spots, which the murderer must cover up."

He paused a moment, put his hands in his pockets and, leaning back against the mantelpiece, went on: "A magician can usually penetrate the secret of a new trick if he sees it twice. Though it may fool him the first time, each succeeding time he views it the odds grow in his favor. He knows what to expect and, from past experience, knows where to look for the chink in the armor. The person who committed these murders is clever, and the weak spot has been concealed very nicely—too well, perhaps. But there's one chance. An illusion without a watcher is like the tree that falls in the forest where there is no listener; its crash sends out sound waves, but no sound is heard. We are faced with certain impossibilities, some of which *must* be illusory. And some one of you who have witnessed the various phases of these illusions has witnessed, without knowing or realizing its implications, that weak spot. I want to dig into your minds and get at that evidence. The tell-tale observation may be—I rather think it is—so small, so natural, or so innocent, and apparently so unimportant that you don't remember it. I want to discover what it is someone has forgotten."

He waited, and held the rest of us waiting, wondering what the devil he was getting at.

"There exists a way to do that. Hypnosis."

Gavigan looked startled, and began his regretting.

Merlini went on: "Hypnosis would enable us to dive—like Mr. Beebe in his bathosphere—deep into the subconscious mind and bring to the surface that one essential clue, that missing jigsaw piece which we need to dispel the illusion. The plan has but one drawback. Hypnosis, as you know, requires the consent of the subject. The unwilling subject who doesn't want to be hypnotised and fights unavailingly is a popular myth. If you will all consent to such an experiment, I'm confident that we can solve these murders and clear away the suspicion that now rests on so many of you. Duvallo, here, is a capable operator, and would, I think, do it for us." He turned to the latter questioningly.

Duvallo was thoughtful. "Yes. I could, and it's worth a try. But suppose I'm the person who has forgotten this minor detail you want to get at? I'm not sure that a self-hypnotic trance would go deep enough."

"If we have no luck with the others, I'll let my friend, Dr. Brainard, the psychoanalyst, give *you* the works."

There was an uneasy air on several faces, including Gavigan's. Malloy and Grimm wore expressions of frank skepticism. Alfred LaClaire was the first to object. "You can count me out, please. The whole idea is screwy. Suppose Duvallo is the murderer. I know enough about hypnotism to know that in a trance—well, he couldn't make me admit murder—hypnosis has its limits—but he could make my answers sound damned funny. No thanks."

"All right," Merlini countered. "Would you submit if it were someone else, someone quite outside, Dr. Brainard, for instance? I only suggested Duvallo because he's handy and he's the only one here who could do it properly."

Alfred spoke. "The answer is no. I don't trust the police, nor you, since you seem to be hand-in-glove with them. They always have to have a fall guy, and I'm not accepting the nomination."

Watrous, who had returned in time to hear most of Merlini's speech, spoke up. "I agree with Mr. LaClaire, very decidedly. I will not submit to any such unorthodox procedure, and I most emphatically cannot allow Madame Rappourt to do so. Both for the reasons Mr. LaClaire has mentioned and for the further reason that any hypnotic tampering with her delicately attuned, inner psychic self might be disastrous."

"I think we can let Madame Rappourt speak for herself, Colonel," Merlini said.

"The Colonel," she said, "is wrong. Your idea is a sound one. But why do you beat around the bush? You do not need to hunt for some small thing that someone has incorrectly observed. That is foolish. Why not find the murderer? Hypnotize each of us and ask, 'Did you kill Sabbat? Did you kill Tarot?'"

That had occurred to me too, but I didn't want to horn in. It was Merlini's show, and I suspected he was fully aware of the possibility, but had some secret reason for approaching it circuitously. I couldn't tell whether or not Madame Rappourt's incisive going to the point bothered him.

"Yes, of course, there is that," he said matter-of-factly. "Jones, what about you?"

"I don't see that an innocent person has any choice. Yes, I'll do it."

"Judy?"

She nodded without speaking, but the cool face under the warm brilliance of her hair was troubled.

"Mrs. LaClaire?"

"Yes, if you keep your questions within bounds."

"Duvallo?"

"Yes. I think it might work."

"Ching?"

"Suits me."

"Care to change your mind, Watrous?"

"I do not."

"Alfred?"

"No, dammit. I don't trust you. Zelma, you're a fool."

"Well, that's that," Merlini said. "I might add that if anyone thinks the test is off, unless everyone consents, they're mistaken. I shall make arrangements with Dr. Brainard for this evening. If anyone has any other engagement—"

"You're forgetting, Merlini," Ching said, "the S.A.M. show is tonight."

Merlini snapped his fingers. "Oh, yes, of course. All right. We'll make it after the show. Suit everyone?"

No one said anything.

"Fine," Merlini said. "We'll meet at the show and go from there. I'd like to have you come as my guest, Madame Rappourt, and the Colonel, too, if he will."

Watrous started to protest but, noticing Madame Rappourt's nodded assent, said, "Yes, I'll come. If she's going to go through with this in spite of my counsel, the least I can do is watch to see that you don't try any tricks." The emphasis he put on that last word was thoroughly uncomplimentary.

Merlini was impervious. "I think you'll like the bill," he said brightly. "Duvallo, Ching, the LaClaires, and myself are on it. And Jones has something rather special to present. He's doing Ching Lung Soo's famous trick. He . . ."

"Can I say something?" Gavigan put in.

Merlini nodded. "Yes. Time's up now. And thanks for your forbearance."

"Hmmpf! It's old age creeping up on me. Merlini, do you realize that whatever you may discover with your hypnotic Aim flam won't be admissible in any court as evidence?"

"I know that. But evidence obtained with the Third Degree isn't either, and yet the police of this country still resort to that medieval technique. It sometimes gives them leads toward evidence that is admissible. You'll admit that."

Gavigan scowled, not wanting to put himself on record. "Okay, if you want to play Svengali, I don't suppose I can stop you. You'd do it anyway."

"If that's all then, Inspector, suppose we adjourn until tonight at eight." He frowned at Gavigan, signalling him with his eyes to say "yes."

The latter agreed somewhat reluctantly. "Okay, but if you people are smart," he said, addressing the others, "you'll each accept the escort of one of my men until after this monkey business is over. If the murderer should happen to agree with Merlini that one of you knows something that hypnosis may reveal, then that person is in obvious danger."

Watrous asked, "Then I can go?"

"For the time being, yes," Gavigan said, "*with* one of my men."

"I don't think that's necessary, thank you, since I'm going to have nothing to do with Merlini's test."

"I wasn't thinking of that. My man goes with you, whether you like it or not. Grimm, you're delegated. And don't let him take it on the lam out any back doors. Better have someone with you."

The Colonel threw him a look that needed its face washed, and then, gathering up Madame Rappourt, he went out. Grimm followed doggedly.

"Malloy," Gavigan ordered, "get out there and detail men to nursemaid this bunch."

Duvallo was speaking to Judy. "You come with me, kid. I'll just see to it you have two nursemaids. Merlini, you've certainly managed to cook up a situation. If it wasn't for Judy, I'd enjoy it. It has everything. Drama, suspense, and danger. I wish you luck."

Merlini said, "Before you go, Dave, I'd like to see you a minute. The Inspector will look after Judy. Come here."

Merlini took him by the arm and led him into the study.

As the others got up to leave and were going toward the door, I edged back nearer the study. Merlini and Duvallo were leaning out the window, talking in low tones. They were examining a hook set into the outside frame of the window; a hook from which dangled a rusty pulley that some tenant had used to hold a clothesline. Once Merlini pointed toward the far end of the yard, and I caught two words, ". . . *the tree.*" But that was all. When I saw them pull in their heads I moved away.

The others had all gone now. Merlini and Duvallo returned to the living room, and when the latter showed signs of staying, Gavigan sent him off.

"What," he said then, "were you two up to in there?" Merlini picked up his hat and tried balancing it on his forefinger. "It's a secret, Inspector. A deep, dark secret."

The Inspector grumbled. "Going mysterious on me again, are you? Dammit, I'm old enough to know better. There should be a year-round open season on amateur detectives. I might have known you'd set off a lot of melodramatic fireworks. Hypnosis! Bah!"

Merlini grinned. "But, oh, my friend, and ah, my friend, Roman candles give off such a lovely light."

"And very little illumination," Gavigan came back acidly. "I'm beginning to wonder if the murderer is among that list of suspects after all. God knows they all act suspicious enough, but I don't see a theory that'll explain half the puzzles we've got on our hands."

"And that's just the trouble, Inspector. The murderer is among that list of suspects, but the evidence is too flimsy. A defense attorney, even one fresh out of college, could take that alibi list as it now stands and say, 'The murderer must have been two other guys.'"

Gavigan stuck out his square under jaw, and there were cold lights in his blue eyes. "Who is it? You tell me that and I'll get a confession."

Merlini shook his head. "No, Inspector. Your bright lights, your torturing, incessant questioning, your Third Degree wouldn't make a dent. You'd find that Hauptmann was a talkative old woman compared to this murderer. You'll see that the psychological make-up of our culprit will explain a lot of things, but he's not the sort to fall for that. We've got to trip him up some other way."

"Okay, and since you're the Great Mysterioso—he sees all, he knows all—suppose you tell me how to do that. But remember, hypnotic confessions don't count."

"If my little trap works, your worries will be over," Merlini said.

"Your little trap?"

"Yes. That's what I was busily working at. Didn't you notice?"

"Yeah, but the way you said it, I thought maybe it wasn't what I think it is."

"Very clever of you, Inspector. I don't believe it is."

Merlini's innocent, pleased expression was that of the cat who has just swallowed the canary. Gavigan's expression was the canary's. He snorted and went out to the hall where he conferred with Malloy. Merlini put on his hat, and then, instead of leaving, stood silently looking out the window at the fading light in Van Ness Lane. I gave myself up to a survey of my alibi list, but it had all the aggravating obstinacy of a scattered Chinese Wood Puzzle, one of the more devilish ones.

Absorbed in that futile occupation, it was only afterwards that I remembered having been vaguely conscious of a phone ringing and of Gavigan's answering it. Standing just this side of the study door, he was suddenly saying, "If anyone else gets killed, Merlini, it's your fault. Trouble is, I'll have to answer for it."

"What's happened, Inspector?"

"Jones! He went home with a detective, left the man in the bedroom, stepped into the John, closed the door, and dropped out the window on to the fire escape. God knows what he's up to now."

That announcement made me unbutton my ears, and then something I glimpsed in Merlini's face left me with my chin hanging. I was closer than Gavigan to where Merlini stood in the shadow, and I caught something I couldn't quite define, the barest flicker of a smile playing at the corners of his lips, perhaps, or just a faint hint of artificiality in the surprise he showed at the Inspector's news. At any rate I was sure of one thing—Merlini had expected that.

Chapter 23
The Most Dangerous Trick

".. . and sometimes vanishes in the midst of multitudes
that go to take him . . ."

THE GUEST night programs of the Society of American Magicians
are presented in the twenty-fourth-floor auditorium of the
McAlpin Hotel on Broadway at 34th Street. As I entered the main-
floor lobby I found the Inspector, with Captain Malloy, Grimm,
and half a dozen detectives gathered near the door.

"Something brewing?" I asked.

"Looks like it," Gavigan said. "Merlini phoned H.Q. a while ago
and told me to have all the exits from the twenty-fourth floor covered during the show. Then he announced—as off-handedly as he
could manage—that he'd found Jones, and hung up. I called him
back and he simply let the phone ring."

The Inspector turned to the others. "You boys have your orders. Go to it, and keep your eyes open. Come on, Harte."

I followed him across the lobby into the hotel manager's office.
Gavigan introduced himself and said, "I want you to issue orders
to the elevator operators that, once the S.A.M. show upstairs has
started tonight, no car is to stop for any reason whatsoever at the
twenty-fourth floor, except at my order."

Having completely upset that gentleman's peace of mind, we
left.

"Looks as if we were going to be properly marooned for the rest of the evening," I commented. "More of Merlini's recommendations?"

"Yes," Gavigan said gloomily.

We stepped from the elevator into the twenty-fourth-floor lobby, a T-shaped corridor, with elevators lining both sides of the downstroke. The right arm of the T held the checkroom, and at its end, an exit led to the roof. The left-hand corridor stopped at the large door, now closed, of a banquet room. Directly before us, opposite the elevators, was the auditorium door and before it a small table where an S.A.M. officer stood taking tickets.

The lobby was crowded, and from the animated buzz of conversation that filled the air my ears several times filtered out the word *Tarot*. To many of these people, I realized, the murders were headline news that had come close and touched them.

I noticed again what had struck me on a previous reportorial visit. With the exception of one or two men that had overdue haircuts, all looked about as mysterious as—well, as Gavigan did. And yet, I knew that among them were many famous exponents of the wand, master of the innocent face and the deceptive hand. There were, too, the amateurs, whose skill in some specialty often equalled that of their professional colleagues—professors, jewelers, brokers, florists, mailmen, doctors, lawyers, newspaper cartoonists—who at night turned to wizardry and deception. Sprinkled here and there were perhaps a dozen or so decorative blondes, those glamorous and indestructible ladies whose bodies are nightly severed from their heads, pierced with swords, divided into halves with a crosscut saw, and burned alive.

Merlini stood near the ticket taker's table, talking to Colonel Watrous. Standing very still beside him was a woman wearing dark glasses—Madame Rappourt. Aha, I thought, she's shy among the conjurers.

Merlini saw us as we started toward them, and with a warning shake of his head, he quickly steered Rappourt and Watrous through the door into the auditorium. After several moments he hurried out again and took us under his wing.

"What's the idea of that?" Gavigan wanted to know.

"I want your presence as little noticed as possible. You wouldn't wear a disguise." Merlini winked at me.

Gavigan made a sour face. "When I get a case that necessitates my dressing up like the House of David, I'll resign."

"Always so forthright and direct," Merlini said. "A little deception is sometimes a good thing, Inspector, and it's lots of fun. But perhaps we'd better go in. I've saved seats down front and the hocus-pocus is about to begin. Are your minions in their proper places?"

"Yes, but I'd enjoy myself a lot more if I knew . . ."

"That's what *you* think. Besides, there'd be no dramatic suspense, no climax."

"Hang your suspense, Merlini!" Gavigan began, but Merlini shut him off by introducing us, as we passed, to two card kings, a sword swallower, and the Man with the X-Ray Eyes.

Merlini had three seats reserved on the center aisle in the sixth row. Watrous and Rappourt, I noticed, were sitting two rows further forward on the other side of the aisle, and in the end seat of our own row, near the wall, I saw Judy Barclay.

I glanced at my program, and Gavigan scowled at his.

GUEST NIGHT

The Society of American Magicians

Masters of Ceremonies

Al Baker and Dennis

1. Jossefy   The Skull of Cagliostro
2. John Mulholland   Magic of India
3. Bernard Zufall   The Human Encyclopedia
4. The Mystic LaClaires   Mysteries of the Mind
5. David Duvallo   Nothing Can Hold Him

Intermission

6. The Great Merlini   The Devil's Hat
7. Max Holden   Shadowgraphs
8. Signor Ecco   Something Old, Something New
9. Ching Wong Fu   Darn Clever, These Chinese

"Merlini," Gavignan said sharply, "Is Jones backstage?"

"Yes, but you sit right where you are. Before the evening is over you can have at him all you want. But not now."

The auditorium lights faded. Al Baker stepped from between the curtains carrying Dennis, a harsh and utterly irrepressible ventriloquist's dummy, who interrupted violently every time Al tried to speak. Dennis finally M.C.'d the show, introducing Joseffy's act as a masterpiece of skullduggery.

The skull—Cagliostro's, so Joseffy said—rested on a glass plate held by a committee from the audience and indicated, with a gruesome clicking of its white teeth, the names of cards surreptitiously chosen by the audience.

Gavigan's disgruntled comment was, "Maybe I should ask *him* who our murderer is."

John Mulholland caused a rosebush to grow from nothing and mysteriously blossom. Bernard Zufall instantly memorized a list of fifty words supplied by the audience and repeated them forwards, backwards, and then singly as they were called for by number.

Dennis then introduced the LaClaires and challenged Zelma to read *his* mind. Dressed in white and blindfolded with a black bandage, she was apparently in constant communication with Alfred, who silently went up and down the aisles, glancing at the various objects held up for his examination, which she immediately described, and listening to whispered questions, which she answered. The act was well done, faster paced than most, and it finished with a clairvoyant climax that consisted in Zelma's addition, sight unseen, of several six-digit figures written by members of the audience on a slate.

Duvallo's act took some time to set. We could hear the thump of heavy apparatus being moved into position as Al Baker, before the curtain, put one over on Dennis. The latter pooh-poohed Duvallo's skill, boasting that he could do as well. Mr. Baker, taking him at his word, produced a miniature strait jacket, laced the dummy in, tied a handkerchief securely over his protesting mouth, and commented, "That's the best gag of the evening, if I do say it myself."

When the curtain went up on Duvallo's act, I saw the Inspector sit up and take notice. I dropped my cigarette on the floor and ground it out nervously with my heel. Was it coming now? Would we get a hint of the way in which someone had escaped from those two apartments? I looked about quickly. Judy, the Colonel, and Madame Rappourt were all present and accounted for.

On the stage I saw a great box whose sides were large rectangles of heavy plate glass, bound along the edges with steel bands. A fire hose from off stage was rapidly filling the box with water. Duvallo's offering was obviously going to be the escape from the Chinese Water Torture Cell, a creation of Harry Houdini's, and the secret of which was lost with his death. Duvallo had successfully re-discovered, if not the same, then an equally efficacious method of release. An assistant hoisted a smaller steel box with an open top and a steel-barred front up and into the water. Duvallo, stripped to bathing trunks, came on, and the separate top of the glass box, a heavy metal affair having two leg holes in it after the fashion of the Puritan stocks, was locked securely about his ankles. With block and tackle this was raised high, and then lowered over the box. Duvallo, hanging head down, was completely immersed in the water. Several large padlocks were quickly placed, locking the box and its top together, the keys being thrown into the audience. A concealing canopy was drawn around the Torture Cell and the assistant stood outside peering in through a slit in the curtains, holding a fire axe in readiness should anything go wrong.

For three minutes the audience, sensing the danger that was on the stage before them, sat very still, tensely searching the assistant's face for some clue to what he saw. Then, at a sign from him the piano player stopped in mid-bar, and the curtains were flung wide. Duvallo, last seen upside down and smiling through thick plate glass, steel bars, and water, was sitting outside the box on the stage floor. He dripped water and was breathing heavily, drawing in the air with great gulps. The box remained inscrutably locked and was shy of being filled with water only by the amount his body had displaced. The applause of the audience expressed relief.

As the curtains closed, Merlini rose and excused himself to go and prepare for his own act. The audience got up to take a stretch and wandered about, smoking and chatting. Gavigan and myself went to the lobby and walked to the end of the corridor where he rapped lightly with his knuckles on the banquet hall door. It opened a crack and Malloy peered out.

"We're bored stiff, Inspector," he whispered. "Anything doing yet?"

"No, but sit tight. Merlini acts confident as hell."

"Doesn't he always?" Malloy asked and closed the door. As we came back, I noticed a man standing before the elevators, trying hard not to look like a detective. He paid no attention to us, nor Gavigan to him. The Inspector repeated his knock on the door leading to the roof, and got an answering reply. I recognized Brady's voice. I asked, "What about exits from backstage?"

"There aren't any except for the two doors on either side of the stage that lead from the dressing rooms directly into the auditorium. And I've got a couple of men backstage, anyway. Merlini had me place them everywhere, short of behind the woodwork."

We slid back into our seats again, just as the lights dimmed. I saw Gavigan glance anxiously at the still empty chair where Judy had previously sat.

Merlini stepped on to a stage that was bare of everything except two or three small spindly-legged tables. He announced that, in his opinion, it was high time someone revived Joseph Hartz's great trick *Le Chapeau du Diable*, neglected since that conjurer's death in 1903. Borrowing a collapsible opera hat from a member of the stock exchange in the fifth row, he proceeded calmly and with smiling deliberation to produce from its empty interior the following objects in order named: a bushel or two of large silk handkerchiefs, six bottles of champagne and a dozen goblets, enough playing cards to fill three hats, an electric table lamp whose bulb burned brightly with some infernal energy of its own, a canary complete with cage, and a large goldfish bowl brimming with water and fish.[1] And finally, as he returned the hat to its owner in the audience, it collapsed with a snap, disclosing the inevitable rabbit.

Inspector Gavigan sat back in his chair, one finger tapping impatiently on his knee. Whatever he had expected had not happened. Had something misfired, or was it still to come? There were two acts yet which might have possibilities, Jones' and Ching's.

---

1 The electric lamp was a modern variation of Merlini's, Hartz himself having produced several lanterns containing lighted candles. A description of his original routine may be found in Hoffman's *Later Magic*, the editions of 1925 and 1931.

I'm afraid I didn't pay much attention to Max Holden's dextrous shadowgraphy. Instead, I watched Judy's vacant chair and eyed Watrous, who was whispering excitedly to Madame Rappourt as she sat stolidly behind her dark glasses, possibly watching the performance, but giving every impression that, except for her body, she was lost in some other world. That woman's dead-pan attitude got on my nerves.

Under cover of Dennis' boisterous kibitzing, Merlini slipped back and took his seat again.

"Won't Jones' ventriloquial act be a bit flat after this Dennis kid?" Gavigan asked him.

"He's doing something else tonight. Keep your eyes open."

I didn't like the way he said that, and a cold shiver coasted down my spine. So—now it was coming.

When the curtains parted the audience were still smiling over Dennis' final remarks. But when they saw the bare, black-draped stage and the solemn, strangely pale expression on Jones' face as he walked out and stood motionless near the footlights waiting for quiet, something stilled them.

He began quietly, in a soft, flat voice that accentuated the dramatic import of what he said.

"Ladies and gentlemen, this evening I shall present one of the most famous feats in all magic—and yet one that is rarely seen. It has been attempted by but few performers, for the very excellent reason that its presentation must always be absolutely perfect. Make just one mistake—as almost all its performers have eventually done—and it's your last. It is the most dangerous trick in magic."

His speech was somewhat stilted, as if memorized, and, as he paused, something of his nervousness passed across the footlights into the audience. There was a stiffening of attention, a hushed absence of those rustling, stirring noises that indicate lack of interest.

"Captain Carl Storm, formerly of the United States Army," Jones continued, "is here tonight at my invitation. Will you please step up, Captain?"

From an aisle seat on the other side of the auditorium, a man in uniform rose and made his way toward the stage. Under his arm he carried several implements that had, in their smooth, machined lines, an efficient, deadly look. The polite applause was hesitant, apprehensive.

"I requested the Captain to bring with him from his collection three army rifles which he was instructed to choose at random. Did you do that, Captain?" The man nodded.

A mumbled undercurrent of excitement wavered through the audience, many of whom apparently guessed what was to come.

Jones faced the footlights. "I would also like to have several gentlemen from the audience form a committee to assist me on the stage. Particularly those who may have some knowledge of firearms, though anyone at all is quite welcome to volunteer. Perhaps I should add that whatever danger exists does so for myself only and can in no way touch anyone else."

Before any ordinary audience Jones would most certainly have made this request prior to any hint of danger or any display of armaments. But volunteer assistants come easily enough from an audience of magicians and their friends. There was a slight hesitation; then, almost at once, several persons rose from different parts of the auditorium. In a moment or two Jones had to hold up his hand indicating that that was enough. There were five men on the stage besides himself and the Captain.

Two of them I recognized immediately. One was a detective I had seen outside with Gavigan before the show, the other was Dr. Hesse. Then, as I watched them line up under Jones' direction on the left side of the stage, a man in evening dress, the last to go forward, turned, and I saw that it was Watrous. I looked about quickly. Gavigan, bent forward, and scowling heavily at the stage, obscured my view; I couldn't see Madame Rappourt. Judy was still missing. Duvallo, Ching, and the LaClaires were, I supposed, still backstage.

Jones spoke again. "Captain Storm, will you tell the audience if, since you chose those rifles, I have had any chance to examine or handle them."

The Captain shook his head and answered in a parade-ground voice, "This is the first time you have even seen them."

"You brought ammunition?"

The Captain placed the rifles on a table and drew a box of cartridges from his coat pocket. At Jones' suggestion he slit the box open and poured the bullets in a heap on the table.

Jones, keeping some distance from the table, motioned to the committeemen. "Will you kindly step over and examine the bullets. When you are quite satisfied that they are genuine, will you select two and stand them on end, at the edge of the table away from the others."

When this had been done, he asked, "Does someone have a pocketknife?"

The man whom I recognized as a detective produced one and offered it.

Jones indicated the selected bullets. "Will you choose one of those," he said, "and scratch your initials on the nose of the bullet and on the case."

As the man did this, Gavigan curled a few words from the side of his mouth at Merlini. "*You* would think up something like this, dammit. I've a good notion to break it up right now."

"Easy, Inspector," Merlini whispered. "We're going to get a nibble."

Jones spoke to Watrous and Dr. Hesse. "Will you gentlemen please select one of those guns."

They did so, examining each and agreeing on one.

"Who, beside the Captain, knows how to load this gun. You, sir?"

He looked at the fifth committeeman, a shy professorial looking man who wore thick lensed glasses and a short Vandyke. He stepped hesitantly from the background, and in a low voice that barely got across the footlights, said, "Yes. I think I can."

"Will you take the gun then and load it with the bullet that is left, there on the table."

As he did so, Jones picked up a white dinner plate from the table and placed it in a metal holder at the right and rear of the stage.

"Captain Storm, will you please take the gun and fire at the plate."

The Captain nodded, took the gun and raised it. I saw a woman in front of me put her fingers to her ears. The gun cracked and the plate dropped, a shower of small pieces that rattled on the floor.

An odd sort of sound rose from the audience as more than one person gasped involuntarily and caught at his breath.

Jones held the tension steady. He quickly took the marked bullet and held it in turn before each committeeman, asking that the initialling he noted. He passed the bullet to the man who had loaded before, and as Captain Storm held out the gun, the latter threw back the breech, ejecting the spent shell. As he loaded the gun again, Jones turned his back, walked across stage to where the plate had been and faced his audience.

"The trick I am about to present, is, of course, the Great Bullet Catching Feat."

His voice was strained, with a tight piano-wire vibrance in it that sang. Was he acting, building up his effect, or was he scared to death? I couldn't tell.

"Ready, Captain?" Storm nodded.

"Then you will aim the gun, which everyone has seen loaded

with a freely selected and marked bullet—*at my face*. When you fire I shall try to catch the bullet between my teeth. Can you score a bull's-eye the first time, Captain?" The man nodded slowly. "If you say so." Somewhere a woman giggled, the loose foolish sound that precedes hysteria. Jones was putting on a good act.

I saw Judy come through the door from backstage and make her way through the dark back to her seat.

"I must have complete quiet, please," Jones cautioned. "Everything—my life, perhaps—depends upon the Captain's aim." He wiped his forehead with a handkerchief, then faced the Captain and stood stiffly, like a store-window dummy, his movements jerky and mechanical.

"I shall call, 'Ready—Aim'—and, when I drop this handkerchief, you will fire. Is that clear?"

Captain Storm nodded almost imperceptibly and frowned. The handkerchief dropped—but stopped short. Jones still held an end of it. That drew another gasp from the audience. Jones, arms rigidly at his side, appeared not to have heard. He pulled his chin up and said: "Ready!"

The Captain half raised the rifle. Merlini, oddly, settled back somewhat in his chair, a queer half smile on his mouth. Gavigan had one hand in his coat pocket, his arm flexed, ready. Judy moved slightly and glanced toward us, her eyes dark and large. "Aim!"

The gun snapped to the Captain's shoulder, one sharp, clean movement in a blurred slow-motion film. A cold high light glinted brightly down the long barrel that pointed steadily at Jones.

The silence was complete, breathless, and the chalky faces of the committeemen were like a row of white holes in the dark backdrop. Watrous shifted on his feet uneasily. There were damp high lights on Jones' sharp, tight face.

At last, after what seemed an interminable pose, the tableau moved. Jones' fingers jerked wide, convulsively and the white blur of handkerchief fell slowly, almost floating, to the floor. It touched the stage and the rifle cracked! The report still rang in my ears; Jones fell backwards, and slowly swung halfway around, his body twisting above the knees. His legs gave loosely like a marionette's and he slumped forward to the floor on his face. And was still. A faint halation of dust rose upward around him. For a brief second no one moved, no sound came. Then instantly the place was in an uproar. "Come on, Inspector," Merlini cried, but Gavigan was halfway up the aisle, running. In the back of my head some automatic adding machine foolishly did a sum. Where there had been five committeemen, there were now but four!

Simultaneously a heavy voice from off stage at the left shouted, "Oh, no you don't!" Then I heard the sound that accompanies a smashing impact of fist against bone.

The missing committeeman tumbled backward from the wings on to the stage. Detective Janssen, whose voice I had recognized, jumped out after him, plunging forward in a flying tackle to wrap himself about the falling man's knees; they went down together. The uproar became pandemonium.

"He tried to sneak off into the wings," Janssen yelled at Gavigan as the latter vaulted the footlights.

Merlini, climbing up, said, "Grab him, Inspector. *That's your murderer!*"

With that, a movement on the opposite side of the stage caught instant attention.

The still body of Jones rolled over—and sat up! The audience stood and stared.

My hands that were gripping the chairback before me started slowly to relax. It was all over now; there was no need for that tight, strained feeling or for the pounding of my pulse—and then, as the Inspector drew out a pair of brightly glittering handcuffs, the murderer's foot swung up and caught him in the groin. With almost the same movement he swung a haymaker against Janssen's jaw and, leaping forward, threw himself into the air across the footlights. He landed, falling to his knees and, without rising, pivoted. There was a revolver in his hand.

Gavigan's was out too, but he didn't use it. The man's voice came, hard, rasping, with a deadly sincerity.

"If anyone moves, I'll fire into the crowd. I'm going out, and, if you try to stop me, someone'll get hurt. I mean it! Clear that aisle!"

He started sideways down the aisle, watching over his shoulder, his gun moving at the crowd. The people before him fell away; a path straight to the door opened magically. Halfway back, a woman gave a small yelp and fainted, falling across the aisle. He stepped over her and went on, his gun waving from side to side menacingly, the tendons of his jaw standing out in hard ridges.

I saw Janssen half raise his gun. Gavigan knocked his arm down and ordered loudly, "Let him go! Everyone keep your seats!"

As the man reached the doorway, he turned and backed into it "Thanks, Inspector—and good-bye."

He was through it, and the door closed after him. There was a thump from outside as of a table overturned.

Gavigan cried, "Quiet, everybody, and sit still. The exits are all guarded and the elevators aren't—"

"Crack!"

The report of a gun came from the lobby outside. Gavigan and the two detectives were suddenly running down the aisle. I slipped out of my seat as Merlini went past, and followed. In spite of the Inspector's command, the spectators were milling desperately amid a welter of overturned chairs.

The Inspector threw himself at the door, pushing it open against the table that lay there. Outside, the detective I had seen before the elevators lay on the floor with a dark wet-shaped stain on the carpet beside him. From doors at either end of the lobby the other detectives came with drawn guns. But I saw no sign of any murderer.

"Where'd he go?" Gavigan shouted frantically.

"Who?" Malloy asked. Brady, from the other door, shook his head blankly.

Gavigan looked at the coatroom as a girl's white face came up above the edge of the half door.

"Did you see him?"

She nodded dumbly, he mouth working. "I—yes—I saw him come out—and shoot . . . and I ducked. I don't know . . ."

The Inspector didn't listen to the rest. He turned about once, completely, surveying the empty lobby, the bare lobby that held no hiding place at all.

I'll never forget the blank astonishment on his face and the empty teetering in the pit of my own stomach. The murderer had done it again! He had vanished into thin air, from a room whose exits all were guarded!

Merlini, after one quick look, bent over the fallen man and then, straightening, glanced at the elevator indicators. He took two long strides and yanked a hand phone from the box in the wall.

"Starter!" he shouted, "Starter! Police speaking. Quick! Number Two car. Start it back to floor twenty-three at once. Don't let it stop! And for God's sake don't let it go *above* twenty-three!"

The dial hand moved on—6, 5, 4 . . . However between 3 and 2 it stopped, hung briefly and began to reverse.

"That does it!" Merlini cried, "Quick, Inspector. At each side of the door and have your guns ready. He plays rough."

We flattened ourselves against the wall. Someone pulled the fallen man out of line, and the damp smear streaked the floor.

Merlini was talking fast and low. "I don't smell any brimstone, so there's only one place he could have gone. The top of that car. He must have found it parked at twenty-two or three and jumped to its top, intending to get off at the second floor when it arrived at the first."

The dial hand moved on . . . 21 . . . 22 . . . 23 . . .

Merlini inserted the end of a pencil into the small, round hole in the center of the sliding doors. He levered upward and the doors moved half an inch. Gavigan got his fingers in the opening and pulled the doors wide, staying flat behind them.

"All right," he said grimly. "Throw out that gun!"

His words fell into silence, and then, finally, the brittle tension in the air shattered and a voice came, calm as always, but tired and flat, empty of the old cocksureness.

"Pick up the marbles, Inspector, you win."

A revolver flashed dully, turning as it fell, and bumped across the carpet. A pair of glasses and a false Vandyke followed.

Then, his greasy hands raised, a sagging weary expression on his lean gray face, the shy committeeman who had loaded the rifle, David Duvallo, stepped out into the light.

Chapter 24
Rolang

The Performance of all this is fair . . . as always the juggler confesses in the End that these are no supernatural Actions, but Devices of Men performed by Dexterity and Nimble Conveyance.

Henry Dean: *The Whole Art of Legerdemain, or Hocus Pocus in Perfection.*

HIDDEN AWAY on the top floor of one of the elderly buildings surrounding Times Square is a door that bears this inscription: THE MAGIC SHOP, *Miracles for Sale,* A. Merlini, Prop. Behind that door is a queer sort of shop, a shop that is somehow all at once gay, festive, bizarre, spectacular, weird, showy, and comfortable. There are the usual glass-topped counters, shelves rising high on one wall, and a cash register; but there the usual ceases. A white rabbit hops about on the floor and the merchandise is a strangely incongruous assortment of cards, thimbles, silk handkerchiefs, tripod-legged tables, billiard balls, slates, ribbons, flowers, alarm clocks, crystal gazing balls, red and gold cabinets and boxes, bird cages, fish, bowls, a half dozen toothy papier-mâché skulls, and several hundred books. The right-hand wall, from above a comfortable divan that stands against it, upward to the ceiling is covered with framed and autographed photos of magicians, and grinning foolishly down from the top row of shelves is a brightly painted set of Punch and Judy figures.

Inspector Gavigan and I were sitting on the divan the morning after Duvallo's arrest. Merlini leaned on the counter scratching the head of Dr. Faustus, an enormous black cat who stretched luxuriously on the glass.

"How's Hunter?" Merlini asked.

Hunter was the casualty of the night before.

"It was damned close," Gavigan answered, "but the report this morning was that he'd pull through."

"And what happened at headquarters after the fireworks last night? Duvallo talk?"

"Yes, once he knew it was no go, he talked plenty. Oddly, too. He'd get so enthused at times that he's forget he had come a cropper, and he almost boasted of the way he'd fooled us."

"He would; he's an egomaniac. That's also why he's such a good magician. I've a little theory—I don't discuss it with my customers—that conjuring as a hobby appeals most to people with inferiority complexes. And the more they over-compensate the better magicians they make. Even the display of parlor tricks at a party imparts a glow of superiority, quite false of course, but not all of us realize that. Duvallo didn't. He fooled himself thinking he was smart enough to deceive the police. And when a magician starts fooling himself, he's on the skids."

"Yes," Gavigan agreed, "that's criminal psychology. Most of them think they're too smart. And I noticed how Duvallo took Miss Barclay for granted, not being able to understand how anything in skirts could resist him. She was down at headquarters last night, and, though pretty cut up about it, I don't think it's anything she won't get over shortly. She had suspected him all along, which explains some of her actions."

Merlini nodded. "Professionally, though," he went on, "Duvallo's egotism was a decided asset. It gave him a devil-may-care air of confidence and bravado that impresses an audience."

"I wonder how long it'll stay with him. That statement I got last night is going to hang him unless some simple-minded jury-falls for the extenuating circumstances he'll probably plead and lets him off with life."

"Oh, then you know the motive? I'm interested. I think I could hazard a good guess, though I haven't had time to dig up any corroborative details. I'd intended to look through the daily papers for the last week of May 1935."

"You'd have wasted your time," Gavigan said. "But I'll trade you that information for some of the things you know that Duvallo didn't. In fact, there's a lot of answers I want."

"And what about me?" I protested. "You're both bursting with information, and I'm about to explode. Come on, talk."

Merlini leaned over and picked the rabbit from the floor. He rang up "No Sale" on the cash register, took a carrot from the drawer, and held it before the twinkly nose of the bunny.

"Breakfast, Peter," he said. And then, to the Inspector: "We'd better enlighten Ross before he plunges us into another murder case, one that neither of us will be in a position to investigate. Which answer do you want first?"

"I'd like to know how that bullet trick was stage-managed last night. Realizing that the murderer was on the stage and up to funny business when he loaded the gun, what the hell made you think Jones wouldn't be killed, and why wasn't he?"

"Duvallo was the only one who took a chance, Inspector. We had the cards stacked, and dealt him four of a kind—all jokers. Captain Storm, who rates tops as a trick shot, had instructions to aim a foot to the left of Jones' head."

"I thought so! *You* were responsible for Jones' disappearance last night!"

Merlini nodded, "Guilty. Yesterday afternoon at Duvallo's I sneaked this note to him." Merlini handed over a folded scrap of paper. It read: *You and I may be able to trap the murderer, if you'll sit tight and follow directions. Agree to anything I say about your act tonight, and, when you leave here, shake the detective who'll be on your tail, and wait for me at The Shop.*

"He had planned his usual ventriloquism for the show, but I changed that when I announced that he was going to do Chung Ling Soo's famous trick.[1] Your query about the hall light told Duvallo that the radio gimmick had been uncovered, and he didn't like my hypnotic plan a little bit. Things were getting warm. The Bullet Trick was a made-to-order chance for him to have his neck. But it was made-to-order more than he knew. He put on that scholarly committeeman disguise in his dressing room, and went out into the auditorium during the intermission ready to volunteer during Jones' act. Backstage he passed as just another of the many performers' relatives that were milling around. Judy almost threw a monkey wrench in my little trap, when, not knowing what was up, she went backstage once to look for Duvallo and couldn't find him. I was afraid she'd raise a hue and cry, but luckily she was still giving him the benefit of the doubt. It's always hard to believe one of your best friends is a murderer."

"There's one thing I want straightened out right now," I said. "How could Duvallo agree to let himself be hypnotized? Wouldn't that have let the cat out of the bag?"

"No," Merlini explained, "being a hypnotist himself, he was confident that he could fake it, even though it meant fooling Brainard. It's not an easy thing to do, but he could have gotten away with

---

1   Chung Ling Soo (William Elsworth Robinson) was killed while performing the Bullet Trick at the Wood Empire Theatre in London in 1918. A verdict of Accidental Death was returned at the inquest, although some commentators have pointed to certain evidence, still unexplained, that would seem to indicate suicide or even murder. Of the dozen performers who have featured the trick, half were killed, the others injured. The only present-day performer who dares it is Theodore Anneman.

it if anyone could. His colossal self-confidence has pulled him out of some pretty tight spots. That time in Milwaukee when his Buried Alive stunt went wrong, he—"

"Then Jones was the absent-minded suspect who had forgotten something vital?"

"Yeah," the Inspector replied, "if Merlini's psychoanalyst friend had hypnotized Jones, Duvallo knew we'd find out that—"

"Hold it, Inspector," Merlini broke in. "If you're going to let Ross in on the pay-off, don't begin with your climax. Build up to it."

I reached over the counter and picked up one of the heavy glass spheres that were labeled "Finest Crystal Gazing Globes. Specially Priced. $6.50." I hefted it menacingly.

Gavigan said, "All right, you take it. And while you're at it, I want to know how you doped it. I still don't see what the tip-off was. You weren't even there yet when Tarot—"

"There you go again," Merlini objected. He served Peter Rabbit another carrot. "Let's begin at the beginning, with Sabbat's murder. The main problem there was one of escape. The Inspector wouldn't have Surgat, and both of you thoroughly snowed under my davenport suggestion with obviously valid objections. And, anyway, I'd found no traces under the davenport, as I'd previously admitted. There was nothing left except Duvallo's hanky-panky with the string."

"Damn!" I said heartily. I know enough never to believe a magician and, in spite of all his protestations to the contrary, I'd half expected him to come through at the last with a nice new escape for that apartment. "But if Duvallo's explanation is correct," I went on, "the murderer had to be in the apartment to throw that bolt sometime between our breaking in and the arrival of the police. Duvallo doesn't qualify."

"Take it easy, Ross. Forget Duvallo for a moment. Just assume that the murderer must have been there, and put yourself in his place. Suppose you were the murderer and had yet to finish off your monkey business with the kitchen door. First, you'd go over there supplied with a couple of witnesses. Secondly, you'd not welcome any unpredictable elements in your little act, and when neighbor Harte from across the hall put in his two cents' worth you'd not be pleased. And you would certainly object to his phoning the cops before you had even broken into the place. Furthermore, you'd try to keep yourself in command of the situation, directing and controlling the actions of others, and, most important of all, you'd damn well see to it that you, and you only, were the first person into that kitchen. Right?"

"It sounds swell. But it was Tarot who did all those things!"

Merlini smiled mysteriously. "And you gave him a couple of nasty moments. Your announcement that you had already called the police, for instance. They might burst in at any moment, and he hadn't even started for the kitchen. He went into action at once. He suggested that the murderer might still be lurking about, and, to emphasize the danger, and to provide a good reason for his being the only one to go look, he pulled out that gun and waved it about. Then, you rushed in where angels wouldn't have poked their noses. He had to think fast and shunt you off into the bedroom. All those things were highly indicative. Tarot was the only suspect of the lot who acted at every turn as if he wanted to get that kitchen door."

"And with his alibi he couldn't possibly have been the murderer," I said, wondering where the hell this was taking us.

"But, as far as we knew at that time, he might have been the murderer's accomplice. It looked very much, in fact, as if he *and* the murderer were trying to frame Duvallo. There were all those heavy-handed clues cocked and aimed at Duvallo, the business card, his picklocks, and the fact that the crime seemed to call for an escape artist."

"Yeah," Gavigan put in, "I thought that, too, until Tarot began acting up, not leaving his fingerprints, vanishing from that taxi, having Sabbat's gun, giving the wrong address, and all that. It didn't make sense. When you're trying to frame someone it's customary to try and keep your own skirts clean. But I never thought—"

"And then," Merlini interposed hastily, "the apple cart was up-dumped properly. Duvallo walked in, nice as you please, and two things happened that were as subtly suspicious as all the evidence against him was overly obvious. The business card turned out to implicate not Duvallo, but Tarot. That was bad. As long as it pointed at Duvallo, his position was relatively sound, but when it about-faced and we discovered it had been pointing at Tarot all along, Duvallo was in dutch."

"Do you have your own private brand of logic?" I objected. "Take those paradoxical jumps a bit slower, please. I'm falling off."

Merlini scratched the rabbit's ears. "The card was planted, of course. Gavigan told Duvallo as much, and he was dead right. If it was not planted and was a straight-forward clue, we'd have had to assume that the man it implicated, Duvallo, was a sixteen-carat bungling idiot. But the crime itself gave the lie to that.

"The only question was, did the murderer plant the card in order to throw suspicion on Duvallo, or did Duvallo plant it in order to give the appearance of being framed by some murderer not himself? Duvallo wanted us to think he was being framed, and that phony, phony phone-call from a mysterious Mr. Williams was for the same purpose. Duvallo got a jolt when Gavigan surprised him by going straight to the truth. He hadn't given the cops credit for that much penetration."

"He'd probably read too many detective stories," Gavigan muttered.

"Not only that," Merlini went on, "but he suspected the police might be so obtuse that they wouldn't deduce that he was being framed. He was performing that most dangerous trick, murder, and he became over-cautious. He used a card which had Tarot's erased writing on it—a card, by the way, which *he* could have filed away for future use as easily as Tarot might have done. The erasure was fairly obvious, and if the police hadn't seen it, he'd have pointed it out. That was where he made his mistake. As soon as I realized that the card had never really implicated him, I was sure he had planted it. If anyone else had wanted to implicate Tarot they'd have left Tarot's calling card, not Duvallo's. There would be no reason for a delayed action clue."

The Inspector said, "You don't mean to tell me, Merlini, that you knew Duvallo was guilty because of any highfalutin' complicated reasoning like that?"

"No, but it made me good and suspicious. Besides, the business card was only a subtle error in reasoning alongside the glaring blunder that followed. He tried to prove, without damaging his professional reputation, that *he* couldn't possibly have gotten out of *that* apartment. What sent me into a tail spin was the fact that he did exactly that. He did prove that he couldn't have been the one to bolt the kitchen door, and *at the same time he admitted that he was the murderer!*"

"He did what!" Gavigan was startled.

"He gave himself away completely. He explained far too much. More than he should have known. He borrowed the Inspector's handkerchief to use in demonstrating how the key-holes might have been plugged up, and he put the pencil marks on it *before* he had been told that any were found on Sabbat's handkerchief!"[2]

The Inspector stared, his blue eyes popping. Then he growled, "Damn!"

"But," I wanted to know, "why the pencil marks anyway? If the murderer had only poked the cloth into the keyholes with the

2 *See* pp. 123-124.

eraser end of the pencil, he wouldn't have needed to switch the handkerchief later. The bolting of the door wasn't really necessary; it was locked. The murderer wouldn't have needed to come back, or send an assistant at all. Sounds screwy to me."

"Sure, it would. You're a simple and more direct person than Duvallo. He's a magician and his wiles are devious. He's in love with mystery, and a Grade A impossibility wasn't good enough for him. He had to make it a super-production—and it boomeranged. He began with a sound original idea. He'd commit two murders, make it clear to the dumbest nitwit of a cop that they were—that they must have been—committed by the same person, and then he'd be prepared with an unshakable alibi for *one* of them. You might commit a whole series of crimes using that technique; just be sure that your one alibi is strong enough. His was. It consisted in being with the police when Tarot was murdered. He should have left it at that, but he didn't; he tried to cook up an alibi for Sabbat's murder too. He over-elaborated. The pencil marks made the switching of the torn handkerchief necessary, and that proved that the murderer must have come back to the apartment during a time when it seemed fairly obvious that Duvallo had not been present."

"I don't follow that," I said. "If you two have jugged the right man, if Duvallo is the murderer, then the pencil marks prove, not that the murderer came back, but that he had an assistant, Tarot. But that doesn't . . . I don't see—"

"And at that point," Merlini continued, "neither did I. If those two were in cahoots, why in the name of sanity did Tarot accuse Duvallo and vice versa? That certainly didn't look like teamwork. And they couldn't both be double-crossing each other. A murderer and his accomplice usually prefer hanging together to hanging separately. One line of reasoning said that they must be colleagues in crime, and another equally valid chain of logic said the exact opposite. The logical snarl that left us in was as bad as any rope-tie Duvallo ever escaped from. And then," Merlini flung his hands wide, fingers spread, "the whole set piece exploded right in my face with a loud Whoosh! The incomprehensible Tarot is killed, and his body is surrounded on all sides by evidence—the method of murder, Sabbat's dressing-gown cord, Dr. Dee's crystal, the *Grimorium* page, the very position of the body—evidence which could only mean that there was but one killer. And at the time of Tarot's death Duvallo was in plain sight talking to us, busily curving the suspicion back toward Tarot! Even if we supposed that he had really learned the neatest trick of the Tibetan week—being in two places at once—and had admitted that his astral double killed Tarot in order to remove a double-crossing accomplice, we should still have to explain Tarot's damnably inconsistent actions. On top of all that, Tarot dead presented us with a new puzzler—his disguise. Each new discovery was a setback. Our retrograde motion was a sight to behold. In spite of his giveaway blunder, the Great Duvallo drew further ahead of the bloodhounds every minute."

"Merlini," Gavigan kibitzed, "stop blowing up toy balloons so they'll make a big bust when your devastating logic starts to pop 'em."

"But, Inspector," Merlini argued, "they weren't toy balloons at the time; they were more like stone walls. *You'll* have to admit that."

I broke in peevishly, "You're forgetting that I don't know the answers. Get on with it. I'm a nervous wreck."

Merlini went on calmly: "I'd had a quick peek behind the scenes, a passing glimpse of the rabbits hiding in the hat, and still he fooled me. The mystery got progressively deeper until finally we resolved one impossibility. We found the gimmicked radio, and we knew that the murder had taken place earlier—apparently a half hour earlier—sometime between Tarot's arrival and the beginning of the snowfall. We knew then why there were no footprints in the snow. But did that help any? The murder took place in Duvallo's own rooms; he had by far the best opportunity to hocus that radio; and I was sure that, not expecting the snow, he'd left that ladder against the open window so that we'd think someone had gone down it—someone not an escape artist. But his alibi was as iron-clad as ever. A half hour before, at ten o'clock, he had already arrived at Sabbat's and placed himself where there could be no doubt of his presence, right under our noses."

"And then Jones turned out to be the guy who started the radio," Gavigan added disgustedly.

"Yes, he looked like off-stage assistant number two, only he was the wrong man for the part. Not being a complete idiot, he wouldn't go down there at Duvallo's request and poke that light button, knowing that his ventriloquial ability would put him smack on the spot. But I felt morally certain that somehow, in spite of Space and Time, Duvallo *had* managed to strangle Tarot. So I asked myself this: could Duvallo have made Jones stop in and flick that light switch at precisely the proper moment, without Jones realizing that he was acting in any way except of his own free will and by chance? Put that way, I saw it. The answer could be yes."

Merlini grinned maliciously, looked at Gavigan and said, "Ross, here, is going to sit right up on his hind legs and howl that it's too shilling-shockerish, that it's too trite and whiskered a device to go well in the story he's itching to write. My answer to that is: why, those criticisms being true, didn't he tumble to it? We talked about the method enough, both during the investigation and now, just a few minutes ago."

I tried, not very successfully, to cover my chagrin with nonchalance. "I'll be damned! Duvallo hypnotized him!"

"Exactly." Merlini chuckled. "That's the only thing that could have happened other than a ridiculously impossible coincidence. Duvallo persuaded Jones to try a hypnotic experiment, and, during the trance, double-crossed him. He gave Jones a post-hypnotic command to show up and turn on that light at 10:30 sharp, and then told him that on awakening he'd not remember having been hypnotized at all. That's what the absent-minded suspect forgot, and that's what Duvallo knew that another spot of hypnosis would uncover. Duvallo admit that, Inspector?"

"Yes. I thought for a minute he was coked up when he confessed that. But then I remembered something I'd read in Sodermann and O'Connell's book.[3] They mention a case in which two young men hypnotized a girl, raped her, and then, through suggestion, compelled her to forget what had happened. If that's possible, then I guess Duvallo could have made Jones push a light switch."

"Go on," I prodded. "How do you get over the next hurdle? You've still got to get Tarot killed."

Merlini got down off the counter and put the rabbit in his pen on the floor. "I know," he said. "That's what gave me the jitters. Somewhere along the line Duvallo had pulled a fast one. The murders were tricks, and he was a magician. If my pet theory of deduction was true, we must have slipped up somewhere along the line; we hadn't caught the tell-tale manoeuver when the rabbit was loaded into the hat. I'd caught him out over those pencil marks, and that something I didn't find that I wasn't looking for at Tarot's apartment held intriguing possibilities, but it was all too vague and uncertain. I needed something more conclusive. So I had Ross write down in full detail what had gone before, what I had until then only heard verbally. It worked. The clue was there, and suddenly all the trap doors and the secret springs were laid bare. Duvallo's house of cards fell, flat as yesterday's uncapped seltzer water.

---

3 *Modern Criminal Investigation,* Funk & Wagnall's, 1935, p. 31. Hypnotism was one of the two things Duvallo could have done that *none* of the other suspects were able to do. *See* p. 4.

But since the evidence still wouldn't be sure-fire with a jury, and I wasn't certain that you'd accept it, I set the Bullet Trick trap."

Merlini had that half dollar out again, and as it twinkled in his hands, I saw that he'd worked out a new one. He balanced the coin on the tips of his fingers and slapped it into the palm of his left hand, which he shut tightly. Gesturing cabalistically at the closed fist, he slowly opened it, and in pretended amazement poured out change for the half dollar—a quarter, a dime, two nickels, and five pennies.

The Inspector carefully took no notice. "Was it something I saw, too?" he asked appehensively.

"Yes, I'm afraid so. It was a common enough action, ordinarily quite innocent, but this time it was positively pregnant with possibilities. Harte's report said—and he mentioned it twice—*Tarot pushed back his cuff and glanced at a silver wrist watch.*"[4]

I saw comprehension creeping over the Inspector's face, but I didn't feel any yet on my own.

Merlini turned and pulled down a book from the shelves. "Harte doesn't get it, Inspector. Do you mind, now that it's all over and the culprit has been apprehended, if I help him out with just one last spot of witchcraft?"

I had never expected to see Inspector Gavigan smile at the mention of that subject, but he did now. "I haven't figured out any way of stopping you, Merlini, short of assault and battery."

"I see no objection to that," I said acidly.

Merlini grinned and ignored me. "We've had occasion," he said, riffling through the book and finding a turned down corner, "to mention this work before. It is Madame David-Neel's *Magic and Mystery in Tibet*. There's a description here titled 'Rolang, the corpse who dances.'" He read quickly:

The celebrant is shut up alone with a corpse in a dark room. To

---

4   *See* pp. 24 and 33.

animate the body, he lies on it, mouth to mouth, and while holding it in his arms, he must continually repeat mentally the same magic formula, excluding all other thoughts.

After a certain time the corpse begins to move. It stands up and tries to escape; the sorcerer, firmly clinging to it, prevents it from freeing itself. Now the body struggles more fiercely. It leaps and bounds to extraordinary heights, dragging with it the man who must hold on, keeping his lips upon the mouth of the monster, and continue mentally repeating the magic words.

At last the tongue of the corpse protrudes from its mouth. The critical moment has arrived. The sorcerer seizes the tongue with his teeth and bites it off. The corpse at once collapses.

Failure in controlling the body, after having awakened it, means certain death for the sorcerer.

The tongue carefully dried becomes a powerful weapon for the triumphant *ngagspa*.

"And," he added, closing the book, "Duvallo failed to control the body of Tarot after he had awakened it!"

"What the blue blazing hell!" I thought, and scowling said, "If you're all very good boys and girls tomorrow I'll tell you all about how Uncle Wiggley outwitted the Skillery Sealery Alligator and the nasty, bad old Werewolf. Boo! And nuts!"

"Go ahead, laugh, but that's what happened. It's the only way to untie all the water-soaked knots that snarled up that alibi list. We couldn't escape the dilemma by assuming two murderers—two people working as one—because of the evidence. But there wasn't anything to prevent the assumption that one person had worked as two. Duvallo killed Tarot and then brought him back to life. Our not so triumphant *ngagspa* had two accomplices; Jones, who wasn't aware of it, and Tarot, who was dead."

"My God, a zombie!" I groaned.

"Exactly." Merlini had put aside the book and was playing with three walnut shells and a pea that lay on the counter. "Duvallo impersonated Tarot. And I don't understand why you didn't see it, Ross. You know that impersonation, like hypnotism and secret exits, is, in a detective novel, as hackneyed as all get out. When the gentle reader notices in Chapter Two that Lady Van Wigglebottom was a shining light in her high school dramatic society, you know immediately that she's going to turn out to be the mysterious stranger with the red beard who was seen putting a white powder in the soup. But this time there wasn't just one amateur actor in the case, *they were all actors,* most of them professionals. *That was the one thing that they all really had in common.* Impersonation was written all over the case. Gavigan thought of it once when what was supposed to be Tarot's voice didn't sound right in the Xanadu broadcast, and, for a moment, he had truth by the tail. He shouted that someone must have been impersonating Tarot. Later, when Tarot vanished, the cab driver impersonated him for a block or two; and, finally, I told you that Tarot had impersonated Duvallo in the Mystery of the Yogi. It could work just as well the other way about. *And Duvallo was the only person who could possibly have played the part of Tarot!*[5] All the others were too short or too fat, too old or too young, the wrong sex, or they had appeared simultaneously with Tarot. But compare the descriptions of the two men in the resume Harte wrote for me. They are alike in all the fundamental essentials of build, general facial structure, same color eyes, and hair. Their differences lay in those superficialities of voice and dress that are the things most easily noticed in a dimly lit room, and the easiest to imitate."

"You mean to say that we never saw Tarot alive at all?" I asked.

Merlini nodded. "We decided that Tarot couldn't have been killed any earlier than ten o'clock because that seemed to be the earliest hour at which he could have arrived at Duvallo's. We were

---

5   See p. 4.

wrong. He had arrived, had been admitted and killed by Duval-lo almost four hours earlier. Duvallo brought him back to life for Watrous, Rappourt, and the rest of you by impersonating him and in doing so literally managed to be in two places at once. It was while I was telling you about Tarot's impersonation of Duvallo in the Yogi-in-two-places-at-once trick that I first tumbled to it. Gradually it dawned on me that here was a hypothesis that explained away all our difficulties."

He checked the points off on his fingers. "One: It offered Duvallo a way of being present at Sabbat's to throw that bolt and switch the handkerchief in the keyhole himself. Two: It would explain why Tarot avoided being fingerprinted and never removed his gloves even when doing card tricks—he couldn't go around leaving Duvallo's fingerprints. Three: It would explain why Tarot, who ordinarily went out of his way to get publicity, when he left Sabbat's covered his face with his arms and bowled photographers over right and left. Four: It gave a reason for the pennies in the light sockets—the less light during the impersonation the better. And to see Duvallo as himself. Point number five concerned—"

"Wait a minute," I cut in. "During the time 'Tarot' was on the scene Duvallo said he was alone in his booking office waiting for Williams, but he heard the detectives come and knock on the door. How do you explain that?"

Gavigan answered, "That's easy. As Tarot, he heard me order the men to go there."

"And that," Merlini added, "was the only thing that made his 'waiting alone in the office' story even faintly plausible. Point number five concerns the towel with the cold cream on it that was found at Tarot's. Tarot wouldn't have smeared a towel with cold cream *putting on* that sun-tan disguise, but Duvallo would have done just that *removing* his Tarot disguise. Six, was the mysterious suitcase which had been cached in the lockers in Grand Central.

That could have held Duvallo's own clothes, which he would need when he discarded those of Tarot. Seven: The impersonation would explain why Tarot had given a false home address—Duvallo wouldn't have wanted the place cluttered up with cops before he'd had a chance to get there, accomplish his Tarot-to-Duvallo metamorphosis and leave Tarot's clothes strewn about the bedroom. Point eight made me pretty sure I had something. The impersonation would answer that whopper of a question I kept insisting on why had Tarot escaped Janssen with a vanish that was as fancy as a birthday cake instead of using more ordinary bread-and-butter methods? The taxi-vanish, as worked, sent Janssen off on a wild goose chase and not only gave Duvallo time to make his change but with any sort of luck, time to get back to Sabbat's and report to us as himself *before Tarot was listed as missing.* If we hadn't penetrated that inspired bit of conjuring we would have been out on the end of a long, long limb. We would have been sure that Duvallo and Tarot were present and accounted for simultaneously, Duvallo at Sabbat's and Tarot in the taxi. And finally, point nine. I had felt all along that Tarot acted as if he expected to be killed and knew he wouldn't have to answer for his tall stories and mysteriously suspicious actions."

The Inspector said, "You had all that under your hat and you were afraid to present the impersonation theory?"

"There wasn't any really concrete evidence for a prosecuting attorney to get his teeth into, nothing so far but nice, neat speculation. And I couldn't quite believe it myself until Ross convinced me with his written resume. He turned up three more things that pointed to impersonation. Ten: I discovered that Tarot had receded modestly into the background and become suddenly and unnaturally quiet as soon as the LaClaires, who knew the real Tarot, came on the scene. And eleven: he had hurriedly left Sabbat's as soon as he heard I was on my way for the same reason."

Merlini placed the pea on the counter, covered it with a walnut shell, and put his hand over that. He smiled, removed his hand, and, strangely enough, the pea was still there—but the walnut shell had perversely vanished into some limbo of prestidigitation.

"Point twelve," he went on, "consisted in another lamentable boner by the Great Duvallo. When I read in Harte's account that Tarot had worn a *silver* wrist watch, I remembered that Tarot had bribed the cab driver with a gold watch and chain. Odd assortment of timepieces for the impeccably attired Tarot to be caught out in. Added to this was the fact that no wrist watch was ever found, either on Tarot's body or in his apartment, and the fact that Duvallo wore one. Might not Duvallo have dressed himself in Tarot's clothes, gold watch and all, and forgotten to remove his own wrist watch? Like glasses, one is apt to forget that they class as wearing apparel.

"Twelve points, plus one, the unlucky thirteenth, that something I wasn't looking for at Tarot's apartment which I didn't find . . ."

"The medicine cabinet!" I exclaimed suddenly, and Gavigan, startled, eyed me like a suspicious psychiatrist. "So that's what was so odd—Tarot was stocked with flesh-colored sticking plaster, but no adhesive tape!"

Merlini grinned. "Yes, Duvallo was caught out there too. He'd tried to make it too good again. The adhesive wasn't really essential, though it did serve two purposes. It helped his disguise as Tarot, and, later, it distracted anyone's suspicion that strangulation had changed Tarot rather too much. Same principle the conjurer uses when he has you initial the card you've selected. He nicked Tarot's face just after death, applied adhesive, and then, dressing in Tarot's clothes, put a similar strip of adhesive on his own face, but with no cut under it."

"And what we thought was Tarot's disguise," I said excitedly, "was made necessary because Duvallo, having taken his clothes, couldn't very well leave Tarot in his underwear at Van Ness Lane, and later leave the evening dress for us to find at 50th Street. It would not only have indicated that someone else must have worn his evening dress, but it would have left us with the odd picture of Tarot, the Beau Brummel of Broadway, travelling crosstown on a cold winter's day clad only in his unmentionables. So Duvallo dressed Eugene in an old suit of his own (minus laundry marks) glasses, and a mustache to suggest a disguise and offer a reason why the immaculately tailored Tarot should be caught dead in a suit of old clothes. Then he smashed the lamp, put Dr. Dee's crystal in Tarot's pocket and the *Grimorium* page under the body, left the floor lamp burning, Sabbat's dressing-gown cord around Tarot's neck, the ladder at the window with the intervening study door left open, and all the radiators turned for the body's rigor being so far advanced—and then he fared forth to gather up Watrous and Rappourt, and finish the kitchen door sequence. Sabbat, I suspect, hadn't invited Watrous and Rappourt over at all; that was Duvallo's doing. The gun he swiped when he strangled Sabbat the night before; Jones had already been given his hypnotic instructions, and the radio was set. But how did he entice Tarot into his parlor? Something as simple as inviting him over for tea, I suppose?"

"Not quite," Gavigan said. "It was a lot surer than that. It has to do with the motive. You said you could make a guess, Merlini. Let's hear it."

"The $100,000. It was blackmail after all. I said that none of our suspects were wealthy enough to pay out that much hush money, and as I said it I was hit, all of a heap, with the realization that Duvallo could get it if he wanted to. With his knowledge of locks and how to overcome them, it would be pie . . ."

"It evidently was," Gavigan admitted. "On May 10, 1936, one hundred thousand smackers in cold cash disappeared as neatly as if it had melted from the vaults of the American Consolidated Oil and Petroleum Company. May 10th was a Sunday. The money was there Saturday night, and it wasn't there Monday morning. There was absolutely no trace of forced entry, and six locked doors, plus the door to the vault itself, stood between that money and anyone from the outside. The officials of the company were half crazy; the treasurer slid right off into a nervous collapse. I checked all this last night with Inspector Barnes, who had charge of the investigation. Figuring it must have been an inside job, the officials pulled some wires so that Barnes got orders to keep the whole thing a deep dark secret—none of the papers carried a line. The employees were given a royal going over; they even tried the lie detector and caught two or three small-fry grafters with their pants down. But information about the missing 100 grand? Not a thing! An investigator for the insurance company took a job with the company and worked there almost six months before he gave it up, knowing exactly as much as he did when he started. Duvallo was doing his full evening show at the Majestic in Chicago that week-end. He took a plane after his Saturday night show, came here, did his burgling early Sunday morning, handed the dough over to Tarot and Sabbat, and flew back in time to give a radio talk that evening over WGN. A couple of weeks later when all seemed safe and quiet Tarot and Sabbat made their bank deposits."

Merlini nodded, smiling. "There's another little sample of Dave's attention to detail, Inspector. I remember that broadcast. He gave his usual lecture exposing the tricks of con men and crooked gamblers. It was called *The Right Way To Do Wrong*."

"He knew his subject," Gavigan said. "He got himself into hot water first by pulling the same stunt before, in Paris in '30. That was before he made such a rep for himself and he was stony broke. He cleaned out a back safe there one night, but he had to tangle with the night watchman on the way out. The watchman inconsiderately tumbled down a flight of stairs and fractured his skull. That story did make the papers, and Tarot and Sabbat, who were both in that neck of the woods at the time, put two and two together, particularly after he paid back loans they'd both made him. Tarot and Sabbat sneaked into his rooms one night and found the cash he hadn't dared bank. He had to split with them, and they had him cold. Two years ago Sabbat, his money spent, returned from Europe, hunted up Tarot, and they started to work on Duvallo again. They told him he'd have to do a return engagement of his burglary act. They had him by the short hairs; he had a reputation now that he didn't want to lose. One slip off the straight and narrow, one hint that he'd been engaged in burglary, would properly sink his professional career as an escape artist. Forced to quiet them, he got the dough, and he took what he thought was enough to keep 'em good and quiet from then on. But Sabbat promptly went off on an orgy of rare book and curio buying and Tarot's sleight of hand was no match for that of the boys in Wall Street. In the last few weeks Sabbat, particularly, had to have more; and Tarot wasn't averse to the idea. At least, if Duvallo was going to get more, he might as well have his cut. They put it up to him just after he got back from the road. Duvallo stalled, told them they'd had plenty and they could go to hell. But Sabbat got nasty and threatened to tell Miss Barclay. That tore it. And Duvallo realized now that Sabbat was just bats enough so that he couldn't be trusted, even after getting more money, to keep his mouth shut. There was nothing else for it but murder—and it had to be both of them. He sat up nights trying to figure out a safe and sane method. Then, at Miss Barclay's one evening he read one of Tarot's *Crime Doesn't Pay* scripts which she had brought home to work on. The irony of Tarot's furnishing his murderer with an alibi didn't escape him either. He saw that argumentative '*the police will never know*' bit of dialogue, and he had his radio idea. I've seen the script, and some of the dialogue Grimm didn't catch was even more appropriate. From there on the rest of the trickery was all in the day's work for a magician. Tarot

290 · CLAYTON RAWSON

came running over to see him that afternoon because Duvallo said he had got the money and was ready to pay off."

Merlini took a cocktail shaker from one of the shelves behind him, removed its price tag, showed us that it was empty, and promptly poured out three Martinis.

"And that," he said, "is that."

"Oh, no, it isn't," I objected. "What was that whispering huddle you went into with Duvallo yesterday afternoon in the study? I saw you looking at that clothesline pulley and heard you mention the tree, and I was sure you had figured a *seventh* method of escape from that place."

Merlini grinned. "I had. For Duvallo's benefit. But I didn't know I'd misdirected you, too. I suggested that the murderer might have re-installed the clothesline—the usual endless affair running around pulleys between the window and the tree—and asked him if he thought the murderer might not have grasped the clothesline and coasted, like one of those old-time department store cash boxes, out across the yard and into the tree. He could have then cut the line, pulled it after him, and dropped over the wall into the next yard, and away. Duvallo jumped at the idea. It was a good substitute for the ladder theory he had meant us to adopt and which the snow had queered. And it left him thinking that I didn't suspect him at all. I had to put him at ease on that, or he might not have thought it worth while to eliminate Jones. Satisfied, Ross?"

"Then Judy of the scarlet tresses," I said, "was just a red herring, and the LaClaires—say, why did they have to show up at Sabbat's when they did, anyway? Got an answer for that?"

"Yes," Gavigan said, "I spent an hour or so this morning collecting loose ends, and I talked to her. She'd tried to reach Sabbat by phone several times with no luck and had begun to worry. It occurred to her that maybe the night before she'd flown off the handle a bit too soon when she had pounded on his door and cussed him out. Perhaps something *had* happened to him. She left that Tudor City cocktail party ahead of Alfred, and he trailed her, catching up just as she came in the front door. They had a bit of a scrap downstairs, and he followed her up. He says he intended to tell them both where to get off. When they found Sabbat dead, Zelma realized the sounds she'd heard inside the night before must have been made by the murderer and that she had exactly no alibi. And Alfred immediately suspected her and hinted as much to us."

"What about Rappourt and Watrous?" I asked. "Are they on the up and up, or not? Is she medium or fraud? And wasn't there something more behind that fake faint she pulled when you started questioning her, Merlini?"

"Yes, I'm glad you asked that. She'd had a good hard jolt when she saw who the corpse was, and she got another when she found me nosing around, hand in glove with the cops. Svoboda was her maiden name, and she knew that if I recognized her you would, in checking back, discover her connection with Sabbat. The trance was for the purpose of stalling my questions and getting herself some time out to plan a course. She realized that unless she sidestepped me she was in a tough spot. As for her mediumship, I've had a look at her act. I'm going to do that soon somehow."[6]

"And what about the pentacle invoking Surgat and that levitation in full light that Duvallo told us about? More of his fancy embroidery—or was it?"

"That," Merlini said in his best ghost story voice, "is something we can never know. What strange secrets of the mystic occult, what recondite mysteries of Gnostic science Sabbat had explored, we cannot—"

"Applesauce," Gavigan snorted. "Tarot—I mean Duvallo—lied. Duvallo drew that pentacle on the floor just to thicken the mys-

---

6 He did, sooner than he thought. We were to meet Colonel Watrous and Madame Rappourt again, later, in the strange case of *The Footprints on the Ceiling*.

tery, gladden the hearts of city editors, and annoy the police. As for Sabbat floating in midair—Duvallo thought he was so damned clever he could make murder give off a byproduct. He had a new levitation illusion planned for his act. He knew he could pretend he was heir to an occult method of Sabbat's and could broadcast the story to the reporters without anyone being able to disprove it this side of the Styx. He figured that a couple of fancy impossible murders like these would splash across every front page in the country and carry his picture with it—the policeman's little friend, the conjurer who had explained to the dim-witted cops how the unknown murderer must have escaped from Sabbat's apartment. And—well, does all that classify as A No. 1 publicity, or doesn't it?"

"It does," Merlini admitted. "And if Jones had been killed on the stage last night, and if Duvallo had, according to plan, successfully stepped off into the wings and shucked his committeeman disguise, to reappear immediately as himself, the triple murder would have been climaxed by the most dramatic vanishing-man stunt of them all. It would have been a city editor's dream, and Duvallo would have been able to sell standing room eight weeks in advance."

"Yeah," Gavigan said, "he didn't miss any tricks, did he?"

"No, but a couple of them misfired." Merlini lit a cigarette and, turning, began to make some adjustment in the strings of a marionette that hung on the wall. Over his shoulder he said, "By the way, Inspector, did you take the precautions I advised?"

"Yes," Gavigan answered. "He's in the tightest cell we've got. Doc Hesse stripped him stark naked and examined him thoroughly. No picklocks in his mouth, hair, on the soles of his feet, or in any of the body orifices. We kept his clothes and gave him others. There's a light outside his cell door that burns nights and day, and two guards on duty every minute. He escaped from the Tombs once, but in the face of conditions like those."

"That sounds pretty thorough, but just the same I'd keep a sharp eye out. He's as slippery as—uh oh! I forgot!"

Merlini snapped his fingers with a sharp click. He wheeled to face Gavigan and the cigarette, hanging forgotten from his lips, bobbed as he spoke.

"Houdini, when he was about to get a particularly stiff going over, used to conceal his picklock by a method he'd learned from the old-time carnival freaks, the men who ate frogs and poisons, who swallowed glass and stones. He swallowed the picklock and regurgitated it when needed. Mediums have also been known to conceal and produce fake ectoplasm in the same—"

"Hand me that phone!" Inspector Gavigan ordered in a thunderous voice. "I'll get an X-Ray outfit down there and—"

Rapidly, furiously, he dialed Spring 7-3100.

The weather outside was mild. Through the room's one window, raised two or three inches, came a sound that always sends a tingle of excitement stirring with me. Mingled with the cough and rattle of the traffic that swirled about Times Square, but rising on a higher pitch, I heard the long drawn cry of newsboys.

"Extry! Extry! Uhx-treee!"

AMERICAN MYSTERY CLASSICS
from PENZLER PUBLISHERS

Established by Otto Penzler in early 2018, the American Mystery Classics series is a line of newly-reissued mystery and detective fiction from the years between the first and second World Wars, also known as the genre's Golden Age.

Our carefully-curated titles include celebrated classics by authors including Erle Stanley Gardner, Ellery Queen, and Mary Roberts Rinehart, each one refreshed with attractive new covers and contextualized with original introductions.

With more than forty years of experience as an editor, critic, publisher, and bookseller, Otto Penzler's selections are made with unparalleled expertise, meaning that the series is sure to please both long-time fans as well as newcomers to the genre.

Visit penzlerpublishers.com to see more upcoming authors and titles.

Available Now:

Ellery Queen
The Chinese Orange Mystery
An Ellery Queen Mystery

"Without doubt the best of the Queen stories."
—*The New York Times Book Review*

Introduction by Otto Penzler

The offices of foreign literature publisher and renowned stamp collector Donald Kirk are often host to strange activities, but the most recent occurrence—the murder of an unknown caller, found dead in an empty waiting room—is unlike any that has come before. Nobody, it seems, entered or exited the room, and yet the crime scene clearly has been manipulated, leaving everything in the room turned backwards and upside down. Stuck through the back of the corpse's shirt are two long spears and a tangerine is missing from the fruit bowl. Enter amateur sleuth Ellery Queen, who arrives just in time to witness the discovery of the body, only to be immediately drawn into a complex case in which no clue is too minor or too glaring to warrant careful consideration.

Reprinted for the first time in over thirty years, *The Chinese Orange Mystery* is revered to this day for its challenging conceit and inventive solution. The book is a "fair-play" mystery in which readers have all the clues needed to solve the crime. In 1981, the novel was selected as one of the top ten locked room mysteries of all time by a panel of mystery-world luminaries that included Julian Symons, Edward D. Hoch, Howard Haycraft, and Otto Penzler.

PB ISBN 978-1-61316-106-7, $15.95 • HC ISBN 978-1-61316-110-4, $25.95

Available Now:

Mary Roberts Rinehart
The Red Lamp

"There are a few masters in the field of crime who never stale, and Mary Roberts Rinehart is one of the select group."—*Kirkus*

Introduction by Otto Penzler

An all-around skeptic when it comes to the supernatural, literature professor William Porter gives no credence to claims that Twin Towers, the seaside manor he's just inherited, might be haunted. So, though his wife, more attuned to spiritual disturbance, refuses to occupy the main house, Porter convinces her to spend a summer in the lodge elsewhere on the grounds. But not long after they arrive, Porter sees the evidence of haunting that the townspeople speak of: a shadowy figure illuminated by the red light of Horace's writing lamp, the very light that shone on the scene of his death. And though he isn't convinced that it is a spirit and not a man, Porter knows that, whichever it is, the figure is responsible for the rash of murders—first of sheep, then of people—that breaks out across the countryside. When the suspect eludes his pursuit, Porter risks implicating himself in the very crimes he hopes to solve.

Written with atmospheric prose and tension that rises with every page, *The Red Lamp* is a hybrid of murder mystery and gothic romance that shows the "American Agatha Christie" at the height of her powers.

PB ISBN 978-1-61316-102-9, $15.95 • HC ISBN 978-1-61316-113-5, $25.95

Available Now:

Craig Rice
Home Sweet Homicide

"The doyenne of the comic mystery"
—Kirkus

Introduction by Otto Penzler

Unoccupied and unsupervised while mother is working, the children of widowed crime writer Marion Carstairs find diversion wherever they can. So when the kids hear gunshots at the house next door, they jump at the chance to launch their own amateur investigation—and after all, why shouldn't they? They know everything the cops do about crime scenes, having read about them in mother's novels. They know what her literary detectives would do in such a situation, how they would interpret the clues and handle witnesses. Plus, if the children solve the puzzle before the cops, it will do wonders for the sales of mother's novels. But this crime scene isn't a game at all; the murder is real, and when its details prove more twisted than anything in mother's fiction, they'll have to enlist Marion's help to sort them out. Or is that just part of their plan to hook her up with the lead detective on the case?

The basis for the 1946 film with the same name, *Home Sweet Homicide* is the novel that launched Craig Rice to literary fame. The book, a comedic crime story that pokes fun at the conventions of the genre, finds "the Dorothy Parker of detective fiction" at her most entertaining.

PB ISBN 978-1-61316-103-6, $15.95 • HC ISBN 978-1-61316-112-8, $25.95

Available Now:

Stuart Palmer
The Puzzle of the Happy Hooligan
A Hildegarde Withers Mystery

"*The Puzzle of the Happy Hooligan* is a book that
will keep you laughing and guessing from the first
page to the last."—*The New York Times*

Introduction by Otto Penzler

Hildegarde Withers is just your average school teacher—with
above-average skills in the art of deduction. The New Yorker often
finds herself investigating crimes led only by her own meddlesome
curiosity, though her friends on the NYPD don't mind when she
solves their cases for them. After plans for a grand tour of Europe are
interrupted by Germany's invasion of Poland, Miss Withers heads to
sunny Los Angeles instead, where her vacation finds her working as
a technical advisor on the set of a film adaptation of the Lizzie Bor-
den story. The producer has plans for an epic retelling of the histori-
cal killer's patricidal spree—plans which are derailed when a screenwriter turns up dead. While the local authorities quickly deem his
death accidental, Withers suspects otherwise and calls up a detective
back home for advice. The two soon team up to catch a wily killer.

At once a pleasantly complex locked room mystery and a hilarious
look at the foibles of Hollywood, *The Puzzle of the Happy Hooligan*
finds Palmer, a screenwriter himself, at his most perceptive. Reprinted for the first time in over thirty years, this riotously funny novel
shows why Hildegarde Withers was among the most beloved detectives of Golden Age American mystery novel.

PB ISBN 978-1-61316-106-7, $15.95 • HC ISBN 978-1-61316-110-4, $25.95

Available Now:

Dorothy B. Hughes
The So Blue Marble

"Extraordinary . . . [Hughes's] brilliant descriptive powers make and unmake reality."
—*The New Yorker*

Introduction by Otto Penzler

The society pages announce it before she even arrives: Griselda Satterlee, daughter of the princess of Rome, has left her career as an actress behind and is traveling to Manhattan to reinvent herself as a fashion designer. They also announce the return of the dashing Montefierrow twins to New York after a twelve-year sojourn in Europe. But there is more to this story than what's reported, which becomes clear when the three meet one evening during a walk, and their polite conversation quickly takes a menacing turn. The twins are seeking a rare and powerful gem they believe to be stashed in the unused apartment where Griselda is staying. Baffled by the request, she pushes them away, but they won't take no for an answer. When they return, accompanied by Griselda's long-estranged younger sister, the murders begin...

Drenched in the glamour and luxury of the New York elite, *The So Blue Marble* is a perfectly Art Deco suspense novel in which nothing is quite as it seems. While different in style from her later books, Dorothy B. Hughes's debut highlights her greatest strengths as an author, rendered with both the poetic language and the psychology of fear for which she is known today.

PB ISBN 978-1-61316-105-0, $15.95 • HC ISBN 978-1-61316-111-1, $25.95